Capital Resolutions
Blessings, Balance, Courage, Control

Dawn Wright

This novel's story and characters are fictitious. While the businesses, locations, and some organizations are real, they are used in a way that's purely fictional. The opinions expressed are those of the characters and should not be confused with the author's.

ISBN: 978-0-9980787-4-8

Dedication

Well, I did it, Ryan! I completed the trilogy as planned. This confirms that I can write any book now going forward. Polishing a trilogy can be daunting, but your dedication and commitment to your lengthy journey to fitness through Wu-Shu served as my guiding light of inspiration. Thank you for showing me what it looked like to achieve a paramount goal when the journey appeared inexhaustible. May you continue your Wu-Shu kicks in Heaven among the bright blue skies. I'll see you when I get there.

table of contents

1: new life

Summer

I burped my baby in my arms after breastfeeding her. Her tiny hands grabbed and released my uncombed strands. Still, I wanted to eat her up while shielding her from the pain she would undoubtedly feel one day upon experiencing life without knowing her biological father. Despite it being just the two of us in her room, the situation suffocated my energy.

Holding her in the rocking chair, my eyes darted around her room, from wall to wall, embracing the pale green walls with animal strips lined at the top. All of her eggshell-colored furniture blended well with the décor and style of Oliver's condo. From the crib to the changing table, every piece of Autumn's furniture colored her spacious room. Oliver was at work, so the knock at Autumn's door had to be my mom, since she'd come back yesterday for a quick visit.

"Come in."

"Trying to shut me out?" she reluctantly joked, easing closer in her jeans and button-up sweater in August. Her attire hinted that perhaps our home was a bit too chilly.

My expression softened. "No. I'm sorry. I just feel like her room is my private oasis."

"Are you in loooove?" She grabbed the tiny pillow in the chair placed next to the window and sat down, hugging it snugly.

"More than I ever thought possible. I feel like being the best person ever. I feel so connected to her." Cleaning Autumn's mouth, I cradled her in my arms and sprinkled motherly kisses over her cheeks and forehead.

"Motherhood does that." My mom watched us through narrowed eyes and a homely smile with her fingernail pressed against her chin. "Oliver's on cloud nine." Her sandal-clad foot flung over her knee.

I agreed with a few nods.

"Something's on your mind. I'm only here for a few more hours." Even though she gave up the habit fifteen years ago, I would be able to recognize that slight smoker's tone in any diner among waitresses who smoked. I loved her so much.

"Are you moving here or not?"

"If Oliver can find me something cool like you said he found his mother."

"Mom." The room suddenly felt hotter. "Let's not rely on Oliver for everything, okay?"

"Summer." She weaved her fingers together and dropped her foot to the floor. "What is that supposed to mean?"

I exhaled, unsure as to whether I should reveal my feelings now or withhold them. "*Mom,* I feel like a jerk, but I can't help but feel a tad more alive after giving birth to Autumn. I should feel like a white-picket fence, a dog, a husband, and, heck, who knows, maybe even a minivan. But I feel . . ."

"Yeah?"

I felt like a patient in therapy with a nursery setting. It was one of those rare moments when you actually welcomed your mother's advice, especially since we barely saw one another.

"Autumn's birth, Ruben's death—" The heat of loss inflicted my chest. A sea of tears ebbed into my throat. "It put everything into perspective. My daughter taught me that life is precious, and he reminded me that life is short."

"And what does that mean to you?"

Tears welled and fell onto my white camisole and onto Autumn's pink onesie. My mom leaned forward and motioned for me to pass her granddaughter. With my hands free, I clutched the arms of the rocking chair. "That I need to be true to myself. Life's too short to live a lie or someone else's dream." I gasped once; my chest heaved sharply.

"And what does that mean for Oliver?" she asked in a soothing tone.

"It means—"

"Summer! Rebecca!" Our heads jerked to the open bedroom door. Oliver had returned earlier than expected. One look at my mom communicated a request for confidentiality. She nodded with silent allegiance.

In no time, Oliver showed up at the doorway. Instantly, he noticed my upset face. "Baby, what's wrong? Sorry. That's a dumb question considering the recent events." He moved to stand beside me.

"My mom and I were comparing after-birth notes, that's all." Lying felt like the best option.

He stroked my hair. "Hi, Rebecca. Autumn being good?"

My mom smiled. "Always. How was your short shift?"

"Oh, got home earlier than expected. I wanted to get back to Summer and Autumn. I missed them."

My widened eyes stabbed my mom's face. She bit her lower lip as an interpretation of my expression. Luckily, she had to hit the road in a few hours. Being caught in the middle of my and Oliver's situation had to feel uncomfortable for her.

"How sweet." I tried to sound appropriate to his sentiment. Tearing away from his touch, I stood. "I'm going to Starbucks for some coffee. I need a quick walk."

"I can go with you if you can hold up."

"Oliver, I'm fine. Really. You just unwind or . . . something."

He nodded. Standing, my mom passed Autumn to him. "Maybe I should hit the road now. I can come back three weekends from now." She straightened her sweater at the waist.

"Ohhh, noooooo," I whined. My heart clotted with sadness. "Why so soon?"

My mom reached out to hug me. "I can go to Starbucks with you, or I can leave now." Since her departure was inevitable, I decided to set her free. I wanted her to beat dusk anyway. "Go, Mom. I don't want you crossing that nasty Bay Bridge at night. Please call me when you cross it."

She squeezed me tight one more time and kissed my cheek before running her fingers down my hair. "I love you, sugar foot."

The ball of dread in my throat compromised easy swallowing. I, too, was a mother now. It was important to transfer my energy to my daughter and not waste it on sadness and attachment.

I held hands with my mom and squeezed hers gently. "I love you so much, too. You're the best." It reminded me of the days when she held my hand as we walked together into the school building on the first day. As we stood in my daughter's nursery, throwing a temper tantrum felt tempting as I felt her hand slide from mine. Even as an adult, she was my backbone.

I gave her one last quick hug and stepped away. "Drive safely, Mom."

"I will, baby."

Oliver turned to bring Autumn to her grandmother. "Here, say, 'bye' to her so she won't cry in the night for you." His gesture melted my heart.

My mom giggled as she took Autumn into her arms again. After communicating with baby-talk and showering her with affection, Oliver took Autumn back and placed her into the crib. My mom gave Oliver a hug. In some way, I felt like my decisions would let my mother down.

My mom held our hands as she walked with Oliver and me to the front door. Before reaching the door, he grabbed her bag and purse from the sofa. She spun to tell us, "You guys take care of my little baby in there. And, Oliver," she added, poking him in the chest, "you take care of my original baby right here."

"I will," he pledged.

A pensive smile crossed her face. "I am one lucky woman. Good job, Summer."

"Yeah." I wiped a stupid tear from my eye.

She slid her bag from Oliver's shoulder and accepted her purse. "Thanks, honey."

"No. Let me." Oliver took her bag back and headed for the elevator to follow her down.

As my mother blew a kiss at me and disappeared behind the door, I tried to pretend that I didn't feel the hole in my heart.

Brooke

The hot and steamy bathroom hid two lovers behind an ajar door. Italian jazz played overhead through Brooke's speakers, setting the mood among the foggy mirrors. Lavender floated through the air like an intrusive ghost. In her oval Jacuzzi tub, Brooke's manicured feet pressed against Jackson's defined torso. Each red toenail tap danced across each squared muscle stacked across his abdomen.

Easing her torso against the tub with her hair pinned on top, Brooke cocked her head back with closed eyes. "Mmmmmm. So, so good."

Jackson grabbed her foot with a firm grip and began to press his thumb into the sole of her foot with one hand while squeezing her heel with the other.

"Relax, baby, I got you."

"That, you do. Thank you, baby."

"I know things have been tough, you know, with Summer and all."

"Her, the business, the clients. I need a freaking vacation, Jackson."

"Can you hold off till the honeymoon? I can't get out of work till then. You wanna vacation with your friends instead? Maybe Summer could use one, too."

Jackson's fingers stopped working when Brooke's head straightened. She snapped her fingers at him, eyeing her feet. "Hey, bruh, get back to work there. Who told you to stop?"

Following her orders, he chuckled. "Sure, sure."

"And you're the sweetest fiancé, you know that?"

"Can't wait to make it official. Then I can ditch this wack-ass title."

Brooke smiled at him through loving eyes, still wrestling with the reality that they'd found their way back to each another. "I can't wait to become Brooke Sloan." She warned him with a finger. "But I'm keeping my maiden name for business, okay?"

"I got cha." He playfully rolled his eyes.

"You know, Emily was too excited that I asked her to be my maid of honor. Since she has a wedding coming up, and I have Haysia, she doesn't have to worry about having anything extra on her plate."

"Oh, that's cool."

"Yeah. I mean, aside from the two of us being so close, it was a clear option. Summer has too much on her plate right now . . . Ruben . . . Autumn. And, Amber, nah. Nope-di-dope. Never qualified."

"Damn that's harsh." He grinned.

"No. She'd be out of her element. Really. If I needed her opinion about style or *anything*, I—we're just on two different pages. Emily is safe. She gets me."

"Well, sounds like you got it all worked out, even if she's got the job in name only and by default." He chuckled.

"Stop it. Besides, when I told Amber and Summer, they totally supported my choice."

"Glad to hear there's no catty drama."

"Not on my day. And Jared is cool with being your best man?"

"Oh absolutely."

"Nice. We are smooth sailing so far."

"Good to hear."

The steamy water massaged Brooke's skin while turning her fingers into prunes. "Will we always make time for these bathtub moments?"

"Under one condition." He lowered his chin to kiss the bottom of her toes with eyes that never disconnected from hers.

"What's that?"

"I get to do this . . ." Jackson released her foot, grabbed her outer thighs, and pulled her close. The water fought against her body in one flat wave as she locked groins with her man. With her knees pointed toward the ceiling, Jackson stared at her through a lascivious smile.

"I want you. I wanna make an ocean up in here."

Brooke giggled. "Jackson—"

"Shut up," Jackson ordered with an almost ascetic expression. Brooke didn't quite know what to make of his sudden change in demeanor until he lifted her leg high enough to expose the inside of her thigh. He tasted the glistening, moist skin with a tongue flick. Smacking his lips together as he processed her taste, he moved in close again to repeat the action, but pushed his full lips tenderly into her skin, releasing slowly, sensually, lost in his own world.

Jackson spoke to her leg. "Mmmmmm, baby. This is what daddy looks forward to after sitting behind the screen all day." He rolled his eyes to Brooke's as he went in for another kiss in the same spot, this time, releasing his tongue to smooth over her moist skin.

Sucking in air between her teeth, Brooke's vagina responded with a tingle to their arrested gaze. Sacrificing a hand from her leg, he moved it to her nipple and pinched it for added pleasure. Brooke closed her eyes and eased her head back. She couldn't stand to face him. He could eat her pussy through his stare alone.

"*Ahh.*"

Easing her leg down and sliding a hand between her legs to massage her inner thighs, Jackson closed the space between their chests to place his chin on her shoulder. Tilting his head, he kissed her neck several times and whispered, "Do you wanna come?"

"Yes," she barely managed.

Teasing her, he asked, "Are you sure?"

"Please. Do it. I wanna come for you." Brooke wrapped her arms around him until her nails skated over his back.

"I love you," he whispered.

Brooke felt the mist of a tear, even with closed lids. A tear ran away from the comfort of her eye and headed for her chin. Jackson must've seen it, because he abandoned her thighs and grabbed her face.

Staring into her eyes, Jackson asked, "What's wrong, baby?" His hand eased down her throat, between the hills on her chest, and over the flatland and back under the ocean to find her hidden treasure.

"I'm so . . ." She rolled her neck with dopey eyes until they fluttered before closing. "Happy. Mmmmm."

"Good." He placed a gentle kiss on her neck. "Good. Let's get you ecstatic." Jackson's hand crossed his chest to turn her face in his direction to get what he wanted—her lips.

Brooke opened her mouth to let his tongue in. They tasted one another, knowing no boundaries, grabbing all the flavor that each one had to offer. She squeezed the back of his neck for release while resisting any ideas of mercy to welcome the pain of gratification. She moaned as his tongue worked her mouth and his hand worked her shelter of power. He manipulated it with his upside-down index finger until it woke up to send sweet lightning bolts throughout her groin. Feeling his ax grinding against her stomach, Brooke was ready to beg for it. Ready for take-off, she wanted that rocket into her space.

Jackson gave up her lips to watch her face contort beautifully under his incantation. Wriggling under his control within the water, Brooke arched her back, welcoming him inside of her. His finger, rubbing between her folds, caressing them up and down, inserted itself into her galaxy. Using his other hand, he pushed one of her breasts from under the water to draw the allure from her nipple into his mouth.

As his teeth clamped around the base of it, Jackson sucked hard, sandwiching her nipple between the roof of his mouth and tongue. Drawing his mouth away, he stared at it before diving back in with a circling tongue that tasted her water-sprinkled areola while playing her guitar under water. Brooke's feet drove up and down the tub like a car, each one going in the opposite direction.

Yasssssss, daddy, yassssss. Give me that sweet dick.

As if he could hear her thoughts, relinquishing all sexual ties to her body, Jackson eased her back, so he could straddle her. He positioned himself perfectly; he was the airplane, she was the landing strip. She waited for his next move, anticipating his dip into her pool as she grabbed his cock to play with its length and tip. She felt the slant of his tip, allowing her thumb to play over his hole. He released a long grunt with a tightened jawbone.

"Dive deep, baby. Dive deep," she told him in a husky whisper.

"Do you own a mop, baby?"

Puzzled, she blinked a few times. "What?" She chuckled. "You know I do."

"Good, cuz we gon' need it." Jackson eased onto her body and kicked her hand to the side with his hand. Balancing his weight with one arm on the edge of the tub and his other hand planted on the floor of the tub, Jackson lined up his business and filed it in the right place.

Brooke accepted his length with squeezed eyes and an open mouth while tilting her head back. "Ahhh, *hell yeah, baby*. Yeah."

She felt the expansion of his width, the tension of need stuffed into her like sand in a cup. Jackson took up all possible space, brushing against her walls and alerting her senses. Brooke squeezed her core around his penis, clapping against him with her own manipulated beat. Moving her head forward, she wanted to capture the look of sweet pain written across Jackson's face. With his eyes closed, he reacted with furrowed brows and a tightened jaw.

"Damn, baby." Jackson opened his eyes and aimed for her lips. "I need this. I need you."

Brooke captured his loving and painstaking stare. Resting inside of her before continuing any motion, he searched for something past her eyes. Brooke barely placed her fingertips along the sides of his jaw, wishing that this moment could last a lifetime.

"Jackson?"

"Yeah?" he whispered.

"Baby, you better wear this pussy out like it's the last slice of the century."

Jackson's eyes widened with a stare of stone. Arching an eyebrow, he used the outer arm propped on top of the tub to support his elbow as that same hand gripped her face. Sliding back and forth into Brooke, he covered her mouth with his, sucking hungrily on her lips.

"Mmm, mmmm, mmmm!" Brooke whimpered under the delicious capture of her fiancé.

Jackson anchored himself with a knee as he lifted his hand from under water to wrap his arm behind Brooke's head. Relinquishing her face, he searched for her hand and yanked it up past her head as he drove into her with such a devoted thrust. Locking her into a safe haven, Brooke felt her lover's shaft push deeper into her, knowing that there was no limit, and that there would never be one. She didn't need to wait until marriage to give herself over to him completely. That happened the day he sat down at her table in Starbuck's. She just didn't quite know it then.

Rolling her neck around once they disconnected at the lips, Brooke's eyes could barely sustain sight as he almost knocked the vision out of her. She did understand why he'd asked for a mop. The water from within ferociously lapped at the rim of the tub until one strong wave jumped over the porcelain and onto the floor. Catching each other's gaze, he smirked, hiding his face into her neck.

Brooke felt Jackson's kisses against her damp skin with grunts in her ear as he struggled to catch a devoted breath. One of her hands gripped his butt cheek, allowing her to feel his dedication to the gym every time he pushed inward. She wanted to make sure she didn't miss an inch with every pump. Calling his name, he became more intense, even though she didn't think this man would have more to give. That good burn started a fire between her legs. Brooke's clitoris started to get the shimmies. She felt the butterfly of life coming to as it prepared to leave the cocoon.

Fly away, baby, fly away.

Starting from her toes, Brooke felt the power of that dick releasing the chains of pleasure, saw the water rain on the floor in heaps, felt the skin on his shoulder under her teeth as she took a bite for mercy, released a cracked sound from the pit of her throat, heard his suppressed cry for goodness hum like a needle skirting a vinyl record at the end of the album.

When her body hit a point of sensory overload, Brooke's orgasm exploded like a shaken can of an opened soda.

"Ohhhh, Jackson!" She clawed her fingernails into his butt cheek and squeezed his hands and fingers with the other. "Ohhhhh, shiiiiiit!" Brooke knew that Jackson let his balls bust when he dipped into her with intermittent thrusts that pressed into her for seconds at a time.

Collapsing on top of her with a throbbing heartbeat and pulsating chest, Jackson whispered, "Damn," before barely moving to her side.

With her arms slung carelessly over the tub, Brooke eyed the floor with eyes of horror. "Oh, my." Barely able to speak, she turned to look at a grinning Jackson, whose eyes fell elsewhere. "We made a mess, baby. We better get up."

"Oh, please." He shook his head. "Relax."

She wished that she could adapt his nonchalant attitude about things, but it wouldn't be who she was. Sometimes she got the feeling that he liked to do things to test her, to call her out on her own freakish, controlling ways. Brooke knew her man and was onto him. She turned at the waist and slapped both hands over the rim of the tub and said, "But, honey, my floors will be ruined," and then turned back to Mr. Carefree. All he needed was a hammock and pineapple juice with a leg dangling to the side. "But you couldn't care less."

"*Brooke*. You know I will get it, Ma." Jackson turned to her with a smirk. "In the meantime, roll your sexy ass over here and take this dick for another spin, so I can bust all up in ya again."

Still worried about the water but unable to resist this man, she smirked as she felt the attitude leaving her body. "Well, you know I'm achy, baby." But she twisted her body to transition to a straddling position.

"That's the best kind of pussy." He bit on his folded lips as Brooke settled onto his lap.

"Oh, yeah, Zaddy? Oh, yeah?" Brooke rocked over his groin, knowing that he'd need some time.

"Lemme get that nipple real quick. Let's get you happy again." Jackson slipped one hand under Brooke's vagina and inserted his thumb between her curtains to find the lightning rod. Leaning forward to take a damp breast into his mouth, he massaged the nipple with his tongue and mouth. Brooke closed her eyes to focus on the sensation. It traveled down to her groin, like lightning hitting the ground, electrifying things around it. He worked her clitoris, moving his thumb in circles, sending fuzzy feelings of a sugar rush all over her body. It was like the effects of something too sweet, but nothing about this had side effects.

Enjoying the play, Brooke rocked her hips from right to left to help agitate the feeling. She played in her wet hair with one arm behind her head with closed eyelids, wanting to focus on the feeling. She felt her strong man's arm grab her close with his forearm pressed against her back. Jackson's thumb moved away as another finger slid in to take its place.

"You like that, baby?"

Brooke opened her eyes long enough to see a man staring up at her with a smirk. She cupped her other breast with her hand and replied, "I dooooo."

With smoky eyes, Jackson said, "I wanna eat your pussy."

Sucking air between her teeth, Brooke whispered, "Go, 'head, baby. It's yours."

"Come here, then."

Brooke wiggled away from him to place her back against the tub, placing herself beside his feet. Jackson stood like a Greek god emerging from the ocean with water escaping his skin and diving back into the tub. Towering over her and peering down over his nose, his damp muscles glistened from the kisses of water like sun hitting gold in a pile of dirt. He stood strong, manly, and in charge, ready to take his queen from the filth of a day's labor to a lair of reward and pleasure.

Stepping out with one foot touching the wet wood at a time, Jackson's big, powerful shaft swung like a rope from a tree. Brooke bit down on her lip with a desire to grab it for dear life to do things to it that no woman should.

Her eyes rolled up to his, daring him to do something about his desire. Throwing her hand up for him to grab, she rose to her feet letting the water escape from her body and stepped out beside her king. Bending over to scoop her up, Jackson hugged Brooke close, allowing her to smell the traces of lavender from the soap suds. She'd chosen the scent, promising to serve as an aphrodisiac, to which he'd insisted was pointless given his residual need to have her.

Leaving foot trails from the bathroom to her bed, Jackson eased her onto the middle of the mattress, as he climbed in between. Opening her legs in one aggressive motion, Brooke watched her man with an appetite for the serving between her legs. Standing on his knees and over her, he licked his lower lip, staring with eyes that hit hers before looking at what she had to offer.

In a husky tone, he told her, "Ahhh, mama. I'm ready to feast."

Remaining silent in anticipation, Brooke bit down on her finger as she longed to feel the steamroll of pleasure. Her hips danced a little with excitement, the walls of her pussy throbbed as it expected the familiar rush from enduring Jackson's tongue. That feeling of waiting and feeling his wet muscle tasting her made her heart race faster than a Nascar driver.

Jackson laced his arms under her legs with his hands relaxing on top of her thighs. Waiting to feel that first lick, Brooke held a deep breath in the pit of her stomach until she felt her man's tongue tickle the inside of her folds. Sucking in a quick, sharp breath, Brooke released the air between her lips as her toes curled and stomach shivered. Brooke loved watching the man she loved going to town in the secret location.

Not only did Brooke love this man, but he knew what he was doing. Every. Single. Time. Moaning under the work of his mouth, she gripped the sheets as Jackson's mouth kissed and nibbled her labia. His tongue wiped her inner and outer lips before reaching her pleasure pearl.

Jarring her hips upward, she cried, "Jackson!"

Paying her no mind, he rubbed his beard over her naked vulva, erupting small flames to her follicles. She wiggled hard underneath his body. Jackson inserted two fingers into her mouth of arousal and worked in circles and sliding motions. Gripping one arm around her leg and perching his chin on her knee, he watched her with a grin as her gaped mouth released sounds of approval. She eyed him with a hazy stare, tweaking her nipples with hands pressed against the outer form of her breasts. The pressure from his fingers exploring her walls only intensified as Jackson lowered his head for round two.

Two golden, glistening shoulders showed movement above the horizon of her vulva. The top of his head faced her, while he sucked on her clitoris, gently, with his soft, full lips.

Panting, Brooke wriggled under the extreme sensation. "Mmmmm. Mmmmmm, Jackson, *please*. Oh, baby. I can't. I can't." Brooke's nipples became rock-hard. She swung a leg over his back and arched her foot as she coasted her heel up and down his skin. She felt his tongue move from her clitoris and down to her vagina. Removing his fingers, he inserted his tongue into the hole of wonders as he worked her clitoris with fingers.

"Ah! Stop! Mmmmm. Please, Jackson, *please*, Jackson." Brooke's heart jumped so hard she thought a bunny would pop out of her chest. She clawed the top of his head, grabbing for hair that wasn't long enough to pull while feeling herself being killed softly at the hands of his skill level. The whoosh that started at her toes came again, causing her feet to wildly travel up and down her sheets as the pit of her womanhood erupted a sweet energy that sent deep shivers over her being, while pooling at the cause. "Damn!"

Jackson continued to work, lapping up her milk like a cat at a bowl. Wiping his mouth clean with the back of his hand, Brooke struggled to breathe with a spinning head and pounding chest. It was all too much. Her limbs felt like spaghetti attached to her frame. Noticing his hard-on, Brooke knew he wasn't done and wondered if she could survive. It really didn't matter. He could get it again, especially after that performance.

Two smacks against her thigh and an order of, "Turn over," placed Brooke on all fours after Jackson helped her flip with impatient hands. Collecting herself without seeing what was going on behind her head, she felt Jackson slide in from behind, working her pussy again with his raw cock. Smashing repeatedly into her, Brooke felt a good vibration hit her groin. Biting her lower lip, she heard him say, "You've been a dirty girl, coming all over my face like that." Jackson reached for her damp strands and pulled them tight, sending her head back. "You want this, huh? You like it rough, don't you? I told you I was gonna get you. You can't escape."

Whipping into her ass with his package, Brooke cried out as she struggled to stay up on her knees even though Jackson had a grip along her side. Her fingers worked tirelessly to keep a hold on the sheets. She winced with each shot, liking it, hoping to capture another orgasm.

"I like it, I like it," she cried.

Jackson slammed faster and harder, and Brooke knew he needed to bust after what felt like too damn long. She could hear his gritted teeth when he said, "You bad, pussy."

Grunting and slowing down, his hand moved to her breast and grabbed it with several squeezes as he released.

"Ohhhh," Brooke cried as she accomplished a third vaginal victory.

As they settled into the ideal position across her bed, she knew the chaos of life had just been released within the last hour.

Amber

Trying her hand at the domestic life, Amber dully straightened Daniel's tie. His large hand rested on her butt, which was clad in shorts that barely covered her cheeks. She firmly patted his chest when she was done. "Have a nice day, sir."

"Kiss, kiss, my chocolate bunny." When Daniel puckered his lips with closed eyes, Amber rolled hers as she went in to kiss him. "Good. What are you going to do today?"

"Hmmmm," Amber twisted from side to side at the waist. "Class starts tonight."

"Oh, yeah?" He raised his brows. "Which one?"

"English. How exciting," she replied sarcastically.

"Am*berrrrr*," he said. "Be positive and do your best," he lectured, picking up the briefcase beside his feet.

"Bet."

Daniel smacked her butt before turning to leave. "Bye, precious."

"All right, Daniel."

Anxious to have private time, Amber felt relieved to see him go through the double wooden doors. She took a seat on the bottom of the fancy staircase and dialed Emily. She threw her waist-length braids over her shoulder and waited for Emily to pick up the phone.

After the line rang four times, Emily finally picked up. "Hello, Amber."

"What up, sis?"

Sounding happy, she replied, "Enjoying life. Waiting for Eric to finish up in the shower. We just . . . you know." She giggled.

"Ahhhh, well believe me when I say I'm happy to hear that. Hey, listen, have you heard from Summer? Do you know how she's doing?"

"Ummm, briefly. I decided to give her a quick call last night. She's home, but she wasn't too chatty. I feel so bad for her. I wish there was something we could all do for her."

"Same here." Amber rubbed her leg. "Poor baby. She ain't herself right now. I know she wanted her daughter to have that bond with her father though. I loved having a relationship with my dad; it was priceless." The emotion started to stir in her chest. The mist developed in her eyes.

"You know, you and I have that in common, and I agree. My dad is my hero. So, I couldn't imagine . . ."

Amber wiped an unexpected tear from her eye. "It still hurts that I don't have my dad, let alone parents. But at least I had them."

"Oh, Amber, I'm so sorry. I didn't mean to upset you."

"No, no, no, Emily, please don't take it that way. I'm glad you have somethin' the rest of us don't have: two parents. Oh, God, I could never ask that you apologize for that blessin'."

"Thanks. Hey, how's your new house?"

Amber appreciated Emily's effort to change the topic.

"Chile, lemme tell you. You guys have to come over one day. It's a big, beautiful house. It's a mini mansion. He even said that he can't wait for Mara to come and visit me."

"You sure he's not expecting a threesome?" Emily fell over laughing, and Amber had to join her at the sick thought.

"Ohhhh, you know I'm a freak, but not that much! I don't think we need to bunk up in a five-bedroom home."

"You sure? You sure?" she teased. "Oh, hey, listen, Eric cut the water off. But, yeah, arrange something for us girls, and we'll come over."

"Enjoy your corporate romp."

"Yes, trollop, you should know."

"Puh-lease. I'm sure you got some hot, Latina moves that you can teach me. Don't act like I'm the only one."

"Oh, come on. In twenty-eighteen, is this the best stereotype you could come up with? I can teach you money principles and teach you English."

"Bye, Ho-lita. Bye."

They chuckled and hung up. Even though she felt better after speaking with Emily, she wanted to speak to one more person who sat above everyone else: Mara.

"Hello?"

"Hey, sweetheart."

"*Amber*. I didn't look at my screen before picking up. What a surprise."

"How's school?"

"School is better. Staying here for summer courses helped. I'm not so lonely anymore. And you?"

"That's what's up, baby! I moved. I ain't in the hood no more." Amber cackled with jerking body movements.

"Whaaaaat?" Mara sounded so happy for Amber. "You got a high-paying gig or something?"

"Nah, baby girl. Slow your roll." Amber released a strained laugh. "Ummm, Daniel, you know the one who hurt me?"

"That jerk, yeah. Go on."

"He came back into my life and asked me to move in. He apologized, so I did. So, I'm in school, and he's helpin' with my bills." Amber heard the silence on the other end of the phone. The one criticism that she couldn't stand, was the kind that came from her sister.

"Oh, well, that's . . . good. I am so proud of the school news. Really, Amber, education can never hurt. What's your major?"

"Being that numbers ain't so bad, maybe accounting. Not sure. And then I can do music on the side."

"Right. That does sound good, Amber. Guess what?"

"Yeah?" Amber was perfectly aware of the fact that Mara hadn't commented on the fact that Daniel was back in her life.

"I'm like, ten pounds lighter. I'm throwing out my older clothes as I go. Then I have no choice but to keep losing or to at least maintain. Salads are my friend now. But, my girl Nyla and I walk together, too. She's sick of being a twenty."

Amber beamed with pride. "That's my girl. Keep it up. Yo, Mom and Dad would be proud. And, hey, Daniel wants to know if you tryna stay with us."

"Umm." She paused. Amber could see Mara with a pensive finger over her chin. "Are you sure about him? He did treat you badly."

And there it was. "I'm a grown woman. I'm gettin' my bills paid, I have transportation, a nice home—I'm happy, Mara. Please don't overanalyze this. Be happy for me."

"It's hard to get excited for you when this is all provided for you by a man. Okay, okay. Just save your money. If you two break up, you'll need to have money in your corner, not just good credit."

"I'm lookin' forward to good credit. That's a strange concept to me."

"Amber, I have to get to the registrar's office to straighten something out."

"Oh. I hear you, baby. But hold on. How were the grades?"

"Columbia's hard, but I'm rocking with the As and Bs right now from freshman year. Think I did well for the summer, too. Thanks for asking, though."

"Aww, shucks! That's how we do, baby. That's how we do."

Mara giggled. "Please take care of yourself, sis. I love you sooooo much."

"Don't make me cry. Wait. Are you gonna come visit me one weekend or nah? Remember, Brooke and Jackson are gettin' married, and so are Emily and Eric."

"Yeeeeah. I'm not sure just yet. Depends on school. I can*not* believe E & E are getting back after what happened with you and him."

"Right? But, hey, at least I don't feel like I ruined them forever."

"True. How's Summer coping?"

"We only guessin' she's gettin' by all right. We don't really know. But, she got Oliver and that bundle of joy."

"Please tell her I'm thinking of her."

"I will."

"Okay." Mara exhaled loudly. "Alright, well, lemme get going before I miss this lady again. But, sis, you take care and be safe."

"I will, hon. Love you bunches, and good luck."

"Thanks, sis. Talk to you real soon."

"Alright."

They hung up.

Amber stood and looked around her new three-level home, taking it all in. As she paced the dark, wooden floors to admire his home in private, she made her way to her Steinway piano placed in the living room corner. She sat and played a piece with her eyes closed. Flashbacks of her life played in her mind, from wearing Sunday's best to church, to her family eating dinner in their 1300-square-foot house. A tear rolled down her cheek once she opened her eyes upon completing the piece. Expecting to see the surroundings of her own apartment, Amber saw the 5,000-square-foot home instead.

"Wow," she whispered.

She knew she would do whatever she had to do to maintain her new lifestyle with Daniel in his $2 million northwest home. Maybe she would come to love him, maybe not. However, love was not at the top of her list like it was for most women, especially since her recent attempts resulted in dead ends. They quickly reminded her that she was not a woman with an interest in love. Daniel could provide a life without worry in exchange for sex and companionship. Getting up from the piano while carrying her thoughts with her, Amber approached the wooden stairs and headed to their spacious master bedroom to take a nap.

Emily

Emily watched Eric adjust the tie to his Brooks Brothers' suit in the full-length mirror, as he juggled his stare from her eyes to his tie.

"It's August, baby, and you have to come to grips that it's the end of the summer for you. Ready to head back to work?" He gave the tie one last tug before spinning around. With outstretched arms, he asked, "How do I look?"

Emily crawled to the edge of the bed on her knees to meet him. Her long, heavy hair whipped from side to side behind her. "Like a million bucks." She kissed him on the lips then massaged his shoulders. In a husky, whispery voice, she replied, "I *am* ready to go back to work."

"I'm ready to do you here."

Dressed in bikini panties and a bra, Emily brushed her skin against his suit. "Come on then."

Eric caressed a cheek. Clenching his jawbone, he rejected her. "I can't. I have to go to work. I'm still new here; I have to gain their trust."

Emily pouted and sat against her heels. "Eric. I'm sorry again about that childish stunt."

"Emily, don't even think about it again. I betrayed you one too many times, so I had something coming. Now come give me a kiss bye-bye."

With raised spirits, Emily threw her arms around Eric's lean shoulders and told him, "You're great. Have I told you that before?"

"Now you have." He smiled.

She kissed him. "Well, remember this, and I will tell you over and over each day. Now get going."

"Yeah, I can't lose this job. It was hard enough trying to land it." He bent at the knees to pick up his briefcase. "Ems, I'm not sure if I'll be back tonight. I may crash at my place. I'll call you."

Emily nodded and waved. She really hadn't realized how much she missed Eric, until he came back into her life. The last thing she wanted, was to experience that type of emptiness all over again.

2: her undoing

Emily

"I'm glad you could come over," Emily said as she opened the door to allow Zach through.

He removed his baseball cap and took a seat on her white three-cushioned sofa. He grunted as he sat. "Working on houses, you know, remodeling, it can be taxing on the body sometimes."

Emily flashed a perfunctory smile. "Water?"

"That'd be great, thanks."

As she headed toward her modest-sized kitchen, she realized how disconnected she felt from Zach. She couldn't help but realize that he felt the same way, too. "I have to warn you," she told him with her hand on the faucet. "My filter expired, and I don't buy bottled water. Is tap okay?"

"Oh. Well, yeah, oh hell, it's all the same."

Emily couldn't disagree more, but she cringed on the inside as she let the water from the sink fill his glass.

"I should really invest in a fridge with a built-in ice maker and water sprout. Really sick of buying filters."

She took it to him and sat on the other end of the sofa with her body pointing in his direction.

Zach thanked her and took a long sip. His suspicious eyes rested on the middle cushion between them. "What? Do I smell like hard labor or something?"

"No." Emily let out a short, dull laugh. "I have something to tell you, so I'm glad you stopped by."

"I'm listening." Zach didn't seem full of life as usual. He seemed reserved, and Emily's suspicion that it was work-related didn't seem to explain it either.

"There's no way to say it but to say it. Eric and I are back together."

He grinned. It was a bitter grin. The kind that hid the fact that the wind had been knocked from him. He scratched the top of his head with a finger. "Gee, Emily."

He peered at the ceiling with squinted eyes. "With you, I always wait for the other shoe to drop."

Emily felt slightly insulted. "What is that supposed to mean? That's not fair."

"Neither is life . . . apparently." With hostility, he placed the glass down on the end table next to him and turned his body to face her. One of his hands grabbed the other. "Emily. You and Eric are chaotic. You know that? Do you see me running back to Heather? No. That woman brought nothing but drama and confusion into my world."

"I don't have kids," she replied defensively. "If I'm going to make mistakes, now is the time." She pointed a hand at her chest. "I can take care of myself."

"Soooooo, not having children is an excuse to treat yourself badly?"

"Look, Zach, I'm sure that you had to do what was best for Enzo. You're a parent. Children grow up to judge and assess their parents' methodologies in the department of parenthood. I'm not there yet." Emily could feel the heat rising from within. "So, please, get off my back."

"And what happened to the handshake, Ems? You know, the one we had after sex in *your* living room? Did that not mean anything?"

"Of course, it did," she squealed. "But that was then, and this is now. Besides, we're not blood brothers who made a pact or something. We're adults."

"*Exactly*, Emily. As adults, we oughta be people of our words." In pain, Zach stood slowly.

Emily did the same, not knowing what to say. Maybe there was nothing *to* say.

He shoved his hands into the pockets of his fitted blue jeans with a look of regret and exhaustion. His eyes met hers. "You know . . ." He took a break to choose his words wisely. "Give a person one more chance and you're sweet. Give a person another one down the line, and you're creating a pattern."

The gaze behind his eyes wasn't condescending, but one of pity. As he moved toward the door, Emily froze, certain that he could see the words floating over and away from her head.

Before he yanked the door open, he turned to her one last time to say, "You think about that tonight. I'll be in my neck of the woods carrying on with life."

Emily followed him to the door when he had one foot out. She held it open long enough to deliver a message. "Hey, Zach?" He spun slowly. "Tell Enzo good luck this coming school year. And I hope you take care of yourself. Try not to work too hard."

"Somehow I get the feeling that that will be you."

"Just go to hell, Zach." Emily slammed the door behind her. She turned, then flattened her back against it while pretending not to be haunted by his words of caution.

Brooke

Watching her fiancé in the kitchen after waking from a nap in the bedroom, Jackson swung a dish towel over his shoulder. He placed the roasted duck and sautéed vegetables on the plate. Balancing the two plates, he approached the table to set them down in front of their chairs and beside the glasses of sparkling cider. Wearing a silk nightgown slip, Brooke groggily eyed the two plates resting on the table. She could see the steam escaping the roasted duck.

Jackson grinned when he saw her yawn. "You look pretty in purple.

Leaning against the kitchen wall, she said, "Thanks, babe."

"Come on. Sit with me." Smiling, he ushered a hand at the chair she always dined in.

"I don't . . . I have never eaten a duck. I can only eat birds that begin with the letter *c* and *t*. Duck seems too strange."

"Well, tonight you have to try." Jackson gazed at her with unwavering eye contact that would melt any woman.

Working on being more fun and less rigid, she took her place beside him at the table. He sat at the end and she sat on the corner. Studying the golden duck with eyes of admiration, she asked, "Can I hire you?"

Jackson grinned and grabbed her hand. "Let's give thanks. Bow your head." Jackson blessed their food with a prayer to God, and afterwards, he tucked his cloth napkin into his collar.

Brooke sprawled hers into her lap. "Do you always say grace?"

"I try to. You?" He sliced into his duck and when he saw the moisture, he said, "Perfect."

"I should."

"Guess you should simply work on it. How was your day off?"

Brooke sliced a knife into the duck and decided to be a trooper. "Wait. Let me get this duck into my mouth." A vision of a duck in the water attempted to hold her back, but seeing the trouble that her man went through allowed her to push past her reluctance. "Here we go." Placing the fork into her mouth, she chewed and allowed the flavor to hit her tongue. It was excellent, and all her idiosyncrasies seemed to melt away with the bite. "On point, Jackson. So on point." She closed her eyes with an, "Mmmmmmm." When she opened them, Jackson wore a grin as he watched her. "Wow. My day was fantastically boring. Thank you for asking. And yours?"

"Bastards wouldn't let me off today, because I was the only one who could do what they needed. I wanted to be with you."

"They needed you like I need your cooking?"

"Every night when I go home, I cook for myself. I only eat out on dates and other rare occasions. Cooking gives you all the control from the beginning to end."

Brooke washed her food down with a sip of sparkling cider. "Speaking of control, we need to talk about living arrangements and the wedding. Oh—the honeymoon as well."

Nodding and chewing, Jackson replied, "Like who should move in with who? Or maybe we should buy something together?"

Brooke pointed a finger at him with a smile. "But let's get something straight. I'm not selling my condo."

His eyes quickly shifted from his plate to her. "Well, neither am I. I've always wanted something at the Harbor."

Brooke's fingers tapped the table. "Then what? I have two extra rooms, one being my office." She shrugged.

"Look." He placed a hand on hers. "I can move in here. I work in DC, you have friends in DC, and your office is right across the street. I don't want you commuting to your new office. All I have is a condo across the way. Everything we do is here. Besides . . ." He went silent. Brooke waited for him to continue with a crinkle in her brow. "If—I said *if* we have a baby—" Brooke's heart skipped a beat as she realized his walls of doubt had a crack in them, "—this apartment would be best in terms of space and layout."

Brooke placed a hand over her chest, making sure to avoid going overboard with emotions. "That is so kind of you to consider everything that matters to me. I feel a little stingy."

"Brazile, if you're gonna be my wife, my father would smack the back of my head if he learned I didn't place your happiness in front of my own."

Brooke slightly tilted her head as she caressed his hand in silence. Tenderly, she told Jackson, "Well tell him 'thank you.'"

A knock at the door made them jump. Brooke stood up wearing an irritated expression as she marched toward the door. "These stupid guards are bad at giving me a heads-up when I have visitors."

"Maybe I need to have a word with them," Jackson said. "You want me to answer that?"

Brooke called from over her shoulder, "That's all right, babe. I got a peephole."

Standing on her toes to check the face on the other side of the door, she yanked it open when she couldn't discern anything else aside from it being a black woman. Brooke froze. Her jaw dropped when she saw who it was. *Anyone else but her. Anyone else but her.*

"What are *you* doing here?"

Amber

Curled up beside Daniel in the bed, Amber relaxed against him with her naked thigh placed over his legs and her hands under her face on top of his puffy chest.

"Ahh, *The Sopranos* is always a treat to watch," Daniel told her, caressing her upper thigh and butt cheek. Cringeworthy in Amber's eyes, she thought his hands were awfully rough for a man who sat behind a desk all day.

When her stomach growled, Amber sat up abruptly. "What we havin' for dinner?"

"Well, what do you want Amit to cook us? You've been here for a few weeks now. Whatever you want from him, speak up." Daniel returned his attention to the men playing pool, resting one hand on top of his sizeable belly and the other behind his head. "But he should have it prepared by now."

Amber nodded and headed for the door. She turned to face him. "Are you hungry?" She realized her question was stupid, since he never rejected food.

Daniel never broke his gaze from the television. "I'll devour whatever you bring back. But bring me back something."

Amber nodded before heading downstairs to find their help, Amit. Amit was a very young and handsome man, with whom Amber didn't bother to acquaint herself. Usually, he came in the evenings and left by midnight, just to return at dawn before leaving by noon. Amit's main priority was to feed them, if nothing else.

Now that Daniel wasn't by her side, Amber figured it was an ideal time to get to know him. When she turned the corner, she spotted Amit crushing pepper. The back of his dark hair brushed his collar, but he couldn't see Amber with his hair covering the side of his handsome face. He stood in the middle of the kitchen at the island, hard at work.

Creeping toward him with a smile, Amber asked, "Whatcha cookin'?"

His head jerked up to see a braless Amber standing there in a white tank top over shorts that barely covered a few inches of her thighs. Amit smiled, and with a slight accent replied, "I am making a crab salad for you and Mr. Crosby." His amber-colored eyes glistened as he spoke, perhaps grateful for the company.

Amber couldn't wait to try it, so she joined him at the island. Tasting crab would be reminiscent of her visits to the Waterfront next to her apartment.

"I thought we weren't getting fed," she said, lightly laughing. "I came to check things out. How do you do that crushing pepper thing?" Amber rested her fingertips on the edge of the island's granite countertop.

Amit paused. "Well, here." He passed the mortar to Amber. "Hold the mortar in one hand and take this pestle," he passed it to her, "to crush the black peppercorn. Make it as fine as possible."

Amber pressed with all her might. "Wow."

"No, no." His soft voice interrupted Amber. "I muddled it. You're banging it. It's almost done. It's becoming powder-like."

"Oh." She pounded it aggressively with the pestle. "Like this?" When she looked up, she noticed that his eyes were focused between her breasts. "Or should I muddle it now?"

"Like this." When he gently took it back, he showed her the stirring motion. When he passed it back to Amber, she continued the process. She noticed her breasts moved seductively with a jiggle. As she worked, she gave him a quick smile. Clearly, Amit liked what he saw.

"There." Amber released the pestle and took her hands back.

When Amit examined it, he said, "You did great. See the powder?"

"Did you go to school for this?" Amber asked.

"No." He sprinkled the pepper generously over both salads. The fresh smell of the salads teased Amber's nostrils.

Reluctantly, he added in a melancholy tone, "My nanny taught me how to cook to distract me from my barely-there parents." He turned his back to her as he hovered over the salads before retrieving wine glasses from the dark cherry cabinets above his head. "They worked from sun-up to about nine at night. They owned their own restaurant and worked as partners. They wanted me to stay home and study for school. I wanted to be with them." He turned back toward her as he looked at his fingers while tugging at the tips. His mind seemed to drift. Amit cleared his throat. "Well." He flashed a quick smile and for the first time, he seemed shy. "Mr. Crosby may not want me talking to you." Amit turned to grab the bottle of wine and glasses to organize them on the tray.

"Oh, don't you worry about Daniel. I can deal with him," Amber said, sounding like a Hollywood woman of the house.

Amit nodded with a wan smile then headed toward the oversized arch of the dining room before returning for the salads. Amber wanted to help him. "I can at least buzz

Daniel." She pressed the button on the wall intercom and told Daniel to come down for dinner.

"Thank you," Amit said shyly. The switch of demeanor almost made him appear gregarious earlier. Amber couldn't help but feel slightly perplexed. She figured he must've felt that talking with her meant flirting with unprofessionalism should Daniel ever catch wind of it. Amber realized that she must never share that interaction with Daniel.

Minutes later, a shirtless Daniel joined Amber at the Medici dining room table. She secretly rolled her eyes at the sight of his bare belly as they dined. It was an unnecessary attack on her appetite. His throat ejected the one harsh cough—to which Amber had miserably grown accustomed—as he flattened the cloth napkin across his wide lap. For one thing, Daniel failed to cover his mouth every single time. Secondly, the crackle of phlegm in his throat came to mind when he lodged his tongue in her throat during sex. Amber realized that there was a reason why some couples couldn't exist beyond the move-in phase.

During dinner, Daniel tried to make slight conversation as the food managed to remain in the clenches of his teeth. The dressing from his salad formed a bridge between the roof of his mouth and his bottom teeth. Amber struggled to retain her appetite. Nodding, she pretended to care about the work stories he shared.

"I don't know if these people were properly trained or what?" The passion in his voice irritated Amber.

Placing a gentle hand on his hand, she admitted, "Danielboy, let's get something straight. I'm not the kind of woman to indulge you in the tales of the office life and politics. I can't keep up with stiff men and women in suits. Not my style." She ended her revelation with a weak smile.

Embarrassed, Daniel replied, "Oh, well. That's a shame. But okie dokie. You got anything you wanna talk about?"

Amber wanted to eat. She wanted to enjoy the delectable crab salad prepared by the handsome, Amit. She decided to be frank and shook her head. "Nah, I'm good. Just wanna eat. I'm starving like a mug."

Chewing, Daniel smiled. Realizing that she needed water, Amber jumped up. "Be right back. I need water."

"Honey, let Amit—"

Without looking back, Amber called, "That's okay. I can manage." She turned the corner to see Amit retrieving dessert from the oven.

When he saw her, he asked, "Do you like chocolate soufflé?"

Amber licked her lips at the sight of it and inhaled its promising aroma. "Among other things," she replied in a flirtatious tone.

Amit snickered. "Oh, more water?"

Amber opened the door to the refrigerator, making sure to bend over as she reached for a lime on the bottom shelf. "I think I want this lime, too. It brings out flavors in food." She knew it was naughty, but Amit was like that naughty gardener that the housewife was bound to bed.

"Yes, it does. Then next time I will remember to serve it to you and Mr. Crosby."

Amber turned to see him eyeing her with masked desire. His hands clenched the dishtowel in an effort to remain professional and unreadable. The knot in his throat dipped with a hard swallow. Amber knew she was getting to him, but she chalked it up for now as having fun. Walking on her way out of the kitchen, she realized she forgot the water, and so did Amit.

"Go. I will bring it to you." Before Amber could fuss, he held up an assuring hand, "It's okay."

Smiling with a nod, Amber left one stud in one room, as she regretfully joined a dud in the other.

Brooke

"Why are you here?" Brooke demanded.

Staring back at her was a worn-down-looking woman with scars of wrinkles settled into her brown skin.

Immediately, the blood shot to her head and stewed like a pot of soup left on the stove for way too long. Her vision almost doubled in anger causing a rage to burn in her chest with legs that could barely serve their purpose. She couldn't stop shifting from one foot to the other.

This is a nightmare. What a nightmare.

Brooke clutched the bright brass lever for support until pain settled into her hand. This was the last person she'd ever wanted to see.

The woman gripped her oversized handbag with shame. "Brooke. I-I'm sorry. But I need to talk to you." Seemingly timid, the woman found it difficult to make eye contact with her.

Brooke pointed a hasty finger at her. "No! No, no, no, no, no! You do not get to pop up on my doorstep unannounced. You know that!"

"You woulda hung up on me." She seemed devastated at the rejection, but it came across as pathetic to Brooke.

Brooke's attention rapidly turned from the woman and to her right, desperate to keep Jackson from seeing this moment. "Lilly, *you cannot be here*," she emphasized through gritted teeth. "And if you do—"

"What's going on here?" Jackson asked with furrowed eyebrows as he came around the corner.

This was a moment in life that Brooke never wanted to have. She had every intention of keeping her past where it belonged. Embarrassed and overwhelmed, Brooke backed away from the door in horror. The woman stepped through the entrance with the ajar door pressing against her shoulder. Lilly and Jackson witnessed Brooke's collapse against the wall behind her. She slid down the wall until her knees met her chest. Her fists slapped the wooden floor.

"Noooooooo," Brooke cried. She didn't have enough energy to yell or raise her voice. No amount of control prevented Jackson from laying eyes on her visitor. He stood in front of Brooke with a frozen gaze, interpreting the reaction. He squatted down in front of her.

"Baby. Baby. What's wrong? Who's this woman?"

"Her mother," the woman from behind replied.

Jackson turned his head to the side, so he could hear Lilly better.

"I only wanted to speak with my daughter. I have something to tell her."

Jackson turned his face back to his fiancé. "Brooke? You don't wanna talk to your mom?"

Brooke wasn't sure she could focus during her meltdown. Her mom's presence tainted her home. "Get her out," she pleaded with her mouth buried in her knees. "Get her out. Please, Jackson, *do* something."

"Brooke, baby. Come on, baby," Jackson pleaded softly. "You know I'm here for you. Calm down, sweetie. I got you." He kissed her cheek and stood. Brooke raised her face to capture what she could through an averted stare. She refused to acknowledge that woman's presence.

Lilly stared at her daughter through glassy, coffee-colored eyes. "I'm so sorry. I didn't intend to . . . You guys have a lovely home. I should go."

Jackson stopped her. "Wait. Do we have your number?"

He turned to see Brooke crinkle her nose at him. She couldn't understand why he thought being decent toward Lilly was going to fly with her. She expected him to handle things *her* way.

Lilly shook her head. "I doubt it. I'm Lilly Hopkins. I live in southeast. You can look me up that way." She folded her lips inward with a melancholy expression. "Sorry for this. But I have some information that I think my daughter needs to know."

Jackson nodded. "I can't make any promises, Lilly. But I'll talk to her. Do you need help to the elevator?"

Brooke couldn't stand the amount of compassion Jackson showed this woman, especially since he had an idea of what Lilly had put Brooke through as a child. Compelled to do something, she jumped up. Brooke appeared next to Jackson with urgency, screaming hysterically, "No, no, no! Don't you dare help her. Don't even touch that lady." She saw her mom flinch.

Alarmed, Jackson grabbed her by the waist. "Calm down. *Now*. Calm down." Jackson nodded apologetically to Lilly as he shut the door. "Yo, girl, why the hell you wildin' out like that, Brooke?"

Brooke failed to digest how he could look at her with such disapproval, especially when she felt it should've been directed at her mom. "Are you serious, man?"

Jackson raised his hands in the air. "Was she that bad?"

Brooke smacked her palms against her forehead. She pointed at the door. "That lady is not some innocent old lady, Jackson. She's the spawn of the devil himself."

Jackson folded his arms. "Okay, so tell me about it."

Brooke walked to the sofa. On her way there, a very unflattering glimpse in the mirror revealed runny mascara. She vowed to make sure that Jackson would never see her that ugly again, inside or out.

Plopping on the sofa, she waited for him to take his place next to her before speaking. "She ruined my appetite." Brooke looked away from Jackson. "I thought I told you that that lady," she turned to face a concerned Jackson, "—Lilly was colder than any winter I'd ever endured. When I turned eighteen, I changed my last name to match my father's. She only told me my father's first and last name. Told me nothing else about the man." Brooke choked up.

Jackson's face melted in subtle places with sympathy. "Okay, that explains the difference in last names. I know you said she was cold, but exactly how, baby?"

Brooke exhaled years of frustration from the bottom of her throat. "Jackson. Okay, okay, okay." She held up both hands before explaining and placed them against her chin. "Lilly treated me like a stray cat. If she felt her walls crumbling, like a tender moment, she would recede into her hard shell. Do you know that as a child, she only played with me five times?"

Jackson winced. "Wow."

Brooke exhaled. Holding up a finger with each listing, she said, "Uno, Go Fish, Jacks, Monopoly, and Uno again." Brooke shook her head in disappointment before she burst into tears. Jackson pulled her head into his chest. In some way, getting this off her chest with the man she loved and trusted was therapeutic. She only wished that someone told her that her name had been signed up for a session tonight. "Jackson, it was horrible," she cried. Her walls fell as fast as a waterfall and the impact stung at the core of her heart. "All I wanted was a mom. I couldn't even get friendship out of her. She would go on dates and leave me home alone at ten until midnight."

Jackson caressed her back and shoulders. "Baby, I'm so sorry. I'm here for you."

Brooke thought his chest felt warm, like the home she should've found when she was that lonely, sad child.

"I wish I was a neighbor who coulda taken the pain away. Ohhhh, baby."

Brooke pulled back to face him. She glanced tenderly at his eyes and lips as she played with her fingers. "I used to watch scary black-and-white movies on some Friday nights. It was a new tradition that I'd started when I ran out of magazines to cut wedding dresses from until I got new ones. On those nights, it was me and my favorite plastic green bowl with popcorn. It was hideous, but it was my favorite bowl. You know, something you would let your dog lap water from."

Jackson chuckled. "Awww."

"I'd be in the living room, but my mom would be sleeping in her room. It all started one Friday night when I couldn't sleep. I snuck into the living room to watch a scary movie. There was this one very scary movie in particular that I couldn't turn from. I was bored and intrigued, but I knew I would regret it. And that's how my tradition started." She sniffed and wiped her nose.

"Wait." Jackson jumped up and grabbed her some tissue from the other end table. "Here, baby." He sat back beside her.

"Thank you." Brooke blew her nose. She was past embarrassment. "Sorry."

He waved a dismissive hand at her.

"Well, one night she was on a late date and that movie plagued me. I thought my heart was going to burst. I was too scared to be in my room, so I jumped in her recliner with a blanket over my body. Do you know what she said when she came home and saw me in it?"

"Can't imagine."

"She shook my shoulder so rudely. I woke up to her scorning me. She pointed to my room and told me to scat. Lilly reminded me that that was her chair and told me that she'd better not find me in her favorite chair again."

"Did you have anywhere else to sit in the living room?" Jackson leaned forward, listening intently.

"Nope. Just the television, green nasty carpet, and her recliner. I mean, yeah, there was the floor but, uhhh . . . You know." She shrugged.

Thinking, Jackson looked away. "I'm glad you let your childhood propel you and not turn you into a statistic of any kind. What do you think she wanted to say after all this time?"

Brooke's gentle shrug told Jackson that she hadn't a clue. "And I don't care." Brooke stood and crossed the room to study her graduation picture. She took it in her hands. "When I left for college, I washed my hands of her and swore off all communication with the lady. It was liberating." She replaced the picture.

"So, who came to your graduation?" His eyes suddenly seemed full of pain.

Brooke's usually beautiful, brown eyes had been replaced with a blank realization of how lonely her life had been. Her mouth fumbled for words while pushing the pain away. "No one." She crossed her feet at the ankles and folded her arms.

Jackson approached her.

He gingerly grasped her elbows. "No family? None?" He searched her face for a hidden revelation, or maybe he was waiting for her to scream, "Joking!" But he ended up swallowing hard when he realized Brooke had no joke to bare.

Almost inaudible, she replied, "No one."

Speechless, Jackson yanked her close. With arms still folded, Brooke buried her face into his chest for safety, as he chanted how sorry he was, over and over again.

3: ride on

Summer

We called it an end-of-the-summer dinner party hosted by Amber at her new shared residence. The four-level brick home sat on a corner hill like a modernized castle in an urban setting. The grass that blanketed the lawn was perfect in color and nicely trimmed, a far cry from her cramped southwest apartment. Amber had become a reflection of me: a modest-earning woman who moved up in the world because of a man, unlike my mother who did it all on her own.

My mother maintained a modest roof over our heads, fed us at every meal with leftovers to spare, clothed me as needed, and paid every bill on time. It was never easy, but my mother never grimaced or nibbled at my happiness with complaints. So, to think of myself as a woman rescued by a man and to see my friend do the same, I couldn't help but think that our formula could've used some tweaking. Perhaps we needed to rip a page from Brooke's manual of independence.

I stared at Jackson and Brooke's interaction at Daniel's ten-piece dining table. His arm draped over the back of her chair, and when they talked, the other would stare at the other with admiration.

We laughed when Jackson told us, "Yeah, she didn't find it funny that we were at the staircase in Georgetown." They sat happily at one end of the table as Brooke chewed on the baked chicken she opted for instead of lobster.

At the opposite head of the table sat Amber and Daniel. When Daniel shared stories, especially the ones involving Amber, she would put the glass of champagne against her lips and grin uneasily. The strain in her eyes sold me on the real truth. Daniel tried too hard to make them appear as a couple who'd finally found each other.

"I hate the days when I come home to find Amber still at school. But I'm proud of my muffin for getting a grip on education." He shoved the fork into his mouth to chew on his lobster.

A noticeably somewhat smaller-framed Mara sat on the other side of the table with the corner separating her from her sister. Her reserved expression proved that she didn't care for the sudden shacking up of Daniel and her sister. The glow she had in her eyes the first time we met at Emily's dinner party was missing tonight.

"Well," she replied, "I read that a great education can take one far in DC." Mara took a bite of her asparagus.

"That's right, Mara. And I'm so proud of my little Emily for laying the foundation down for these children in the capital." Eric wrapped an arm around Emily and squeezed her shoulder with one big grip. She smiled with puppy eyes, a look I never thought I'd see coming from her eyes to his again.

And then there was us: Oliver and me with my baby in my arms. When we first arrived, everyone including the men, took turns fussing over her. Autumn was doing a good job and barely cried when being passed from Oliver and me. If it weren't for my arms tiring, I would've held her all the way through, although I didn't want to be one of those moms who hogged the baby. My mother warned me about that and how it could lead to an overly attached baby.

"You guys gonna make it through dinner?" Daniel asked.

Everyone chuckled.

Oliver and I felt like zombies most days, and tonight was one of them. Many nights were full of interruptions between the feedings and the diaper changes. Oliver pitched in as much as he could, but since he had to be up for work, and I didn't, I tried to take over as much as possible.

"Oh, we are gonna do this," Oliver declared with humor. He set his fork down as he gestured with his hands. "Hey, guys, true story. I woke up one night to a baby's cry. Summer had just slipped into bed, but I didn't know it."

When I realized the story he was going to tell, I fell over laughing as he continued.

"She looked at me like, 'what are you doing?' because I woke up saying, 'The baby. She needs to be changed, I heard her crying a moment ago.' Summer tells me that she wasn't crying and that I was dreaming it, because she'd just put Autumn down ten minutes ago."

My friends laughed with us.

"I was a mess," Oliver confessed. "Our daughter's cry followed me into my dreams."

"It was a good nightmare," I pointed out.

Oliver smiled. "True."

"You guys are so cute," Emily told us.

"Yeah," Oliver said. "I think we've all been through a lot since the last time we sat together.

I noticed a nod of agreement between Brooke and Jackson and the locking of eyes between Emily and Eric. Mara bit down on the inside of her lip as she avoided any eye contact while her sister took a long swig of champagne. Their handsome hired help added another bottle of champagne to the table. I think I heard Daniel call him Amit.

"I think we should make a toast," Daniel suggested.

Amber slid an arm over the back of his chair. Perhaps it was the champagne that made her lower her guard to act more like a couple.

"To love and staying together," Daniel said.

"And friendships," Amber added. She looked at each of us ladies.

"To love, staying together, and friendships," we all repeated, tipping our glasses at the ones sitting closest to us.

Through the night, we carried on with dessert over passionate opinions about politics and current events. The sad thing was, given the history between certain people in this group, politics actually seemed like a safer topic. And the heavy discussions told me a little bit more about the men with whom I'd had limited interaction prior to this dinner.

Daniel had a lot to share, sometimes sounding like a page from *The Washington Post*. I could picture him now: the middle-aged man with his nose between black and white pages with one ankle over the knee having toast and coffee. Daniel didn't seem to know much about the real world, except for what he'd read and what his status had provided.

Eric seemed to have lived in a more realistic realm. Somewhere in life, it'd seemed as though he'd gotten his hands dirty somewhere, perhaps in college during a summer of community outreaching, but at least he had first-hand experience with points he attempted to defend. Still, Eric remained mysterious. He managed not to disclose too much personal information while hiding behind random kisses placed into Emily's cheek as he held her close.

And as hot as Jackson was, that didn't stop him from having a brain that could pick another's until it bled. He was that modern, black man armed with knowledge that only self-initiated trips to the library could provide. What made this man dangerous to women wasn't just his gorgeous phenotype, but his swag and impeccable taste in choosing *GQ*-ready garments. Brooke had indeed done well and had better prepare herself for the THOTS lurking to snatch this man up. He was that unicorn trotting around in DC—the one capable of giving love, financially holding his own, anchoring political memos to the brain, giving you the black history lesson that your teacher wouldn't tell or didn't know, while taking you home and eating your pussy like it was the last meal of the century. Just sayin'.

Then there was Oliver. My dear, sweet Oliver. This man could only respond with head nods, grins, and unintelligible sounds as he struggled to follow along. Autumn caused him to lose the extra sleep he needed most nights after work, either because I would fall asleep shortly after his arrival, or he'd want to spend time with her if she were up. He didn't care about sleep, just about getting the quality time that he craved to bond with her. It was adorable. Autumn needed that, especially since she would never know Ruben. However, Oliver did the best he could to contribute tidbits of knowledge and opinions among us. Brooke picked up on his lethargy and eyed him with a broken smile and eyes of pity. She flashed me a pouty mouth at one point, to which I smiled.

After dinner, I fed Autumn in another room before joining everyone in the living room. Everyone broke into chatter in different parts of the spacious living room decorated with beige walls complemented by off-white furniture and the biggest television I'd ever seen. The flat screen was so big, the furniture had to be positioned on the opposite end of the living room. Standing up-close in a huddle, Daniel turned it on to show the gawking men an oversized ESPN replay of a touchdown.

I took a seat on one of the sofas, and the girls came to join me. Mara sat on the chaise lounge chair while Amber and Emily sat on the loveseat. Brooke sat next to me.

She sighed. "Well, you guys won't believe who came to see me and caused me to melt down."

When she had our attention, she explained how devastating the unexpected visit from her mother unfolded. Our mouths had dropped to the floor.

"Hey, Brooke." We all looked up when Daniel called Brooke's name from the other end of the room. "Did you know your man played on a high school football team?" When she shook her head with a half-hearted smile, he replied, "No? Well, I bet you were a cheerleader, huh?"

Wearing a regretful grin, Brooke replied, "I couldn't. My mom made me quit once I made the squad."

Instead of replying, Daniel just turned back around with a hand shoved into a pocket and resumed his conversation with the men. Jackson looked back and flashed an expression of quick pity. Brooke stared at the floor before she continued. "Yes, that same mother let me try out and all that, just to make me step down when I received my uniform. I hate that woman."

Emily took her place beside Brooke and then rubbed her back. "It's okay. You will be a better mother than your mom."

Amber said, "Dang, sis. That blows. What are you gonna do now?"

"Keep away from her." Brooke grimaced. "I haven't seen her since I left for college. Now she happens to resurface when I'm happy in love to crap all over my parade? I don't think so." She knocked my knee with her hand. "How are you holding up, you know, since the thing happened?"

With a soft expression, I told Brooke, "You can call it what it is. It's his death. Since Ruben died."

Brooke's mouth tipped downward as her shoulders slumped.

I wasn't prepared to talk about that, but I really didn't mind her concern. If I couldn't talk to them, then what did our friendships matter? One quick glance at my daughter's face, and I knew how to answer her. "It sucks that Ruben lost his life at such a young age. He was so happy to be a dad. For her sake, I'm sorry. But, I also know what I have to do as an adult and as a parent."

"And what's that?" Amber asked.

"I have to do everything right. I have to be strong. I have to put her first." My stare averted everyone's eyes as I lifted Autumn and placed her against my chest to rub her back. Feeling the beat of her heart against mine was the best feeling in the world. She was all the strength I needed.

Seconds later, the Italian leather shoes that I picked out for my man to wear tonight stared back at me. Looking up, Oliver stood above my daughter and me with hands in the pockets of his tanned slacks. "Ready to go? I'm tired, and I know she is." He stretched his arms out to take Autumn.

"Yeah. Thanks, babe." I picked up her pink diaper bag and rose to my feet.

"Awww, oh noooo," Mara said. "The only baby in the house has to go now?" She pouted, and I lowered myself to embrace her. I kissed the top of her black curly hair.

"Bye, sweetie. It was *so* nice to see you." My heavy bag almost smacked into her, but I managed to stop it.

"Whoa. Close call," Mara chuckled. "You, too. I'm leaving tomorrow. So, I guess I won't see cutie pie anymore on this trip." Oliver lowered Autumn quickly, so Mara could shake her tiny hand in a brief goodbye.

"Then come back soon," I told her. Nodding, she assured me that she would. I turned around to hug all of my girls. The broken look of confidence and safety in Brooke's eyes made me sad. We exchanged hugs with an extra squeeze. "Thank you for asking about me."

A quick tear fell from her eye as she nodded. Brooke's emotional Band-aid must've fallen off, because all of her scars hit the surface. Whatever her mother's visit did to her made it hard for my friend to shake.

Eric gave me a one-arm hug with a pat on the back. "Take care, Summer. I hope motherhood gives you all the happiness you're looking for." I thanked him before accepting a regular hug from Jackson.

"See you later, girl. Take care of that angel." He leaned into my ear and said, "I'm sorry for your loss. Brooke and I are only a phone call away if you need anything."

I nodded. "Thank you, Jackson. I appreciate it." I took one look back at Brooke, who was chatting with Mara. "And, please, take care of my girl."

Jackson responded with one nod and gave me the 'okay' sign with his fingers. He turned around and said, "Come on, Brooke. Let's get you home."

I turned to see Daniel beside me. He held out a hand for me to shake.

"Thank you for that yummy dinner," I told him. "That lobster was on point."

"I'm glad to have met all of Amber's friends. We can definitely do this again. Drive safely." He placed his other hand on top of our clasped hands before letting go. His eyes were genuine, and despite all of our initial misgivings, I was happy for my friend. She had a man who took an interest in her life. The question was: Did Amber have a genuine interest in Daniel? But I think I already knew the answer to that.

Brooke came over to shake his hand, too. "Thanks for having baked chicken for me."

Oliver popped up beside me. "Ready, baby?" I couldn't help but chuckle at the sight. A minute more, and Oliver would've probably needed one of the men to carry him out to the car.

"Baby, I'm gonna drive," I said. Heading out, he didn't put up a fight.

Emily

Eric helped Emily into his Mercedes. She secured herself as she waited for Eric to enter. The night felt like a success. It was the first time all of her friends had a partner at the table. Even though Mara didn't, Emily took comfort in reminding herself that she was an extended guest.

Eric eased inside the driver's seat and started the engine. "Did you have a good time?" His seatbelt clicked before he pulled away from the curb.

"I did, honey. And you?"

"It was nice. Would it be a bad joke to say that it went better than last year's effort?"

Emily puckered her lips to the side and squinted her eyes. "Yes. Bad joke."

"I don't know how you did it tonight, sweetheart, but thank you for being a trooper."

"Was it hard for you?"

Steering, he looked at her briefly. "Uncomfortable, awkward . . . but I decided to put the debacle with Amber out of my mind. I only really remember it because of her connection to you."

The night, the scarce number of cars on the road, and being with Eric in the car, came together to make a perfect scenario. DC pedestrians were few and far between at midnight on this Thursday night. While Emily wasn't in need of a sexual rush, she wanted Eric and she wanted him now. "Pull over." She pointed to an alley filled with parallel parked cars. "Pull over," she repeated with urgency.

Eric pulled into the alley. He looked utterly confused. "What, Emily? What's going on?"

"You have to park this car right now."

He sighed as he parked. "Emily." Turning off the engine, he looked at her with annoyance. "Emily, what's the problem? Am I in trouble again?"

With a mischievous smile, Emily shook her head as she unbuckled her seat belt. Raising her hips, she slid her fitted, long dress above her thighs. The tip of her tongue rested against the top of her lip.

"What are you doing?" he asked in a smoky tone.

"Unfasten your pants right now, buddy." She slid one heel at a time out of her blue panties as she watched Eric follow her orders. He slid his chair back and unbuckled his seatbelt.

"Ahh, here's my fiery little kitten. Don't start what you can't finish." Both of his hands were ready to grip Emily by the waist to help ease her over his lap.

"Stop? Keep dreaming."

Once she straddled him, Eric's hands moved freely over her thighs and butt as their lips fastened with caresses of passion and need. Eric's breathing picked up, causing tender puffs of breath to brush her face. Emily's heartbeat trembled inside of her chest as her vagina throbbed. She wrapped her arms around his neck and locked them behind the headrest of Eric's chair. He moved his impatient hands from her body long enough to set his package free from his pants. It became a one-man race, him against the buckle, button, and zipper. Emily waited with an ache that'd developed between her thighs.

"I need you to bend your neck down, so I can raise my hips real quick, Ems."

Emily leaned over his shoulder to accommodate the fast motion that would liberate his love muscle. While next to his ear, she whispered, "Mmmmm, *papi chulo, mi cuerpo es solo para ti.*" Eric moaned. Placing her hand over his bare groin, she felt that his dick had come to and was ready to play. Straightening her spine, she peered down at him as she released her hair from a pin.

"Let me put it in that wet pussy of yours." Eric licked two fingers and slid them between her thighs and into her parted lips.

His hands worked to ease into her. Moving up and down slowly, Emily rolled her head, leaning back and moving her hands provocatively against her breasts. Even suspecting she looked like a cliché didn't bother her.

"Ooooooooooh." Eric stroked deep into Emily with fingers that convinced her he was made for her. She slid up and down the length of his fingers, squeezing them with her core. "Baby," he whispered, with hands that moved wildly about each butt cheek.

Breathing heavy, they both spoke in husky voices.

Emily cupped his face with her hands. "What, baby?" She leaned in to kiss his thin lips.

"Mm," he moaned.

Alternating between kissing and talking, she barely managed to ask, "What, baby? What, baby? What, baby?"

"I wanna slide my dick into ya."

She pressed her forehead against his and heisted her hips to release his fingers. With her eyes closed and mouth parted in agony, she replied, "And I want you to, baby. I do. Please."

Eric grabbed her by the hips to line her up until he slid into her with precision as Emily wiggled down his shaft. Closing around his penis like a cave, Emily was ready to take Eric's mouth into hers. She bit his lower lip with hungry aggression. Tasting the wine that once coated his lips earlier that night, she sensed his appetite to do the same with her.

"You always had that tight pussy, Emily."

Emily rewarded what sounded like music to her ears by snatching at her sweetheart neckline to release one of her ample breasts to shove into his mouth.

"Suck."

Eric didn't need her instruction, and like a newborn with his mom, he already knew what to do. He flicked the tip of her nipple before sucking it into his mouth. Despite the pain of resting on her shins and feeling car parts sticking into her skin, she trooped through it, since the reward would be high. Eric handled her breast with one hand and sculptured her ass with the other.

Singing sounds of pleasure from her throat, Emily cried for mercy in the seed of her brain. "This dick is so good, *papi*."

Examining him from over the bridge of her nose, Emily saw a man have at it like a vampire on flesh. The way he'd sunken into a place of private lust turned her on. His tongue danced across her sand-colored areola, and his mouth squeezed over her sensitive tip.

Releasing his mouth, he looked up at her and asked, "You wanted other women to gawk at my big dick, huh? Is that why you spread my pictures everywhere?"

Not understanding why he had to know that now, Emily stopped rocking and shrugged and replied, "No, baby, of course not."

Tapping her lip with his finger, he said, "You're a wild one. Maybe we'll have to make other women jealous and let them watch me bang you out from behind."

Flattered that he'd want to use her to show women that she was the lucky one, Emily grabbed him by the lapels and brought her lips to his and whispered, "Perhaps," as she continued to ride him again.

Wiggling his brows at her, he said, "Thatta girl."

Knowing he was joking, Emily cast that thought to the side in favor of finishing up before any spectators ruined the moment or better yet—cops!

Eric became more aggressive in his movement, so Emily had to match him. As she did, her butt moved faster and harder, and every time she pushed back, her generous bottom hit the horn on his G-Class Coupe. Every other second, his horn sounded once with each press from her ass. It should've given her pause, but it didn't. It only intensified the moment and experience, swelling the imminent pleasure that was bound to surface with each thrust. She cradled his head against her bosom with his nose buried deep into the split of her breasts. Emily's pink, manicured nails stroked the tiny hairs on the back of his head.

"Damn, Emily. What are you doing to me?"

Beep! Thrust. B*eep*! Thrust. *Beep*! Certainly, neighbors had to emerge from the dark just to light their rooms with anxious hands to see whose car alarm had become a nuisance. Perhaps, someone called the cops on them. A man with a badge would show up on Eric's driver's side with two strong knocks against the glass and a big, cock-sized flashlight. They'd flash a badge like detectives in movies and ask with frowns and furrowed brows to step outside. Her heart pitter-pattered against her chest, her vagina pulsated as a warning that something was about to happen. The payoff was coming. Eric would have to use his clout and money to hire lawyers to bury the case before her teacher reputation had a chance to become besmirched.

She rocked faster as Eric pumped harder and before she knew it, her orgasm erupted like a dormant volcano. She pooled over Eric like lava on surrounding land.

"Ahhhh, a-a. Yessssss," she cried. Emily's toes curled the best they could in her heels with intensity that matched the shivers that ran over her whole body.

Wanting to move to the side but frozen by a heart running its own marathon, Emily had to collect herself with a dry mouth and broken breathing. When it was over, she opened her eyes to see a man drowning in his own world of intensity with bitten lips and sealed eyes.

Running through the course of his sensation, Eric opened his peepers and patted her thigh. With struggled breathing, he told her, "Okay. That was good. I just hope we didn't wake the neighborhood."

Emily grinned then carefully maneuvered back into the passenger seat with achy skin that had been pierced by hard material.

"For that feeling, I think we should wake them each night." In the dark, she used a hand to fish around the floor until she managed to locate her underwear. She slid them back over her legs and butt before securing her body again with the seatbelt.

Eric smirked. Emily looked out her window. Smiling, she didn't know what'd come over her, but the idea of trying to figure it out didn't appeal at all. Just like her sexual encounter, she decided to sit back and enjoy the ride.

Amber

Amber held her breath as Daniel leaned in to kiss her goodnight. Dealing with his bad breath still proved to be a chore, but her new lifestyle made her jettison these "minor" concerns.

Throwing a hand up in the air, Daniel said, "Goodnight, sugar. Goodnight, Mara."

Mara nodded once at him. "Thanks for the good dinner and for having me as a guest."

"Come again," Daniel replied. "And if I don't see you tomorrow, safe travels."

"Thank you, Daniel. Goodnight."

Amber crossed her legs on the chaise lounge chair. "Goodnight, babe." Wearing purple silk shorts and a matching top, she and Mara were comfortable in their nighttime attire.

When Amber heard him stump up the stairs, she asked her sister, "So, what do you think?"

Still wearing her reluctant expression, Mara replied, "Amber, I still think that you're an intelligent woman who can do shit all by herself. There, I said it." Donned in pajama pants, she twisted the excess checker-patterned material hanging loose at the knee between fidgety fingers.

Amber felt a little put off. She felt her sister's lack of real-life experience didn't qualify her for realistic feedback. But she appreciated her sister's input nonetheless. "Mara. This part of the country is so formally competitive. New York had more oddball opportunities. But now, I eat well, I dress better, my bills are paid, and I have no worries. I just go to school and come home to a man I enjoy."

Nestling into the couch, Mara appeared slightly guarded. "Amber, you don't even love him. How long do you wanna continue to do this? Don't you want real love, honey? This ain't it."

One look into her sister's eyes, and she could see the concern nibbling away at Mara. "I ain't worried about love.

I want security a-and to be able to let my hair down. I'm in school. Ain't that good enough right now?"

"That's awesome, but it would be even more awesome if you did this in your own apartment. I don't understand why you brush off love when you saw Mom and Dad so close. Where does all this detachment come from, Amber?"

Amber inflated her cheeks as she swallowed a sigh, averting her sister's eyes as she thought. "Their passing hurt me. I feel so betrayed, Mara. Is this what love is? Loving someone to lose it all in a blink of an eye? You saw Dad. He shut down without Mom as each year passed. Then *he* passed."

Mara gestured with her hand. "But that's life. And there's nothing to say that you and your man—someone you love—won't live to grow old together in rocking chairs. You wanna pigeonhole life experiences?"

Amber shook her head, because she wanted Mara to believe that she just didn't get it. Deep down, she knew that her sister was undeniably spot-on. It just didn't matter; her mind was made up. Life was better with money, so love had to wait. "Mara, one day you will understand. I ain't gonna make my life harder than it has to be when someone stepped up to the plate to make it easier." She shrugged nonchalantly. "Sorry."

Mara stood. "Well, sis, Daniel's a nice guy, so I hope he makes you happy and that it works out." She bent down to kiss her big sister on the forehead. "Goodnight. See you tomorrow. You not tired?

"Hm-um. I'm wide awake, baby. Goodnight, Mara. Luh you."

"Love you, too."

Once Mara headed away, Amber stood and headed to the kitchen to search for fruit. The unexpected sight of Amit stopped her in her tracks. "Hey, you. What are you still doing here?"

Using a dish towel to dry the last square dinner plate, Amit looked over his shoulder and flashed her a warm smile. "Mr. Crosby wanted me to do some overtime."

Amber spotted the leftover strawberries on the counter next to Amit. Her eyes lit up as she reached for one. Folding the dish towel, he turned in time to watch her bite into one with subtle seduction. Knowing that his eyes were focused on her lips, she teased him with an, "Mmmmmm. Have you tried one?"

With a sideways flick of the wrist, he tossed the folded towel onto the countertop. "Mr. Crosby doesn't want me eating the food, so, no." Amit stood on the other side of the island with his hands folded in front of him. Partially out of uniform, Amber decided that he never looked so irresistible in his white button-up shirt and black slacks.

"What a shame," Amber replied. She eased around the island to meet him.

Amit froze, cleared his throat, and placed his intertwined fingers against his body. Apparently, she'd made him slightly uncomfortable.

Reaching for another strawberry, she held it up in the air. "Take a bite," she teased with the tip of her tongue resting against the back of her top teeth.

Amit didn't move. His eyes glinted with doubt and a hint of fear about being reprimanded by Daniel. "I can't, Ms. Hamilton."

"Amber. Just, Amber. And don't you mind what Daniel tells you. Come on. Bite." Amber closed the gap between them. As Amit struggled with the decision to bite the strawberry or not, Amber did a bit of her own emotional wrestling. Perfectly aware that she was in Daniel's home with an arrangement and not a relationship, she was able to build a case that supported her desire: She was a woman who acted on impulse. Worrying about consequences wasn't her strongpoint, and she wanted Amit.

With her breasts brushing up against Amit's chest and the feel of his uneven breath fanning her hand that held the fruit against his lips, she inched it closer to his mouth and encouraged in a seductive whisper, "Don't be scared."

"He said I can't eat here. I must obey." His eyes locked into hers.

"Bite it," she whispered. Raising the stakes, she placed a palm on the side of his neck. The other hand gently shoved the strawberry into his mouth, leaving her satisfied as he bit.

Wearing a naughty smile, Amber watched him chew as neither averted the other's gaze. She stood on her toes to place a kiss on his lips. With sealed mouths connected, Amber decided to take the first step. Parting her lips slowly, she wrapped her full lips around his and tasted remnants of the sweet strawberry.

Amber rested both palms against Amit's chest to ease into a more intimate kiss. Throwing professionalism to the wind and giving in to his desire, Amit slowly lifted his hands and placed them on Amber's hips. Amber reveled in the fact that there was a man in the house who could really give her what she needed—a level of desire and need she couldn't find in Daniel. No amount of money could replace the basic instinct of attraction, and she just didn't have it with Daniel. Amber had no clue that she'd missed it and didn't remember what she was giving up until she kissed Amit.

While kissing Amit, Mara's crinkled face from earlier danced around in her head. Feeling his pleasure race into his manhood and knowing that the warm feeling burning between her legs was a fire that Amit was not allowed to put out, Amber decided to pull out from the poker game before losing to a full flush.

Backing up with exhausted lips and heavy eyelids, Amber saw the confusion across Amit's face. Touching her lips, she raced out of the kitchen and allowed her desire to burn with the realization that she needed an extinguisher. Rejecting the help of the fireman downstairs, she made her way to her bedroom and saddled the horse waiting in the barn, as she took it for the ride of her life with Amit in mind.

4: truth and honesty

Summer

It'd been two weeks since the dinner party at Amber and Daniel's house. That was the last time we came together. Yesterday, Autumn and I strolled down the tight streets of Ballston after purchasing books, which included an erotica and parenting book for me and a few children's books for her. The time spent with weeks of bonding even more as each day passed wasn't lost on me. We made it outside briefly every day this week, whether it was just a simple trip to the grocery store or a peaceful moment in the park.

I decided to spend this Friday with my daughter with a trip to Starbucks. But knowing that I had to speak with Oliver tonight about something, prevented me from relishing in my celebratory Friday sentiments. Securing Autumn in the baby sling across my chest, I picked up her diaper bag along with my keys and wallet and headed for Starbucks. Dressed in a pair of pre-baby jeans and a cap sleeved t-shirt, I ambled down the street amidst joggers, walkers, and shoppers.

Ballston was always a pleasure. The stores were lined up one after the other, and most of them were as close to each other as townhomes. Traffic lights lit up on nearly every corner, and just like DC, many streets were designed as a one way. The people crowded the streets as they would Georgetown, with their shopping bags, groceries, or stuffed bellies from an eatery. Ballston housed people with high salaries, or at least people with a great appreciation for fine living in a clean environment. At night, college students gathered for drinks with friends in pubs or to play at a billiard hall. It was youthful and full of life.

Yanking the door to Starbucks, the smell of milk and coffee traveled to my nose like a tight competition to fill my nostrils with steamed dairy or grinded beans. I welcomed both. Inhaling deep to bask in the one-of-a-kind aroma, I wasted no time to be first in line, even though the coffee shop housed multiple people at the tables sipping drinks while chatting to another person or sitting behind a computer screen. Feeling the stare of the chubby cashier as she gripped the sides of the register, I glanced over the menu behind her shoulder even though I pretty much knew what to order.

"Grande iced coffee with four shots of caramel, please."

The happy lady smiled and nodded as she repeated my order before instructing me to swipe my debit card. After completing the transaction and giving her my name, I moved to the other end of the counter to wait for my drink. My hand caressed Autumn's back, my lips kissed her forehead. Waiting for his drink, a thin man who barely towered over my head appeared beside me.

"Summer?"

Turning to face him, my eyes squinted in an attempt to remember from where I may've known the brown-haired man. "Yes?" I replied with reluctance. The longer I stared into his blue eyes, the more I began to recognize him. "Wait . . ."

"Do you remember me? I was your client when you presented me with three candidates."

A quick flash of me sitting in a black and white three-piece suit at his desk with candidate profiles came to mind. "Ohhh, *right*. I'm sorry."

He chuckled with his fingers to his chin.

"Summer," the woman called. I thanked her and grabbed my drink before returning my attention back to my former client.

"Simon Jack?" He cocked a brow.

I pointed a finger at him. "Yes, that's it. How are you doing Mr.—"

"Nope, call me Simon. And looking at your baby, I guess I should congratulate you. Congratulations, Summer. She's pretty."

"Thank you—Simon. Thank you."

"Well, listen. I would love to chat about that beautiful baby of yours, but I'm glad I ran into you. I emailed you to no avail, but I wanted to tell you about the candidates you sent me that I hired."

"Oh, okay." Curiosity nibbled at me, so I wanted to know what he had to say. "Oh, yeah, I'm sorry about that. I just . . . you know . . ." I couldn't even justify my lack of communication in a way that would make sense to him.

"Oh, no, I'm glad to have this moment with you."

"Simon," the barista called.

Grabbing his drink with hands that proved they were used to holding pens at a desk as opposed to doing anything associated with tough labor, Simon took his drink and immediately sipped it. Pleased, he said, "Mmm, good."

I smiled, doing my best to hide my impatience. It would be lovely if Simon went ahead and got to the point. Any minute, Autumn could become fussy, and sitting in Starbucks wasn't in the plans.

Ushering his hand toward a table, he asked, "Sit?"

"Sure."

We located an empty table a few feet away, despite the coffee shop being packed. "Look. Let me make it clear. You sent me three great candidates, and they ended up being dynamic workers. All three of them have panned out. Your eye for top talent shows."

"Well thank you, Simon." I felt so flattered that someone other than Fran acknowledged my work. Besides, she did set out to ruin my career, and according to Ruben, she accomplished that mission. My heart dipped when I remembered him, but I shook it off. "Glad to hear that."

"Look, we need your results as a regular. Are you working now?" Once he leaned forward, I knew what that meant. He couldn't hide his desire to recruit me no more than a pump of cologne could mask a musky body.

"Ummm, no. I had to stop to adjust to motherhood. But I'm dying to get going again as a recruiter."

"And you once said that you have agency experience, right?"

"Yes."

"Can you give me a little background about yourself?"

Obviously, I had become a tad fidgety. Autumn began to make small cries, so I cradled a hand behind her head and tried to bounce her slightly while still in the sling.

"Oh, I'm sorry, Summer. Is this a good time?"

"Sure. She'll be fine. As long as we can do this in ten minutes or less."

"Absolutely. My mind is pretty much made up. I just want to learn more about you, if you don't mind." He sipped his drink.

"I graduated from American University with a degree in business administration. I worked for some years in retail and became a manager within two years. I got tired of the ceiling effect in retail, and, one day, my former boss came in and handed me her business card at the end of her transaction. She loved the way I sold some merchandise to her. She wanted me to get my toes wet first by observing the culture and nature of her company, so when I came on board, it was as a receptionist."

Simon's short brows furrowed. "A receptionist?"

Nodding, I continued. "Also, there weren't any openings at the moment within the staffing agency, but she wanted me there at any capacity—the agency was small. But I appreciated it, because I wanted a break from sales. I mean I was in retail for five years. So, when an opening came a year later, my boss promoted me to junior recruiter because of my sales experience."

Simon rested a hand on his five o'clock-shadow chin as he settled an ankle over a denim-clad knee. "And how did you come to branch out on your own?"

"To be frank, we didn't work out."

He held a hand up. "No problem. I've seen you in action from the short time we spent together, but you were really polished. Your insight was spot on. What did she pay you?"

I hid the fact that I was taken aback by his direct question during this impromptu interview, but it was also exciting to know that my career had a heartbeat again. "As a receptionist, thirty-two thousand. As a junior recruiter, on average I was taking home about two grand every two weeks."

"Shy of fifty a year." Simon exhaled as he leaned back in his chair. "Not a lot to make a living with in this area."

I nodded and shrugged.

He drummed two fingers on the shoe resting on his knee. We lost eye contact as he seemed to tussle with a private consideration. "Okay, look." He placed his foot on the ground and pulled at the brown lapels of his jacket. "This position pays more than what you last made. I can't seem to find someone who can nail this position, and no offense, but I'm willing to do what I normally wouldn't and that's taking a chance on a newbie. I mean, I *did* see your potential. I got a good feelin' but, I gotta call your last employer at the agency."

And just like that, I felt my heart clench. My hopes were smashed as quickly as they were built. I just couldn't let Simon see my nerves unravel.

"You don't have much experience specific to what I'm looking for, but I also have no doubt you will perform as well as I'm expecting." He finally flashed me another smile. "I just have to see what your boss says about your performance. I'll email you a consent form before calling her. But first send me your resume. If you get this in to me within an hour or two, I can call her today and have an answer for you right away." He checked his watch. "Gotta get back to the office, Summer." He held a hand out for me to shake before standing.

"Thank you, Simon. I'm so glad we ran into each other. I'll head home now and get started on the documents." I stood and picked up my coffee.

"Excellent. Take care of that beautiful baby." He waved once and exited through the glass door. Confident I wouldn't see him anymore, I still decided to give it an old college try and follow through with my word.

Amber

Irritated, Amber slammed her textbook shut. She couldn't focus, and before Daniel came out of the shower, she decided to give Emily a call.

"Hello?"

"Mornin', boo."

"Good morning, girly. Well, it's about noon in a matter of minutes. But, hey, happy Friday!"

Leaning against her headboard, Amber chuckled dryly. "Thanks. I need your opinion. Need it badly." She scratched the back of her head.

"Sure, what's up? This is my last day of freedom, so I'm using it wisely. This is a wise moment," she joked.

"Right. How should I start? Okay, can life exist without love? You were bitter when Eric left you, but you still wanted to fall in love, right?"

"Whoa. Throwback situation, huh?" She laughed. "And Amber calling me about love?"

"*Emily?*"

"Okay, what's—what's this about, Amber?"

Amber couldn't respond right away. "I ain't in love with Daniel, and I don't think I'll ever be. But he's willin' to live like this with me, you know, sex for money. Like, I have sex with him, and he takes care of my bills."

"I know."

"Emily, for the *first* time in my life, I don't have to worry about expenses. This bruh done wiped my slate of debt clean. I'm startin' to think this pussy is made of gold."

She heard Emily sigh. "Honey. Any *pussy* on this earth with the age below the man piercing it is gold to them. Get to the point."

Amber moved the phone away from her ear and studied it with a frown. She rolled her eyes before placing it back to her ear. "Well anyway, we ordered my credit score and, do you know, he shelled out fifteen thousand dollars to pay off my debt? Money is nothing for this man. Nothing."

"Gee. How many blowjobs did that cost ya'?"

"Ha-ha. My jaws are sore. Happy?"

"No wonder you didn't talk that much during dinner." Emily fell over laughing. Despite Amber's downbeat mood, she couldn't help but join her.

"Shut up. Emily, please. Give me guidance."

"You're asking me if you *should* . . .?"

"I had a talk with my sister. She pointed out that we grew up with two parents and lost them both. She made me realize just *may*be, I avoid love to avoid the hurt that may come down the line."

"Like if you lose the love in any way, shape, or form?"

"I guess."

"I lost Eric, yes. Forget about me getting him back. But I don't know why I have a weak spot for him. I guess that's love. Since his apology was sincere, that made all the difference. But when I lost him, Amber, I still really wanted love and children in my future. I figured: Why punish myself because he didn't want me? I figured another man was still out there."

"But mourning Eric . . . didn't that, like, kill your spirit?"

"Absolutely. But not your hope. If it does, it's usually temporary. But, Amber, love is an essential part of humanity. It brings pain and pleasure, but without it, we whither in some capacity. So, we take a leap of faith. And that is why they say it is better to have loved and lost than to not have loved at all. Make sense? Because at least before the heartbreak, I felt love from Eric."

"Hmm."

"Amber that money will only take you so far. Are you still teaching piano?"

"Yeah. He lets the students come here."

"And that's not an inconvenience to your students?"

"I moved. People move. Businesses move." Amber shrugged her shoulders as she drew her knees to her chest.

"Well, honey, I have to warn you. I'm not comfortable with a man paying all of your bills. You made the debt, you should have solved that yourself."

Amber was thrown off by Emily's blunt words. She would've expected that from Brooke, but not Emily. Emily was the gift that just kept giving. With her, it was one surprise after the other. "Wow."

"You called me."

"Hey, I'm a New Yorker. I can take the blunt stuff. That's all I know. And, besides, he has the money. Why not?"

"Dependency."

"You depend on a man to give you a baby."

"*Amber*. No thank you. That's a process that takes two. Debt does not. Look, you live with this, but I gotta go, *cariño*."

"Ca-who?"

"Bye, girl."

"Wait. Thank you, Emily."

"Oh, no problem. Yoga class. Gotta run."

"Well, stretch on, honey."

"Take care, *chica*." Emily hung up.

"Sweet bunny?"

Amber looked up suddenly to see Daniel come around the corner wearing nothing but a white towel around his oversized waistline. His short hair lay wet and matted like the trail of hair on his chest. Water beads lit his skin up like a Christmas tree.

Ugh. Did he even bother to dry off? "What's up?"

He approached her with a smile. "You talking to someone?"

Amber cussed under her breath upon seeing him since it made her think of Humpty Dumpty wearing a towel. "Yeah, just Emily."

"I see." A chubby finger scratched his head. "Hey, listen. I'm already late. I almost yanked, ummm, you know. I almost pulled the lunchmeat from the package in the shower." The crooked smirk across his face was no subtler than a little boy who'd pulled a despicable prank, telling Amber that he had something on his mind. In one swift move, he snatched the weak knot on the side of his waist, so the towel could drop to the floor.

"Whoa." Amber held up both hands. "Not now, please. I'm not in the mood."

Daniel placed one hand under her chin and looked down at her through expectant blue eyes. "I'm not taking care of you to be in the mood. Do you think I was in the mood to drop thousands on a whim on debt I didn't create? Hmm?" Waiting for her to answer, he tilted his head. Amber swallowed hard. "I stuck to my bargain, now you stick to yours." He stroked her braids.

Mentally, she said every cuss word she could think of, in hopes that Daniel couldn't read her mind through her expression. A stressed smile spread across her face as she reached for his lengthy penis with one hand. Amber had given him so many blowjobs that the skin on his shaft even appeared chafed. Yuck, she thought. It was hard not to gag, especially since she was a debt-free woman for the first time in her adulthood. The only motivation now would be not to become homeless. As she reached, she eased her mouth around his penis. Suddenly, she found herself jealous of Brooke and Emily for having their own places.

For the first time while performing oral sex, Amber wanted to cry. His cold penis in her mouth mixed with the imprinted memory of his chafed shaft proved too much to bear. Refusing to look up at him and not wanting to stare at his oversized, pale belly, Amber closed her eyes. She begged her brain to give her something to fight for in order to hang in the moment. Obviously, he was looking down at her, because as he stroked her hair with one hand, she could smell a whiff of his malevolent breath as he whispered, *"Good job."*

With her mouth plugged and his breath trapping the unpleasant airways to her nostrils, Amber felt suffocated! Involuntarily, a stifled cough interrupted her ability to continue. Her gag reflexes kicked in, so she jumped to her feet and ran to the bathroom to spit. After rinsing her mouth with warm water, she reluctantly turned the corner to find that Daniel had moved on. To her dismay, his unfastened pants were on as he struggled to weave his arms into his dress shirt.

Amber pretended to be disappointed. "Awww, you leavin'?"

With a shoe in his hand, Daniel paused to stare at her. Approaching her with a pointing finger, he said, "Amber, this is my home. Mine. And unless you want to find yourself back in the hood, you need to do your job. I'm allowing you to go back to school instead of going to work. If this arrangement is making you too spoiled, then . . ." At a loss for words, he shrugged.

With folded arms, Amber bit her lower lip to keep from crying like a shamed child. She responded by doing what she did all her life: fighting back. "You still haven't taken care of that breath."

Daniel's eyelids dropped in disbelief. "I'm working on that. Okay? My dentist is doing all that he can to—" He waved a hand through the air. "You know, make it go away. But this is not about my—that, Amber. I gotta run." He waved an irritated hand at her, then approached his drawer for a tie. "Tonight, I want you on all fours, Amber." Hastily, he buttoned up in the mirror before starting on his tie. "We're gonna do the backdoor thing. My co-workers rave about that, and I wanna try it, too." After tucking in his shirt and approving of his look, he turned to Amber, who stood nervously with a finger in her mouth. Her worrisome eyes darted about and then to him.

"I—" Amber tried that once with a man, and it hurt. She vowed to never do it again, especially if the man didn't come with a Kodak smile and military muscles.

"No." He slid both hands into his pockets as he approached her. "I pay good money to have you around, Amber. Don't let me down," he warned. He kissed her forehead and grabbed his briefcase and jacket from the chaise chair beside the wall. "Tell Amit I want halibut for dinner."

"You are the halibut," she mumbled to herself.

Amber didn't watch him leave, but she knew she was alone and not just physically. For the first time since her parents' passing, she felt alone in every way possible.

Summer

A few hours later, I picked up my cellphone when it rang. A number that wasn't programmed showed up on my screen. It had to be Simon.

"Hello?"

"Summer."

He sounded happy. But if Fran had given him bad feedback, why would he call me in a positive tone?

"Simon, hi." Moving into the kitchen with my hand on my head and then on my hip, I waited nervously for the embarrassing feedback.

"Fran DuBois confirmed your employment with her as well as your work ethic." Here it comes, I knew it would be horrible. With squeezed eyes and gritted teeth, I felt like I was on a roller coaster ride going down a massive dip. All Simon had to do was say the word, and then I would feel the cart drop down the rails of the biggest dip of the ride, sending my heart into my stomach.

"Fran said that you were very dependable, thorough, and learned the ropes very quickly. She agreed that you had a keen ability to match and make placements."

"Wow. She did?"

"Surprised?"

"Uhhh, well it was just so nice to hear that." *Fran? Fran!* She came through for me after I destroyed what was left of her marriage. Why would she back me up? We couldn't be talking about the same Fran. Had I really made such an impression on that woman that she couldn't deny my performance no matter what?

"Well, you said you almost made fifty. I can do better. With your several years of sales experience, and agency and independent recruiting experience, how does seventy-five sound?"

My heart did a backflip. "You mean thousand? Seventy-five thousand a year?"

"Yes. It's generous for someone without more years of direct experience, but you do have sales, and I do like what you did for us. Plus, I considered the cost of living and child expenses. We do have an on-site childcare center. I'm hoping the salary will incentivize you to move mountains since your predecessors couldn't. Our human resource department is missing someone like you. We need to stay on top, but we can't do that if we don't have top talent. Since this is salaried, you will need to stay motivated, so I need you to have a salary that can carry you for at least a year. Then we can discuss keeping you and increasing that if you really wow us. But you will have to sign a contract."

"I can do that. I need stability." My heart raced with several unstoppable thoughts speeding through my brain like a New York City subway. I couldn't believe it. It was as if the heavens were finally moving for me. This was the independent woman I'd always imagined myself to be, minus the kid. However, now that Autumn was here, my vision would mean nothing without her. I was determined to take care of her just like my mother did for me.

"You can learn more about all the perks when you come in to sign the contract."

"Okay." I had to place a hand on the counter to help balance myself.

"Okay, well, see you Monday, Summer, for the paperwork. Then we'll discuss a start date and what not."

"Thank you so much, Simon. See you then."

"Have a nice weekend. Bye." He hung up, leaving me standing in awe with my cellphone against my chest and my heart in my throat. On the other hand, I knew what I had to do. Drawing the phone from my chest, my finger scrolled through the list of contacts until the name I needed appeared.

"DuBois Staffing, this is Fran."

The voice didn't sound any different, but hearing it still evoked that reminiscent feeling of the day she chewed me out in her office and kicked me out on my ass. I cleared my throat. "Um, Fran?"

Pausing for a few seconds, she chuckled bitterly. "Summer."

"It's me. Hi." Grimacing, my teeth dug into my bottom lip. Standing was harder than I thought, and between Simon's good news and this unexpected phone call to Fran, by butt needed to be planted into the sofa.

"What can I do for you?" Straight to the point. It wouldn't be Fran otherwise, especially once on her bad side.

"I called to thank you. Thank you for giving me the recommendation that impressed Simon Jack." I sounded timid, but it couldn't be helped.

"Summer, I stated the truth. I didn't give blood."

"But you didn't have to, considering what I did to you."

"You did nothing to me. I'm not a victim. You're a single mother with a mouth to feed. I can't get in the way of a woman trying to make it in a man's world."

"Thank you, Fran." My voice cracked. Her words actually spoke to my heart. It was a man's world, and women had to fight like hell just to swim in their ocean.

"Just make this job work with this company, because your name is still mud with the local agencies."

With that last warning she hung up, quickly reminding me that she was still Fran, and I was still the woman who screwed myself.

Emily

Sweaty, Emily came from yoga class with her mat rolled under one arm as she unlocked the trunk to her Jeep with her alarm. She held the cellphone up to her ear with her other hand.

"So, Eric said to make the wedding small and easy for me to plan. We are getting married in two weeks. We don't even have a lot of time left. We need to get married, because Eric's schedule will get nasty soon at his new job. They have a lot of plans for him, like sending him on business trips and what not." Emily threw her mat into the trunk and closed it. She climbed into her car and used the rearview mirror to fix her hair.

"No honeymoon?" Brooke asked.

"He said after his first business trip. I mean it, Brooke. He will be getting on a plane right after the ceremony, or reception, I should say."

"Then why not wait longer and do it all right?"

"We've done this before. We are seriously one step away from eloping, but Eric won't let us." She started the engine. "In fact, we are having dinner at my place tonight."

"Is he moving in?"

"Yeah, because I just bought my place. His place is full of boxes. Do you know that he already starting packing to move in with me? I think we will need a new place. I guess I shouldn't have sold our last one, huh?"

"You didn't know. Hon, Jackson is moving into my place next week. We're gonna use his place as a weekend and holiday hideout."

"That's awesome. Both of us getting married . . . wow. To men we thought we were rid of."

"That is crazy. Love is crazy, and I love it."

Emily could hear the glow in her friend's voice. "And, so, your wedding is marked on my calendar in three weeks."

"Three weeks. Haysia is amazing. Honestly, I had to do a little helping out, but I feel like I've met my younger sister or something. She's learning well, but there's no way I could ever be hands-off on my own wedding, especially my first and only one."

"Have you heard from your mom?" Emily started the car and headed for her building's parking garage. She felt guilty driving such a short distance from her yoga class but hated the idea of walking around with a mat.

"No, and God, I hope I don't. No one needs her around. I'm happy."

"Oh, well, maybe you can reconsider giving her another chance. Parents are important people, you know."

"Emily, I have to go."

Brooke's tone told Emily that she hit a nerve.

"Take care."

Brooke

"Baby!" Brooke came through the door. The silence told her that Jackson wasn't there. Standing in the foyer wearing her grey Armani suit, she sifted through the mail. The knock at the door stole her attention. Opening the door without checking through the peephole, she saw the guard from downstairs in a panic, standing beside a feisty Jacqueline Laurent.

"Ms. Brazile, I tried to stop this woman."

With raised eyebrows, Jacqueline demanded, "Tell this fool that we know one another."

Puzzled, Brooke tossed the mail into the basket on the end table and placed her hand on her hip. "Jacqueline. Wait. First of all, how do you know where I live? Secondly, he has every right to stop you. You need to follow the rules just like everyone else."

"Brooke, please." She gave a side eye to the guard beside her, daring him to put a hand on her.

"Paul, it's fine. I know her. But next time, follow procedure. I don't appreciate being surprised. That's why I pay to live in a guarded building. Come in." She widened the door for Jacqueline. "Thanks, Paul."

Closing the door, she turned to Jacqueline, who was dressed in black leggings and a leopard-print blouse. An unflattering hue of blue colored her eyelids, and the red lipstick applied on her lips appeared to have been drawn on by an undeveloped fine motor-skilled preschooler. Her golden-brown hair fell sloppily past her shoulders. Brooke sometimes wondered if the lady owned a brush.

Brooke folded her arms and raised an eyebrow in question. "Jackson will be here any moment. Do you wanna tell me why you're on my doorstep on a Friday night? Why didn't you just call? I woulda met you."

"No time, dear. May we sit?" Jacqueline seemed scattered. She juggled her purse between her hands in her too-big blouse.

Unfolding her arms and leading Jacqueline to the sofa, she asked, "What would you like to drink? And how do you know where I live?"

Jacqueline took a seat on the sofa and held her head. "Water would be fine. Although after our talk, I suppose I may need a shot of liquor."

Brooke grew concerned but didn't show it. Instead, she just nodded and headed for the kitchen. She heard her visitor say, "This place is exactly what I'd imagined it to be: high maintenance, clean, and modern. Smells nice, too."

On another day, Brooke would've been flattered. Today, it was hard to appreciate the comments when she was expecting to be alone with Jackson. She wondered where he was. Brooke handed the glass of water to Jacqueline and headed back to the foyer to retrieve her purse and check her phone. Jackson had texted that he would be late because of work. Brooke replied that she had a visitor and not to worry about being late.

Joining Jacqueline on the couch, she asked, "So why the ambush? Are you okay?" Her irritation had begun to melt as she deduced from Jacqueline's undone demeanor that something was wrong. Why not call her daughter, Veronique? Brooke was very confused. Maybe she owed Jacqueline after pouring her heart out to her over Jackson, and now Jacqueline had finally come to collect.

"Brooke." Jacqueline closed her eyes as she chose her words wisely. "You may hate me after this."

Brooke was done with the mystery. "Can you just say it?"

"Remember when you asked why I cared about you so much?" Sighing, she placed a palm on her leg.

"Yeah." Brooke turned her body to face her.

"You wanna know how I know where you lived?"

"Ummm hm." Brooke's curiosity fought against the desire of her heart to beat faster and won. Remaining calm, she just wanted it over with. Jacqueline needed to spill the beans.

She sighed loudly. "Your mom told me."

Brooke gasped and asked, "Excuse me? What did you say? You don't know my mom. Don't be silly." She barely pulled off the calm façade, unsure of whether or not Jacqueline bought it.

Jacqueline's hand flew to her forehead with fingers that gently tapped her skin. "I do, and she did."

Stunned, Brooke didn't know what to say. Shooting to her feet, the room began to spin as her heart pounded in her chest. "Excuse me?"

"I know your mom and very well, in fact." Jacqueline took a long desperate sip of water, as if it were liquor. Her shaky hand gingerly placed the empty glass on the end table.

With pinched brows and a sunken spirit, Brooke demanded a response. "Oh, really? What's her name?"

Folding her arms over her stomach and hunched over, one of Jacqueline's knees started to bounce. "Brooke, please."

"*What's her name, Jacqueline?*"

Nodding uncontrollably, Jacqueline refused to look in her direction. "Please don't—"

"Name!"

"I don't—"

"—tell me now or—"

"—Lilly!"

Feeling the wind knocked from her gut, Brooke's lashes fluttered. "Wh-what?"

"Lilly Hopkins."

With a gaped mouth, Brooke felt betrayed, like she'd never known this woman. Tears came to the rims of her eyes without falling. Truth was, she really didn't know this woman. "How long have you known that she was my mom, if this is the truth?" Panting, she hated every second she felt out of control.

"I think I need more water."

Brooke pointed a feisty finger at her. "No. No more water. No more anything. Who are you to her?" Brooke demanded in a broken voice. She sealed her lips into a tight pout.

What is she doing to me? Don't let her get to you, Brooke. It's all a game.

Jacqueline took a deep breath. Her eyes searched the apartment in an effort to find strength. Exhaling, she raised a pair of reluctant eyes toward Brooke. With a look of shame, she replied, "Lilly Hopkins is my sister."

Brooke's jaw dropped. Her limbs felt weak. Nothing felt right. Jacqueline had punched her in the throat with her confession. *Is my whole life nothing but a lie? What happened to the refrigerator mother that I knew growing up? According to her, we didn't have any family.* Lilly Hopkins was all she knew! Lilly Hopkins *was* her only family. Therefore, Jacqueline Laurent wasn't telling the truth. In fact, she was messing with her, but for what reason, she hadn't a clue. "You liar! Get out!"

Jacqueline stood. "Brooke, *please*. Why would I lie? You're my niece, I'm your aunt."

Through gritted teeth, Brooke replied, "No." Dread tainted her usual buoyant eyes as her defined eyebrows squeezed inward.

With crossed arms, Jacqueline declared, "I will not. Not until you hear the whole story."

Summer

Oliver and I took turns pushing Autumn in her stroller through the closed park in Old Town Alexandria. It was a small park with a view of the Potomac River. A sporadic cool breeze gently hit us. My hair brushed in front of my eyes, and I fought to keep it at bay. We leisurely walked toward a stone bench.

"How was your day?" he asked.

"You wouldn't believe it if I told you."

Grinning, Oliver said, "Try me."

Unable to contain my secret and excitement, a smile appeared on my face from ear to ear. I stopped walking long enough to blurt out, "I have a job."

He stopped walking. "Really?" He stared at me with nothing but pride.

"Really." Nodding and giggling, I told him every single detail, including my phone conversation with Fran.

Oliver squinted at me. "Guess he had to call that bitter bitch."

"Yup. And she behaved. Can you believe it?"

"I think she knows better than to mess with you."

He lost me with that statement. Fran was the one with leverage, not me. "Oliver. I'm the one who screwed her over. She really wasn't trying to wish me well. But at least I got a fat salary and a great referral because of her."

"I see she behaved herself. That's good. And let's get something straight: You pulled your own weight, so try not to lean too much credit her way."

Nodding, I replied with, "True. You-you're right."

We took a seat.

Oliver placed a hand on my knee. "Autumn is proud. I told her you would make her proud." He smiled and, for the first time in a while, I didn't want to see the smile in his eyes. In fact, with all the chaos, Autumn was the only one to bring it out in him. It was nice to see it solely for me, but it also broke my heart.

"You make me so happy, Summer. You and our little season." After giving my knee a squeeze, he took his hand back. All I could do was nod.

I cleared my throat. "So, Oliver. Don't you miss your space? I've totally taken over your home."

"For you? Nah. You two make it feel warm. The single life ain't all that, unless your woman is a psycho."

We shared a laugh. As good as it felt, I had to stick to my plan. "Oliver—"

"Summer, wait."

"Yes?"

An expression of seriousness swept over his face. "I think we should discuss taking what we have to another level."

"Level?" My lungs constricted. His words had boxed me into a corner without a light. It took everything within me not to reach into my purse for the inhaler that I didn't own. His words made me feel emotionally claustrophobic. "What level?" I tried my best not to sound nervous, but I failed.

"I love you, Summer. I love, Autumn. I love our life and what we have. I don't wanna lose this."

"Oliver." I closed my eyes as I struggled to be strong. "You are moving too fast." And then I opened them to a man with nothing but hope coloring his face.

"I don't think so. We've known each other—"

"Barely a year."

"But we're getting there. Look at all that we've achieved so quickly that most couples can't manage to achieve in years. What woman wouldn't glow at my words?"

I slapped my chest. "I'm not most women. Oliver, listen."

With a tilted head, he asked, "What?"

There was nothing else to do but to take the verbal plunge. It would never get easy, it would never feel right. "I think I should move out. I need to be independent."

Oliver slid his head back to look at me through a set of suspicious eyes. "Because you have a job?"

My hands gestured wildly. "No. No, no, no. I was going to offer you the money I made earlier this year and start recruiting with the new company."

"Oh!" he scoffed. "She has it all figured out."

"Please stop. I couldn't have made that money without you." Autumn's short spurts of noise hinted at her becoming upset. I placed a hand on her tummy to pacify her. "Shhhh, Mommy's here. Mommy's here."

"Oh, please," he snarled. "I don't want your money. And why the sudden change of heart?" Upset, he stood to his feet.

Sighing, I tried to find the right words. "Oliver. I do love you. I do. But I need to know that I can do this on my own first." Why did I feel like a mad person with a sword who just kept on stabbing people, only to cry when there was blood on my hands?

Perplexity monopolized his face. "*Do what*? What is 'this?'"

"Raise my girl, handle my bills, have a career. When I'm in your home, I feel rescued." I wanted to inhale, I needed to inhale and capture the bubble in my throat, but it wouldn't happen. "At first, it was all a fun blur, then when Ruben died, and Autumn was born, I realized that I could become too comfortable and dependent on a man. My mom did it alone, and I think I can, too."

Oliver angrily placed both hands on his hips. "I can't believe this."

"No, wait." Suddenly, I felt like crying and telling my daughter to move over, so I could share her stroller. She wasn't the only baby. "Oliver, listen. Why did I end up in your home, huh? Because I became homeless. It wasn't love that made me pack up and leave my own apartment. I was in a situation, and you rescued me. I loved you, you loved me, but the circumstance was odd. I've put you through constant hell since being with you."

"And we got over that."

I reached out to touch him, but he raised his hands and took a step back.

"I'm good, I'm good. I'm a big boy, all right? Don't look out for me," he snapped.

"How could I not? Look at this. I have a baby from another man who is dead, I'm in your apartment and, frankly, I couldn't have made it this far without you. That's pathetic. I've realized that I've been riding your coattail, and that's not me. I shoulda moved out when I made money from—"

"Summer!"

My head jerked. "Please don't yell in front of Autumn."

"Summer," he repeated softly. "From the beginning, I've been nothing but your cheerleader. I've never judged you, made you feel like you owed me, or treated you or Autumn badly; I've done none of that. But I've stuck by your confessions, late truths, and constant yanking me around. And now, you say you wanna move out, and for what? To prove that you're strong? Instead of taking that salary and building an empire with me, you'd rather uproot our little girl to prove a wack-ass point that makes no sense to me and probably not even to yourself."

Suddenly, his words embarrassed me. I didn't know what the hell I was talking about or feeling. What did I want? To be a single mom, or to be a woman with a devoted man to me and my baby?

"Summer, do you think your mom would advise you to raise her without a daddy? I ain't tryna make visits to your new home and play daddy to her. Either you and Autumn stay put, and I become the active daddy, or you leave and don't look back." He licked his lips. "Baby. You will not jerk me around for nothing and try to come back. So, you sleep on it. Even if you're convinced right now, that's fine. But sleep on it, because once you wake up, that's it. It's either heads or tails, baby."

His all or nothing stance caused me to wake up. An evaluation was in order to figure out what I'd be leaving behind. My intentions were not to let him go. I just needed my own space and to know that I was still independent. Standing, my sweaty, little hand grabbed the handles of the stroller to turn it around. I was ready to go home. "Let's go."

I felt like an infant trying to make sense of the world. Sometimes when you think you have it all figured out, you realize that you don't know anything. One day I would have to tell my daughter what no adult likes to admit: Being older, doesn't necessarily make you any wiser.

Emily

Eric came through Emily's front door. "Emily?"

She emerged from the kitchen with a spoon of rice and beans and approached him in a curve-hugging, black halter dress. "Taste this."

Eric grinned upon seeing her. He dropped the duffle bag full of casual clothes next to his feet. Emily placed the spoon in his mouth and watched him process the taste. "Mmmmm. My Latina. My tasty Latina." The sparkle in his eyes told her that he genuinely enjoyed the taste.

"I've been throwing myself into cooking, telling myself that maybe this time you will stay and be good if you came home to good food. My mom warned me that cooking was essential." Shaking her head, she walked toward the dining room table. "I should have listened." The problem was, she knew that their problems ran deeper than a missing bowl of rice and beans in their marriage.

"Stop. No more about the past." He lifted a straightened arm and pointed ahead of them. "Just look straight."

She nodded. "You're right, baby."

"I'm gonna go change. Can I wear shorts and a white t-shirt?"

"I guess it will go well with this dress. I know you've been suited up for too many hours now. Go change."

"Thanks, honey." He placed a slow kiss on her forehead.

Emily watched her tall man disappear into the bedroom. About five minutes later, he joined her at the table.

"Ahhhh. Comfy at last." Emily pointed to one of the empty chairs with a smile. He sat, and she positioned herself in the chair across from him. "Smells fantastic, Ems. What are we having?"

"Red beans and rice, pork chops, and green beans with a side of your favorite dinner rolls."

"Yesssssss. Nice and hearty. Thank you, honey." He picked up a roll and held it beneath his narrow nose to inhale. "No fast food for me tonight. Feels good to eat at home."

She giggled. "You poor thing."

"How's our wedding plans?" He chewed on a piece of pork.

"I have the chapel booked for two Saturdays from tomorrow."

"Good. Good. Move it right along, because I promise, my boss is cooking up a back-to-back trip for me once we jump the broom."

Emily pouted. "Will I see you much?"

"No." Biting down on the forkful of red beans and rice, his eyes didn't blink when he said, "Not much at all."

Amber

Amber found Amit cooking the halibut in the pan. When he looked up to see her watching him with fingers against her lips, he smirked.

"Hi there."

Amber heard the sizzle and smelled the delicious aroma. "What you got there besides the halibut?"

"I have your halibut and asparagus."

Amber smiled. "Amit, that won't be necessary."

"Huh? Why not? Is Mr. Crosby not coming home tonight?"

"No. I mean, he is, but I won't be here."

"Oh. Okay. Then there will be an extra piece?"

She nodded and stood across from him at the island. "Amit, I have to tell you that I'm sorry. Well, I am and I ain't."

"For what?" He worked the pan to skillfully sear the halibut.

"I shouldn't of flirted with you, and I definitely shouldn't of kissed you. You coulda lost your job because of me."

Disagreeing with a shake of his head, he grinned at her and said, "I rather enjoyed it. I knew what I was doing."

"No, I was in no position to provide you with another job if you woulda lost this one. I wouldn't of been able to forgive myself. And as a matter of fact, I need to think of others for a change, not just myself. I'm sorry for my actions."

"Very well—Amber. Dinner is served. Well, for Mr. Crosby."

Suddenly, cooking her own meals sounded right as well as natural. Amber smiled. "I wish you the best. I'm outta here, playa."

"What do you mean?" He waited with narrowed eyes as he shut off the stove by pressing a digital button.

"I'm leaving. I'm moving out, tonight."

Nodding thoughtfully, he told her, "I'm sorry to hear that. His loss." Amit smiled then plated the meal with a dish towel over his shoulder.

"No, it's fine. Really. At least I know how to grind fresh pepper."

Amit snickered.

"But take care, Amit." Amber stuck out her hand for him to shake.

"And you as well, Amber. It was a fine pleasure waiting on you." A hint of naughtiness polished his grin. Amit's eyes flirted with her one last time as he slid his hand into hers.

She wished she could've acted on the chemistry that sparked when their hands met, but she was glad to behave with restraint. Pulling her hand back, she saluted with one last look before making her way to the stairs to wait on Daniel.

Reflecting on the past, she remembered when she tried to redeem herself with Emily. Between Daniel making her feel like a fool, and Emily taking back their friendship, Amber felt compelled to make a change. It wasn't as organic as she'd thought. It was a cheap chance at assimilation among her friends to atone for sleeping around and with the wrong men. But something about life and living it her own way only made her realize that control was a false comfort that she'd used like a security blanket. She decided to throw that blanket away and cuddle with hope. She'd rather fall and get banged up for trying life like an adult, than to be dependent and still come out bloody.

Instead, Amber had traded one debt for another. Monetarily, she was finally in the clear, and that came with the price of achy knees and a sore jaw. On the flip side, she'd become indebted to a man and all of his demands, and for the first time, owing the bill collectors didn't look so bad. She stood up when she heard the jingle of keys at the front door. Daniel entered with a look of exhaustion.

The first words out of his mouth were, "What the hell you doing there with those bags at your feet?" A suspicious and irritated Daniel studied her as he waited for an answer. The door slammed behind him.

Amber dug her hands into her pockets as she prepared to inform him. "I'm leaving, and I don't wanna be stopped."

"Leaving?" Daniel scoffed. She could hear every breath he took. "And go where?" He threw an annoyed hand in the air. He didn't want to hear of it, but clearly, he thought she was helpless without him.

"Daniel." Amber took a step closer toward him. The smell of his foul breath grazed her nostrils. "I can't play house anymore. My heart just ain't in it."

"Oh, you mean because you have good credit now?" She hated the way he peered at her through patronizing eyes. "What do you know about life? Huh?" He placed his chubby hands against his muffin top formed by the tightness of his belt.

Amber took a step back with a tilted head. "More than you think. I knew that this arrangement was too whimsical to work. Think about it, Daniel. You like that I'm dependent. You want me to feel trapped. You think that I can't manage on my own because at the end of the day, you still don't have any respect for me. I'll always be the poor minority girl who was rescued by the rich, white man in exchange for sex. Nah, man. Ain't nobody gotta rescue me." Amber threw her hands up and realized that all of her epiphanies involved Daniel.

Desperation plagued him as he closed the gap between them. With a softened tone, he said, "Amber, my bunny. Please, cookie, I like having you here. Why do you wanna go, hmm? Stay here. Stay."

"Why? There's no love. There will never be any love."

Moving his hands to her jawlines, his eyes were coated with ruffled emotions. "You don't know that."

Amber felt bad, and for the first time, she was really convinced that he may've actually loved her. He did spend a lot of money on her and moved her in. Daniel didn't have to uproot her from her dire neighborhood, but he did. No! She berated herself to stick to the plan. She blinked slowly. "I do."

Daniel's sweaty hands hugged the sides of her neck. "I do respect you. I know I shouldn't belittle you, but fear is the only tactic I know in order to win."

Shaking her head, she replied, "You can't bully me."

"I know. I know. And that's why I like you. Where will you stay?"

She shrugged. "With a friend."

"No. Don't. I will pay for your hotel room until you find your own apartment, on your own."

"Daniel—"

"Amber, look. It's a cruel, cruel world out there. And if you're not prepared, you'll never get ahead. I can't sleep if you're out there. I won't bother you. I promise."

"Nah. I'm good. I'm a New Yorker. These streets can't teach me nothin' new. Besides, I can't fly if I keep borrowing your wings." Touched by his concern and constant generosity, Amber's firm stance began to slide as fast as quicksand.

"Yes, you can, and you will. I started this whole sex for money mess this time around, and now I need to fix it. But first, I have to confess something to you."

Biting her lower lip, Amber nodded for him to continue.

"Amber." His hands slid down to find her hands. Tied like a rope, their hands joined in a shaky union. "I, uhhh, don't know how to get what I do in life without using fear or some dirty tactic as a card. I knew you wouldn't want to move in with just me as the prize. I could only bend your arm back with money. In the back of my mind, I figured if I showed you love, you'd love me back one day. So, I let you think that I gave you money because of sex, but you woulda had all of me, and my things, regardless." He kissed her on the forehead. "Maybe you'll come back to me. Someday."

Amber felt tears race down her cheeks as she wondered if he could've been the one. But as quickly as she pondered the lost possibility, it found its place on a shelf like a book in a library. Putting it away, she shook her head and told him, "No. I'm not looking for love, or the one. I'm just looking for . . . myself." Amber bent at the knees with slight effort to grab her bags. "I'll send someone to pick up all of my things and the piano when I get the money. But everything of mine is packed for them to take into the guest bedroom."

Feeling defeated, Daniel replied, "Take your time, cookie. I'll guard it with my life." He grinned and crossed his heart.

Reaching for the doorknob, Amber turned around and said, "Daniel, thank you. You are kind and warm, and I wish you all the best. Thank you for everything."

Realizing that she wasn't leaving behind a man with whom she had sex, but instead a friend, Amber dropped her bags to hit him with a sincere hug around his waist with her face pressed against his chest. Then she felt his arms lock behind her back. They stood there, finding closure, somewhere between the place of a rich man's poor sense of self and a poor woman's rich outlook on soul searching.

Brooke

Brooke wished that she could head to the bathroom to find a Band-aid that was big enough to cover the fresh wound that Jacqueline had inflicted. But no company made such a product. Fortunately, love was the best first-aid kit, and Jackson was the brand of her choice. The only question was, did she really want him to step in the middle of the battlefield?

Exhausted with defeat and watching the floor become a blur, Brooke held her head with both hands. Realizing that a fight was pointless, she decided to humor Jacqueline's demand for the spotlight with a, "You win, now talk," as she took a seat in her white armchair.

Relieved, Jacqueline said, "Thank you." She took a seat on the sofa. "I'm just going to start from what I believe is the beginning."

Leaning forward with an elbow on her leg, Brooke supported her chin with her fingers. Her eyelids had become heavy, her stare hit the floor. Since when did Jacqueline's shame become her own? "That's fine."

Jacqueline cleared her throat. "It was your mom and me. We grew up with two parents—your grandparents." Brooke felt a needle-like ping at her heart at the sound of the word "grandparents." She grew up in a home where those labels weren't used. How strange it felt. Though it felt warm, she refused to look at her aunt. Another term she wasn't used to.

"Our parents weren't perfect. Our mom worshipped the ground our father walked on. Your mom was the oldest sibling. I got my light skin from our dad, and your mom got her dark complexion from our mom." She took a break.

Intrigued, but not willing to show it, Brooke turned to her with a neutral expression and said in a dull voice, "Go on." She crossed her legs and tapped a foot in the air nervously.

"Well, your grandmother didn't treat your mom with the kind of unconditional love she should have. When I came along, my mom clearly favored me. I had the golden-brown hair, the light skin, the lighter shade of eyes. I was my father. Your mom was her mom. Anyway, Mama didn't like Papa giving us too much attention, especially to your mom. So, needless to say, your mom grew up with a complex."

Brooke sighed as she tried to digest Jacqueline's words. "A complex?"

Nodding, Jacqueline replied, "At seventeen, she met a light-skinned man as well, just like Mama. Met him at our corner ice cream shop."

"I see."

"I suppose they were in love, because your mom split faster than a banana once Papa died. She was only eighteen, knew nothing about the real world. Papa suffered a heart attack one day at work. His charisma had held our family together." Briefly aloof, Jacqueline shook her head at her own thoughts. "Last thing Mama and I knew, Lilly had left abruptly with that same man." Jacqueline held up a quick finger. "But we never knew you existed. She broke all ties with Mama and me. Not that I could blame her. She was jealous of me, because, Mama, treated me better."

"And how and why did you find your sister?"

Wiping tears from her eyes, Jacqueline swallowed hard. "Brooke, I knew you were my niece when I came to you for your services. I was determined to never let go."

Brooke never felt so betrayed and so lost in her own life. No one seemed to be who she'd thought. She clasped her hands together. A wave of stress clenched her chest causing her voice to reflect a hint of excitement. "You still didn't answer my question."

"I got tired of wondering where my sister was. With all the technology now, it wasn't hard. In fact, I think she wanted to be found."

"I was in France my whole adult life after college. Had to get away after losing Mama and not knowing where Lilly was. I wanted an escape, a chance to start over and build my own life." Slight energy had returned back into Jacqueline's eyes. A distant smile eased across her face. "I fell in love over there. We married, but when we divorced, he gave me enough money for two lives."

"Compensated for heartbreak."

"Nothing measures the love of your life, Brooke. You know that, thanks to Jackson."

Brooke snarled. "I really don't want you to say his name right now. Not you."

"Fair enough." Jacqueline's lips tightened. "My life in France was done. It was simply time to come back home and face my identity. My daughter and I came back, and she fell in love while I hunted down Lilly and reconnected with her. We had so much that needed to be built."

With the realization that her newfound aunt had seen her around at events at least a year before their initial meeting in La Madeline, Brooke became livid. "Wait." Her hand shot up. "You and I have run into each other, and you never said a word?"

"Your mom begged me not to. She convinced me that I owed her some kind of happiness."

"How is staying silent a way of making her happy?"

"She wanted to reconnect with you first. Convinced that you were happier without us, she could never manage the strength to face you. I tried to tell her that withholding my identity was wrong, and that you needed some kind of family in your life, so she compromised. Lilly said I could get next to you as long as I didn't tell you who I was. So, since I felt guilty about our childhood, I felt I could do this one thing for her."

Brooke sighed as she uncrossed her legs. This all seemed too messy and idiotic to her. She sat with squared shoulders and balled fists deep into the cushion at her sides. "How did she take your reunion?"

"Actually, after all these years, she was happy. She told me that she'd been tracking you since your graduation from Pepperdine. She claimed she owed you your space." Brooke wasn't surprised that she sat back in the shadows like a coward. Her only regret was that her mom stepped out of them. "Lilly knew you were a wedding planner with an amazing reputation. I told her it wasn't fair for me to keep talking to you while leaving you in the dark. Finally, she agreed, but she wanted to tell you everything. Your mom raced over here to beat me to the punch to do so. You kicked her out, but she has something else to tell you."

Brooke couldn't stand on her feet fast enough. "Not interested. All I've heard was this circus of you two jerking me around and laughing behind the curtain."

"Honey," Jacqueline struggled to her feet, "no one is laughing at you."

"Then how do you explain where my dad is? How do you explain me growing up without a family?" Brooke could feel her chest fighting a collapse.

"I'll tell you. Your dad loved you, but your mom couldn't handle it. Your mom confessed that she didn't like being second to you, because it was like her childhood playing out again, and you were just a baby."

"That's so pathetic."

"It is, it is. Regardless, your dad was arrested for embezzlement shortly after she kicked him out."

"I guess that's why he didn't bother to come see me, right?" Brooke asked facetiously.

"Well, there is something else." Jacqueline placed a finger on Brooke's arm. Brooke's eyes widened with fear.

"According to your mom, Greg Brazile was stabbed to death in prison . . . right after you went to college. Your mom paid him a visit once you left so he knew of your accomplishment. Still . . . your mom needs to tell you something."

Used to growing up without worrying about a father, Brooke didn't know how to feel about his possible pride in her going to college. It was all her mother's fault. Regardless of not having a bond with him, her heart tore a little when she heard confirmation that she could never have anything with that man named Greg Brazile.

Brooke snapped. "No, I'm not speaking to that woman about anything. She is the reason why I grew up without a loving father. Do you even know how embarrassing it is to tell my fiancé about my life when he grew up with such a nice family?"

"Greg was ashamed for his crime. *He's* the one who asked Lilly not to tell you about his imprisonment."

"Doesn't matter. If it weren't for my success, I'd be one pathetic creature, Jacqueline. There would be no one to thank for that but her."

With a tone of empathy, Jacqueline assured her, "And a victim you are not. I'm not making excuses for her—"

"Good," Brooke curtly replied. "But my father wasn't a saint either. He got himself into prison."

"And you don't have to be embarrassed, Brooke, because she fueled you with the desire to take care of yourself. It could've gone the other way."

"Who knows, Jacqueline?" Brooke was stumped with realization. "I mean, maybe I would've been this driven if she were a terrific mom. Look at Jackson. His family was sweet to him and look how well he turned out."

"Did you live in his house? You don't know nothing but what this man tells you."

"I know he's not a liar like you." A teary-eyed Brooke looked at Jacqueline with raised eyebrows.

"*Touché.*"

"I had so much respect and admiration for you. Look at this." Brooke pleaded heavenward, shaking angry fists in the air. "See? I have a cousin. A *cousin.* I planned her wedding. Oh, my gosh." She placed a hand over her heart. "Does she know about this?"

Without hesitating, her aunt replied, "No. Well, yes. Just last night, I told her. I never wanted to put her in the middle by making her bear this secret with me and Lilly. That's why I couldn't contain myself any longer, because she's anxious to come see you."

With her tongue pressing into her cheek and a foot skirting over the floor in thought, Brooke placed a hand on her hip staring downward. Looking up, she calmly told Jacqueline, "I feel like you're telling me all this now because you feel compelled, but not because you really want to." A hurt expression creased her face.

"No. No, no, honey." Her aunt scrambled to pacify her. Jacqueline seemed just as lost as Brooke, even though she knew the truth a while ago. "I—I just couldn't move like I wanted to. I had your mom and her request, and then I had to think about you and what my place was in all of this. This," she threw her hands up, "this is horrible." Jacqueline raced to the couch to plop down with a river of tears.

Brooke told her, "Man, Jacqueline. I go through my life with just a mom. No grandparents, no cousins, no aunts, no dad." With a thumb and index finger, she measured an inch, adding, "You know, I was this short of being an orphan. And now you barge in here after my mom and tell me that you're my aunt and that I have a cousin. But, you know, the funny thing is, where was everyone on Christmases and Thanksgiving dinners and, you know, all those family vacations? Huh?"

She could feel herself losing it. Her head began to throb, her heart began to race.

Jacqueline raced to be by her side. "Brooke . . ." was all she could manage. She tried to place a hand on Brooke's back, but a flinging hand pushed it away.

"No. I'm not done." Brooke could barely catch enough breath to fight back. "Y-you let me down just like her." A rip of pain shot through her head. An electrical jolt of irritation shocked her like a lightning bolt. "I'm *disgusted*. You actually felt like family to me *before* you told me the truth. And now? Now I hate you, and I want you to stay away. If your and her blood is what's running through me, keep it. I don't need a family at this point."

Standing, she peered down at Jacqueline's awestruck face. Feeling lightheaded, she was determined to tell that lady how she felt before it was too late. In a low tone, Brooke proclaimed, "Jackson is my family, so are my friends. I'm good. No blood needed. From now, till the day I die, Jackson and the children I have yet to bear will be my only family." Saying that made Brooke feel good, before she saw black.

Summer

"I need to see you. Now."

My eyes shot around the kitchen in an effort to locate the digital clock on the stove. It was pushing ten. With the controller on his chest, Oliver had lost the battle with sleep while watching TV on the couch. Autumn rested quietly in her room.

"Now?" I whispered in shock.

"Now. Like, if-you-are-a-good-friend-see-me-now kind of situation."

"Damn. That serious?"

"Goldilocks, I ain't gon ask you again. Meet me at that late-night diner we go to sometimes."

I sighed. Only this one girl in particular would call me with this kind of demand. "You are so lucky that I have—" Wow. I had to complete my thought not only because it was the truth, but for my own sake as well. "Oliver. Hang on. Let me tell him. Bye." Trudging across the floor, I smiled at the sight of the famous male sleeping pose: crossed arms and a tilted neck. I nudged him gently and whispered his name. "Oliver." One push didn't do it, so I did it again. "Oliver." His eyes flickered, and he observed his surroundings as if to see whether or not his environment had changed. *Only men.* I snickered.

"What's up?"

"Amber needs to see me. But she wants me to see her at the diner. Can you watch Autumn?"

Sitting up, he licked his dry lips. "She doesn't wanna come here?" His voice came out raspy and low.

Shrugging, I answered, "I guess not."

"Sure." He picked up the controller and turned from the basketball game.

"Thank you, baby." I kissed his forehead. He grabbed my wrist. Before I could straighten, I became paralyzed mid-way.

"Don't forget that you have to think about that decision by tomorrow morning." Without blinking while issuing his reminder, he released my wrist.

Nodding, I mumbled, "Okay. Um, bye." It was impossible to forget that I was with a business man. His methods were woven into our relationship.

In an instant, I spotted Amber eyeing the menu. Her brown, blonde-streaked braids spilled over one side of her shoulder. She whipped her neck in an effort to remove it without her hands. Her lids flicked and revealed eyes full of relief upon seeing me. It wasn't hard to notice the luggage beside her. I waved, approaching her with a grin. Once nestled into her booth, I greeted her with a happy, "What's up, boo? What's up with all the luggage here?" I cleared my throat before picking up the menu. My eyes looked over the print to see the selection of hot drinks.

"Well, I ain't headed for the Bahamas, if that's what you wanna know. By the way, thanks for meeting me," she blurted in deep appreciation. She hugged the menu against her chest.

Suspiciously, I lowered the menu with mock fear in my eyes as they darted from side to side. "Ohhhh kaaaay. What is going on with you?"

"Can I get you ladies started with something?" the mature, blonde server asked.

"Espresso," Amber answered without hesitation. "And fish and chips." She passed the menu to the server without looking up as her gaze burned intensely into mine.

The server chuckled. "Got it. And for you ma'am?" She tilted her neck to catch my stare.

Making eye contact, I replied, "Well, yes. How about hot chocolate with whipped cream and a toasted bagel with cream cheese. Both plain, please."

Amber joked, "Hot chocolate? What are you, four?"

"Starting to feel like it."

Snickering, the server took my menu and headed off.

"Lady, don't start with me. Now. Do you wanna tell me why you took me away from my infant and man on a Friday night?" I cocked my head to the side with furrowed eyebrows. "And why do you have your runaway gear with you."

"Sure." Amber sighed and sat back. "I'm homeless." Before I could respond following my dropped jaw, she placed a hand in the air to silence me. "And it was my own doing."

"Why? Why would you wanna do that?"

"Because my life was fake, and I couldn't take it, Summer." Amber seemed frazzled, and that was new.

"In what way?" My curiosity showed in my squinted eyes.

"I don't love that man. It was too much." Using her fingers to count, she listed aloud, "The sexual demands, the money for the sex, the five-star house, the getting an education, our chef—all of it. We weren't a couple in love. It was all BS."

"Honey, I saw that at the dinner you hosted." Concerned, I asked, "You're gonna quit school?"

"No, I'm not. I'ma hold to that commitment." Amber pouted.

"Good. Good for you, Amber. We knew you could do it alone. Now I'm thinking of taking your advice for the same reason. I want my independence back, too."

Amber snapped out of her tunnel of worries when she heard my response. "What? Why? Are you stupid?"

I scoffed. "Maybe. Yeah, you know, it's just not right. I moved in with him because I was homeless, and I couldn't take Fran and Ruben anymore."

"But who cares how you two got there. All that matters is that you did." She glared at me as if I couldn't perform single-digit addition. I felt stupid.

"My mom held her own. I feel dependent. My course of independence has been interrupted." I tried to fight, but I felt like a lawyer without a shred of evidence at a murder trial trying to put away the bad guy.

Amber leaned forward with her hands hitting the table as she spoke. "Listen up, kid. Don't be stupid," she warned. "You been livin' on your own for years, with or without a roommate, but without a man. You been makin' your own decisions on your own. You did the college and entry-level job thing and have nuzzled your way into a career. Before I left, Daniel reminded me that it's a cruel, cruel world out there. And he's right. That doesn't mean that we shouldn't embark on independent journeys, but only when necessary. And, sis, I don't see this one as necessary."

Troubled, I could only blink as I stared away. Was my dear friend right? Could I not see my own milestones? A plate and mug slid in front of me, but I couldn't touch them. I only cared to indulge in Amber's wisdom and opinion. "But you're leaving right as we speak."

"Honey, I already left." Amber unfolded her cloth napkin hastily as it parachuted into her lap. She was ready to eat. "Look. I didn't love him. You love Oliver, right?" I nodded, to which she replied, "Then stay. What would leaving achieve? The real deal is, maybe you don't want him at all, or you're worse at commitment than me." She bit into a French fry.

The ball was in my court.

"Yes, you are right. I do love him. And I do want him. At times I feel like I'm in an oversized fish tank with room to move while feeling trapped at the same time." I paused before admitting, "I don't know."

"Right." Amber devoured her fries in between bites of her fried cod. "You don't know anything." She smirked.

I shot her a playful, stank face. "Coincidentally, we're both here because we're seeking independence, but ironically, I'm considering leaving for the very reasons you couldn't stay. I mean, I have the love, the passion, a salary to work with, and the history showing that I'm capable. Still, when my little girl comes along, I try to relive history by playing out my mom's life after my dad died."

A light bulb went off in my head.

"I think I don't feel like a real woman unless I've attacked the hardest tasks, like motherhood, without a man." Confounded, I asked, "But why did I feel like something had to be proved?"

My unyielding trance-like eye contact with Amber watched her chew as she shrugged. Obviously, she couldn't chew fast enough, so with a full mouth she replied, "Cuz you stupid."

Reaching across the small table, I placed a hand over her hand to genuinely express my gratitude. "Thank you. From the bottom of my heart, thank you."

Lost with wide eyes, she shook her head and asked, "Bitch, what? What did I do? I think you figured this out on your own."

"I am stupid. You pointed out that I was releasing a good man back into this world, and for what?"

"For some other THOT like me to come snatch him up?" She cracked herself up, I just shook my head.

"True. But for real, all because not only my fear of commitment, but I think I thought of help or relationships as being weak. I wanted to be the strong, free bird."

"Yeah, who woulda chirruped alone till death." Amber snickered before attacking her cod with another bite.

I tipped my head to the side mocking a wicked stare. "Oh, shut up."

"Does he know you thinkin' about this?"

"Yup. And he made it clear that if I go then our course ends here. I have until the morning to tell him."

"Good for him, but good for you, too. I know what you were trying to do, Summer. The truth of the matter is, independence is more than money. It's having your own life, schedule, set of friends, career, all of that. I gave up on myself, sold myself out for money, but this all taught me something." I bit into my cream cheese-covered bagel while she kept going. "Ain't no shortcuts in life, baby. Success requires hard work or blood, sweat, and tears, as they say. I gotta quit lusting over my have 'nots' and build my empire slowly. You know, day by day." With a matter-of-fact nod, Amber grinned.

"I think so, too. But I feel that," I ripped off a piece of bread, "through you, I know that it's okay to be with him."

Amber threw a hand up and closed her eyes. "Wait now." She then opened her eyes. "What does your heart say?"

My eyes darted from right to left with the realization that I never really considered that pumping vessel. "Well what did yours say when you left Daniel?"

Without taking a moment to think, she answered, "That I was better off alone. So, I didn't question it."

I didn't have to think. The flip I felt in my tummy every time I saw a flash of me leaving with bags in one hand and Autumn in the other told me the truth. "My heart tells me that I would be devastating too many lives. Mine, his, and Autumn's." There. Saying the words in all honesty out loud closed the book on confusion. I sat back in the booth with my hands resting in my lap with a piece of bagel in one hand. Staring at the floor, it all occurred to me what I would've been giving up.

"Then stay," Amber said softly.

I nodded and met her gaze with a tender smile. "Thank you, Amber. Thank you." After she nodded, I asked, "Hey, where you gonna stay?"

Pursing her lips like a duck and widening her stare, she replied, "Bitch, I was hopin' you was gonna tell me. Shiiit."

Amber was crazy, so I had to chuckle. "Saved any money this time from your lessons when you were living with garlic breath?"

"Oh, okay, Brooke Brazile." She pointed two fingers between our eyes. "I see ya'. And, yes, I did."

I placed a hand over her hand that gripped her cup of espresso. "Amber, when I lost my home, you took me into your little one-bedroom. And on top of saving me from

making the dumbest decision of my life, that earns you a
reward of staying with Oliver and me."

Amber chuckled. "And what would he say?" She tilted
her head at me.

"Does it matter? If he and I are gonna be a family like
he says, then as the woman, I have rights," I teased.

"Well, okay." She bit her lower lip devilishly. "I guess
it's the least you can do for me since I took you in, huh?"

I winked.

I paid the bill twenty minutes later and drove us to my
place. When she and I took the private elevator to the
kitchen, we spotted him immediately heading into the
living room.

He squinted when he realized I wasn't alone. "Hey,
Amber!" Oliver scratched the back of his head, no doubt a
little thrown off by my sudden company.

Amber waved and smiled. "What it do, Oliver?"

"It's good, it's good." He crossed the room to meet us.
"Just making these two my priority. And, you? How are
you and Daniel going?" He placed a kiss on my forehead. I
grabbed his hand.

"We . . . we're not. I left him today. It wasn't working
out." Amber appeared shy, which was unusual. It made her
look cuter than she already was.

Intrigued, Oliver replied, "Oh? I'm sorry to hear that,
Amber. What can we do to help you?"

I couldn't help but to bite down on my lip to keep from
giggling. Turning to look up at him, I warned, "Well, that is
what we need to discuss. I need to see you in the other
room." I gingerly tugged at his forearm. Taking the cue, we
headed to the bedroom. "Be right back," I called to Amber.
Shutting the door, I said, "She needs our help."

Oliver raised an eyebrow. "I gather that. But in what
way?"

It was like a train that I was pretty sure he could see coming. Suddenly, I felt nervous about telling him, but with each silent second that passed, the walls moved in on me more. "You said that if I leave tomorrow, then that's it, right?"

"I did. That's right." Oliver crossed his arms and stood his ground like a grown man.

"I concluded that there's a condition that must be met in order for Autumn and me to stay." I enjoyed teasing him and trying to play hardball.

In the dim room, I could see that he was trying to study my face. "What kind of condition?"

"Amber took me in when I lost my apartment in the flood, and she *is* like a sister at this point. I would like to do the same for her. Agree, and Autumn and I will stay." My chin tilted in the air, my arms folded across my chest. Suddenly, hearing the words come out instantly made me feel like a jerk. Perhaps I'd gone too far in the teasing department. At first it felt harmless to play that game with him, because he would much rather take her in than to lose me. I should've told him my decision to stay before mentioning Amber.

"Summer." His head hung low in thought before speaking . . . something I should've done. He rubbed his head with both hands in distress or confusion. I couldn't tell. "I don't get it. Is this a game to you?" He raised his head and crossed his arms. "One has nothing to do with the other."

I didn't know that tears had developed until I opened my mouth to speak. "Okay, this came out all wrong. I wanna be with you, Oliver." Ambushing him with a hug, I repeated, "I just wanna be with you." My arms squeezed the back of his neck.

He peeled me back, so he could look into my eyes. A grin appeared. "You telling me you wanna stay?"

I wiped a tear as a nervous half-laugh escaped. "Yeah, I do. I can't walk away. Can you forgive me for being stupid?"

"Wait. So Amber needs a place to stay?"

"Well, yeah. She's kind of homeless right now."

"Hell, yeah, she can stay. Know what? Ten of your friends can stay as long as you and the baby do, too."

He picked me up with his arms gripped around the bottom of my butt. Lifted off the ground, I bent my legs back at the knee and squeezed him tighter. "Oh, baby. You are so sweet."

Placing me down, he said, "I can't believe I can wake up to you and the baby."

"Our baby. She's your daughter, too, you know."

The smile plastered across Oliver's face disappeared, making me feel nervous. Did I say something wrong?

"Summer, I have money, education, and a home. But nothing feels like a real accomplishment than having your own family." Nodding and trying to choke back the emotion, he finished with, "I feel complete now that I have you and our daughter. Our daughter? I have a daughter," he realized as it registered. Oliver yanked me close with his strong arms as I reiterated his happiness.

"You have a daughter. *Our* daughter."

Pulling me away from him again, he joked, "But I bet she was just your daughter when you were ready to dip, huh?"

Grinning from ear to ear, I replied, "Shut uuuuup."

Holding my face in his manly hands, he pressed his lips against mine. I was in love, and it felt good to be honest without allowing fear to play on my thoughts. A soft knock on the door floated us back down to earth.

Before we could say anything, the door opened slowly. "I-I'm sorry," Amber said hesitantly. "If this is gonna be a problem, please, don't let me—"

"What?" Oliver and I asked simultaneously.

"No, no, no," I assured her, grabbing her arm. "Get in here. Like, no, *get in here,* because you are staying."

Oliver added, "You can sleep in the guest room as long as you need to, Amber." He pointed a thumb at me. "I have this woman, so life is good."

Amber looked at us with a dull expression. "So, no Ramada Inn for a sis?"

We both shook our heads at her.

She wiped her forehead. "Phew. A girl had visions of an ice bucket and vending machine snacks."

We laughed.

"Look, though. In reality, I know there's an expiration date to this stay. Let's just say I appreciate this, guys, I really do, but I'ma use every day as an opportunity to get back on my feet."

"Give me the keys to your car so—"

"I don't have a car—yet."

"Yeah, her stuff is in our truck." I pulled the keys from my jeans pocket. "Here."

"I should come and help you," Amber suggested.

Oliver brushed her off with a look. "Nah, I'm good. Stay put."

"Oliver." Amber plucked at her fingers. "Thank you so, so much."

He grinned. "It's really no problem, Amber." We both watched Oliver leave the room.

When he was out of sight, Amber turned to me and pointed an acrylic nail at me. "Look. Screw this one up and I'ma have to come kill you myself. Don't you put that man back on the market for some ungrateful ho to snatch him up."

Laughing, I replied, "No. I'll choke myself first. How 'bout that?" Calming down with all jokes aside, I said, "No. I'm not letting this one get away."

Brooke

Brooke heard voices as she came to.

She could hear a frantic female voice. "I don't know what happened. She just . . . blacked out."

A nervous but strong masculine voice that she recognized without fail followed with, "I think she's gonna be fine. She's coming around." Brooke felt strong hands grip her arms. Jackson. "Brooke? Brooke? Are you all right, sweetie?"

Brooke replied with a moan as he helped her to her feet and eased her onto the sofa. He sat next to her, and her vision came into clear view. The handsome and chiseled face brought the quickest sense of peace to her like never before. "Jackson." His strong arm embraced her from behind. Caressing her back, she knew that everything would be all right.

"Shhhhh. I'm here, baby. Jacqueline told me everything. Relax, baby. Relax."

Turning at the waist, Brooke smashed into him with a sudden and desperate hug. "I don't know who anyone is. I don't understand these people who are supposed to be my family."

Slightly rocking her from side to side in his arms, he replied, "Nothing has to make sense right now. Just take it easy, sweetie. Everything's gonna be okay. I got you."

Brooke pulled away, so she could take comfort in the sight of his face. "I don't know how you do it, but you always know what to do." Brooke noticed a petrified Jacqueline standing off in the distance. With a nod of the chin, Brooke demanded to know, "What is she still doing here?"

Biting on the nail of her index finger, Jacqueline looked over her shoulder at Brooke but chose not to answer.

Instead, Jackson responded, "Brooke, I know this is your aunt. She briefly told me what happened. I think you should go easy on her, okay?" He tried to placate Brooke with both arms around her.

"No." Brooke could feel the heat rising from within again. "This lady involved herself in my life under false pretenses. Get her out. Now!" Brooke's normally charmed eyes were full of disdain and impatience.

Jackson appeared awkward as he resisted her demands. "No."

Brooke couldn't snap her neck upward fast enough. A look of disbelief burned into his eyes. "Excuse me? This is my home, and I say she's not welcome. Do you wanna show yourself out with her, too, Jackson?"

"Calm down. *Now*." Jackson shot her a firm look that told her that he would be wearing the pants in the family and that any other way would present a problem. She swore, with him, the pants may have ended up in her hands at times, but in the end, he always had a way of making her place them back on the hanger before stepping out of her skirt.

"Well. She lied to me. And I don't like that one bit."

Jackson inched his face closer to hers. His pleasant breath brushed her cheek. "Look, baby. I know this is a sticky situation. After many years of thinking you know who you are and where you came from, you wake up and find that everything ain't the same. You have family now. Count your blessings and think about the future. If we have kids, this is who they'll have on your side." Lightening the mood, he joked with a grin, "Because I swear that one day my family is gonna drive you nuts, and you won't wanna see them another year in a row for Christmas." Brooke managed to chuckle along with him. "So, I'm telling you, you can be mad, but one day you'll need to get over it. But right now, let's go see what your mom had to say."

Jackson's eyes stared intently into Brooke's. She had to look away. Amidst the pain, she could still feel the natural pull he had on her.

Reluctantly, Brooke allowed her eyes to search for her aunt's gaze. It drove her crazy that Jacqueline pretended not to peer at them. Putting her resistance and irritation to the side, Brooke decided to put on the biggest pair of big-girl panties that she owned to handle things like an adult.

Marching to the other side of the room to face Jacqueline, through gritted teeth, she said, "Let's go see Lilly."

5: baring it all

Brooke

    Jackson's muscle car gargled down Seventh Street as they headed toward southeast. In the passenger seat, Brooke wiggled uncomfortably as she realized that her fiancé would see the ugly and bad part of her life: her past. When her face formed a zit, she'd reach for her trusty concealer, and no one would ever know of that ugly spot but her. She wanted so badly to find something to reach for, something that would cover up what was about to be revealed: Lilly. Brooke didn't want to see her past, and she surely didn't want Jackson to go there with her. There was a concealer that came with life, and it was called 'lies.' Lies were meant to hide the ugly spots. If she wanted something special with Jackson, then she'd have to leave that concealer in the makeup bag and let him see her blemishes to preserve the natural beauty of what they shared.

    Brooke felt like a model, and Jackson was the agency. Would he really want to sign her on after seeing how imperfect things looked without the makeup? Her condo, her job, the way she acted, and the way she presented herself in garments that the kind of money she earned could buy. It was all her makeup. People saw her in the light in which she chose to reflect. Now with Lilly only yards away and her aunt in the backseat, that light was about to spotlight something that even Broadway wouldn't want to touch. No one wanted to see this show. If only she could pull the strings to keep the curtains from drawing.

    In the backseat, Jacqueline remained silent. The only words spoken in the car were the quick directions mumbled by Brooke. No matter how much she wished, she couldn't forget the directions to her mom's house that faithfully sat on the other side of the nation's capital.

    A quick and sudden rub on her knee from Jackson distracted her from the sights passing outside of the window. She smiled wretchedly at him. A quick meeting of the eyes assured her that this moment was real. In less than ten minutes, she would come face to face with the woman in a house she hadn't seen in several years. There was no going back. Jackson and Jacqueline were committed, too.

Now, thanks to her mom and Jacqueline's shenanigans, her whole life had been uprooted in one night, with Jackson as her witness. How embarrassing! Brooke realized that the past never rests, even in an effort to escape it. It seemed that if they weren't going to leave her alone, then she would have to make them. Jackson was her family now, and they would all have to accept it.

"Right here," she directed him.

They made a left to ease into southeast. Brooke could feel her body responding to the sight of her past creeping up on her. By all means possible, she avoided this side of DC, even as a resident. It'd been years since her eyes touched the sight of this side of town. A shock of pain hit her spine as Brooke realized they were inching closer to the house she grew up in. Her chest felt tight and a nasty breath of anxiety slid up from her chest and into her throat. The little, green, one-level house would soon be into view. Before seeing the house, they would have to see the black men standing on the sidewalks in groups, talking, cackling, and drinking. The depressing sight of hanging garbs drying on the lines in the backyards and flipping in the light breeze stung her pride.

God.

She could see the pitifulness in the dark. *Why can't the past just stay where it should? Behind me!*

"So, we're almost there," Jacqueline observed.

Brooke released a dry and sarcastic, "Hooray."

"Brooke," Jackson whispered without taking his eyes off the road.

Unbeknownst to him, she rolled her eyes.

Falling behind on her duty to direct him, Jacqueline cried out, "Oh, right here, Jackson. Make a right."

Agitated, Brooke shook her head. Turning into a neighborhood that seemed all too familiar, but more in despair than when she lived there, her heart smacked against her chest as she fought to admit that she was a child from the ghetto. At the time, the economic status of her neighborhood didn't feel real, and maybe it was because she'd spent so much time in her head dreaming about the future and thinking of ways to make it happen.

When they stopped at the little green vinyl house on her right, Jackson parked against the curb with the engine purring quietly. Brooke felt his eyes on the side of her face.

"Are you ready?" he asked calmly.

Clutching the seatbelt, Brooke stared straight ahead. Her normally pretty eyes were horror-filled. Air barely escaped between her pouty lips. She gripped the seatbelt for dear life, finding it impossible to answer her fiancé. Flashbacks of her childhood bombarded her head. Coming home from school and heading toward her room . . . sitting in cheap wooden chairs at a quiet dining room table across from her mom . . . watching black and white horror movies on late Friday nights . . . begging her mom at the foot of the woman's bed to play a game of Uno . . . getting dressed to go to church just to end up staying at home . . . hearing her mom giggling like a fool in the arms of a random silly man on any given night . . . and, finally, reading fashion magazines under the covers, in the dark, to cut pictures and create collages to serve as a vision board.

Closing her eyes and feeling a tear hit her cheek, in a fragile voice, she replied, "Yeah." Brooke didn't know what "ready" meant, but she knew nothing would come of her sitting in Jackson's car. Staring without seeing, she fumbled to locate the latch so that she could set herself free. She wondered why life didn't provide humans with latches that they could press to free themselves of any pain and suffering. She guessed for the same reason it didn't provide seatbelts for impact just as she'd wondered the night Jackson broke her heart.

A few seconds later, her door popped open when Jackson pulled on the handle. A hand from behind touched her shoulder.

Jacqueline told her, "You can do it." But to Brooke, her words meant nothing. She didn't need encouragement from someone who'd broken her trust.

Brooke willed herself out of the car with the helping hand of Jackson's. "Thanks."

He helped Jacqueline out and locked his car with the alarm. "Are you ready, baby?" He stroked Brooke's hair before cupping her face.

"Do I have a choice?" she asked with a raised eyebrow.

"Brooke, your mom will be so happy to—"

"Goodness, Jacqueline, could you just please stop with all the cheerleading? I get it, okay? We gonna do a quick, fake family reunion, and with my fiancé, no less. Let's just get it over with."

Alarmed, her aunt stood stock-still. "Okay. I'm sorry."

A weak grin painted across Jackson's face was like a silent apology to Jacqueline. He placed a hand above Brooke's ample bottom. "Let's keep our cool for your mom, all right?"

Brooke rolled her eyes and huffed. "No promises."

"This way then." Jacqueline waved a hand toward the front door.

For Brooke, it felt like a walk of shame. The patchy grass on either side of the concrete was unruly but not too long. A rusted, abandoned bike with streamers hanging from the handlebars leaned against the raggedy wooden fence on the side of the house. Brooke stopped in her path to examine it from afar. Jackson paused by her side.

"You okay, boo?"

"Ummm"—she froze with squinted eyes—"yeah. Uh-huh. I don't know why a little girl's bike would be in her lawn."

"Maybe the bike belongs to a neighbor," he suggested casually.

Brooke shrugged and proceeded to walk. "Maybe." They caught up to Jacqueline, who stood at the wooden door hidden behind a white screen door, waiting for them to catch up.

"Should I knock?"

Brooke nodded, and her aunt went through with it. Until the door opened, Brooke's eyes darted about to see what else was the same or different. The same three bushes held their own in front of the kitchen window. Overall, the little green house stood identical to the one in which she grew up, and the house still hadn't received much love.

Jackson squeezed her hand and covered it with the other, studying her demeanor. Brooke cleared her throat nervously and squeezed his hand back. Moving a piece of hair from her face, she stared forward and waited for the door to fly open. Jacqueline knocked again. Brooke didn't understand why she was so nervous when she'd seen her mom recently. Besides, she didn't even care about the woman. Seconds later, the door slowly creaked open to reveal the same woman who'd stood on the other side of Brooke's door that night: Lilly Hopkins.

Emily

Emily donned a sheer lace and net baby doll lingerie top over matching red underwear while Eric showered. Modeling in front of the body-length mirror with a naughty smile on her face, she stopped when her cellphone rang. Surprised but nervous to see that it was Zach, she peeked over her shoulder before answering it even though Eric's shower water was still running.

Full of caution, she answered with a shaky, "Hello?"

Zach cleared his throat before speaking. "Hello? Emily?"

"Hey . . . hi. How have you been?" Emily wasn't quite sure how she felt about him calling, but she could admit that it sure felt good to hear from him.

"Good, good. It's just been a long time since we've connected. I wanted to see how things are going with you and . . . you know. Him."

"We are doing pretty good, thank you. And his name is Eric."

"The infamous Eric," he replied dully.

Emily's knee stabbed into the bed as she held the phone up to one ear. "Oh, come on. Not all of the memories were bad." She couldn't stop smiling. She appreciated his call.

Unconvinced, he replied, "Whatever makes you sleep at night."

"Hey, if you don't behave then I won't be inviting you to our wedding." Before she realized what she'd blurted out, her hand flew to her mouth to censor the words that were already floating in the air. "Ooh."

Zach sounded uneasy. "Wait. Did you say something about a wedding? Are-are you re-marrying this jerk?"

Emily didn't need to ask if he was upset. With her back to the bathroom door, she sat on the bed. "Yes."

The long silence on the other end spoke volumes. No matter what he said, Emily knew that she would go through with the ceremony, but she didn't know why receiving a positive response meant so much to her.

"Why? Why do you want to do this, Emily? He's gonna hurt you. Again."

"Why would I worry about being hurt if he is going to marry me? That doesn't make any sense. That is like the ultimate display of love and commitment right there.

"Was it the first time?"

Right then, she knew why his approval meant so much to her. It was because she valued his opinion. He usually made good sense. And if Zach had reservations, then perhaps it was because he only wanted what was best. Emily just couldn't convince Zach that deep in her heart, she knew that the worst was behind her and Eric.

"Get out now. He's gonna hurt you."

"Look, come or don't come. I will send you an invitation and the rest is up to you. Thank you for calling. I gotta go." Without waiting for his response, because she didn't have any more heart to deal with his broken heart, Emily hung up.

"Who was that?"

Emily froze and lowered the phone slowly before turning around to face a wet Eric with a towel tightly hugging his waist. He waited for an answer while working to dry his hair with a hand towel.

"Zach." Emily remained seated on the bed. So much for modeling sexy lingerie, she thought.

"Is that the guy you told me about? Your friend?" He gripped the towel in both hands, shifting his weight onto one side.

"Yup." Emily nodded with an averted stare.

"Well what did he want? He doesn't like us getting married?"

"Nope." Emily sighed as she looked up. "He feels that you've hurt me too much, and he feels that he can do a better job at making me happy." Emily walked to the foot of her bed on her knees to meet her tall and lean fiancé. "But I don't want him." Emily tossed her cellphone behind her and onto the bed before working both hands on the knot of the towel until it dropped. "I want this." Biting her lower lip in desire, Emily yanked him close, hoping to change his mind to sex and away from Zach while feeding her insatiable lust for him.

Eric placed his intertwined hands behind his head. She knew what that meant and what he wanted. However, he still wanted to talk about it. "Do you agree?"

Emily shrugged as she reached for his groin. "It's in the past," she said in a flirtatious whisper. "We both did things that we are not proud of."

"Well, maybe he wants you back and there are some unresolved feelings on both ends." His eyes peered down at her, watching her lips hit different zones of his six-pack.

"Did you like my lingerie?" She refused to give in to his game of Twenty Questions.

"Well? Do you want Zach?" Though he acted calm, she could sniff out his suspicion.

She wouldn't fold. With folded knees, she sat back against the heels of her feet and toyed with one spaghetti strap. "Do you want me?"

Eric smirked and was probably impressed that he couldn't provoke anger or trap her. "So, you won't answer me, huh?"

Emily stood on her knees and decided to go in for the kill. Maybe she would piss him off, but she wanted to dig herself out of the corner he was trying to pin her in. Lowering the strap that was under her fingers, Emily placed a hand over one breast and rubbed it seductively while the other played in her hair.

"Do you want me, or do you want Zach?" Emily traded playing with her hair for another playground. His eyes followed her lower hand, and his erection told her that he'd made his choice. Evidently, Zach was no longer a factor.

Emily pushed her breast up toward her mouth and tickled the tip of her nipple with her tongue. Keeping her eyes on him, she watched his internal struggle, noted by his tightened jaw line and furrowed brows.

"Mmm," she teased, smiling at him with her eyes. Pushing her breast upward, she said, "Taste."

"Oh, shit, Emily. You're making me wanna bust all over you." Eric bent down to take her breast into her mouth, sucking her nipple, placing kisses all over her breast.

"Wait," she moaned. "Wait, baby."

Eric straightened with breathing crippled by desire. She loved it when he wanted her like this.

"What?"

"I know that you want me, and I'm glad that you do. But first . . ." Emily reached for his hard cock and aimed it at her mouth. Staring down at his delicious pink tip, she covered it with her mouth and sucked his head like it was a strawberry-flavored popsicle.

She knew Eric's flavor, and it was the one she'd choose. Every. Single. Time. Emily had a quick flash of her trying to wrap Zach's penis in Saran Wrap. Simply put, it was the wrong dick. No, she could only do this with and for Eric. To her, she still carried the marriage vows in her heart and heard them in her head. This was her man, and she was more than happy to please.

Emily located that special vein and placed her thumb over it. She wanted to suck his cock like it was the last one on Earth. Running circles around his tip, she slid his shaft into her mouth like a canoe into a cave. Her tongue was like the ocean, lapping against the underside of the boat.

Eric sucked in air through his teeth, coping with his sensation overload by stroking her hair with one hand and doing something unbeknownst to Emily with the other. Emily used her other hand to massage his sack as she continued with her head bobbing. Eric moved his hips to guide his property in and out of her mouth. Even though his length required a high gag tolerance, Emily was prepared. Her desire to please and need to taste overrode any difficulties that would prevent her from getting the job done.

Emily pulled his muscle from her mouth and stared at it while firmly holding it with one hand. *How many pussies have gotten a raw run-in with this cock? Not on my watch, not anymore. He's all mine. Now and forever.*

Eric asked, "What? What's wrong, babe?"

"Not a damn thing, anymore." Emily went into killer mode, determined to make him realize what he'd given up. She'd never opened her mouth so wide in her life, not even for the dentist. Inside of her mouth again, Emily made his dick a snack, sucking his shaft, tracing the tip with tongue flicks, massaging the vein of love in a circular motion, kissing his balls and licking the hairs with her tongue.

"Errrm. Emily! What are ya . . . what . . .?" Eric couldn't finish his sentence, and Emily knew why. His manhood started to pulsate in her mouth, and she was ready for the eruption. Right in time, she took him from her mouth and slid his penis down her chest and watched his semen ooze out like lava, all over her skin.

Emily looked up at his heavy-lidded eyes and with a wink, said, "Checkmate."

Brooke

Lilly Hopkins faced the tiny crowd on the other side of her door with a smile across her wide face. The small-framed woman that Brooke once knew was now slightly plump. Aside from the wrinkles, everything went unnoticed when she shocked her daughter by appearing at her doorstep.

Lilly's eyes surveyed the faces that waited to discuss pressing matters with her, especially Brooke's. They locked stares as her mom slowly opened the screen door before saying, "Please, come in."

Standing with folded arms and a tight mouth, Brooke realized just how much time had elapsed between now and the last day they saw each other since Brooke headed off to California. The progression of time was evident in her mom's looks. Aside from the weight gain and wrinkles, Lilly's smile appeared stressed even when sincere. That look was foreign to Brooke, because the mom she knew barely smiled once a week. Her hair retained its dark color, though Brooke wasn't sure if her mom used a box of dye to achieve the look. Brooke always suspected she must've taken after her dad's look, because even as a child, she could never quite see the resemblance in her mom. At that moment, Brooke had to study her mom's face to see if she could find a similar feature or two. At best, Brooke could see the full lips and shape but nothing more. Brooke wasn't sure if lips were enough to convince her that they indeed shared the same bloodline.

"What a pleasure." Lilly's tongue flicked her lips with excitement that she failed to suppress. She stepped back to accommodate them. Jacqueline went in first; they exchanged brief greetings without hugging. Jackson placed a hand on Brooke's lower back to urge her to proceed. After taking one look up at his confident face, Brooke felt secure after he nodded back at her, so she took the next step and braced herself for impact. She lifted one foot on the single step to take a walk down memory lane.

The dim house used to have a neutral smell. Now, it smelled like one big closet full of old furniture and carpet, and a build-up of loneliness. Brooke didn't know where to look. One choice was to look forward and face the flashbacks from the past, and the other was to look at her mom. Entering the house, she noticed that her foot landed on the same ugly brown tiles that covered the kitchen floor. The same cheap wooden table from childhood sat to her left. Nothing had changed here since her childhood.

She could feel her mother's gaze burning into her skin. Without changing her stern expression, she turned to her right to say, "Mother."

Her mom attempted to conceal her zealous demeanor to keep from overwhelming Brooke. Brooke appreciated that, because she really didn't want to embarrass her mom right away. There was no way she could possibly share the same joy as her mom from seeing one another. It was definitely a one-sided sentiment.

"Brooke. I can't believe I get to see you again, and in our home."

Brooke stopped in her tracks to straighten her mom out. "Your home, Mom. Your home." She sighed and stepped further into the kitchen to make room for Jackson.

"Good to see you again, Ms. Hopkins." Just like the man she knew she had, Jackson smiled and shook her hand. For Brooke, having him there felt like a double-edged sword. She loved the support of having someone from her inner circle; otherwise, she'd feel outnumbered. On the other hand, she didn't like him seeing where she came from. If she had her way, Brooke would rather take that knowledge to her grave.

"And a pleasure to see you as well." Lilly shut the door and asked them if they would like something to drink. Everyone initially declined.

Jacqueline changed her mind after Lilly ushered them to the adjacent living room. "Actually. I'll take coffee, Lilly, if you have it."

"I do. Let me get a pot brewing." Lilly left the room.

Brooke and Jackson stood in the room, but Jacqueline sat on the loveseat that Brooke had never seen before. It was a shabby green couch that looked like its better days were far behind it. Parallel to the loveseat sat another loveseat, but brown with floral print. Jackson and Brooke chose to sit there, enabling them to face Jacqueline and the miserable recliner chair that was her mother's throne during Brooke's childhood.

Brooke watched her mom come through the entrance to sit beside Jacqueline. She was sure she would have chosen the forbidden recliner seat. Trying to avert her mother's face, Brooke studied the carpet that allowed a flood of memories to rush into her mind. The nasty green carpet was just as much a part of the house as her mother. She shivered and located the television to her right. The set had rabbit ear antennae.

"Does that thing still work? I used to watch television on that," Brooke blurted out.

Almost ashamed, her mother shook her head with eyes cast downward.

"Then how do you watch TV?" Brooke insisted.

"I have a tiny one in the bedroom. A neighbor gave it to me. Once I pay utilities and buy food, I'm all spent out," she explained quietly. Her mom crossed her hands on her lap.

"What do you like to do for fun?" Jackson asked, trying to cut the tension in the room.

Her mom shrugged. "Ummmm." She stroked her hands up and down her legs, which were covered by a long, light blue skirt. Brooke noticed that her mother had a hard time with eye contact. She was probably nervous, too. "I think . . . ummm, well sometimes I read the newspaper. I like *Jeopardy*. I read a lot of books. I swap books with my neighbor. She's a good friend of mine." A smile spread across her face when she acknowledged that.

Brooke had had enough. She didn't come there to connect with her mom, but to find answers to explain away her bad childhood. More importantly, she wanted to know why her aunt felt the need to bring her there.

"You had something to tell? Spit it out," Brooke demanded.

Jackson turned to her. "Baby."

"No," Brooke replied to him. "I did not come all the way across town to talk about crossword puzzles and game shows. Jacqueline and Lilly said that I was supposed to find something out *and I want to know what that is*."

"We're sorry." Jackson licked his lips and sighed.

Brooke faced her mother. "*No. We* are not *sorry. We* were in the middle of the best time of our lives when you arrived uninvited on my doorstep after all these years and after messing up my childhood."

"*Brooke*," Jacqueline called out with closed eyes and one hand up. "That is enough. Your mother is old, and you have developed into a very successful woman. Can't we just heal?"

She squinted her eyes at Jacqueline. "Were you there? Huh?" Standing up, Brooke said, "I just found out about your connection to me tonight, and you think you have rights about my life? No one understands that all this woman provided me with was shelter and food." Brooke didn't want to cry, but she couldn't stop the heat from within manifesting into tears of anger and pain. "I was neglected. I didn't understand why I had a mom and a home, but no love. That was so confusing to me. I didn't understand why I didn't just get placed into an orphanage instead. Knowing your parent, seeing them day in and day out, but being ignored felt so disgusting as a kid." Brooke placed a hand over her heart.

"Because my other friends were able to come to school and share wonderful stories about their parents. Instead, I had an occasional tale of how I beat you in a game of Uno or something. That's all. Where were my hugs? Where were my moments with you? I raised myself. My God! You never took me to church like I asked. When I did go, it was because a friend's mom took me. What is it like to go to church as a kid with a parent? Even my friend Amber knows that, and she had a rough life in New York. So, there is no damn excuse, lady. None." She sniffed and hastily wiped her finger under her nose.

The room fell silent. Her mom nodded. Brooke sat down. Her chest slightly heaved. She couldn't estimate how many pounds lighter she felt. Releasing years of pain off her chest to the right person felt more than good. It felt great. Necessary.

Jackson rubbed her back and then wrapped his arm around her waist. He kissed the top of her head. "Oh, baby. I'm here for you," he whispered. They were secretly in their own world for a moment. Brooke hadn't even noticed that her mother had gotten up to retrieve the cup of coffee for Jacqueline. Brooke sniffed. Jacqueline passed her niece a few pieces of tissue retrieved from her purse.

"Thanks." Wiping her nose, she looked up to see Jacqueline staring into her cup of coffee and her mother looking at the hands she wrung in her lap. Brooke straightened, and Jackson took his arms back. She cleared her throat. "I wish to God that I didn't feel as hostile toward my own mother as I do." Her voice had become scratchy. "Tonight, I look like the bad guy. I look like a bratty kid, because all you two see is that 'I have made it.'"

"No. We didn't say that," Jacqueline replied.

"Yeah," Brooke replied. "You're right. Because she doesn't say anything. She hasn't said a thing, but yet I'm the one who got into a car to come."

"I did come to see you first, you remember?" Lilly asked.

"Why? And what *do* you have to say for yourself?"

Lilly cleared her throat. She sighed and rubbed her legs nervously again. She struggled with making eye contact with her daughter, but when she was through averting eyes, she boldly faced Brooke.

Her voice was barely a whisper. "I was a horrible mother, and there is nothing that excuses that. You are absolutely right, Brooke." Lilly stopped talking to collect her thoughts. "The only thing that helps me sleep at night is knowing that you made something of yourself. You exceeded in what most people strive to achieve. I cannot take the credit for any of that. You are someone that I deeply admire, Brooke. The right to call you my daughter is the best thing that I own."

Brooke nodded as she wiped a tear. "The right? The *right*?" She pointed at the wall. "You have about as much right to call me your daughter as that wall beside us. And as far as credit goes, you can take some credit for my fight, because I fought so hard not to be like you."

"I think that you're being too harsh," Jacqueline said. "Your mom sounded like a horrible person to have as a mother, but what you don't understand is the raggedy childhood that she had, and the guilt that I had to carry around all my life because of that. She didn't know how to be a mom."

"I was a classic case. I passed down bad parenting skills based on my own experience." Lilly shook her head and looked away. Again, no one said a word.

Brooke bit her lower lip in anger and shook her head. She exhaled. "I feel like we're just sitting here, passing the Nerf ball of avoidance."

"What do you want from her? Blood?" her aunt asked with furrowed eyebrows.

"Please stop defending me," Lilly requested quietly and calmly.

"If I have to tell you what I want, then it must not be coming," Brooke replied with a raised eyebrow and tight mouth. "Take me home, please, Jackson. This is enough and a waste of my precious time." She stood and pointed a finger at her mom and aunt. "You two have managed to ruin my night with my man. These next two weeks in Jackson's and my life should be great and carefree. Instead, you guys are pissing all over that. Get up, Jackson, let's go."

Jackson stood slowly. "No."

Brooke studied him with a confused expression. "No? Honey, I'm not playing. I wanna go home."

Jackson didn't bend. "And I said 'no.' I'm not playing either." Standing his ground, her fiancé shoved his hands into his pockets.

Looking humiliated and becoming increasingly agitated, Brooke relented. "Fine. Then you stay here and enjoy coffee with a biscotti. I'm going."

When she turned, Jackson calmly said, "You leave, and the wedding is postponed indefinitely."

Brooke stopped in her tracks and froze. She spun around and said, "Our wedding has nothing to do with my moment here."

Jackson met her and placed his hands on her narrow shoulders. "Baby. I love you to the moon and back, as they say. No doubt I will be the happiest man alive with you. But this moment in your life is in your face, and you can no longer escape it. It has torn your spirit into two, and until you address it, you're gonna wake up with this in your face every morning. So, my dear," he said as he cupped her chin, "I love you enough to push back our wedding until you're able to get on with your life. Otherwise, everything you do as a wife and mom will always be about your childhood, and from a place of disdain rather than a lesson. You have lemons right now. We need lemonade, not lemon peels." Jackson squeezed her shoulders before stepping to the side.

Brooke looked at him with an empty stare. She couldn't blink. Feeling frozen by too many emotions to the point of losing control, Brooke turned to her mother and asked in a hushed voice, "Why didn't you come to me all these years?"

Lilly stood, but she didn't move closer toward her daughter. Even in her old age she towered a few inches above Brooke, who was already considered to be somewhat over the average height. "Brooke. I didn't interfere in your life when word got out that you were a top-notch wedding planner. I owed you that much. Didn't wanna seem like the mean parent who comes crawling back looking for a payout."

Brooke blinked slowly. "Thank you."

"And I don't quite know why I couldn't connect with you as a mother. I think I didn't feel good enough for you, in fact. I don't think I was born with the maternal gene like Jacqueline. I just didn't know how to love. I can't explain it." Her voice quivered. "I was happy for you when you left me."

Brooke swallowed hard and felt a slight kick in her stomach upon hearing those dreadful words of admission. But why should she care? It was only Lilly Hopkins. However, she felt relieved for some reason when Lilly stretched a hand forward and added, "But not because I didn't want you." Lilly released a nervous giggle as she sniffed. "No. Dear Lord, no. I wanted you, but it woulda been selfish of me to try to hang onto you. You needed better than me. I wasn't it, honey. Although you left me, and even though I was somewhat relieved, the little spirit I was born with was crushed, because the best thing that had ever happened to me left." Tears fell from her eyes, and her voice struggled to continue. "And I didn't know if I wanted you to come back. What could a wretched woman like me do with a precious jewel like you?"

Brooke's heart shattered. Nothing made sense anymore. Was her mother saying that she'd imagined all of her bad memories? Brooke pointed a finger at her mom. "Just stop right there," she demanded, crying through tears of hysteria. "Don't make me feel like what I went through wasn't real. Like I was playing life out only in my head."

"Nooooo. No, no, no, no, no," Lilly assured her. "I'm not." She watched her daughter hold her stomach and then her head. "But come on, Brooke. The best thing I did for you was sit back in the distance."

"Why now?" Brooke shouted. "Why didn't you let me keep going at it alone? I was fine!"

"You call this fine, Brooke? Is this fine to you?" she asked as she stepped forward, finding her voice. "You have to be carrying around such hatred for me and your childhood every single day, because I know I do. I don't even wanna look in the mirror. My own *sight* makes me sick. Would you really prefer not seeing me again? Because I think we both needed this. I needed you to cuss me out to my face. I needed you to hate me, yell at me, do whatever it is you have to do so I can see my punishment. Punish me," she pleaded with arms thrown outward.

Brooke was losing it all: her composure, her perfect demeanor, her ability to feel. Screaming at her mother she let the rage go. "What? What do you wanna hear? That it hurts me to think of my own mother as a bitch? That when I stepped out into the real world, I felt like I had to be a woman on the outside but a man on the inside just to keep my emotions in check?" She balled her fists. "I hate trying to control everything. I don't even know why Jackson wants any part of a woman so predictable. When did I live? When did I *ever* let my hair down? I never partied. All I did was work! I was so afraid that if I felt relaxed for *one* moment that I may like it too much and become a slacker. Who else would have my back? Huh? No one! I feel so freaking fake all the time!" Her hands flew to her head. "I'm so sick of being a poster child for a princess. Now, the whole town is watching me, and no one wants to see a businesswoman with flaws. Congratulations, Lilly. You succeeded in raising a wreck." Shaking, Brooke couldn't stroke her hands through her hair fast enough. "I gotta go, I gotta go, I gotta go," she cried as she paced.

Jackson grabbed her abruptly and shaped her into his arms. "That's enough. We can go," he told her.

Lilly said, "Brooke?"

Brooke slowly peeked out of Jackson's chest and at her mom at the sound of her name. "So, is this . . . all about you? Did you want to do this to make you feel better?"

Brooke pushed Jackson's arms away. "Am I here to be your therapy? This is an atonement for you?"

"No." Remaining calm, Lilly said, "I never once told you this."

"What now?" Brooke asked as she tossed a piece of hair from her face.

"I'm sorry."

Everyone in the room stood still and silent.

"Even if this apology does nothing for you and has little or no worth. But I am. I am sorry." Lilly placed a hand over her heart. "I don't think I have much time left on this earth, so I didn't want you to ever think that how we lived was okay by me. I'm sorry. I'm so, so sorry, baby girl. I do . . ." Her mother bit her lip as a new stream flowed from her eyes.

"I do love you. I love you more today with no recent memories between you and me than I did when we had them. Just know, if I can't get a hug or if we never see each other again, just know that I am sorry I wasn't there for your graduation, or for any fine moments in your life. I would love to be at them now. Brooke, I love you with every fiber in my being, and I am sorry that you weren't handed a better mother."

Brooke didn't know what to say. The words sounded funny to hear, and she felt uncomfortable. But the apology stung her heart, although she couldn't tell in what way or why. With folded arms, she watched her mom limp down the hallway to her room. She didn't know if the limp had always been there or what could've caused it. Nor did she know if she would ever see her mother again.

Amber

Waking up with a yawn on a Thursday morning, Amber was greeted by the sound of a quiet home. She knew Summer was at her new job, and that Oliver had to be at one of his laundromats. She didn't hear Autumn or any other rustling in the condo. Amber wanted to start apartment hunting, but with all the changes that her old quadrant was under, she didn't know if she would even qualify to live in her prior residence.

She knew she couldn't take living in Virginia a second longer. The people were way too stuffy and the state wasn't as raw as DC. This New Yorker liked it raw, even if that meant getting it from a revamped nation's capital. Some type of city life was better than no city life she supposed. Maybe a bite of the New York bug had finally caught up to her, but regardless, there was no going back, at least not now. Amber enjoyed new horizons and she'd yet to conquer Washington.

Stretching, it was time to shower and pound the pavement. Amber hadn't a clue as to where she was going exactly, but she knew progress couldn't be made within these four walls. Speaking of these four walls, she had to remind herself every morning when she opened her eyes that they didn't belong to her. It got her thinking how good Summer had it. She had a rich man, a beautiful baby girl, and a home that looked like a picture from a catalogue. As a guest, Amber enjoyed her stay. The bed had to be expensive, because it was the most comfortable one she'd ever rested on. The room upheld the picture-perfect image with its private balcony that complemented the white decor.

Making her way to the bathroom before slipping out of her oversized t-shirt and shorts, Amber realized that she was out of soap. She forgot to ask Summer for a new bar yesterday after showering with a skimpy leftover amount. Combing through the cabinets, Amber's mouth twisted when she realized that she might have to steal some from her friends' bathroom. She'd never gone in there without Summer's presence, and she felt odd going into someone's intimate space. Deciding that she didn't have a choice, Amber closed the cabinets in the bathroom and reluctantly made her way to their bedroom.

About to knock, Amber realized that it was pointless since she was alone. Turning the knob slowly, and uncomfortable that she was even in that position, she yanked the door open and screamed at the sight before her eyes.

Oliver stood naked beside his bed and unfortunately, his penis stood out first. "Whoa!"

Amber slammed the door shut just as his hand flung over his groin. She chanted on the other side of the door, "I'm sorry, I'm sorry, I'm sorry, I'm sorry. I just needed a bar of soap," she called. "I thought I was alone. I swear!"

"Wait! Hold on, then!" A few seconds later he yelled, "Stand away from the door."

"Okay." Amber did as directed and saw a box of soap fly through the air. Embarrassed, she couldn't help but acknowledge that Summer had, in fact, hit the jackpot.

Emily

Emily hung up the phone with a squeal after her father told her that the family had arrived at Reagan National Airport in anticipation of the wedding. She couldn't wait for their arrival. She hadn't seen her family since the holidays, and there was no excuse. Though they lived in separate states, everyone still resided on the east coast. They had to do better as a family when it came to seeing each other, a concern that she planned on bringing up.

She'd spent the whole day tidying the place to make sure that it'd meet their approval. For the first time, she actually wished that she had the house that she and Eric once shared to accommodate her family. This new place failed to hold more than a few people, unfortunately.

An hour later, she'd just placed a dish of ham on the table when a loud knock on her door alerted her to their arrival. Checking herself out one more time in the mirror on the wall outside of her kitchen, Emily approved of her look. She'd chosen a purple sleeveless pantsuit with a ruffled collar and a high ponytail. Her heart pounded with anticipation at the thought of seeing her family on the other side of that door. Knowing that they must've been hungry, Emily couldn't wait for them to catch a whiff of her various dishes.

Emily pulled the door open with massive excitement. Leading the pack stood her dad, Quito. Standing eye to eye to her, but only because she wore heels, her dad posed with arms wide open. Emily didn't have time to survey her family. Instead, she flew into his arms.

"*Papiiiiiiiiiii*," she cried. Emily could only hear cries of joy as the excitement took over.

"*Mi hija.* It's been so long. Too long." Quito rocked her in his strong arms. Emily's eyes stung from tears and eyeliner. Wiping her eyes, she learned to go with her gut the next time and apply makeup *after* doling out the hugs.

"I know, I know, I know," she agreed. Pulling back to study him, she invited everyone in.

Locking the door and turning around, she clapped her hands together just to look at everyone before handing out hugs. "Look at you guys. Just look."

"What?" Lourdes joked. "Only *papi* is good enough for a hug?" Lourdes, her baby sister, stood with a hand on her very skinny frame. They shared the same hazel eyes as their mother. Lourdes resembled Emily very much, except her nose was narrower, as well as her lips. Everyone always joked that Lourdes was nothing more than just another Emily in a smaller body with smaller features.

"Oh, of course not. Get over here!" Emily waved a hand at her baby sister and squeezed her tiny frame in her arms.

"Ouch, you bastard. You tryna kill me?" She laughed. "I know you missed your hot sister and all but come on. Bring your ass to Jersey sometime, and you can see a sister."

"Ho, please. She misses me most." Valentina marched toward Emily and clawed the back of Lourdes' brunette-covered head with her hand. "*Mueve lo*, stupid."

"Ouch," Lourdes pretended to complain. "*Mamá.* Get your *hija.*"

Valentina pointed a thumb over her shoulder at their sister before she hugged Emily. "See? She's twenty-eight and still telling *Mommy.* Get over here, nerd."

Valentina and Emily didn't always have the best bond. Her older sister had an overbearing personality as the first child and, with five years between them, Valentina had a hard time sharing the spotlight growing up with Emily. It took them living in separate homes to actually grow closer.

Regardless, it felt good holding her curvy sister. Ponytails must have been the trend that day, because all three sisters wore them high on their heads. Valentina's red-dyed hair smacked across Emily's lips as they embraced. She was the Brooke Brazile among them. A high-maintenance perfectionist. The two would appreciate one another.

Valentina sold real estate in New York City, bitten by the same bug as their dad. Emily admired the drive and guts that her sister possessed ever since childhood. This was the same sister who confronted a group of five guys who picked on an eleven-year-old Emily in their neighborhood. Granted, they were sixteen years old just like her sister and she knew them, but Valentina was ready to throw rocks at the dickheads if that's what it took. Since then, Emily saw something more in her sister than just jealousy, a rowdy mouth, and a beautiful face.

After Valentina placed a kiss on Emily's cheek, she smacked her butt and gripped it. "Look. Our sister actually has an ass now."

"*Mujer*! *Tu eres loca.* And this butt has been here for a minute." She lectured them with a finger. "You guys would have known that if we met up more." She missed their crazy ways.

Valentina opened her arms. "Trick. Don't act brand new cuz you drove up last over the holidays."

Emily scoffed. She didn't want to argue. "Move it so I can see, *mamá.* Saving the best for last." Emily spread her arms with a tilted head, watching her plump, grey-haired mother walk toward her. Covered in a floral, light blue dress, Emily couldn't recall a day when she'd seen her mother in pants.

Helena gripped her daughter's hands and gazed into her eyes with a smile. "*Mi hija.* Ohhhhh." She placed a hand over her heart and smiled lovingly at her daughter. "I haven't seen you since the holidays. Way too long." Helena placed her hand under her chin, admiring the sight of her daughter.

"I know, *mamá.* So, so sorry." Emily felt tears lick her cheeks. She wiped them away aggressively. Her heart felt so full having her family standing in her living room. "Gimme a hug, *mamá.* I want to feel you." Pulling her mother close, Emily squeezed her while resting her head on her shoulder. "Thank God that you are here. I've missed you so much."

Helena pulled back. "Emily?" When she placed a hand on Emily's head, she knew what her mother was about to ask, so she beat her to the punch.

Giggling, Emily answered, "Yes, *mamá.* I do go to church. I miss some Sundays, but I do go."

"Good."

"Mmmmm, mm." Quito skirted around the dinner, resplendent in his Hawaiian shirt. "Look at this food. My baby girl knows how to keep a Puerto Rican happy!"

"Oh, *pernil?*" Valentina's head shot up to examine Emily. She pointed at the dish with a sassy finger adorned with a gold ring. "You know how to cook *pernil* now? When did this happen?"

Emily grinned. "Hahaaa. Surprised you, huh? I made myself practice over the years. Sometimes Eric wanted more cultural foods."

"And she even got *mofongo?*" Lourdes asked. "Whoa. This child cooks now?"

Valentina's mouth dropped. "This is not the same sister we know, because growing up she denied her roots. Now this heffa knows who she is. Amazing." She threw a hand of long nails up.

Growing up, Emily was always teased by her family and some of her relatives about her eye color and complexion. Warned her not to let those two attributes make her forget where she came from. Yes, she struggled with finding her place in society, and maybe she didn't boast about or announce her roots like her sisters did, but that didn't mean she didn't appreciate them.

Emily was used to Valentina's mouth, but she didn't want to fight, so she took a passive approach. "People change, Valentina. And I was never ashamed."

With folded arms, Valentina left it at a shoulder shrug and a doubtful expression.

Changing the subject, Quito said, "Hey." He placed both palms on his chest. "Look at this. We have *arroz con salchichas*." He rubbed his hands together with his tongue hanging out. "I'm ready to go. Let's join hands and get ready to pray. Emily has prepared us with about eight dishes. I cannot believe it. Our Puerto Rican has come home."

"I know, right?" Lourdes chimed. She pointed a thumb at Emily. "I thought this girl was white growing up. Glad she knows that she's one of us."

Emily placed a hand on her hip. "Guys, come on. I never once thought I was too good to claim my roots. You know I'm proud. Let's just pray."

Joining hands, they bowed their heads as Quito led them into prayer in a circle next to the table. "And finally, God, thank you for reuniting this family as a whole, all nice and healthy. Amen."

"Amen," they all repeated and took a seat.

Playing catch-up, everyone started asking Emily a flood of questions, and she did the same to them over dinner.

"Why haven't we all called each other more? I mean, we seem to call *mamá* and *papi*." Valentina seemed concerned at their lack of contact.

Happy to see that it mattered to someone other than her mom, Emily agreed. "I think we should really do better after tonight. And by the way, where is your new boyfriend?"

Valentina asked, "You know about that?" She placed the forkful of pork and rice into her mouth.

"I do." Emily nodded once before sipping on her glass of wine. "What's his name?"

"Carmine."

"What's he look like?"

Valentina's face immediately lit up at the question. "Tall. Tanned. Italian. He's a mortgage broker. You'll meet him at your wedding. He's flying down."

"Mmmmmm. Sounds like a winner," Emily replied. "How about you, Lourdes? What's new with my little booger?"

"This little booger got a new man, too." Chewing, she smiled at Emily. Without swallowing, she replied, "*Papi* met him. His name is Marc. But *Papi* hatin' because he thinks that he's not serious about me." She pointed her chin at our dad. "Ain't that right, *pa*?" Looking back up at Emily, she added, "But he's wrong."

"You have to live and learn." Emily's face betrayed a blink of pain. For a moment, her family didn't say anything. Taking slower chews and moving hesitantly, they took a moment to process Emily's shift in demeanor.

"So where's Eric?" Helena asked.

Emily knew that her mother brought him up out of sheer curiosity and for the sake of being polite. Her parents were never big fans of his. They always felt a sketchy vibe from him.

"He's out of town. Today, he had to go to Baltimore and then tomorrow Bethesda for a client. So, instead of ping-ponging, Eric decided to stay in Maryland. He'll be back tomorrow." Emily feared the question and answer session that was brewing like a storm. She could feel the winds changing.

Helena cocked a brow at Emily. "Sure he's just not avoiding us?"

Emily dropped her head to one side and squinted. "No, *mamá.*"

Quito pushed his plate away, and Emily knew he was ready to be serious. "So. Emily."

Emily responded with a cocked brow. She sipped on her wine as she waited for the grilling to begin.

"Princess, you know I love you, but as your dad, I have a few concerns."

"Okay."

"Eric was never my favorite guy."

With the rim of the glass at her lips, Valentina said to Emily, "Yeah, I'm still selling Carmine on him." She tilted a raised glass in Emily's direction. "So good luck." Valentina sipped.

Quito held a hand up at his oldest daughter. "Please, Valentina." He shifted his body to face Emily. "I'm not convinced that this man won't end up hurting my girl again. I don't know what's going on with these couples these days, but marriage is forever. There is no divorce."

Emily slowly nodded and exhaled quietly, praying that she could make it through this moment.

"Not even if you want to eventually strangle one another?" Lourdes asked with a snicker.

"I'm still with your father, aren't I?" Helena asked.

"What I'm saying, is that marriage is not about quitting. Nor should you just dive in head first because of the way you feel. Don't dive if you can't take the swim." Quito lifted his glass and chugged down his wine.

"Okay, *papi.* All is well, and I hear your point," Valentina challenged. "But sometimes you make a mistake and have to get out. Not all things last forever. We will all be separated by death anyway."

"Baby." Quito slammed his glass on the table; Emily cringed. He didn't even use a coaster, she realized miserably. "Your generation is spoiled and doesn't like to slow down. Everything has to be immediate, easy, and rewarding upfront. Sometimes, the best things are those we have to search for."

"*Papi*, I hear your point." Emily didn't want a lecture about everything that was wrong with "this generation." "I'm a grown woman." She placed a hand on her chest with a smile. "And if Eric and I are not meant to be, then I'll deal with it. Now, in all honesty, I appreciate your concern, but Eric and I are just fine." She raised her glass to her family. "Better than ever."

Brooke

"Baby, thank you for having my back with this packing. I was tempted to hire movers to do this. Glad I didn't," Jackson told Brooke.

"Anytime . . . as long as you remain shirtless." Dressed in a spaghetti-strap negligee that stopped mid-thigh, Brooke skirted around a box to place her hands on her handsome fiancé's bare chest. She decided to come help Jackson pack after work and to spend the night.

Jackson grabbed her wrists and kissed them on the inside. "Emily and Eric are gonna beat us down the aisle. Why'd they move the wedding up?"

"Eric." She shrugged. "He needs to go out of town but didn't wanna wait until his return to marry her. Isn't that romantic, sweetie?"

Jackson pulled her close and gripped her bottom. "Mmmmmm, call it what you want, but I ain't convinced."

Confused, Brooke squinted her eyes and tilted her head. "How is not wanting to wait not romantic?"

"Because it sounds like this wedding is all about his needs and barely hers." He tapped her nose with a finger and went to pull some things off a shelf to pack.

"Hmm. I mean," Brooke placed a hand on a hip and shifted her weight to one side, "I never thought of it that way."

"Emily may not wanna wait either, but you said they won't even have time for a honeymoon? Second wedding or not, that's wrong."

"What would you do then?"

Wrapping paper around a trophy, he paused to tell her, "For real, Brooke? I'd wanna marry you in five minutes, but if I can't do things right and run away with you immediately, then we'd have to wait. Who wants to go back to work after a ceremony? Too busy for love? Come on. No one gets married every day. It's a special time."

Brooke stretched her leg by bending it at the knee and pressing the heel of her foot against her bottom. "I've seen a lot of couples do it. Some people just didn't want to keep pushing the date out. Sometimes, two schedules are hard to coordinate, especially with a boss breathing down your neck."

Jackson chuckled. "What do you know about having a boss? What? Back in your Dairy Queen days?"

Brooke smiled. She placed her foot back on the ground. Shrugging she said, "I do. But it wasn't at Dairy Queen. Listen. I once worked for a wedding planner who would never let me or my co-workers off. That's why she loved me. I never requested off. Not on any job."

"Geek."

"Don't hate." She winked. "Speaking of my past, how do you feel about me after that embarrassing mess at my— Lilly's house?"

Surveying the boxes covering his floor, Jackson answered, "I don't feel anything that I shouldn't. Baby, pass me the tape."

Brooke threw it at him. "I don't get it. Wasn't it a mess?"

"I'm sure that was the day you realized you bleed like everyone else."

Brooke frowned. "Smarty pants. I mean, do you think we are psycho? You know, Lilly, Jacqueline . . . me?" The thought that Jackson secretly felt that she may not have been who he may've initially thought bothered her.

"Your family? Say it," Jackson suggested as he searched for the line on the tape roll.

Brooke chewed on her lip to avoid going there. "Fine. Do you think 'my family' is cray?"

"No. I see humans." He ripped the tape with his teeth.

"Hmm." Brooke tapped a box with her finger. "I'm not the Sleeping Beauty you thought I was, huh?" She played with her nails, feeling slightly embarrassed.

"Brooke, I'll take Cinderella and her dysfunctional background any day over a princess with no problems. Look, you need to get outta your head. So I know you're human." He shrugged. "Congratulations, your shit stinks, too. Tell ya the truth, I'm glad to find out you got flaws. I was a little scared of perfect Brooke. That's a crazy way to come off."

"Well how long were you going to go along with that?" Brooke folded her arms across her chest and grinned. "I mean, you proposed to that 'perfect Brooke.'"

Jackson gave her his full attention. "Well, I couldn't pick at what I didn't know was there. I figured I'd let you crack on your own like the nut you are." He grinned and winked before finishing his packing.

"Oh, you got jokes? I'm sane. Broken, but sane."

"Tell you what." Straightening, he pointed the roll of tape at her. "I'm glad to know that you're human, but don't start ripping farts under the blanket and shit."

"Ewwwwww! *Jackson*? Staaaaaahp." Brooke pointed a finger at him. "You just nasty."

Summer

I took Amber with me for a walk to Whole Foods. As usual, I had Autumn strapped against my chest as we hunted down the pizza.

"I just want all cheese, but Oliver loves the mushroom pizza. Should I get slices or two whole pizzas? They're just so huge though." I needed Amber to help me decide. But I got the vibe that she didn't appear to be in a position to help me out about anything. All night she'd been acting rather strange and sort of jumpy. She shrugged at me.

"I don't know."

"Well, what about you? You still haven't told me the toppings you want?"

"Uhhhh." She placed a finger on her lip as she glanced over the selection.

"Can I help you?" asked the man behind the display.

I craned my neck. "Yes. I'll have two slices of cheese, three mushrooms, and—" turning to Amber I asked, "What about you?"

"Oh. The pepperoni looks good. Ooh, and the slices *are* huge. Get me two, please."

"And three pepperonis," I told him.

The man nodded. "'Kay. Would you like them heated?"

Turning to Amber, I asked, "What do you think?"

"Sure."

"Yes, please." The friendly man nodded and told us to come back in five to seven minutes. "Ooooooh, desserts," I cried. "I can't do it. Whole Foods makes me go crazy. Errrrrrr."

"Well, let's have a look," Amber suggested.

"Some friend you are." Even though I grinned, Amber didn't. "Are you okay?"

Amber sighed and licked her lips. "Guess I have to break the weird news to you since your man obviously didn't."

My heart jumped a beat in fear. My hand covered my mouth. "Damn. What now?" I placed my other hand on Autumn's bottom when I sensed her fussiness.

Amber sighed. She looked reluctant to look me in the eyes. Knowing Amber, I could only imagine what she had to get off her chest. "Okay. Well, ummmm, I thought you guys were both gone when I approached your room."

"Yeah? Well you know, sometimes he sleeps in on days when he helps out with Autumn during the middle of the night."

"Okay, well, I, uhhhh . . ." Amber rubbed her head.

"Spit it out." My wide eyes revealed fear.

"I opened the door and saw him naked."

"Girl, what?" I didn't know how I felt. My best friend saw my man's goods!

She placed a hand in the air. "Hey, look. I shut the door immediately. I didn't mean to see his wrench and bolts."

In a panic, I wanted to make sure that I heard my best friend correctly. "You're saying you saw his junk?"

"Pretty much," Amber reluctantly confirmed.

I placed my hand on top of my head in disbelief. I felt embarrassed on so many levels. "So, you *Emilized* me?"

Her jaw dropped open. "Wha—I did not *Emilize* you. I screwed Eric without knowing it was him." Amber's expression changed to casual. "Well, with Oliver, it was more like—" She tipped her head from left to right as she considered her words. "As soon as we realized what was happening, and that was immediately, he tried to hide his meat and potatoes, and I closed the door promptly."

I thrust my hand into the air and closed my eyes in horror. "Okay, you gotta stop giving his junk these gross references."

"Well, we both felt yucky about it. It was humiliating for both of us," she insisted.

Rolling my eyes, I told her, "Whatever." Then I realized something. "Whatcha need from our room anyway?" I picked up the slice of cake with fresh fruit on top that called my name.

"There was no more soap in my bathroom. I forgot to ask you for a new bar last night."

"Oh, well Oliver does bars, I use liquids. Besides, you should have a back-up case of soap in the armoire in your room. My bad. I forgot to tell you that."

"Oh, gee. After I done saw your man's bush and bolts, now you tell me."

It felt good to stab her in her side with my finger.

"Ow!" Amber cried.

"Let's go get the pizza, Peeping Tom."

6: down n dirty

Amber

Walking outside to mentally whine alone, feeling sorry for herself was a foreign feeling for Amber. A confident woman like herself wore that emotion as well as Brooke wore stonewashed jeans. It just didn't go. Cars zipped past her on the street as she ambled the sidewalk in Summer's busy Ballston neighborhood. Amber couldn't stay in her friends' spare room forever, but she also didn't know how she was going to get back on her feet.

Amber let Daniel talk her out of keeping her apartment. So desperate to be out of her less-than-desirable neighborhood, Amber convinced herself that Daniel was sweet for paying the fee for early termination of the lease. In reality, he wanted her to feel as stuck as possible by stripping away all her options. She knew that she should've listened to her gut, even if it was very tiny. She still had to regain some of her ex-piano clients since she didn't teach as much when she lived with Daniel. Amber shook her head in dismay at her past decisions. She had to admit that she really did a number to herself.

Her ringing phone made her stop in her tracks. Looking at her Note, she decided to answer the unfamiliar number. Reluctant, she answered, with a, "Hel-lo?"

"Amber Hamilton, please."

Amber didn't know if she should confirm her identity. Thanks to her new credit, she felt emboldened enough to confirm her identity with an, "Ummm, yes. May I ask who's calling?"

The man on the other line spoke with urgency. "Yes, Chad Brently here with the Brently School or Arts."

Not knowing what he wanted from her, Amber asked, "Okay. How can I help?"

"Yes, my wife and I own an independent school in northeast. Hope you don't mind me calling you, but a parent mentioned that you teach her oldest daughter, Sydney, the piano. Her youngest child attends our school. This is our first year of operation, and we need to make sure that our costly tuition is justified." Amber listened in confusion as the man prattled on, still not understanding the reason for his call.

"Un-huh," she said.

"Well, our applicant, the lady we were about to hire, decided that she couldn't take the position as a piano teacher, because the pay was too low. We're new and an increase would happen with enrollment. But, as for now, we open tomorrow, and we don't have a piano teacher."

Amber placed a hand over her heart. "You're asking me?"

"Yeeeeeah. My wife and I are scrambling here. We can't play the piano. You're our last hope. We have some funding but, for now, the salary is at $45,000."

"Forty-five thousand?" Amber couldn't hide the surprise in her voice.

"I know, too low, huh? I heard you have talent. I know someone with your talent, but—"

Playing it cool, she said, "Umm, no. That's fine. That works."

Mr. Brently sounded extremely relieved for the first time during the whole conversation. "I know it's a little late, but, Amber, can you come by today? We're in walking distance to the Brookland-Catholic University station."

"Oh, I'm familiar with that area."

"Great, I'll text you the address. Is this your cell?"

"Yes."

"Perfect. Okay, Amber. See you within an hour, right?"

"Oh, absolutely. Ima' head on over there right now."

"Can't wait."

"Wow. Thank you, Mr. Brently."

"No, no. Chad, please, and my wife is Liz. See you soon."

She couldn't believe that she was going to be an employee at an actual company doing what she loved. Opportunities to play at Brooke's weddings were here and there, the Kennedy Center didn't offer year-round work, and she had to rebuild her clientele, but unfortunately that proved harder than she anticipated. Amber told him goodbye and resisted the feeling of dropping to her knees to gleefully shout with outstretched arms, but she couldn't. She would be late for her new job.

Summer

I smacked Oliver on his denim-clad butt with my wet towel. He grabbed the area. "Ouch." He jumped, pretending to be hurt. "What was that for?"

"You didn't tell me my friend saw your balls out." Fresh out of the shower, I sat on the bed in my oversized t-shirt and removed my tiny hoop earrings.

Oliver removed his jeans, stripping down to white boxer briefs. "I was. It never seemed to be the perfect time. What? Over pizza? Hey, baby. Did you know Amber saw my dick today? Our schedules have been kind of funky now with your new job and stuff." He straightened the tangled gold chain around his neck and sat down beside me. "It was a very swift incident. We were both shocked."

I folded my arms and shot him a sideways glance. Pretending to express disbelief, I puckered my lips upward. "Ohhhh, okay. I guess I can believe you."

There was a knock at our bedroom door. I looked at Oliver with a grin, knowing it was Amber. "Come in."

"Wait, girl," Oliver warned quietly. Crossing his arms over his genitals, he said, "See. Look at y'all. Catching men off guard and shit."

"Oops. Hurry then." I helped yank the blanket over his legs.

Amber turned the doorknob slowly and hid her eyes behind a horizontally placed hand. She opened two fingers and peered through them with one eye. "Safe? Safe?" she teased.

"Ohhh, stop," I told her, snickering.

"Yeah, too late for that," Oliver added.

Amber dropped the act and smiled. "I heard some noises but didn't wanna risk missin' you guys in the mornin'. Just wanted to tell you guys somethin'."

"What's up, Amber?" Oliver asked.

Standing in a new black onesie, Amber gestured with wild hands and fists. "Got some good news."

I couldn't help myself. "I like your new onesie. Where'd you get that?"

"Oh. You like this, girl?"

"Ladies," Oliver interrupted. "Tomorrow I will not be sleeping in. Must get sleep."

"Oh, right, right. Sorry." Amber shifted her weight from one side to the other constantly. She seemed fairly excited. "Got a phone call to work at a new performing arts school in DC. You are looking at the new full-time piano teacher!"

"Yeah?" I asked.

"Yeah, girl."

I jumped up to embrace her. While it was a blast having her, now she could move out. Living with the man of my dreams was proving to be tough already, so sharing space with an additional person, even a best friend, really challenged me. However, I genuinely felt happy for her. Amber had endured a difficult year and she could use some relief. "This is hot, Amber. Good for you." Backing up, I pulled all my damp hair over one shoulder. "What happens next?"

"Amber, I knew you would bounce back fast. Congratulations," Oliver told her.

"Thank you." Amber bowed at the waist. She answered me with, "I need to move out. Girl, you know I love my own space. I miss my piano, my furniture, which isn't all that strikin', but you know, I miss lookin' at my own stuff. Even if that shit be low-grade." Amber stuck her tongue out as she bounced her shoulders. "I'm back in the game, baby. I'ma get my own place, get more furniture, redecorate, get a car . . ." she said, ticking off each item per finger with an agenda. "Girl I'm gonna focus on me and my work. Oh. I forgot to tell you and Oliver, and the girls, but I'm gonna enroll in real estate classes. I met a guy today at the job— one of the teachers—he does real estate on the side. I can do that. School classes ain't workin' for me anyway."

"Big dreams to fill, huh?" I asked. Amber's need for success was a relief, considering how far she'd come from recently not being able to see past the shoulders of the man receiving head from her.

"Right quick, then I'm gonna go." Amber tapped my shoulder with a fist. "How was work?"

I laughed. "Ummm, intense. It's serious work, but I'm doing my thing. I love it. Thanks for asking."

"Okay, that's what's up." She pointed at Oliver. "Well, good night to you, sir."

He waved. "Good night, Amber."

Pointing at me, she said, "And good night to you."

"Hugs." I gave her one last hug and watched her close the door behind her. I turned to Oliver with a look of accomplishment on my face. "Wellllllll?" I crawled onto the bed, then moved toward him on my knees and slipped onto his lap, playing with the chain around his neck. "We get some privacy."

He caressed the side of my thighs with both hands.

"Now we just gotta convince Autumn to move out," he teased.

Laughing and then stinging his shoulder with a slap, I cried out, "Nooo. Don't say *that*."

"What? You don't think Mary Poppins won't rent a room out to her?"

"Do you want me to stab you tonight?"

Grabbing my wrists, he pretended to get serious. "Can I stab you? I got a weapon under this blanket."

I patted my chin with a finger to consider his question. "Try not to hurt me too much. Deal?"

"You don't even have any draws on. You hugged your friend without any draws on?"

I shrugged with a giggle. "I didn't know she would come in."

Oliver flipped us over, bringing his body over mine. I bit down on his dangling chain while wrapping my thighs around his body. He placed my hands above my head and secured them with one of his, while using the other one to fondle one of my breasts. Staring at one another eye to eye, I never felt more turned on. We were stronger than ever, and no other time had it been so clear that this man stood solely and completely on my side. I released his chain from the grips of my lips and locked them over his. My arms wrapped behind his neck, and in a quick turn, he ended up back on the bottom. Even in our lives, he always made me feel on top.

I peeled my shirt off and threw it to the side. My full, perky breasts hovered over Oliver with hardened nipples ready to be sucked.

Oliver lifted his neck just enough to take my nipple into his mouth. He started to suck with the same thirst as our newborn.

"Don't take our baby's food," I joked.

Oliver released his mouth, running his tongue one last time underneath the tip of my breast. He tapped my thigh with his finger and said, "Baby, baby. I want to show you something."

Curious, my eyes popped. "Yeah?"

"Hold up." Oliver stretched an arm upward and reached for the remote controller from the nightstand to turn on the television.

"What? The news?" I sucked my teeth, slightly irritated. What was he doing messing up the mood for us? Turning at the waist to look behind me, I remained straddled over his groin.

"Just hold on."

I watched my man press a button that automatically took us to the OnDemand features.

"Can we watch your mafia movies later? Really, Oliver."

"Baby, please. You'll see."

Impatiently waiting with a tilted head, I watched his selection light up. It was an 'After Dark' feature, which told me everything.

My head whipped back around to see a smirking Oliver. "Really, man?"

He grinned. "Hey, don't judge."

Rolling my eyes, I spun back around to watch the plotless flick. A man said 'goodbye' to his woman, and before too long, another woman showed up at the door with a smile and big, perky breasts.

Turning back to Oliver with a frown, I asked, "Oh, so is this what you do when I leave out in the mornings?"

"Ohhh, yeah, you got me, babe."

I shot him a mean look before turning back to face the television. The man took the woman to the bedroom and spooned her from behind with his hand devouring her breasts.

My neck got tired, so I turned to face him.

"So where do you hide this lady when I go?"

Oliver started with a slight gyration. "She lives next door. Her name is Patty."

My grin was evitable. "Patty? Oh, okay."

"Yeah." He tried to look convincing.

"And what makes her so special? What do you guys do when I'm gone?"

"The question is, what don't we do?"

I copied his motion with my lower half with both palms resting flat against his chest. "Like what?"

"Patty don't wear anything underneath her skirt and blouse. I can see her nipples when she arrives. I like to bite her nipples through her shirt."

"That ho." My vagina started to hurt, but in that good way that cried for attention that would lead to a release. "What does she look like?"

"Oh, Patty is beautiful. She's got short, toned legs that she likes to wrap around me. Long, wavy hair that falls wildly. Her skin, the color of gold. She got green eyes that tell any man that she wants to be pounded hard. Her breasts are just right and bouncy. Her lips . . . kissable."

"Is she better in bed than me?" I stared down at him with a raised brow and turned up nose.

"Well, Summer." He sighed. "You have to prove yourself. Patty really knows how to come through. She keeps me satisfied. You see what they're doing now?"

I turned around, wasting no time to see what he and Patty were up to behind my back. When he saw that I noticed that the two rotten characters were in the 69 position, I turned my gaze back to him when he said, "That's the kind of stuff Patty and I are up to when you're away."

"So. You sit on this broad's face?"

"What can I say?" He shrugged with one shoulder. "She smells good."

Chuckling, I said, "You bastard." I reached for the remote and turned the television off.

"Heyyyy. What are you doing?"

"Now you need porn to get off?"

Oliver's expression read, 'oh, come on.' "You know I like to mess with you. Like to have a little different fun sometimes."

"Really?"

"You got me hard and all. I mean, talking about Patty and watching you get horny turned me on."

Laughing, I replied, "Oh, whatever, Oliver, I did not get horny."

He pinched my chin. "Yes, you did, but only because you knew I was describing you. If Patty were a real person, you'd be throwing hands, huh? Don't lie."

"Just be quiet. I'll slap a Patty."

Oliver bounced his hips up and down. "Come on, Summer, give me some of that good pussy. You can have sex now."

Biting down on my lip, I smiled and said, "You know what? This night *will* be special. I mean, I got the greenlight from my doctor, so let's do this."

He lowered his voice with a naughty grin. "Think if we get loud enough Amber will move out faster?"

"Nahhh. It'd probably turn her on."

Oliver snickered. "True."

Our silly moment made me forget about the fact that I hadn't had sex in a while and that tonight would be the best night for it, even though Amber's room was adjacent to ours. I didn't care. She had her strumpet ways prior to turning over a new leaf, and her inner ho hadn't died that much. She'd be aight.

"Summer, let's do this right. I know you gotta go to work tomorrow, but this moment's gotta be special. You choose the music." He eased me to the side, so he could stand. "I'm gonna go look for this special massage oil that I can rub on you." He tilted his chin at me. "You get the music started."

"Okay, cool. Yeah, let's do this." I hopped out of bed.

It was so indescribable to be able to have this special moment with Oliver, especially since we hadn't physically connected in weeks. We could certainly use a stress reliever after putting up with Autumn's random night cries, Amber's sudden but temporary move-in, and just the mental adjustment that Ruben would no longer need to be factored into our lives anymore. We needed sex!

I wanted to find my favorite CD. I couldn't wait to address the longing for Oliver's touch. My vagina missed his tongue . . . his touch . . . his penis. His whole package and all that he had to offer was on the top of my list. It had to happen. It was my turn to be the one moaning like the woman in the dirty film. Where was my turn to be Patty? If Autumn even thought about crying, I'd have to put Amber on "mommy duty" to cover my shift. My porn star moment had arrived.

Ransacking the nightstands, I came up empty-handed. Nothing but some pens, stationary, batteries, and other miscellaneous items covered the drawers of each stand.

Standing in the middle of the bedroom floor tapping my finger against my chin, I mentally accessed the likelihood of its whereabouts.

"Where could that romantic CD be?"

Certain that it had to be in the armoire since there was no doubt that it'd last played in our room, I decided to start with the bottom drawers first. I kneeled down and pulled out the left drawer first, only to see the bottom of the drawer and loose contents floating around. Clearly, it wasn't there. Closing that drawer and opening the next one, I lazily picked through Oliver's folded shirts and knew my CD wouldn't be between the clothes, so I used one hand to neatly line the folded shirts up again, in order to feel good about closing the drawer. About to close the drawer, something shiny stuck in between two shirts stole my attention.

Pulling out the photos from between the shirts, I tilted my head and peered at the items between my fingers. My mouth dropped at the content. I studied the two photos, both of the same woman. My hand shook, my heart stopped. I *knew* this woman! The question was: What was she doing in Oliver's drawer, hidden, no less, and why her? What connection did he have to her?

With my mouth feeling as dry as cotton, my head boiled. I was beyond angry. Any moment, my brain would be splattered all over the walls of this room, because it was about to explode.

"What the . . .?"

In my hands, stood a woman in the photo with a proud expression using one hand to dip her sunglasses down the bridge of her nose, with the other hand just flipped off to the side. Standing in underwear and nothing else, she didn't have a care in the world. I swiped the other photo from underneath the one that had areolas staring back at me. This other photo had her sitting on the bed, spread eagle, with nothing covering her body.

"What in the entire hell is going on?" I could barely catch the required breath to sustain an acceptable breathing pattern for survival. The default way of thinking would be that Oliver had some serious explaining to do. Unfortunately, I didn't think that there was anything that could explain why he had pictures of Fran DuBois, in his dresser.

Emily

"Honey, I'm home!"

Emily's face immediately broke out in a happy expression at the sound of Eric's voice saying those words a night earlier than expected.

Emily ran from the room wearing nothing but a laced yellow bra and underwear set. Eric dropped his luggage and briefcase at the sight of his woman. She jumped into his arms and kissed his lips with one long smooch. Drawing back but not getting down, she stared into his piercing eyes and asked, "Did you miss me, *papi*?"

Eric's large hands groped her butt as he replied, "Did I ever. What've you been up to, Ems?"

"My family came by again, and we had dinner. You missed them only by a few hours. How were you able to come back so early?" Emily kissed Eric's lips again.

"The second meeting was cancelled."

"Oh. Umkay. Well, did you have dinner?"

"I did. And right now, I'm ready for dessert."

"Oh. Well I have some leftover—"

"No, no." His eyes widened. "I want you."

Emily grinned and giggled. "Okay. Then Emily on a platter, you shall have."

Eric kissed her long and hard as he struggled to navigate them successfully into the bedroom. "Ouch!" They cried several times as they bumped into the walls and the edges of some pieces of furniture before making it into the bedroom.

When Eric plopped her onto the bed, Emily positioned herself on her side and raised a bent knee to show off her thigh. Caressing it seductively, her hair fell over one side of her face. She licked her lips at him, willing him to hurry up with his attempt to undress.

"I'm gonna do things to you right now, Emily," he said through deep breaths, panting with sexual energy. "Things that you will never forget."

Whispering seductively, Emily replied, "Keep some of your tricks for when we are husband and wife again."

"Oh, honey," Eric replied as he yanked off his tie and shirt, "I never run out of tricks. Now get on all fours and take it. It's gonna be a long ride and a long night."

Emily did as she was told and rolled over, propped up by her forearms and knees. With a heart racing with the persistence of a horse at a race track, Emily felt the ache between her legs while anticipating Eric's entry. She felt the dip behind her feet as blind reassurance that he'd gotten into position and was ready to slide in.

Eric impatiently glided her underwear from her legs with Emily propping her knees up to enable the fabric to come off. Two fingers slid between her lips with ease, and naturally lubricated, Emily was ready to take him.

"Oooh, baby, you're so wet. Mmm." Eric's fingers searched her soft walls with his genitals packed against her round butt.

Emily backed her rear into him. "Come on, baby, get in there." She couldn't believe that she would have so many countless nights in the future with Eric. No one knew her body the way he did. Still, she wanted him to explore her outside of DC. They deserved to get away. They had enough money to do this anytime and anywhere around the world.

Eric pulled out his explorative fingers and moved them over her outer walls in circular motions. He gripped the other hand over one of her dangling breasts and squeezed Emily's lace-clad nipple. Emily cried sounds of pleasure as she sacrificed her stability to squeeze the other nipple with her hand. She felt his hard dick poking between her legs and couldn't take another moment of not feeling his length. Before she could say anything, he'd already read her mind and removed both hands to rest them on either side of her hips. See, he already knew what she needed.

Surprising her, he smacked her cheek and said, "Flip over."

Without question, though she was ready to take him, Emily did as requested, allowing him to part her bent legs at the knees. Eric towered over her, then lowered himself onto the floor and stood on his knees. He gripped the sides of her thighs and pulled her close. Emily anchored her feet behind his head with crossed ankles.

"And what shall we call this dessert?" he asked with raised brows and a smirk.

Emily thought with a finger on her chin. Rolling her eyes upward, she replied, "Hmm, how about crème de la Em?"

Chuckling, Eric replied, "I like that."

She giggled. "Do you?" She was already having fun with him.

"I really do." Eric cleared his throat. "And what can we expect this to taste like, Em?"

"Well," she answered in a low and sexy tone, "we can expect it to be soft to the touch, salty on the tongue, but sweet going down."

With an impressed expression, Eric nodded. "Mkay, mkay. Well, allow me to get a sample before deciding if I should dive in or not."

"Oh, honey, trust me. This dessert comes highly recommended and, in fact, no one has ever taken just one bite and walked away."

Eric angled his face at her with squinted eyes. "So, other people have eaten this dish before, huh?"

"Well, we've had a few critics before, but, uhhh, they're nowhere to be found. Think they had that taste and have died and gone to heaven."

Eric smiled from the heart and winked at her, coming out of role play. "Ohh, Emily, you are definitely a bad girl at heart."

"You like that?" Emily's hip wiggled seductively, just a tad.

"Let me show you how much." With a face suddenly wiped down with a new expression—no smiles, deep eye contact—Eric lowered his face to taste the crème de la Em.

The minute his warm tongue touched her vagina, Emily cried out, "Mm—ohhh." Her toes curled as she sucked air in between her teeth. It felt so good, that she immediately arched her back with her feet.

Emily secretly craved a reunion like this, that is, after she'd seen past the red that flashed every night in her head after learning about his one-night stand with Amber. She couldn't bring herself to admit that she'd masturbated to the picture that she'd sent out to his job before handing it over to Zach the next morning. Her love for Eric made everything that he did to her body a nine on the Richter scale. The quakes that he could send through her body would send her starry eyed to work the next morning. Every time.

Eric eased away from her tasty abyss and smacking his lips as he pretended to process the flavor, he told her, "Yeah, very moist, very moist." Parting her entry again with one hand, he took two fingers and patted it against the opening.

Resting a finger in her mouth, Emily waited for his feedback with a cocked brow.

Placing those fingers into his mouth, he said, "Mm. Yeah. Slightly salty, good flavor. But let's see how it tastes going down."

Emily laughed. "Time to go in for the kill."

Eric dived back down, leaving her with only a view of the top of his hair. Closing her eyes and getting lost with the sensation of his tongue, Emily moaned and wiggled under his hands. His tongue hit her clitoris in circles and strokes while his fingers worked the inside of her pussy. She gripped the sheets for mercy, popping her butt up from the bed and shoving more of her into his face. Was it even possible?

"Eric."

Eric detached his mouth long enough to say, "I want you. I want you, babe."

Caressing her neck with her hand, she pleaded with closed eyes, "Please, let me feel your dick. I want it, baby, *por favor, papi. Mátame. Joder!"*

Eric stood and targeted her opening with his cock. He leaned forward to grab her by the wrists to sit her up, squeezing the undersides of them with his thumbs. "Do you want me to hurt you?"

Emily replied with a slow blink with long lashes that revealed a trusting and surrendering stare from hazel eyes. "Yes."

Eric leaned over until the tip of his nose hit hers. He whispered, "What do you want me to do to you, Emily?"

Emily whispered back, "I want you to push into me with all you've got. I wanna scream, I want the pain."

He tasted her lips with his, foregoing usage of the tongue. Staring into her eyes, he didn't say a word, because his dick did all the talking. Eric entered her, cocking his head back, closing his eyes, straightening his back. Emily rotated her neck and moaned.

"Mmmmmmm, Eric. Mmmmmm, hurt me. Please. I need it. I need this so much." Before she could process the moment, Eric had pulled back just enough to shove his dick hard into her vagina. "Ow!"

Eric repeated his motion, still gripping her by the wrists, refusing to let her go, giving her one thrust after another. He relinquished his grip on her wrists in exchange for her ass. He picked her up and moved her to the dresser covered by perfume, makeup, and hair accessories. Eric plopped Emily's butt over hairpins. A hip knocked into a perfume bottle. He kicked it with his hand, sending it to the wooden floor and creating a shattering sound as a thick aroma of sweetness wafted through the air.

A sense of neediness pulled over Eric like a hoodie on a rainy day. He took one hand and fished it between her thighs and used the other one to remove her hand placed behind his neck. Eric pinned that hand against the top of the mirror behind Emily. He pecked kisses around her neck and chest, leaving his busy hand to explore everything her womanhood had to offer.

"Eric."

Eric could barely sacrifice his random kisses over her mouth, chin, neck, and shoulders, long enough to reply with an, "Mm?"

"They say you'll hurt me."

"Oh, yeah?" He removed his hand from her vagina.

Eric straightened and looked her square in the eyes. He lined himself up again and charged into her like a knight into battle. He placed a hand on the dresser to steady himself, offering her a drunken stare. High on pussy, inebriated by sexual contact.

"I'm gonna hurt you?" He gripped her hand tightly above her head.

"Are you? Are you gonna hurt me?" Emily's tone was slightly tickled with mockery.

"Who says this?"

"People I know." She used her free hand to place it over his mouth, playing with his lips. "Mmmm."

Eric's hand flew from the dresser and to her head, pulling the strands on the side. Yanking them upward, he asked, "You like it when I hurt you, don't you? Keeps you on your toes. And besides, Emily, you've shown me that you like to play dirty."

"I dooooo," she said through pursed lips. "But I also learned from you."

Eric moved his hand to the crown of her hair and yanked her head until her chin flew up. He thrust in and out of her, neither one of them breaking eye contact. Emily felt the pain from his grip, but the two extreme sensations mixed with the burning in her heart was the best elixir for an orgasm that any man could muster. She realized that Eric got off on playing head games with her, but she trusted him. It was the game that they liked to play. There was no rules book, no title, no real established date as to when this game of theirs was created. And he was right; he kept her on her toes, but probably in the sickest way. In a way that Quito, Helena, or her friends could never see or understand.

Eric fed into her so aggressively, that the motion from her body shook the items on the dresser. She heard the remaining perfume bottles clack for mercy, saw the brush dance across the wood, saw Eric's jaw tightened as he brought pain and destruction to and around Emily.

Eric's mouth covered hers. Their hands moved freely and independently now, raiding each other's body.

He gripped her by the sides of her face. "You're mine, and I'll do whatever the hell I want to with you. Do you understand?" he asked.

"I do."

"Don't question it again."

"I won't."

Letting go with an upright spine, Eric placed both hands on top of her thighs. He viciously ran his shaft back and forth inside of Emily, watching her cry in pain.

"So gooooood, Eric. *Yeah.*"

"Who does this pussy belong to? Who does it belong to, Emily?"

"Yooooou. You, *papiiiiii.*"

Emily loved how he demanded all of her, and this time, it meant he was fully committed. She'd never gotten this side of Eric before, a sense of wholeness, a reassuring feeling that he wanted to be there. So, of course, she wasn't going to let doubters into her head, and she never did. She had a right to believe in love with Eric. It took them a while to get there, but they did. Now that they were there, she wasn't going to let the past, doubt, or any type of hate block her from her deserving love with Eric.

Brooke

Staring out at the dark waterfront, Brooke sat on the window ledge of Jackson's apartment with crossed arms. Tired, she still found it difficult to sleep. Jackson's deep voice grabbed her attention. She turned around to see the silhouette of a tall handsome man with a perfectly toned body approaching her in the dark.

"Why aren't you in bed with your man?" He sat next to her, resting a hand on her exposed leg.

She shrugged. "I can't sleep." Brooke turned her attention back to the waterfront. Many feelings ate away at her during the last few days, especially as they inched closer to their wedding day.

"Brooke, I feel left out of your world right now. You don't wanna talk?" Jackson stroked her hair.

"I'm sorry."

"Do you wanna be left alone?"

"It's up to you," she told him without turning away from the window.

"Okay," he said a moment later. He turned and walked away from her.

Brooke didn't want to turn him away, nor did she want to ignore his help. "Jackson?"

He stopped, but he didn't turn around. "Yeah, Brooke?"

"I need you."

"Then that's all I need to hear." Jackson turned and approached her swiftly like a hero in the night. When he arrived by her side, he sat on the ledge opposite of her. "What's going on? Why can't you sleep?"

Broke shrugged, staring downward. "I don't know," she told him quietly. "Something is going on, but I'm not sure what."

"Let's start with being honest, baby. How can we be husband and wife if we can't communicate? I'm never gonna beg you to come to me. That should be natural."

"I'm so sorry, Jackson." Her eyes reluctantly met his. She hugged herself and rubbed her arms as she sniffled.

"Are you cold?"

"A little."

He stood and left the room. When he returned, he wrapped his robe around her and handed her tissue before taking his seat across from her again. She thanked him. "Brooke, I need to know that when things go wrong in our lives, you won't cut me out. We can't be the prince and princess who live happily ever after twenty-four seven."

"I know, Jackson, and I am so sorry for bringing you into this mess of mine." Her head leaned against the window trim.

"Stop, Brooke. Stop it. I can tell you haven't been in a relationship before, or at least a deep one. That's what they're for. You lean on each other in relationships. You don't have to be perfect, baby. That's the last thing I want. Yes, you look perfect to me on the outside, and I appreciate that, but we all have crap to carry."

Brooke nodded. "Oh, really? Then what's your crap?"

He tilted his head forward, and in a dull tone, replied, "I think you already know."

"What?"

"Why did we break up before?"

"Oh, the emotional baggage and not wanting kids."

"Bet you thought I was perfect, huh?"

"You were pretty close in my book."

"Sweetie, things like this take a while to work out. Family issues can be the deepest wound to heal, because blood is involved. But, your love alone is helping me work through my issues."

"Jackson, I just don't know how to feel. My life feels so foreign. I'm going to be someone's wife, I reconnected with my mom, found out I have an aunt who I thought was just a client, and now I have a cousin. My life was so familiar to me just weeks ago. Now, I feel like I'm in a movie or something."

"Truth?" He leaned forward. "You learned that you cannot control everything."

"I'm scared that I'm gonna be a bad wife, when before I thought I would be the best."

"You'll be untouchable, because you're a queen in my book."

Brooke smiled. "You're too sweet, honey."

"Truth."

"Okay, but now I have no clue what to do with this new so-called family."

"Take your time. But if you want my advice—do you?"

She sat up. "Of course. Always."

"All right." He nodded. "Brooke, I think you should embrace them and move on with caution. You say we'll have children. Not giving them a chance to have two additional families ain't fair. Children need all the love they can get."

"Don't I know it," she agreed.

"So, you sleep on it. Listen to your gut. If you feel that they won't hurt you anymore or the children we don't have yet, then what do you have to lose? I won't let anyone hurt you." He placed a reassuring hand on her knee. "I will protect you, Brooke. And if anyone hurts you, they'll have to answer to me. But if you say we need to leave them alone, then I won't question you. It's done, whatever you decide. It's done."

Tears fell rapidly as she bit her lower lip to keep it from trembling. "Thank you." She reached toward him and froze. "Thank you, Jackson. Baby, I feel like you're so supportive of me. You put up with my family fiasco and gave up your home so that I could be close to work. What can I do for you now? What can I do for you? Please. Please tell me. What can I do to give back?"

Jackson grabbed her hands and kissed them with a smile. "Stop it. That's what you can do. Don't measure the give and takes. Just love me with all your heart and remain faithful. All right?"

"I love you so, so much, and I can't wait to be forever yours."

"I think I love you, too, Brooke Brazile."

Brooke embraced him tightly, but Jackson embraced her even tighter.

Summer

The pictures in my hands were barely visible at this point. It felt like my heart had been ripped from my chest, and I could see it on the floor in front of me, pumping with bleeding valves. Where had this thing called trust gone? Like the Metro train in DC, it'd left as soon as it'd come.

Weren't we about to make love? Wasn't Oliver into me, or was I just dreaming? Was I being played for a fool, especially since a picture of Patty had been painted with a deep hue? Perhaps this is what karma looked like, and Fran was more than happy to dish it to me. I just didn't know that she was his type.

"Summer, look." Oliver held up the bottle of massage oil—the thing I couldn't care less about right now.

A sharp inhale of surprise tipped Oliver off.

"Are you okay, baby?" His face rearranged on account of my bewildered expression and heaving chest.

Barely able to stand with jellyfish legs, I managed, waving the two pictures between us. Marching toward him and vehemently flapping the pictures, I yelled, "What is this, Oliver? What is it?"

Oliver's jaw clenched, his eyes steadied on the photos between my fingers. His expression, unreadable. It straddled the line between being angry that he'd been caught by the nosey girlfriend and appearing heartless about my devastation.

"Where did you get that?" His tone came off as calm, but irritated.

Through clenched teeth, I replied, "Oliver, you know damn well where I got this from."

"Put those down," he ordered with a furrowed brow.

Wow. He wasn't panic-stricken at all but rather composed. Had he been wearing jeans, his hands would've slipped right into them, cool as a cucumber. What was I missing here?

"Are you kiddin' me? You jokin' right now? Don't tell me what to do."

"Those aren't for you, and it wasn't any of your business."

My heart dropped like an elevator to my feet. The room started to spin, and I swore that the saying of seeing red was true, because I saw it.

"*What the hell*, Oliver?"

"Lower your voice. We have a visitor and a baby."

"Pshhh. Oh, *excuuuuse* me. First of all, Amber is my friend and knows everything, and you weren't thinking about Autumn when you were kissing Fran's pussy."

Ohhh, I felt like another physical form of myself was emerging. Stronger, muscular, temperamental. I didn't feel like myself in this skin.

Oliver grabbed me by the arm and chucked his chin in the air. We had a staring contest, both of us refusing to break our glares while turning the other into ice. The simultaneous cold-like expression was the dual that could kill the other person. Jaws clenched, mouths tightened. Fran would be rolling over with laughter right about now, and Ruben would . . .

"Sit down, Summer."

"I. Don't. Want. To. I don't want anything from you. Obviously, pictures do say a thousand words. I just thought that I was enough for you." I jerked my arm from his grasp and turned my back to him. Now that the initial shock had passed, my shoulders began to tremble, and tears started to fall. I plugged my nostrils with a sideways finger placed under my nose. My brain wanted to think, but my feelings wouldn't allow it.

"Don't bother crying, Summer, because it ain't what you think."

Oliver was afraid to confirm it, so he stood behind me. *Now* he cared about my feelings and what I thought? I spun around abruptly to face him.

"How could you preach goodness to me all these months and then turn around and betray me?"

"I know. You're right. I . . ." He shrugged with eyes focused on the floor. "Hear me out. It's really not what you think."

"I feel bad for me, for Ruben . . . we were made to look so dirty, and then you ended up paying me back—and him. So, this is Patty, isn't it?" My eyes almost popped out of my head. This was Patty. He had the nerve to describe their sexual behavior to me. He told on himself under the guise of being silly during sex. I was dumb enough to fall for his matching description of me.

"Summer." He sighed with a face palm. Removing his hand, he said, "If this wasn't such an inappropriate time right now, I'd laugh. Listen, Patty ain't real—"

"—Because she's Fran!"

"—I ain't seeing her! I never did!"

"You're such a liar. Liar! Liar! Liar! I *trusted* you. I cut my wings off because of you!"

"Would you just shut up, Summer? This was payback!"

With my chest visibly rising and falling, I barely had enough air to talk, the anger had gripped me so badly.

"What? What are you talking about?"

"Summer. I am your man, your protector. Always was, always will be."

I tilted my head at him with eyes full of confusion. "I don't . . ." I shook my head. "I don't follow."

Oliver planted his hands on the sides of his head as he looked heavenward before letting his hands drop. "God, help me." He turned to face me. "I, umm, went to pay Ruben a visit. And I did it when we were waiting for the paternity test. I was going to get your life back on track."

"You *what*?"

"You had a new baby coming, your job was snatched from you, but most of all, Summer, you were a talented woman with a dynamic career set in front of you. Fran had no right to do this to you. None. One day at work, I made it my business to find out where they lived. Wasn't hard. I started off with her name and Googled it with his first name. Info started rolling in. One morning, after sleeping on it, I woke up and used their contact information. Decided that Ruben was the best bet first. Wanted to get a feel for the guy. You know," Oliver air plucked his head, "see where his head was at."

I tucked my lips inward and shook my head with closed eyes. All this, I was oblivious to. "This sounds crazy." At least my head was starting to make sense of my visuals again.

"Not for the one you love. I wasn't gonna let Fran get away with wiping your career from you. You needed to stay in the competition. I could open up that agency for you, as an investor, but you couldn't walk around with a tainted reputation. You're only in your twenties. That ain't fair."

Still upset, I just felt relieved that, nor Patty or Fran was a threat. "So, what happened next?"

Oliver seemed reluctant to proceed.

I stretched my arms outward. "Well?"

He rubbed his forehead and then covered his mouth with his hand.

"Told him to meet me at a bar, but he said he'd taken the day off and to come to his new condo, so, that's what I did."

My hand smacked against my forehead. "You shittin' me?"

"No, I'm not."

"And, then?" I folded my arms, waiting for the anvil of disappointment to keep dropping on my head.

Oliver sighed. The pressure to come clean washed over his existence and weighed him down like a criminal in a jumpsuit. "Please, sit, Summer."

"No! Don't you tell me to do that! Whatever beans you have to spill, just do it." I was ready to make a soup out of them. It was time to crank up the heat and let the water boil, because something told me that Fran's pictures in his possession came from a very ugly reason. *Am I better off not knowing? No, No, Summer. Suck it up.*

He held up his hands. "Take it easy."

"Don't you dare. You don't get to tell me anything after you have the nerve to be hoarding naked, inappropriate pictures of my ex-boss. Speak."

Losing his patience, Oliver replied, "All right, fine. Fine. I told Ruben that I would be cool with the visitation rights, that I would be encouraging during the visits if he helped me take your power back from Fran."

"How?"

"I asked him if he had any knowledge that I could go public with—something I could leak, regarding Fran."

I face-palmed myself. "Ohhh, my goodness. No you didn't." I removed my hand to face him again.

Oliver eyed me fearlessly. "I did, and I'd do it again."

"Okay," I winded a quick hand at him, "and so what happened next?"

"He was on board. He'd already been declared war on and was salivating at the idea of justice. So, he had the key, went back to the house that same week, we met again, and he gave me the pictures. I'd already explained that whatever dirt he sent my way would be used to confront Fran with."

My chest caved in. "*You saw Fran?*" I couldn't swallow this lump away.

He nodded once. "I did," he answered matter-of-factly.

Giving him my back and pushing my hands against my hairline to move my hair away from my face, I said, "No, no, no, no, no. This is so ugly, so wrong."

He blurted with an authoritative tone, "Listen."

I turned to face him.

"I called her from outside of her building. Told her that when I got up, she'd better make time for a private appointment in her office. She tried to play hard until I told her that if she didn't, it'd be her worst mistake."

Pacing barefoot along the carpet, I chanted, "Oh, my God, oh, my God, oh, my God."

"J-just, just listen."

I stopped and faced him with a frown. He grabbed me by the shoulders. "This is what happened."

Oliver

I approached the receptionist like a man on a mission. Fran was already waiting for me at the door that lead to the corridor of offices. She watched me with crossed arms and a hardened expression to mask her concern. Fran didn't know what deck of cards I held over her, but she refused to let her composed demeanor shatter.

The woman I followed carried so much power on her tiny shoulders. As a man, there was no way she could ever intimidate me, but as a woman working under her thumb, I could see how an inferior could be left shaking in her boots.

Stepping inside her quarter of power, Fran closed the door behind me. She offered me a seat on the other side of her desk as she went to take her place behind it. I rejected, because she had to know that when it came to Summer, there was no wiggle room for cordiality. A man on a mission, I meant business. Obviously, this woman was used to holding firm with men, because she didn't sit either. We stood, which would've been toe to toe had it not been for the desk between us.

Without wasting time, I told her, "You made your point. Summer screwed up. She shouldn't have slept with Ruben. She regrets it. Now, I would like for you to rescind your attempt to blacklist her from surrounding agencies and companies. We have a daughter, and she needs to make a living."

Anchoring her hands on the desk, Fran tapped one mauve nail. Before she replied, she tipped her head to the side and arched a brow. "She has you."

"Summer wants to be a self-made woman like you, and you know that. Give her a fair shake."

Amused, a hand flew to Fran's mouth as she tried to cup a perfunctory chuckle. She placed both hands behind her back. "A fair shake? A fair shake?" Fran nodded as if to consider my suggestion, but I knew she was just having fun at Summer's expense. "Was it fair when she intruded on my marriage?"

"It takes two, and you know that."

Fran pointed one finger in the air. "Ahhh, but she had no problem screwing my husband in my house when I was down the hall. Nor did she have a problem staying with me when her back was against the wall, letting me care for her and fuss over her, loaning out my car, trusting her with my keys, putting the last stake in my marriage."

"I don't dispute any of that. But you know what? You live and you learn, so I'm gonna ask you one more time, Fran. Will you let this go and let her get on with her life?"

Fran inched forward and raised one brow at me. With a look that dared me to request that favor again, she replied, "I think not."

"No?"

Fran whispered, "Over my dead body." She eased back with a stare that showed no fear, but a belief in victory.

"Dead it is." Reaching into my back pocket, ready to show my hand, a part of me was happy for her rejection, just because I wanted to make her bleed for what she'd initially done to Summer. But the other part of me didn't want to go this far and would've preferred to take the civil route.

"Mm." Fran was too ignorant to not be amused. She sat down, donned her glasses, and picked up her pen. Too soon. Holding the pictures in my hand and bringing them

*forward, Fran said, "Playtime's over. I've indulged you
enough. Show yourself—"*

*When I held up both pictures in each hand, Fran
snatched her glasses off with a gaped mouth. She studied
the pictures long enough to confirm her worst nightmare.*

*Banging an angry fist against the desk, she leaned
forward. "What is that?"*

*Wiggling my brows at her with a grin, I replied,
"Horror of horrors. Why, this is you. Didn't know you were
so flexible, Fran." I popped them back into my back pocket
and folded my arms, standing with parted legs.*

Ohhh how the mean bitch foamed at the corners.

"This is private property. How did you get this?"

*"Oh. So, now you wanna talk? I don't think so. Listen, I
got plenty of money to hang with you in court, should you
decide to take a course of legal retaliation. I also got
enough sense to cover my tracks or do whatever it is I need
to, to make your next move go away. But I guarantee you
one thing: If you even think about doing any of the above,
I'll make sure that your lawsuit is worthwhile. My dear, I
will leak these pictures first and deal with you later. Now
what's it gonna be? Do you wanna settle now?"*

*Fran may've walked tall, despite her short stature, but
even in her chair, it was clear that she'd shrunken a bit.
Her lips appeared to have been sewn together, as she just
sat there in deep thought with one hand fingering the side
of her face. Finally, after deep consideration, she looked
upward and relented with an, "All right."*

*"All right, what?" I peered down at her, waiting to
hear a better choice of words to convince me.*

*Blinking multiple times, she said, "You have my word, I
will reverse her besmirched name."*

*I used a very firm voice with her. "When will you start,
and how long will it take?"*

*Bothered, she answered with, "Right away, but this
may take some time."*

"Work some magic, Fran. I mean, I'd hate for your clients to see you open for take-off." Chuckling, I turned to leave but froze as my hand touched her doorknob. "Oh, Fran?"

"What?"

Facing her, I said, "Summer doesn't know about this, and I want it to stay that way. You see, she'd accepted that she had to do the time, but she's a mother. I want her daughter to see her kick ass in this world. She's too sweet to be okay with me holding all the cards, and she'll feel like it's pointless to look for a job, not knowing that she's free and clear now."

Folding her arms, she asked, "And?"

"Recommend her with the highest regard. Send someone her way. Otherwise—"

"She'll never know that she's eligible again."

"That's one way of putting it. The ball is in your court now. Make something happen before the summer ends."

I had to take that seat that he'd asked me to take before he confessed. Dropping my head forward and clawing my forehead, my torso straightened as soon as I realized that my job didn't come to me organically.

"Wait." With my eyes closed and hand held in the air, I repeated, "Wait. Wait. Wait. Wait. Wait."

"Waiting."

Standing, I opened my eyes and warned with a pointed finger, "Don't mock me. You . . . I didn't get this job on my own? Is this what you're telling me?"

"Wait, now, hold up. You're the one who recruited from home. I mean, Summer, look how you turned things around on your own with no help. Technically, you did the work in the past to deserve what you got today."

"That's bull, Oliver, pure bull. You don't wanna say that I got this job with Simon Jack because of you and Fran. She sent him my way, huh?"

"Listen." Oliver raised his hands. "I don't know the logistics. Just sayin' that, Fran was instructed to make things right. Whatever she did—"

"—Oliver!" Tears streamed like a river. I was nothing. I achieved nothing. Once again, a man tried to save me but in the worst way. It all backfired. I found out that he had to play dirty just to get me ahead again. I didn't even dig myself out of the hole I'd gotten myself into. Crying, any strands of strength had already left my body.

"Summer. Let's be realistic. Had I . . . had I encouraged you to apply for a new job, you wouldn't have out of your certainty of rejection. Right?"

Standing, I headed toward the door but then whipped around to say, "None of this is real, Oliver."

"No," he pleaded. "Don't say that."

My face had contorted into something ugly, an expression of devastation. My throat couldn't house the lump of dread anymore. This had all blown up in my face.

"You want an excuse to leave me, Summer! Been looking for one for a while now."

Throwing a finger in his direction, I said, "That's not fair! That's not fair, and you know it!"

"Summer, come on."

My voice was stripped of clarity. "I can't. I don't belong here. Can't do this anymore."

Turning toward the door, I opened it to see Amber standing there with a chicken drumstick in her hand and an open mouth.

"So should a sista pack, *too*?"

Emily

Two hours later, they rested in the bed. Emily checked the clock. "Baby, it's eleven thirty."

Eric cleared his throat. "I'm not done with you yet. I told you we have a long night ahead of us." Emily lay on top of him, enjoying him stroking her hair. She never felt more connected to her former flame before. "I love you,

Emily, and I can't believe I ever let you go in the first place." He gave her a quick kiss on the lips.

"It's all water under the bridge, ain't it?"

"No, not really. Things really heated up between us. I thought we would be enemies for life."

The words pricked her heart. "Well, don't think about it."

Eric smacked her ass with two quick taps; she knew she had to roll over. When she fell beside him, she faced him, propping her head up with a hand. He lay on his back, facing the ceiling.

"We can't act like nothing happened, like things didn't get really sour."

"But why do you even wanna go there if it hurts?"

He looked at her. "Because we need to remember how far we've come."

"I cost you your job. You loved it there. You had so many years with that company, and I embarrassed you."

Eric clenched his jaw. "Yeah, you did. But I'm with a new company. I'm glad they took a chance on me. I don't wanna talk about my career with you. That's off-limits."

"Why? You said that—"

"*Emily*," he said through tight lips. "Please. Let it go. I'm fine, you're fine, we're getting married. Just let that topic go."

Emily bit her lip, narrowing her eyes. "Okay. Okay." She rested on her back, both of them staring up at the ceiling.

"You know, during sex, you said people think I'm gonna hurt you. Who?"

"For starters? My parents."

"Luckily, I'm not dating or marrying them. But I guess I can understand their position."

"Yeah, well, my dad is hard on all men with his daughters."

Eric turned to face her. "And your mom?"

"My mom and dad are so close. She follows his lead. She's not going to oppose him. I guess that's what makes them work."

"Well, she's totally on his team. I respect that. That's any man's dream."

Emily felt like he was taking a subtle stab at her. "From here on out, I want to prove that I can be on your team."

"All my team members ride with me. So get over here," he cracked. Emily flew over his body without being asked twice. "If you really wanna make me happy, fly down south, right now."

Emily saluted. "Aye, aye captain." She wiggled backward and disappeared under the covers, ensuring him that putting a ring on her finger was the best decision he could've ever made.

7: the great escape

Summer

    Dressed up to attend Emily and Eric's Friday night semi-casual rehearsal dinner, we were invited to celebrate at Eric's $1.2 million dollar flat located in Tysons Corner. Eric mingled with everyone at the dinner party in the room behind us, while the girls and I discussed tomorrow on the nineteenth-floor terrace.

    Being here tonight would've been impossible, if it weren't for the arrangements made with my mom weeks ago to be here as my babysitter. I wanted to feel good tonight. Unfortunately, being away from my daughter for the first time, even if in the trusty hands of my mother, still had my stomach doing flips. It took plenty of effort to train myself not to whip out my phone every five minutes to check for missed texts regarding Autumn, or to keep from calling my mom.

    The separation of Oliver and me also had me on edge tonight. Given the unfortunate circumstance of my relationship and despite being a new mommy, it felt like the right choice to be out with my girls and to take a physical break from motherhood duties.

    Emily ran her hand over the rail as we took in the sight. She looked so elegant with her sleek bun and pleated sheath dress. Navy blue never looked so elegant on a lady. Dressed in shiny, black woven pants and a matching sheer floral button-up, Brooke tipped her glass back to finish the last swig of champagne. I went strapless for the night, wearing a blush-colored lace dress. The city was getting chilly. I almost regretted wearing such a short dress every time I looked at Brooke's pants.

    However, nothing made me feel colder than Amber's choice of attire. "Aren't you cold, yet?" I had to ask since her black shorts were shorter than my dress.

Puffing on a cigarette with a glass of champagne in the other hand, she gave me the side eye. "Girl, please, you know where I'm from."

I popped a brow. "You're right. You won't let us forget."

"Never that." She tapped her cigarette against the rail to release some ashes from the stick.

I caught a glimpse of Oliver, Eric, and Jackson standing in a circle talking and laughing.

"Amber, that top is hot," Brooke said. The black studs over the front gave Amber's chiffon tank top an edgy look.

"Thanks, babe." She took one last puff and threw the cigarette over the balcony.

Emily dipped her head at me. "So, what was that Debbie Downer look about earlier when you came through the door? And how come Oliver came after you, and you haven't gone in to greet him yet?"

Well, Emily didn't miss a beat. Made sense as a teacher. They had to be observant and detail-oriented in their profession.

The pebble that I kept rolling underneath my heel stole my attention. "Nothing."

A quick peek at Amber gave it away.

"Then why did Amber grimace suspiciously?" Emily asked.

"*Emily*," Brooke said. "I don't think she wants to talk about it. Trust me, I know those feelings now." She placed a hand on my arm. "But we're here for you if you ever need to talk."

I shook my head to move the hair from my face. "No, it's okay. We can talk. I mean, Amber knows the whole story, because this chicken ho here was eavesdropping on the whole thing."

Amber grinned while wiggling her brows. "Oh, it's good y'all. Juicy, in fact. And by the way, you and Oliver were loud, okay?"

I rolled my eyes. "I can't stand you, Amber."

Brooke leaned forward to rest her weight against the rail. "Oh, really? Well, do tell." She set her empty flute on the rail.

Emily smacked Brooke on the shoulder. "What happened to the privacy clause?"

Brooke smirked. "Well that all went out the door now—or over the balcony—once Amber said the word, 'juicy.'"

I sighed and smiled. "Hate you guys. Anyway, the gist of it is, Oliver isn't the man I thought he was, and he opted to leave the condo for the sake of not uprooting Autumn. Guess he's in a hotel or something. Also, he considered Amber's living arrangement, too. We're not together right now. I can't bear to look at his face."

Brooke's eyebrows hiked up toward her hairline. "Did he cheat?"

"N-nooo." I shook my head. "Quite the opposite, though I thought he did. He's too controlling. All this high-end life with him . . . it just comes with a price tag too high."

Amber chuckled. "Honey, his price tag looks better than Daniels. Shiiiiit."

Emily massaged her temples and Brooke shot Amber a dirty look.

"Be my guest," I offered.

Brooke scoffed, yanking her head back in disbelief. "Y-you don't mean that?"

"No, I don't. But—"

Emily said, "Well, honey, first of all, fill us in. What did the man do?"

I started from the beginning, leaving out information about Patty and dove right into the meat of it.

Brooke and Emily's mouth dropped past the balcony floor.

Brooke rubbed my shoulder. "That's deep, babe."

Emily placed a hand on my back. "My goodness, Summer. What are you going to do? How do you feel?"

"I mean, am I wrong?" My eyes landed on Brooke. "How would you feel if Jackson did that." Then my stare shifted to Emily. "Or, Eric?"

Emily's mouth opened, but nothing came out as she thought about it with her hands pressed together. "I . . . I don't know, I mean . . . it ain't cool, but, it could've been worse." She did a slow shrug. "And he was fighting *your* enemy."

Brooke responded next. "I would hate to think that I achieved something on my own, just to find out my fate had been manipulated. You thought you got the job because of something *you* did right. I mean, I'm a career-oriented woman like you, Summer, so I understand how you could feel robbed by someone you trusted. Come on, night after night, and he didn't say anything?"

I pointed a hand at her. "*Exactly*. So, you get it."

Emily said, "But I have been through worse with Eric, so it doesn't seem like the worst offense. Hurtful? Yes. But enough to walk away? No. You get burned by the person you love in many ways sometimes."

"But who wants to come home to get burned by someone in your own safe space?" Brooke asked with a frown. "There's enough of that going around outside of your walls. And now it's at home with you?"

Emily shrugged. "I don't think my standards are off, just realistic."

Brooke licked her lips and smiled at Amber. She knocked Amber's arm with a finger. "Oh, thee, wise one. You had excellent advice on my birthday. What do you have for our girl now?"

Emily and I directed our attention to Amber with elevated brows, anticipating her response.

She placed both hands in the air. "Well don't look at me? I gotta be crunk before I dish that type of wisdom out again."

Brooke's head snapped to the side. "Oh, please, girl. Help her out. At least tell us what you think."

I told her, "Just try not to make it about his money, okay? Because, I don't care about that. For once, just give it to me straight."

Amber placed a hand on her hip. "Well I never go crooked." She cleared her throat. "Fine." She turned her attention to the men inside talking with one hand in their pants and one wrapped around a champagne glass. Looking back at us, she said, "Each of you is blessed. Having said that, there's a long line of single women, good and bad, waiting to be taken. I think each man in that room loves you guys hard. Deep and hard." Amber pointed in the direction of the men. "To let any one of them go, would be foolish. Listen. Finding the right man goes beyond "things in common." It's being able to take his good with his annoyances. Daniel was annoying, and I couldn't get used to it. Men's bad habits, morning breath, funky gym smell, bad farts, all that. His background, his religion or lack thereof, his family, penis length, and health—I mean every single thing needs a checkmark. You find a new man then you have to go down the whole list again and on top of it, he can't be a serial killer or any other criminal."

We all nodded in silence, listening with eyes that soaked in all her points.

"Yes, I get it. It's not always about cheatin'," Amber said. "Men can hurt us in other ways. But don't think for a second that they'll be crying for long in a corner alone in a fetal position. There's some thirsty hos out there." She took a sip of champagne.

We playfully eyed her up and down, silently throwing shade at her with lips that resisted accusatory grins.

"However, Emily is right. This is the real world, and the real world hurts. As long as a man still loves you, then you got a chance. Worry when there's no more love left."

Brooke stabbed a finger into Amber's shoulder. "And there it is. Thank you. Thank you for that deep advice."

Sober in seriousness, Amber took another sip. "You're welcome."

Brooke added, "But I still say it ain't healthy to lie next to someone at night who operates behind your back." She threw her palms up and took a step back. "Just sayin'."

"I hear ya'," I assured her with a nod.

Amber said, "But you need to understand your man types, and Oliver is a protector. It is what it is, he is who he is. He had her back. Summer wouldn't have let him act if she knew." She tapped a finger in the air in my direction. "Tell you what. I'd rather know that a man would go too far to have my back, than to have a man who hides behind the couch when I need him the most."

Wrinkling my face, I thought about her words. Was Amber right? Was I being too harsh on the man for simply taking care of me when I didn't have the heart to resort to such measures? "I don't know, Amber. I just don't know." I closed my eyes and rubbed the back of my neck for a few seconds.

Emily rubbed her hands together. "My nerves are tangled up in my belly. I haven't been able to silence them all night. I didn't even feel this way the first time around."

Amber rubbed Emily's stomach. "Oh, sweetie. You gettin' married again to the same man, and you two been through an upheaval. That's all."

"Maybe." Emily frowned. She seemed distant on and off through dinner. "I wonder if Eric's mom will make it tomorrow. I know I'm happy that I won't have to see his dad."

"Well, why aren't they here?" I asked.

Emily eased her tensed brows. "He said that his dad was not invited, and his mom is on vacation with her group of friends. She's trying her best to get back from the south on time, so he says."

"You don't believe him?" Brooke asked.

"I do, but I wonder if she really wants us back together. His parents are so uppity, and though they've divorced, I think both would like to see him with a true American girl."

"Honey, you are true. What are you talking about?" I shot back.

"Summer, please. You know what I mean. You're part white, and even you wouldn't cut it. I think they want someone who looks like Charlotta."

"What in the low hell is a Charlotta?" Amber asked.

"Our server for the night," she answered.

"Oh," Amber said. "Who cares about impressing someone else's parents? Someone in the family always gotta be an asshole."

Brooke said, "I will be so glad when I'm married. I just want the ceremony to go perfectly. Every day I'm on pins and needles. I just expect my mom or aunt to come back to my doorstep any day. I'm just not ready for that."

"Maybe we all need cigarettes," Emily said. Since she didn't smile, I wonder if she meant it.

"Tell me about it," I agreed grimly. "Amber has a job with no home, I have a fake job in a messed-up home, Brooke's home got invaded by unwanted family members, and Emily . . ." Taking a second to think, I waved a hand at her. "Well, hell, she don't know if she's welcomed into Eric's parents' home."

We giggled, but then Amber said, "This heffa may actually be the only one at ease, aside from the wedding jitters."

Brooke pointed a finger at her. "But she deserves it."

"Yeah, she does," I agreed.

Emily smiled with outstretched arms. "Time for a hug?"

We shrugged with broken smiles.

"Bring it in," she said, wiggling her fingers, so we obeyed.

"Champagne?" The female server that Eric hired stood at the sliding door with four glasses.

"Yes, Charlotta." Emily took one. "Thank you. Just what I need."

We all took one as well.

Looking her up and down, Amber said, "Oh. That's the Charlotta."

Confused, Charlotta smiled with an uneasy smirk.

Emily's brows shot up. "Oh, thank you, thank you, doll. We're all good."

Charlotta disappeared behind the closed glass door. We all stared at Amber with open mouths and enlarged eyes.

Emily asked, "Dummy, are you trying to start stuff? Sheesh. We can't tell you nothing."

Amber shrugged. "Whaaaaaa?" She sipped.

Brooke pointed a finger at her. "If we end up with poison in our glasses, I'm taking you down."

"Let's make our own private toast," I suggested. We raised our glasses in a circle. "To happiness, all the way around."

"To happiness," my friends repeated. We clinked glasses and sipped.

"I should be so happy, but I feel so distracted," Brooke complained.

"I know what you mean, Brooke," Emily said. "I feel, like, tense. My dad is breathing down my back, my mom is joining him and is not showing one ounce of happiness, and Zach and I are estranged." She scraped her blue heels over the terrace floor. "Maybe I shouldn't have invited my parents. At least my sisters are supportive."

"I love those girls already," I told her. The others agreed.

Amber grinned. "They make me miss mine."

"Makes me wish I had them growing up in that wretched house," Brooke added.

Emily sighed. "Yeah, but, it only got easy as adults. Siblings can be a handful growing up. But, I love them to death. I thank God I had them to call my own. I do love my family. They are the constant blessing in my life."

"I hope I have that with Jackson," Brooke admitted.

"You will, girl." I rubbed her shoulder. "You will."

"How about you, Amber? Are you looking for love?" Brooke asked.

Amber winced as she took a sip from her glass. "No. I won't go lookin'. If it comes, and if it is the real thing," she curtsied, "then I'll be open."

"Honey, you stay open," I joked.

They all fell over laughing

"But I'll attack the future on my own with focus and no stupid mistakes." She nodded and smiled. "I can finally act on my own. I won't hate or bash men. I just won't center my life around them unless it's my husband. Until then, Amber will be Amber, happy and focused with her piano."

"Here, here, sister," Emily said.

We clacked glasses.

A male voice stole our attention. "Emily? Excuse me, ladies." Eric stepped out from behind her and joined her by her side. He placed a hand on her lower back and caressed her ample bottom. "We need to say our goodbyes."

"That means I have to go home," Emily whined. "I don't want to say goodbye to you either."

"I know. I know."

"Awwww," we sang.

Eric snickered. "Then I'll give you a few more ticks once they leave . . . just for me and you."

She pouted but bounced at his idea. "Okay."

We all followed Emily and Eric back inside. They looked so classic together. Eric, the business man, with the provider family-man aura, and Emily, classy and chic. Appearing grown and secure as a union, seeing them tonight killed any of my misgivings.

Eric tapped his glass with a spoon and handed both items back to Charlotta. "Ladies and gentlemen, Emily and I would like to thank everyone for coming to our rehearsal dinner. This woman right here means the world to me, and tomorrow, we will embark on a new journey. Tomorrow at one, please be there promptly to see me marry the woman of my dreams. Good night, and please drive home safely."

Oliver reluctantly eased up beside me, careful not to touch me. After growing accustomed to his hand making its home on the small of my back when we were out in public, it felt strange to have him beside me functioning as a stranger.

"Hi," Oliver said.

Well this wasn't awkward at all. Barely looking at him, feeling shy and guarded, I said, "Hi."

"You look gorgeous tonight."

My heart fluttered, and I didn't know if that was a good or unwelcomed sign. It meant there was still room in my heart for him, but did I still want him to occupy that space? All I could offer was a barely-mustered broken smile. "Thanks."

Well, for the brief second that I looked at him, he did look rather handsome in his suit with the dress shirt underneath revealing the top portion of his chest. The sight reminded me of the fact that we didn't get to make love as planned since I was cleared for intimacy. *Shoot.* I wanted his hands around me, but what he did still eclipsed my ability to mentally unlock the gate to desire.

We stood close to the front door, as others swerved around the room to give goodbye kisses to fellow guests and the hosts. Clutching my cellphone for dear life in one hand, it became the hub for frazzled nerves.

Oliver placed a hand on my shoulder, rubbing circles with his thumb against my skin, waking up my vagina. "Can I just have one moment with you?"

"I guess."

Opening the door to Eric's apartment, we stepped out and to the side to keep from blocking the entrance. Once the door clicked, I slid the strap to my purse into the crook of my neck and folded my arms. His eyes dropped and then raised to meet mine.

"How's Autumn? I miss her."

I let a smile ease across my face. "She's well. I do think she misses you."

"I miss her. A lot. And it's barely been a day."

I nodded with a pensive expression. "Did you enjoy yourself tonight?"

He wore a look of regret. Still, it wasn't enough. Oliver's actions left a lot to question, even though he made my heart get fuzzy.

"It wasn't the same without you by my side."

"Please, Oliver. Don't."

"I gave you a few . . . hours. You've had your space, Summer. What can we figure out under two different roofs and no communication?"

"Oliver—" I shook my head in dismay.

"No." He removed one of his hands from his pants pocket to gesture with. "I moved out of my own home, Summer. Do you think I would've done that for any other woman?"

"Oliver, you keep thinking that doing things in the name of love makes everything right." My hands popped outward. "But it doesn't."

"I wanna come home. Please. I miss you. I miss our daughter. I . . . I don't even know if I can still call her—"

"Of course, you can."

"Okay then, I miss my daughter. I need to come home. Summer. I wanna be with you. This idea of unspecified distance is killing me. Look." He held up both palms. "Learned my lesson. I'll eat crow. I just gotta find a way back to you."

Reaching out to lay a hand against his chest, I said, "I need more time." Craning my neck forward, I placed a kiss on his cheek. "Good night, Oliver."

Turning around to leave my knight and shining armor at the couple's doorstep, I felt like a princess walking away with a broken tiara.

Emily

Emily met Eric's gaze with her head placed against his chest. They slow danced in the dark to the soft sound of a romantic jazz tune. His hands rubbed up and down her spine before resting on her butt.

"Eric," Emily said, "you have made me the happiest woman alive."

"Well do you know any happy dead women?" Eric grinned, flashing perfect white teeth.

"Okay. Touché." Her hands caressed his back. "So how does it feel to have an empty apartment with only a dining room table?"

He snickered. "Feels good. All my stuff is in storage now. I don't need much to move in with you. Besides, I can always go back to get things."

"I guess we need to move into something a little bit bigger in a year maybe?"

"Let's worry about that after we settle into our marriage. I'll be sleeping on the floor tonight with time to think."

"Oh, no." Emily felt horrible. "Why not check into a hotel?"

"Nah. I'm a man, Emily. I can handle it. No worries. Tomorrow I'll be in your bed."

"*Our* bed," she corrected with a smile. "Then we can start the baby-making sessions?"

"Hmmm." He placed his forehead against hers. "How many should we shoot to have while we're young-ish?"

"Two? Three?"

"Okay. I know I was resistant to more than one, but this time around, I will give you everything that you deserve."

Emily stood on her toes to place a kiss on his lips. "You are so sweet. I don't think I deserve it all."

"Oh, Emily Rosado, you deserve all that I'm going to give to you. Don't doubt it." Eric held her close and caressed her head. "Let's make love one more time."

"Before the wedding?" Emily eyed him with doubt.

"Well, don't worry about bad luck. I haven't seen your wedding dress."

She nodded. They were silent for a moment.

Eric asked, "You won't be late, will you? I want our wedding to be perfect tomorrow."

It pleased Emily to hear his concern for perfection. "Nope. I will be there," she assured stroking his shoulders. "On time." Emily frowned. "You still have to go out of town after we get married?"

"Baby, I have to. I'll lose my job. I don't have any leeway, barely got this job after my reputation took a hit. I'll be back in a few days. Then we can take our honeymoon."

Emily sighed and rested her head on his chest. "Fine. I can't complain. It is all my fault after all," she mumbled.

Eric gave her one last squeezed. His fingers gripped her chin, so he could look into her eyes. "Let me make love to you Emily, one more time."

Emily didn't say a word. She turned around. Eric's fingers grazed her back as he lowered the zipper. Her arms crawled out of the dress. Emily turned around to show him her bare chest and taut stomach. She peeled the dress over her hips as he watched it fall to the wooden floor. A hard swallow eased down his throat. She stepped over the compacted dress with both feet. Standing in nothing but black underwear, Emily placed her hands in front of her for Eric to grab. She said, "Take me."

Emily woke up and stared at her reflection in the full-length mirror next to her bed. Her wild hair covered her face, but when she moved it back, the smile on her face became visible. Knowing she should wait, she couldn't. Picking up the phone at 8:15 a.m., she dialed Eric's cellphone number. He picked up on the third ring. Emily instantly felt the butterflies.

"Hello?"

"Hi, Eric." Blushing, she sat on her bed.

"Good morning, princess. How do you feel?"

"Better, now that I hear your voice. When will I see you at the chapel? I'll be there on time. You?"

"Well, I'm getting myself together, but I have to tie some lose ends."

"On our wedding day?" Emily frowned with nervousness.

"On our wedding day. Please, baby, don't worry. Obviously marrying you is at the top of my list. I don't think you get how long I've been waiting for this day."

Emily grinned from ear to ear. "Well in that case, I'll see you at one."

"See you at one. I love you, Ems."

The way he said it made her heart clap a quick, awkward beat. "I love you, too, Eric."

They hung up. Emily stood and reached into the closet to pull out her wedding gown hidden inside of the Wally bag. There was a knock at the door. It had to be her family or the stylist. Emily tossed the Wally bag onto the bed and ran to the front door. She opened it and saw excited women on the other side.

"The bride!" Her mom screeched.

Her mom and sisters greeted her with open arms. Emily invited everyone inside. They all scrambled around her apartment, making her a light breakfast, pulling things out of their bags, and goofing off. An hour later, the stylist arrived with a case of tools for her make-up and hair. Half an hour later, Helena opened the door to Amber and Brooke. They all hugged and headed to Emily's bedroom.

"Where's Summer?" Emily asked.

"She's running late," Amber replied. "Honestly, her mom is comforting her. She was emotional this morning because of the whole Oliver thing. She'll be here though."

Emily nodded. "Ohhhhh, I see. Poor thing. I hope this wedding won't be too much for her."

When Amber's cellphone rang, she raised a finger to excuse herself as she pulled her phone from her purse. After about a minute, Amber placed her cellphone back into her purse. "That was Summer. She said she would meet us at the chapel."

Emily gave her a thumbs-up. "Awesome."

Hours later, it was time to head out. Emily stood in the bathroom alone, checking herself out in the mirror. For her first wedding, she wore an updo, but this time, she decided on a side ponytail full of curls to complement her A-line satin dress. The long sleeve seven-thousand-dollar gown had called her name as soon as she laid eyes on the illusion neckline and embroidery work. The chapel train was the perfect length and not too fussy. The off-white colored dress would make Eric stop dead in his tracks.

When Emily entered her bedroom to a room full of waiting women, they all oohed and aahed over her dress, waiting for a turn to touch it.

"Isn't it a beauty?" Emily asked.

Amber puckered her lips. "Girl, you make me wanna get married."

Everyone fell over laughing.

Brooke had a tear in her eye. "Emily . . . it's all coming together. You look so beautiful."

Emily gripped her friend's forearm. "Thank you," she whispered.

Her mother embraced her tightly. "I hope he makes you happy this time around."

"He will," an emotional Emily assured her in a shaky voice.

"Stupid, don't ruin the makeup," Lourdes said, waving a finger at her. Reaching for the hair pin in the back of her hair, Lourdes gave Emily her favorite accessory from the sixth grade. "Here. Something borrowed."

Emily placed a hand over her bosom as a time-honored tradition started to take place. If felt as though she were marrying again for the first time. There was a sense of maturity that resided within her that wasn't there the first time around.

"I can't. I can't take that. You cried for days when you misplaced it as a child."

"Don't get stupid now. This is on loan." She pushed it closer to Emily. "Take care of it. Take it."

Emily giggled. "You make me sick. I love you, Sticks."

Lourdes pretended to blush. "Yeah, yeah." She gripped her older sister into a tight hug. "Y'all need to retire that old nickname."

Emily shook her head. "Not a chance."

Valentina stood from the bed. "Take this, stinker. This is old." She passed a small wooden box to Emily, which she opened.

Trying to discern the gift, Emily's nose crinkled. She sat the box down on her dresser, erupting memories of Eric giving her mind-blowing sex that rattled the objects on top. She blushed with graphic memories that bombarded her thoughts.

"Huh?" Emily asked as she held up the blue material. Using two hands to unfold it, the material turned out to be cotton underwear.

Valentina swerved her neck. "I wore those in college. Never threw them away."

"Ew! Are you serious?" Emily balanced the underwear on the top of her index finger.

"Dead." Valentina kept a straight face.

"I don't think this is what they meant." Emily offered the underwear back to her older sister.

Brooke's face displayed disgust. "Is it fresh?"

"Well I ain't smellin', Emily replied.

They all burst into laughter. Emily joined them. Valentina pulled out a silver bracelet and grabbed her sister's wrist. "Here, knucklehead. Certainly, you must know that I wouldn't do that to you on your wedding day, right?"

"I should hope not."

"This belonged to *abuela*. She gave these to me when I was sixteen. They belonged to her. She had them when she was fourteen, so this is very old."

The gift touched the deepest corners of Emily's heart. She could feel her grandmother's presence. A tear rolled down her cheek. "Thank you, *hermana*." She grinned and pulled Valentina close.

"*De nada.*"

Emily told them, "Note to self: Apply makeup after all exchanges."

Brooke replied, "There better not be another opportunity for you to get it right."

"True," Emily agreed.

Amber grabbed a bag from the side of the bed and handed it to Emily.

"What's this?" Emily asked swiping a tear with a smile.

"Open it," Brooke told her. "It's the 'new,' from Amber and me."

Emily bounced at the knees. "Oh, goody. Something new."

She grabbed the bag by both strings, then released one of them to enable her hand to fit inside of the bag. Her hand gripped around a hard square. When she pulled it out, she saw that it was wrapped with paper. Placing the bag on the bed, she ran her finger under the taped flap to release the gift from within. Ripping the paper off, she threw it inside the bag until there was nothing left. Emily flipped the lavender-colored photo album over until the opening lined up with her right hand.

"A photo album. Wow. No one uses these anymore, but I should do."

They all giggled with choruses of agreement.

"That's why we knew you'd love this," Brooke explained. "You need to be able to see your new chapter in a new album. Something tangible, you know?"

"I do, and I love it." Emily placed the album down and extended her arms to Brooke and Amber. "Come here." Once in her arms, she said, "You guys and Summer are like having more sisters. I feel rich."

"Aww," Brooke and Amber replied.

Emily said, "Thank you. You guys know me well for ladies who haven't known me for a lifetime."

"Our pleasure," Amber said.

Emily turned to face her mother, because she knew that her mother had something to give her.

Helena stepped forward with her hand balled into a fist. Emily stared at her mom's fist and then into her eyes. "Open it."

Emily nodded and peeled each finger back gingerly until she saw a pair of blue pearl earrings. She sucked in a sharp breath. "Oh, *mamá*."

"Allow me," she said. Helena put them into her daughter's ears. "You're all set."

Emily held her mother close. "Thank you for being supportive. Thank you."

Helena rubbed her back. "My pleasure, *mi hija*, my pleasure."

Summer

A generous amount of concealer helped with the puffiness underneath my eyes. It caused me to be late by ten minutes, but I refused to leave the house until traces of being upset were successfully masked. No way would Oliver be allowed to see the evidence of my distraught heart. And since this day wasn't about me, it was important not to let Brooke and Amber detect my emotional state. Emily deserved every ounce of our attention.

Brooke and Amber escorted me into the bathroom to help jazz me up at the last minute. With three pairs of shoes tucked in a bag, they decided that I should wear my silver heels even though we were wearing floor-length dresses. We all looked like beautiful triplets in our sand-colored renaissance satin dresses. Each of us wore an updo, but mine had tendrils of curls falling from my bun. True, the whole women feeling like princesses kind of thing never sat right with me, but today that feeling was something I could relate to.

"Let's go." Brooke, the A-type wedding planner, kept watch of the time and ushered us out the bathroom in a hurry and on time.

Obeying her, we tried to meet up with Emily. We found her with her sisters in the foyer. Emily had crinkled eyebrows as she watched Valentina hold a phone to her ear.

Emily bit down on the tip of a manicured nail. "He's not answering. If we weren't in church, I would say a few bad words."

Valentina suggested, "Emily, maybe he's on his way and got held up."

"In traffic?" Emily cut her off. "No." In a panic, her accent thickened. "He is never late to anything. That is his number one pet peeve."

"Well, what time is it?" I asked.

Pacing while shaking the nerves from her hands, Emily said, "One fifteen, and I haven't heard a thing from him. Oh my, gosh, oh my, gosh. I feel so sick. I feel so sick. Something has to be wrong with him. He is *never* late."

"Let's wait inside with the guests," Lourdes suggested.

"Lourdes, are you nuts? I cannot go in there."

Brooke raised a hand. "I'm the wedding planner who sometimes feels like a PR rep or something like that."

I tried to play calm. "Then what do we do?"

"Yeah." Emily appeared hopeful for the first time. "You're right. What do we do?"

"Well, because we don't have any facts, we tell the guests the truth without going into specifics. We tell them that we are running behind and to please be patient. Let them wonder why we're late, because otherwise, it makes the bride or groom look bad. There's no need to embarrass anyone in particular or ring the alarm for a false cause. Let me go and do it." Like a trooper, Brooke didn't wait for permission or an objection. Through the small glass pane on the door, I watched her march up the aisle with amazing confidence. She borrowed a microphone, made an announcement, and in a few seconds, she came back.

Valentina didn't give up calling Eric on Emily's phone or on her own. Emily sat in a chair in the corner, bent over, with fists resting on both sides of her head. She didn't want anyone to comfort her. Tears came to my eyes. I couldn't imagine what she might've been going through.

"See," Amber whispered to me with an upset face. "This is why marriages are nothing but a big pile of garbage."

"Please, Amber, not now." I didn't want to hear it. I didn't need to hear her blurt out a list of ten reasons why she didn't believe in love. Based on my recent events, she didn't have to convince me. The sad thing was, Eric's actions just might vindicate our waning beliefs.

Emily sat up, stood, and exhaled with a hand on her stomach. "Guys."

We directed our undivided attention at her.

"It is what it is, whatever that may be." Her eyes darted at us, one by one as she mustered a brave face. "*Que cera, que cera.*"

I wasn't quite sure what that meant, but her sisters nodded.

"I'm not going to keep these guys. I will call the hospitals in a minute, but for now, I must thank the guests and relieve them."

"Are you sure?" Brooke asked.

Emily nodded then marched toward the wooden doors. We shrugged at one another, feeling Emily's pain as well. We followed her inside and lined up against the wall behind the last pew row. Emily walked to the front of the church and grabbed the microphone. The guests whispered indiscernibly, but they stopped when she said, "Everyone. First of all—"

"Emily Rosado?" a voice called from the back of the church.

"Yes?" Confused, her lashed fluttered.

We all turned to see a skinny man wearing slacks and a light jacket march to the front of the church after she answered. He didn't say anything as he headed toward Emily to pass her a manila envelope. I heard him say, "For you." He turned abruptly and left as soon as he'd arrived.

Emily didn't know what to do with the package. Flipping it over to read the front with clumsy fingers, she anxiously fumbled to find the opening before tearing into it like a monetary prize awaited inside. Pulling out what appeared to be a note, she read the sheet of paper in her hand under her breath. Emily tucked the piece of paper back into the envelope. No one knew what she'd learned.

Opening her mouth, the words seemed to have gotten stuck in her throat. It was like I could see her brain racing as she stared out at the guests.

"Ladies and gentlemen, there is a change of plans."

Something was clearly wrong. My heart stopped beating for a moment, as if to wait for permission by way of good news to proceed.

"No wedding." People mumbled and groaned. With slanted brows, Emily hurried toward the doors that led to the foyer. She tried to walk calmly at the hips, but her shuffling feet told a different story. Shoving her hand against one of the double doors, Emily stepped through and disappeared behind the flapping door.

We traded glimpses at one another before following our hurting friend to the foyer. Emily's mom and sisters were close behind.

Hysterical, Emily spun around and shared, "Eric is not coming. The wedding is off. That bastard is not going to ever walk down the aisle with me."

"Excuse me?" I asked.

"What the f—" Catching herself, Amber placed a hand over her chest. She closed her eyes briefly, and when she opened them, she said, "Sorry. What do you mean, Emily?"

Brooke bit her lower lip and folded her arms. "I swear . . ." she grunted with a balled fist.

"*Ay, Dios mío,*" Helena cried.

Lourdes threw her arms up. "Nah, man. You gotta be playin', yo." Her eyes became as glassy as a mirror. "This ain't right. No. How can he do this to you?"

Valentina swung a hand at her heart and then reached for Emily. "What happened? Baby, sis, come here."

Rejecting her, Emily sliced her arms through the air. "It doesn't matter. Long story short, the note he wrote told me that it ain't gonna happen. So," she licked her lips, "I'm outta here."

Before any of us could touch her with our extended arms, Emily had fled from the church.

"Let her go."

We all turned to see the face that owned the authoritative tone.

Quito stood there.

We lowered our arms slowly as we tried to process everything that seemed to be happening too quickly.

"Emily needs time to be alone. We will honor that. We will all go our separate ways—to our own homes and hotels. Give her time. She's not ready to face anyone's questions or scrutiny."

Everyone nodded.

Quito was right. How could Emily answer any questions or determine how she felt when the wound was still fresh and gushing blood?

I patted Brooke and Amber on the shoulders. I swallowed the lump in my throat that I didn't expect to be there.

"Outside, please."

They nodded.

"Of course," Brooke said.

When we were all greeted by the rays of the strong sun, it felt like a mockery. It might as well have been a rainy day. The rays brought no joy to us or to our friend. The fresh air pumped no wind of hope into our systems. Everything felt wrong, and I couldn't breathe.

Needing to get off my feet, I took a seat on the top step of the concrete stairs. Brooke sat to my left and Amber to my right.

"I can't breathe. Why do people fall in love just to get blindsided by the ones we trust? Ruben did it to Fran, I did it to Oliver, Oliver did it to me, and now Eric did it to Emily, God knows how many times."

Brooke held her temples. "This makes me almost wanna question love." She shook her head and crossed her arms, tucking her head downward and into her lap.

Amber shook her head. She pointed behind her. "Can we cuss yet? Or you know, like, is this still sacred grounds? We need to watch what we say, right?"

Looking straight ahead, I answered, "That would be the classy thing to do, Amber."

She nodded. "Got it. And what about cigarettes? You think the Lord would be mad if I smoked a loosie right now? Because this thing called love that you guys claim people need is more stressful than rewardin' if you ask me. Now I'm stressed."

Brooke straightened and turned to Amber with extended hands. "*Amber*. Please stop talking. I can't—I'm not strong enough right now not to cast doubt Jackson's way, and I don't wanna do that to him or us. So, Amber, please. Let's not bash love."

Turning to look at Amber, I said, "I'm a free bird, and I agree. Not now, Amber. Our friend is really hurting right now." The pain seeped through me as well. A tip of my head to the left found solace against Brooke's shoulder. I felt a tear.

We didn't say anything at the moment. We were all looking for some kind of understanding in the midst of silence.

"Should we pray?" Amber asked.

Lifting my head up slowly, I realized that it surely couldn't hurt and that I hadn't done it in a while.

"What should we say?" I asked.

Brooke replied, "Anything that comes to our hearts."

Amber picked my hand up into hers. Then I did the same with Brooke's.

"I'll do it," Amber said.

Brooke and I nodded.

Brooke said, "Wait." She stole her hand back from me long enough to shuffle in her purse for her phone. She accessed the camera, and before pushing the button, she turned to us and said, "Let her see this. She can have something real to hold on to."

"Good idea. We won't be in her face. Plus, she prays," I said.

Brooke and Amber nodded vehemently. Brooke positioned the phone to view us with an extended left arm, while picking up my hand with the other.

We all closed our eyes.

Amber cleared her throat. Then another tear fell down my face. Was this really going to happen? Were the three friends who fought, did other people wrong, and cry a million tears of misery on random nights since the time we've met really going to pray together?

"Heavenly Father, we sit here, on your stairs with three broken hearts, in the midst of . . . doubt. We wanna uplift Emily in this time, and while we don't have the answers, we wanna ask that You offer her a sense of understandin' on the grounds of renewed confidence. We ask that You allow us to be there for her, that we have the patience and wisdom to guide her through this moment. We ask that she sees the beauty and value in herself. God, please throw Eric down—"

My eyes popped open as I squeezed Amber's hand instinctively. "Hey. No, no. You can't ask God for things like that."

"Why not?" Amber frowned. "May he rot—"

"Stahhhp. You're ruining a beautiful thing." I nudged Brooke with my elbow. "Tell her. Tell her that she can't pray for things like that."

Brooke didn't jump to defend my point. She just narrowed her eyes and tightened her lips together into a wide smirk. "Uhhh, he did hurt our girl, but in the interest of keeping the focus on Emily, Amber, let's move on. The man is dead to us."

"Fine."

I shook my head in dismay and watched Amber close her eyes to resume prayer.

"So, God, we come to You, humbled, lost, and with bruised hearts, hopin' that we can guide ourselves and Emily toward better days. We pray that Emily finds the man that matches her integrity, so that she can start a family, we pray that Brooke and Jackson have a long and healthy marriage full of brats to stomp the floor out of the condo, and that Summer works things out with Oliver. And, God, for me, I just want to be self-sufficient. Jesus, we ask that You take the wheel, because we clearly don't know how to drive and done crashed the Cadillac too many times. Amen."

Opening one eye reluctantly before the other eye, I said, "That was beautiful and strange at the same time."

We set each other's hands free.

Brooke turned her attention to her phone to cut the camera. "Right? I mean, to me, it was a beautiful truth. Thank you, Amber."

"Yeah. Thanks?" I giggled and threw an arm over her shoulder to pull her close. Truth was, it was a very beautiful moment indeed.

"Aaaaand send." Brooke hit a button to complete the task of sending Emily some hope.

Amber wiggled a brow. "Reformed hos know how to pray, too."

Emily

Emily took a cab home to escape the wedding. She'd turned a corner to quickly lose her family and friends. Embarrassed, devastated, and humiliated, she needed some much-needed space. Luckily, she'd found an empty cab as soon as she'd turned the corner. It was like her guardian angel, probably *abuela*, had been looking out for her. With empty pockets, Emily decided to tell the truth at a red light.

"Excuse me."

The man responded with an arched brow in the rearview mirror.

"I'm a bride who was stood up by my fiancé. I don't have any money on me, but I think I have some back at my condo."

The cinnamon-colored man turned around, sliding an arm behind the passenger chair and palming the back of the headrest with an ashy hand.

"No?" Judging by his looks and accent, she guessed he was from some part of Africa, probably Ethiopia. "He don't wanna marry a beautiful woman like you? What's wrong with this man?"

Emily barely cracked a wan smile as she shrugged with one shoulder. Her heart was ruffled by an ache, one that she couldn't rub away.

"I don't know, sir. I don't know what's wrong with me."

He turned back around to drive. "Why do you women do that, uhh? The man does something wrong and women say it's their fault. He smacked the back of his hand into the palm of the other. "No. It's their fault. Listen to me. A million men would be happy to see a beautiful woman like you."

Touched, Emily blinked slowly and smiled more genuinely. "Seeing me and being with me are two different things. But, thank you, sir."

"Listen, I pay for your fare."

She nodded and thanked him again. It was nice to know that there were still some decent men in this world. But wasn't that how they always started? Decent? And then they'd shed one skin of a true color at a time like a snake and before you knew it, you'd be in the bed with a worm.

Staring out the window, Emily didn't feel like crying. She felt like shooting someone, and that someone went by the name of Eric. His brief note only read, *"The wedding is off. I'll never marry you."* Emily knew she was done with this man. There would be no amount of begging that could ever convince her to take him back. The contents of the manila envelope contained a tape recorder that she refused to listen to until she arrived home.

Lost in her thoughts, Emily saw something that compelled her to act drastically.

"Stop! Stop the car, please."

"I'm sorry? Is there a problem?"

With no one behind them, the driver came to a screeching halt. Emily didn't bother to take her eyes off the person who captured her attention as she responded, "Just—just give me a moment, this will be brief." Emily gathered her train and opened the door to let herself out. Feeling like a workout just to break free, she finally managed, and once she stood, she left the door open. Marching in her heels to the homeless woman cocooned in filthy rags stretched out on her side, Emily approached her and said, "Excuse me."

The woman hesitated before moving, almost planting a seed of doubt in Emily's head of her existence. But when she did move, her horrible scent responded to Emily before any other signs or sounds of communication. Lifting to attention, the groggily woman wearily opened her eyelids. Emily took one look at her engagement ring and without hesitation, she slid it down the length of her finger and held the sparkling beauty in front of the woman.

"Here. Take this. Hide it. Go to the local shelter, get cleaned up, and sell it. Get off these streets."

The woman slapped a hand against her mouth, tearing up immediately, almost breathless. "I . . . Thank you, thank you. God bless you."

Placing the ring in the woman's hand, Emily nodded once. "Take care of yourself, because no one else will." She stood carefully then shuffled off quickly and slid back into the cab. Closing the door behind her, she told the driver, "Thank you."

Smiling at her in awe, he said, "You are an exceptional person, and I wish you all the happiness."

Emily smiled grimly, watching the scenery scroll past her again. Truth was, she needed that ring off her finger. The sewer was her top choice, but she knew better than to miss a chance to bless someone else who was down on their luck. If it wasn't that woman, it would've been someone else in need.

Her cellphone rang.

"Hi, *mamá*."

"We are worried. Where did you go, *mi hija*?"

"Home. I'm going home."

"How are you holding up?"

"Too soon, Mom. When do you guys go home? I'm sorry that this was all a waste for you guys."

"No. Don't say that. Any time spent with you is precious. We leave tonight, unless you want us to stay?"

"No, no. Don't be silly. Look. I can use a trip up north. I'll come next month. But I want you guys to come say 'goodbye' to me. Can you just give me two hours?"

"Of course, baby. Of course."

"Thanks, *mamá*."

"Bye."

"Bye."

The cab pulled up to the curb in front of her building. Emily could just visualize her face buried into the white, square pillow in the middle of her bed. No amount of anger could erase the pain.

The man turned around and pointed a finger at her. "You are a treasure, and don't let any man make you feel like anything else."

Flashing the man her teeth this time, Emily bent her head to the side and said, "I won't." She reached forward to pat his shoulder. "Thank you so much, sir. God bless."

"You, too, beautiful." He patted her hand and winked before he watched her climb out of his taxi.

With no key to get in with and just an envelope in her hand, Emily stopped by the security desk to ask for her spare key. After providing them with verbal information to prove her identity, the security guard grabbed her spare key and reminded her to return it that same day.

The ride up the elevator felt like an eternity. Her heart felt like exploding every time she thought of the fact that Eric had made a fool out of her. The chiming doors opened, so Emily stepped out and headed for her door. She entered her apartment, dying to bust out of her dress. The whole thing had turned into a mockery of her judgement. She threw the envelope somewhere to the side. Her fidgety fingers unwrapped the tiny black twist from her ponytail. She shuffled her hair into a mess until it sat on her head like a messy mop.

Emily's chest didn't just heave, it boiled with emotions and threatened to erupt like lava. Finally stripped down to her underwear, Emily felt like she could mourn her loss. Given the amount of anger she felt, that seemed impossible. She didn't know where to start.

The envelope. Emily searched frantically with her eyes for the package. It waited for her on the couch. She tore into the package, took out the recorder, and pressed "play" with trembling fingers.

Eric's voice said, "Emily, Emily, Emily." The punch that she dreaded hit her dead in the solar plexus at the sound of that heartless tone in his voice. She could hear him clap slowly three times. Disgusted, she let the tape recorder fall from her fingers and onto her dining room table as if it were a contagion. She listened to him speak.

Emily folded her arms and stared at the recorder, bracing herself for the worst.

"You set out to ruin me, so I had to return the favor. You ruined my reputation with my long-term employer and coworkers, and so it was only fair that I fed you a spoon of the same soup today. How did it feel? Better yet, how did it taste to have something that pleased you be yanked from underneath your nostrils when you least expected it? Were you humiliated? Do you honestly think that I could love you like you wanted after what you did? You are so insecure that you let a meaningless fling between your best friend and me ruin what we could have had.

"No, Emily. You were such a brat, that you didn't hear me when I told you that I didn't know her. And now look. You end up with nothing, like I did. But I did bounce back. You see, Emily, jobs come and go, and yes, I loved mine. It was a second home. Now love . . . love is a tricky son of a bitch. Who knows if you'll get it again and when it will come. But I suppose there's that second-best scrub Zach. Heads up, don't bother trying to find me, because I'll be on a plane to Tokyo by the time you hear this. That's right, baby. I'm moving all right, just not in with you. And by the way Ems, don't ever mess with a business man's livelihood. So, as I will soon be saying, *sayonara*. Or should I say, checkmate?"

Releasing, "Son of a bitch!" with all her might, Emily felt her soul trying to escape from her skin. With legs as stable as oceanic waves, she fought a collapse in the midst of a spinning head. Lost like a character who'd been picked up from one fairytale book and placed in another, she didn't know where she belonged, even in her own home. But this felt more like being misplaced between the pages of a horror novel.

The walls felt too close, constricting her sense of existence. Struggling to see her value, her self-worth had bottomed out in an instant and tanked like the stock market.

She'd hit her Great Depression. In one day, a man had managed to steal her pride, self-esteem, and joy. Emily felt like she'd become the share that no one would want to buy. Considering what she did to him, Emily could only wonder: *Do I deserve this?*

Eric was the man she wanted. But he moved like a burglar, sneaky and calculating. His soul was dressed for the part: black. If valves were supposed to prevent blood from entering certain places of the heart, then why didn't it work to prohibit bad love from breaking and entering the second most crucial organ?

Emily's head teetered on the brink of exploding. She needed an outlet. Falling on her knees, she had to let it out with a loud roar.

"Arrrrrrrrrrrrrgh!"

Surely, the neighbors could hear her loud and painful cry, but she didn't care. Shaking her fists like a fussy infant, she beat the floor as hard as she could with the sides of her fists. Screaming, she stood and threw all her sofa pillows everywhere. She marched back to the dining room table, stared at it with a heaving chest, and took an elongated arm to swipe all that was on top to the floor: two plates, a drinking glass, and a thermos. Meaningless items. Emily's face burned red. Eric beat her when she thought they were done playing. Everyone was right, and she was wrong. She played the fool and deemed herself one, too.

Boom! Boom! Boom!

Turning to face the sound, she screamed at the door. "Go away!"

Boom! Boom! Boom!

"I said *go away!*" Emily watched the door with both hands at her sides and hair all over her face.

Boom! Boom! Boom!

Emily marched angrily in her underwear across the floor until she reached the front door. She didn't bother with the peephole, nor did she remember that she lacked appropriate clothing for whoever waited on the other side of the door. When she ripped it open in one swift move, she saw a familiar and concerned face staring back at her. He barged in past her.

Looking possessed with a heated expression, she could've ignited a fire with a single look. Emily's voice turned raspier and was full of disdain. "What are you doing here now? I am *not*. In. The. Mood."

Zach spun around to face her. With both hands up, he spoke with caution. "One of your friends called me to check up on you, and judging by the look of things, I'd say they're right. What happened, baby?"

Emily pointed her head to one side. "Do you wanna say that you were right? You were. Now leave," she hissed.

Zach shoved his hands into his pockets. "That ain't gonna happen, Emily."

"You're not gonna get a brownie point in my book for staying either."

Zach cleared his throat. "Okay, I can stay here and be as silent as the painting you have on that wall." He pointed to the wall behind her head.

Emily exhaled while rubbing her temples. She dropped her hands to fold her arms. With a softer tone, she asked, "How does that help you?" The door closed gently behind her.

"It's not about me. It's about being there for a dear friend."

"Why would you wanna help someone who dismissed you?" Emily took a few steps away and turned her back to him. He couldn't see her absently picking at her nails. Her breathing began to fall into a normal pattern, but the burn in her chest refused to subside.

"Because, Emily. I'm cut from a different cloth than that square-headed man you so desperately wanted to be with."

She spun suddenly. "Yeah, I was desperate . . . stupid."

"You live, you learn."

Emily cleared her throat, crossed her arms, and stared at her wooden floor. "You don't wanna judge me?"

"How does that help you?" he asked.

"Touché," she replied dryly without looking at him as she spun around to head toward the kitchen.

Without saying another word, Zach approached the mess on the floor to pick up all the broken pieces.

"You don't have . . . to." Emily craned her neck to see him hard at work in a crouching position. She decided to let him be. Instead, she moved the trash can closer to him. "Thanks, Zach."

He stopped for a moment to look up at her. "You don't have to say anything. But you're welcome."

She nodded and went to pour both of them a glass of red wine. When she returned to the living room, he'd already taken a seat on her sofa. She handed him a glass as she took a seat on the cushion beside him.

"Thank you, sweetie."

Emily nodded. "I know I should be in clothes right now, but I planned on being alone, so this is what you get."

"Am I complaining?" he teased.

"I'm just saying . . ." Emily took a long sip of red wine.

Zach took a sip. "Ahhhh. This is good stuff."

"That's why I own it." Emily repositioned herself into a crisscross position. "So, my friends sent you here?"

"She said her name was Brooke." Zach swiped the corner of his lip with a thumb. "I got over here as soon as I got the call."

"What did she say?"

"Nothing much except that I really needed to get over here and see you, because you needed me. And when she said that you needed me, I didn't think twice."

"That was sweet of her, but she didn't have to." Emily propped her chin with a fist.

"What happened exactly?"

Emily didn't feel like talking about it, but she kind of felt that she needed to. Besides, any man who would come on a whim without any question was worth being humored. She sighed in preparation of reliving the nightmare.

"He stood me up at the chapel after all that talk about us and him moving in and not being able to wait for our wedding day. And then he sent me a memo at the chapel, saying there'd be no wedding. Got home and listened to the tape recorder he left. He cut me down, and he mocked me and this entire relationship."

"Wow, that's cold."

"And, by the way, he wasn't packing to move to my home. The bastard was preparing for his move to Tokyo, right underneath my nose. That's where he was headed during our ceremony."

Interested, Zach leaned forward to comprehend what he believed he'd heard. "What happened afterwards? Everyone went home?"

"No." Emily pouted. "I mean, I don't know. I got the hell up outta there." She started to cry, and her head fell on his shoulder.

"Shhhhhh, shhhhhhhh." He kissed the top of her head.

They sat in peace. Emily appreciated having a shoulder to lean on. Zach obviously enjoyed having Emily so close. She felt like sitting up, but as she straightened, his face was closer to hers than she was aware of. Their eyes made contact. The awkwardness between them grew. Finding a solution to the awkwardness, Zach leaned in to kiss her lips.

Emily saw his lips sitting in front of hers, waiting expectedly for something to transpire from that moment. Even though she felt an attraction to Zach, she couldn't give in to it if she wanted to. "Zach," she said, slowly shaking her head. "I can't."

Obviously disappointed, he removed his arm from around her. "I, uhhh, get it."

"You're mad."

"No, Emily, it's not that I'm mad at your rejection. It's too soon, that's understandable. It was worth a shot in my book. But I just wonder why good women always give jerks the time of day *and* the date of the month."

"Well," Emily tilted her head and raised an eyebrow, "you flashed your penis at me and I let you in my house and back into my life."

"Okay. Point taken. Although I can't help but suspect that my son being in your class made you change your mind."

"Made me? No. Influenced me, yes, but you also apologized, too. Remember?"

Zach smiled. "Will we ever have a shot, Emily?"

"You're asking me this after the day I had?" Emily turned her body to face his.

"Yes." Zach turned his body to face hers. "Technically, no matter how much it hurts today, it's in the past. Why can't you ever clear your head of that man and just look ahead and tell me an answer?"

Emily sighed. She knew exactly what she felt. The fact remained that no one had the spell on her that Eric had possessed. However, given today's circumstances, Eric could no longer be a key player in her life in no capacity. Moving on, she could only be open to love when she felt the same spark that she did when with Eric. Considering Zach, when she was with him, she didn't feel that, just a mere attraction. "I can't see it."

Emily smiled half-heartedly through sealed lips. She placed a hand on his knee.

"As much as I want to love, and as lonely as I may become, getting involved with you would only be self-serving, and I won't do that to you. I definitely don't believe in filler relationships. I, umm, I could never have a man just to have a man."

"You're saying you're prepared to be alone?"

Emily thought about that and squeezed her perfectly defined eyebrows. "You say that like that's a bad thing. Alone is not lonely, you know. I can focus on me and get to know life without Eric or any other romantic obligations."

Zach stood. "Tell me. Is this goodbye?" He slid his hands down denim-clad legs.

Emily licked her bottom lip before standing. "I think so." She smiled at him as she realized that everything was going to be all right. After throwing her temper tantrum, she had time to assess the situation. Eric pulled a slimy move on her, but she only got to see who she'd been dealing with before taking the plunge with him the second time around. Emily extended a hand for him to shake. "Friendship?"

Zach stared at her hand and then looked into her eyes. "I'm not sure if that's possible, but I'm willing to be your lifeline. You need someone to talk to, a shoulder to cry on, someone to fix the maintenance around here, a lawn to mow if you move, then call me. I can be that guy. But I can't be that man you call and chat with or take to the movies and go our separate ways. That would hurt too much."

Emily tucked her hand under a bra strap. She shrugged. "Then what?"

He offered a hand and suggested, "Your lifesaver?" He smiled.

Emily smiled back and accepted his terms and label. "Sure." Shaking his hand, Emily agreed. "Lifesaver." At that moment, a handshake didn't suffice for the man who brought her down from a moment in deep despair. His visit was exactly what she'd needed, and she wouldn't be able to thank Brooke enough for going the extra mile. Emily closed the distance between her and Zach with a hug of deep appreciation and one last kiss on the lips and said, *"Thank you, Lifesaver."*

S*ummer*

Amber and I stepped off the elevator after riding up silently, despite the fact that we'd shared multiple conversations in the car during our ride home together. I saw my mom dressed in blue jeans and a checkered button-up shirt holding Autumn close to her bosom as she sat on the sofa.

"She finally went to sleep. Poor thing. I've never seen her this gassy or fussy."

I felt gloomy. I was confident that it reflected in my demeanor, too.

Nodding, I replied, "Her getting relief is good news. Best I've heard all day."

Amber stood beside me with folded arms.

My mom stood and skirted around the coffee table. "Why? Did something happen?"

Amber opened her arms. "I can place her in the crib, so you guys can talk."

My mom's chin hit her chest as she struggled to get a good look at Autumn. "O-okay. Let's just keep from waking her." She handed Autumn to Amber, and after the successful transfer of my baby, Amber left the room.

My mom threw her hands against her hips and asked, "Now tell me. What happened?"

I tossed my purse onto the bar. "Nothing." My hands smacked the sides of my legs. "Absolutely nothing."

"What? Summer, what do you mean?" She gripped Autumn's burping cloth in one hand.

"That bastard left her at the altar. He backed out. She bailed, too, after her announcement that there'd be no wedding."

My mom's jaw dropped with both hands against the sides of her face. "Oh, no. That's horrible. That poor girl. How is she?"

"We don't know too much. Brooke, Amber, and me recorded us praying and sent it to her."

Tilting her head with a look of pity, my mom said, "Aww, that was nice of you guys. I hope she's all right. Poor thing. You know, if he didn't wanna get married, why play games? Why didn't he just say something?"

"He wanted to be cruel? I don't know. Anyway, we'll check in with her later. For now, I gotta go change."

"Sure." My mom stepped to the side.

Once I walked past her, I stopped and turned. "Mom?"

She spun with raised brows. "Mm?"

"Do you think Autumn is crying because she knows things aren't right and she misses Oliver?"

Pondering the question first, she stared off and then looked at me. She threw the burping cloth on the back of the sofa. "Possibly. But, Summer? What are you doing? What do you want? That man ain't gonna live in limbo forever, especially with you living in his home while making enough money to move out now."

"You're right."

"Yes. I think she misses him." My mom spun around and headed for the kitchen.

"What about what he did?"

Wiping down the countertop with a rag, my mom didn't hesitate to respond. "Did he overstep? Perhaps. Was he just trying to make things right for the woman he loves? Admirable. Could he of done things differently? I wish. The important thing to ask is: Can you live with it, and does he understand and respect your feelings in all of this?"

"What should I do?"

My mom shook her head and threw the rag into the sink. "No ma'am. You are an adult, and this is your deal. I'm not in that relationship. This is why I don't do those things. But I wish you all the best." She turned around and reached for the fridge.

Sighing, I headed for our bedroom. My and Oliver's room. I missed him. I did. He'd texted me with an apology after the wedding for not showing up due to our rift. I'd told him, '*neither did Eric.*'

Sitting on the bed, I peeled out of my gown one arm at a time. Looking around the room, some of his belongings caught my eye. His shoes, his bottles of cologne, his shirts hanging in the closet . . .

I had a man who wanted to be here. Emily didn't have that. Oliver was crazy about me, and whenever he could, he'd give me the world before I could ask for it. Despite my current level of distress, the memory of him escorting me to the garage when I'd gone into labor to help me into my new truck put a smile across my face. He thought ahead, showing me just how unprepared I was with the Corvette. If relationships came with a ranking of customer service, I'd have to rank his at the highest level possible.

Standing to step out of the dress, I held it up and ironed it against the bed with my hand before leaving it behind to find a hanger. Yanking its designated hanger out of the closet, I anchored it inside the dress and then hung it up. Walking around the walk-in closet for a pair of jeans and a basic blouse, I donned the two garments, slipped into ballerina flats, and made my way to Autumn's room when I heard her crying.

Amber shrugged as she rocked the crib with a hand. "Girl, I don't know what I did wrong."

"It's not you." I lifted my daughter from the crib and held her close. Patting her on the back, the pressure from being a single mother hit me. She knew of Oliver, and he had a way with her whenever she cried more than usual. He'd figured that side of her out before I had a chance to experience it. He knew he had a more flexible schedule than mine and would answer her most demanding calls.

My mom came hurrying into the room. "Everything good?"

Tears hit my eyes. "No, it's not. I miss him. I miss him, Mom."

"Think you got your answer."

Amber rubbed my back. "I'm sorry."

"I need fresh air, and she needs diapers. I'll be back."

Moving past my mom, I headed to the front door with Autumn, yanking my purse off the bar counter without breaking stride. Driving further than necessary, I needed a longer ride. Instead of going to the same Whole Foods in my neighborhood, I decided to ride into Alexandria to visit the one on Duke Street. Besides, Autumn needed the car ride. She was probably tired of being indoors.

About twenty minutes and several pop songs later, I entered the parking garage and found a space. Removing my daughter from her car seat, I secured her into the baby carrier, facing my chest, and headed indoors.

Grabbing a cart, I headed immediately for the aisle of baby contents, loading up on diapers, creams, and lotions.

"This place is so expensive, Autumn. Mommy's lucky to have this job." I kissed the top of her head. "You're so worth it, baby." I would've never believed anyone if they were to tell me that I'd be happy as a mother. Mothers were right: This was the best job in the world.

"Produce, Autumn, we need produce." Awake and making her usual happy noises, Autumn observed her surroundings based on the immediate content in front of her. Making my way back to the front of the store, I scanned the apples with an extended neck and decided that it'd been a while since I'd had one.

Reaching for a bag, another hand covered mine. It belonged to a woman with a few subtle age spots. Immediately, her jewelry told me that any of her pieces could cover the costs of several trips to Whole Foods. Looking up to see who wouldn't move her hand, I quickly yanked mine back.

"Fran." I held my breath as my heart skipped a beat. Even without being under her thumb, she still managed to scare the shit out of me.

"Pretty baby." Fran spoke with a harsh tone and a tight mouth.

I finally exhaled through my lips. "Uh—yeah, thanks. Thank you. What are you doing here?"

She raised a hand in the air. "As I recall, this is Alexandria. I live here, you don't. Looks like I should be asking you." Fran tore a plastic bag from the spindle. When she opened it, she carefully examined one apple at a time before sliding them into her bag.

"I drove here," I replied matter-of-factly while calmly ripping a bag from the spindle for my two apples. I tried my best not to let her see that she could still get to me.

"Well I didn't think you hiked it." She never did turn to look at me again. Why should she? Hiring me proved to be more trouble than what I was worth.

"Listen, Fran. I need to talk to you."

"Why?"

"I know what Oliver did, and I don't approve."

Freezing for a second, Fran looked at me long enough to say, "Well, of course you do. It got you what you wanted, didn't it?"

"No—I mean, yes, I did get a job, but this isn't how I pictured going about it to get it. And, how did you hook this up—this Simon Jack thing?"

She sighed. "I'll indulge you to ease your tiny brain. Let's just say that Simon is a frenemy whose company is my toughest competitor. He would take my whole staff if he could. Knowing that Simon was in earshot, I dropped your name at the Annual Recruiter's Banquet to a friend and made it sound like you were the one to watch. I saw him salivating when he didn't think I noticed. Took the opportunity to set your name straight with the same people who I trashed it to. When he called me for a recommendation, I could hear his pride over the phone. I gave a stellar review and made it sound like he was lucky to get you. He told me that you two did business at the top of the year. I was surprised. How he found you, I don't know. But headhunters are sharks who can find a way to you, one way or another."

I shook my head. "You Washingtonians. So calculating."

"Well get used to it. It's all about power around here. And who cares? Your name is clear, you got a job." Fran's finger swiped the base of the bag to make it spin before tying it. "Besides, it's all part of the game."

Shaking my head, I replied, "No, no it's not. Oliver and I are taking space because of this crap. I was just a chess piece in all of this."

"And did you keep the job?"

"I need to make a living."

Fran placed her bag of apples into her cart and then turned to me to say, "Smart choice, dumb girl."

Perplexed, I crinkled my brows at her. "Excuse me?"

Given the fact that I was a few inches taller than her, I shouldn't have noticed that she turned her nose up at me.

Fran reached for another plastic bag, separating it from the spindle along the perforated line. Without regards for my feelings, she mouthed, "You're dumb," in a condescending tone.

"Okay, well I see you're still as mean as ever."

Fran reached for the pears stacked beside the apples. I almost doubted that she wanted the pears, and nearly suspected that she just didn't want to stray too far from me. Regardless, she reached for the fruit, scrutinizing them one by one thoroughly.

"Summer, what do you want me to say? Congratulations for acting like an idiot? Would you rather want a man like Ruben, all talk and no action? My little Latin firecracker knew all the right things to say but couldn't back his words up if they were in a truck."

It didn't feel right to speak ill of the deceased, especially since he could never defend himself again and his daughter was in earshot.

"Well, what Oliver did was disgusting. I don't condone that. Okay, he has your pictures."

Fran shrugged casually. "And? How did I look?"

Rolling my eyes, I couldn't understand how she could be so insouciant about this whole thing, while taking the side of the one who blackmailed her.

I lowered my speaking tone. "Fran, why aren't you taking this more seriously? The man has pictures of you posing buck naked."

Grinning with a shrug, she replied, "Look, do I like it? Of course not. But he came to win, and I like that. I never had that with Ruben. Never. As much as I didn't like the fact that Ruben put those pictures in his hands, at least I saw loyalty in Oliver. Look what Ruben did. He helped someone else win against his own wife." She secured the bag of pears with a tie and placed them into her cart.

"But, Fran, you went after Ruben and me. What did you expect him to feel like?"

Annoyed, she replied, "Be a victim or a fighter, but pick a side, Summer. So, it's okay for Ruben to fight, but not you, not Oliver?" Fran walked to the other side of the fruit bin to look for more fruit. "Maybe you should ask yourself that. Summer, you have so much to learn. You think I sabotaged you and Ruben solely out of revenge? No. You guys wanted to play with the big dogs, so I wanted to remind you guys that I'm one of the key owners of this area. You pissed on my turf, now you gotta wipe it up. You and Ruben thought you guys were smarter than me, but you know who played a better game of chess than you and Ruben? Oliver. At least he fought, and it wasn't really his battle." Batting her eyes involuntarily out of anger, she pointed a finger at me. "*He* was looking out for your well-being as a single mother. What did you do, Summer? You rolled over."

I scoffed.

"You know, it's funny that you're holding Ruben's baby, my former and late husband, but you ended up with another man anyway. So, all that home-wrecking was for what?"

Fran's emotional abuse had pissed me way the hell off, especially after seeing enough meanness for one day. Upset, I blurted hastily without thinking, "Well it's not like I can marry a man who is no longer alive now, can I?"

I stung Fran without really meaning to. It'd become obvious, because she took the plastic bag in her hand and harshly flagged it once in the air to snap it open and started to rapidly load it with oranges. With the apples in hand, I abandoned my purse and shopping cart to skirt around my fruit bin to come face to face with her.

"No, wait Fran. I'm so sorry."

"*Move* out of my way, Summer."

"It's just that I didn't mean it that way." The truth was, I had a hard time forgiving myself for sleeping with a married man.

"You have a beautiful baby." She grinned slowly with perverse pride. "It's a shame that she has a whore for a mom who doesn't know how to think for herself."

Startled, I stood there, letting her words float inside my ears. This lady called me a brainless whore to my face, and there really wasn't a way to defend myself. Perhaps she was right. Any woman who slept with a married man deserved such reviews. And this lady had fun reviewing me negatively until the knife couldn't twist any harder. Pleased, Fran could see the misery on my face that she issued.

"That's not true," I protested. "I'm not a slut."

"Oh, *really*? Well, I don't know what you call a woman who sleeps with her boss' husband over and over even when she knows the boss likes her."

"Careful, Fran. We wouldn't want the nation's capital to see you in all your glory."

Fran's grin tightened into an upset pout. "You—"

Done with Fran and not caring to face her any longer, I felt my blood boil and heart punch my chest.

With my angry eyes burning into hers, I threw the plastic bag and apples into the fruit bin behind her and then headed back to my cart to snatch up my purse. I gave her one last look, shaking my head at her concerned expression and left the store with something that I hadn't walked in with: satisfaction.

After securing Autumn in the Suburban, I slid into the driver seat with shaky hands. Anger and bad nerves disrupted any chance of me having a calm demeanor. Fran caused the anger, but the idea of contacting Oliver made me nervous, but it was time.

How will he take me?

Will he play hard to get?

I tapped his name on my phone screen and waited for him to pick up. His voice carried out through the car's phone system.

"Hello?"

Grrr. Why didn't he call me, baby?

Autumn reacted with a noise at the sound of his voice. Taking a quick peek into the rearview mirror, I saw a quick toothless smile in the mirror in front of her.

"Oliver, hey. How are you?"

"I'm good, Summer. You?"

Okay, formal but friendly. He did ask how I'm doing.

"Umm. I've been better. Listen. Can I see you?"

"Everything okay?"

There's the concern in his voice. He still cares. A silent exhale relaxed my chest.

"N-no. It really isn't. This isn't working. Can you come home so we can talk about everything face to face?"

"I can do that. Be home in ten. Lemme tell Trina to take over. Bye."

He hung up before I had a chance to respond. Slapping my forehead with my hand, it occurred to me that he probably thought that me admitting that our arrangement wasn't working meant that I wanted out. Shoot. No wonder he sounded so short toward the end. Oh well. In ten minutes, he'd know better.

Once the entrance to our building came into view, I turned the truck into the property and eased into the garage to find our designated spot.

The diapers! My shoulders collapsed before I cut the engine. "Screw it." Dialing Oliver again, when he picked up I asked, "Hey, I'm so sorry, but could you please bring Autumn back some diapers?"

"Huh?"

Irritated, my face crunched. "Diapers, baby. She needs diapers. We ran out, and I got so distracted I forgot to buy her some."

"No, wait. That ain't possible, Summer. Unless she's been peeing and shitting up a storm, there should be a new box in the closet beside the elevator. You know, in the same space where I used to keep my motorcycle helmet."

"Wait. When did you buy them?"

"Went to Cosco a few days ago and dropped them off when you were at the wedding. Didn't want the whole world to fall on your shoulders just because I'm gone and you're making it work with a full-time job and baby. Anyway, I took inventory of household items and put the box in that closet. Amber can find soap there, too." I closed my eyes and twisted my lips to one side of my face. Wow. I was a jerk. "I'll see you when you get here. Thank you, Oliver."

Sounding defeated, he replied, "You're welcome, Summer."

I found my mom on the sofa. "Hey. You didn't tell me Oliver stopped by this morning to drop off diapers."

Perplexed, she asked, "When?" Then her face settled back to her normal expression. "Ohhh. I did take Autumn for a brief walk this morning."

"Ohhh. Hey, can you watch her for a moment? Oliver's coming to talk."

"Of course."

I waited for Oliver in my room. I paced the floor so much, that a trail of nervous footprints imprinted the carpet. Who knew how many times I wrenched my hands.

Minutes later, the sound of the knob turning stole my attention from my abyss of dark thoughts. Yanking my head in the direction of the bedroom door, Oliver came through and greeted me by jerking his chin in my direction. He closed the door behind him.

Immediately, I slammed into his body and wrapped my arms around his toned physique. "Oliver." My cheek pressed into his chest. But I didn't feel anything around me, just a few hand pats against my back. What the hell?

Drawing back with crinkled brows, I looked up at him. He peered down at me.

"What's this about, Summer?"

"Nothing. I . . . I mean, us. We need to talk."

"I agree. I can't go on like this." He walked away from me to sit at the edge of his bed. He interlaced his fingers and stared at me with a tilted head. "What's up?"

"Nothing." Man, why did I feel so nervous? "I think that we need to talk about the next step."

"Which is?"

Hmm. He seemed so ready for anything. *Is he over me? Has this time away from me backfired? Maybe he realized that I'm just too much. Maybe he's tired of fighting.*

"Don't you think that it's time you move back in? Autumn misses you." I sat beside him and turned to look at his profile. "*I* miss you."

His jaw clenched. One knee shook. I placed a hand on it to stop his nervous energy. He stopped so I took my hand back.

"Come home?"

"Why?"

He wouldn't look at me. This man was tired. "You don't wanna be with us?" A sour bomb went off in my throat at the thought of losing him. How ironic. Now that I was certain that we should be together, he appeared to have placed his pom-poms down on the side of the track that would lead back to us.

Eyeing me with narrowed eyes, he asked, "Are you crazy, Summer? I've only wanted to be with you. But . . ."

"But, what, baby?" I placed a hand on his leg. "You've given up?"

He reacted with a bitter, "Tuh. Summer, I don't know what to tell you. I love you, but this year has been more difficult than it shoulda been. My heart is mangled. I'm getting tired of going up and down. I ain't got no more pep talks to give myself."

I nodded without saying a word, looking straight.

"I came home and realized that I was sad and wiped out. That I didn't wanna throw us away. Being single can be a beautiful thing, Oliver, but only if that's what someone wants." I placed my hand over his and grabbed it. "That's not what I want. You know, looking at Eric's ugly behavior made me wonder if I'm playing on a team similar to his. Emily's feelings are real, baby. Yours are real, too. And here I am, tugging you around like time is nothing, taking my time while you and I try to function with achy hearts. I learned from this, and I think that you have, too. Come home."

Oliver stared at our joint hands. A slow grin rolled over his face. He looked up at me and said, "It feels right."

"Is that a yes?" He had to have seen the hope glimmer in my eyes.

"I think that we're gonna be good this time around. No more misbehaving—both of us." He popped the tip of my nose with his finger. "But, listen."

I straightened my shoulders at attention.

"We need transparency. Agree?"

He slid his hand from under mine to offer me a handshake.

Smirking at him, I slid my hand into his and gripped it in agreement. "Agree. Open and honest for now on."

"Cool."

"Speaking of honesty, guess who I ran into?"

"Agnes?"

I slapped his arm. "Shut up, boy." My eyes popped. "Basically. Yeah, Fran."

Oliver's eyelids drooped. "*Why*? She's like an uncrushable bug."

"That I wanna step on with the point of my heel." I told him the whole story, verbatim.

"Did she really talk to you like that?"

"She did," I replied casually. "But let's not pay her any attention. Let her roast in peace. She needs to be *behind* us."

"Boy, as much as I hated Ruben, I'm starting to think the wrong spouse died."

"*Oliver?*" My hands cupped my mouth then fell to my lap. "No. No more ugliness. This world has enough of it."

"Baby, you right, you right. Besides, we got each other, and she's got misery."

"Score settled."

8: guest who's coming to dinner

Brooke

Feeling emotional, Brooke looked around the room with glassy eyes as she sat shoulder to shoulder with her fiancé at a long table. They were waiting for some of the other guests to arrive at their National Harbor dinner party overlooking the waterfront. They had reserved the private dining area of an upscale steak and seafood restaurant. Many of their guests were having a blast dancing to the loud music under crazy ambient lights that beamed around the room.

"Where's Summer?" Brooke asked, checking her watch. She took her time devouring her steak despite her relentless hunger after an intense day of hammering out wedding details with Haysia.

"Oh," Amber replied. "Work. She texted me saying that she should be here any moment."

"Gotcha."

Amber sipped her champagne. Emily sat beside Amber and continued her story, until Amber interrupted. "But wait. How did Brooke get his number?"

Brooke heard her name from across the table. "Who?"

"Zach," Amber replied.

"White pages online. Started with Emily's street name, and I knew his last name," she answered with a wink.

Jackson heard and added, "This lady can do everything, Amber. Thought you knew." He placed a hand over Brooke's and tightened his grip.

"You guys are amazing," Emily told them. They flashed a look of appreciation that told Emily she made their hearts melt.

"I'm serious," she proclaimed. "I could only hope to find a love like yours."

"You're amazing," Jackson assured her. "Emily, you're a beautiful woman full of grace. You guard that heart for the most worth it."

Emily nodded her head with a wrinkled forehead, taking his words to heart. "Thank you, Jackson. I will . . . I will. But you know who really takes care of me when Eric shatters my world?"

"Who?" he asked. "I may have an idea."

With a quivering voice and teary eyes, Emily pointed to her dear friend with a flick of her index finger. "Her."

Brooke placed a hand over her heart. "*Me?*"

"You got it." Amber pointed back at her.

"Seriously, Brooke. You read all my needs that day when I could barely think or stand straight. I have to thank you."

"Girl, come here." Amber pushed Emily's head on her shoulder and signaled the passing server. "What are those shots?"

"Patron," the server answered.

"Hand 'em over," Amber demanded. She circled a hand to include her friends. "We all gon' need one, sir."

Smiling, the server fulfilled Amber's request before moving on.

Brooke dabbed her eyes with a tissue. "You guys make me sick. So much for staying pretty before the big speech."

Jackson yanked her close to him and placed a kiss on her forehead. "It'll be okay." Brooke knew that he didn't have an ounce of real compassion about the matter, so she shot him a mock evil glance.

Jackson killed his shot in one gulp. Pinching his eyes shut, he hollered, "Whoooooo!"

Everyone laughed. His brave act left Brooke surprised since he wasn't known to be a drinker.

Jackson shook his head. "Hey, ummm, Emily. I have a friend I can hook you up with. He's successful, not a bad-looking guy, and uhh, yeah, I mean, his personality is aight.

You interested?" He raised a dark brow at her. "He's single and looking."

Emily stuck her tongue out and sampled the Patron with the tip of her tongue. "Ew!"

"Don't be a baby," Amber encouraged with her shot glass in one hand. "Take it to the head." Amber finished her portion in one gulp as well. "Whew!" she screamed over the loud dance music.

Brooke giggled and Jackson high-fived her while Emily stared at her unimpressed with a pinched nose.

Emily looked up at Jackson and answered, "Mmm, thanks, Jackson. I appreciate it. I really do, but it's just that—"

"Too soon?" he guessed with a smile.

"Yeah," she confirmed. "Too soon. And I kind of want to court Emily right now and get to know her all over again. I lost myself *too* much along the way."

"I can respect that." Jackson raised his glass again. "Cheers." He lifted his original glass of wine.

"Brooke!" Amber said. "Get on with it."

"I'm not so good at this stuff. Besides," she took sideway glances around the room, "I have guests."

"You need it to loosen up," Amber insisted. "They'll understand."

"We'll see." Brooke played with the glass. She felt so happy inside to know that all of her dreams would be coming true tomorrow after walking down the aisle with Jackson. She felt like the luckiest girl alive. She couldn't wait to escape to Bora Bora with him.

"Hey, you."

She turned to see her fiancé staring at her with intense eyes; she felt shy. "Hi, baby," she said softly. Without warning, he placed a hand on the other side of her face to secure her lips to his. It felt so sexy.

"Woooo," Amber cheered.

"Who are they?" Emily asked.

Brooke broke free of Jackson's kiss to see who Emily was referring to.

"Who?" Before she could wait for a response, she got her answer. There they stood with deer-caught-in-the-headlight eyes. Jackson continued to place kisses on her chin and neck. "Baby, baby, look."

Like lost and shy guests, Jacqueline stood behind her leopard-print hobo bag and matching leggings with an oversized shawl. Beside her stood Brooke's cousin, Veronique, a far cry in demeanor from her wedding day. Instead of being the cheerful girl that she remembered, her cousin stood bashfully, licking her lips as she combed stray golden-blonde strands of her hair over her ears with her fingers. Horrified, Brooke mentally noted that none of them were dressed for her formal occasion. Veronique barely knocked an inch above her mother in the fashion department with her black flats and red pleated skirt. Brooke refused to size up her cousin's upper half. She didn't expect that anything on top would counter the bottom. Her mother emerged from behind them clutching her generic floral bag by its wooden handles for dear life. She wore her proudful smile better than she did her clothes. Bending her head downward, Brooke shaded her eyes with a palm. She hadn't a clue as to why her mother thought it would be okay to come to a dinner party wearing a floral skirt to her ankles over flats with a white cotton shirt. *Why?* Brooke cried to herself. Why?

"Your folks arrived after all," Jackson announced with glee.

Brooke's head snapped up. "What do you mean 'after all?'"

"Grey Goose," the server announced with the second round of shots.

"Well, I invited them here. It's *your* family and my party, too."

Astonished, Brooke didn't know if betrayal was the only thing she felt coursing through her soul. "Jackson," she said through gritted teeth, her eyes glazing with anger. "You said that you would let me decide what to do with them and whatever I decided, you would support. *Remember*? What happened?"

"Uh-oh!" Amber howled.

"Quiet, Amber," Brooke said, quickly glancing at her. Facing Jackson again, she asked, "Well?"

Amused by her irritation, he smiled back at her with dreamy eyes. Clearly, the alcohol had him slightly subdued. Brooke had a feeling she wasn't going to get anywhere with him. "Baby, relax. What's one party, huh? Then after tonight," he held up a hand, "you got my word, ma, that if you don't wanna see them anymore, then I won't bother. Ever."

"You know what you can do with your word, don't you?" she hissed before she downed a quick, long swallow of her Patron. The Patron didn't have anything on her anger, so she barely felt the sting in her throat. Brooke decided to top off the rest.

"All right!" Amber cheered. She hit Emily on the arm with the back of her hand. "Get to it."

Emily moaned and took a big chug with the support of Jackson and Amber hooting. "Yuck!" Brooke examined her friend and realized that Emily's sinuses must have burned because, she held her nose and had teary eyes. "I hate you, suckas." Amber caressed her friend's back to soothe her. "Get off me," Emily playfully demanded. "Where's that nasty Grey Goose?"

Amber and Jackson cheered one last time.

Emily pointed a finger at them. "I refuse to think about Eric tonight!"

Brooke took one last furtive glance at her family who had their attention on the host. "Argh! I don't know why you invited them," she told Jackson feistily. Brooke threw her napkin down on her plate. Rising, she turned to him and added, "*You know they can't dress.*"

Brooke sashayed toward her guests in her strapless feather dress.

The host stepped to the side. "Oh, Ms. Brazile, they're with you?"

"Hi, Brooke!" they greeted in unison.

She swiped her hand once through the air. "Hey, guys." Brooke glanced at his nametag. "Uhh, yeah, Luc. Wouldn't seem like it, huh?" It didn't occur to her that her family may have heard her comment.

Luc bowed before heading back behind his podium. "Very well, then."

Brooke flashed an uneasy toothless smile. "Well." She mashed her hands together uneasily as she tried to figure out what to do with them.

"Thanks for coming." She pointed a thumb over her shoulder. "Yeah, so Jackson told me he invited you to come, so you should eat." She didn't want to sound so contrived because they appeared hopeful and grateful to be there, especially Veronique. Her big brown eyes shined full of excitement. Brooke was surprised at the resemblance they shared around the eyes. She couldn't believe she hadn't noticed it before now.

"I like your dress! Silver looks good on you," her cousin complimented.

"Thank you, but it's uhhh, actually platinum."

Her cousin looked confused.

Brooke pointed a finger upward. "The color." Brooke's gaze swept the floor as she cleared her throat and swiped the bouncy curls behind her ear.

Veronique replied with an, "Ohhhh, I see," and gave Brooke a big grin.

"Wanna eat, guys?" Brooke tried again. She just wanted them to sit so she could be seen away from them.

"What do we have here?" Jackson popped up by her side and dished out hugs to each family member.

Brooke wished that he hadn't done that, because now she worried that she might've come across as frigid.

"This is my cousin, Veronique," Brooke said, making awkward eye contact with her.

Obviously thrown off by his handsomeness, Veronique's wide eyes studied his face. "So nice to meet you," she said.

To let her cousin know that she saw the attraction, though she found herself rather humored, Brooke asked Veronique, "So, where's your husband?"

"He's had a long day and needed to sleep." Veronique managed to turn her attention to Brooke. She figured that reminding her that she had a husband would sober her right up.

"That's too bad," Brooke said.

Veronique smiled. "But he sends his best."

She nodded. Brooke was unprepared to address the elephant in the room, and it happened to be her mom more than anything or anyone else.

"Hi, Lilly." Brooke had to admit, their presence felt like a double-edge sword. On one hand, it meant a little bit to have at least one next of kin on her behalf finally show up, especially since Jackson's family crowded the room all over the dance floor.

"Good to see you," her mother told her in a loud whisper. Brooke appreciated her mother not being pushy about connecting with her. She never tried to hug or touch Brooke, nor did she try to make any additional contact via phone or in person. The biggest thing she currently wished for was the opportunity to whisk them away at a fashion boutique before letting them officially enter. However, she had something on her chest that she needed to get off.

"Jacqueline, can I talk to you for a moment?"

"Sure."

Brooke turned to Jackson. "Can you show them in?"

He nodded. "Of course."

Nipping at her fingers as she struggled to stare into Jacqueline's eyes, she told her aunt, "We had some semblance of a relationship before all of this transpired. It wasn't what I thought it was, but at least I felt like it came from an honest place, that's all." Jacqueline reached to grab her niece's hand, but Brooke moved away. "I'm sorry," she told her somewhat shyly. Besides, she didn't like to be touched by people that much, considering that she didn't experience it much as a kid.

"No, please don't," Jacqueline told her. "We burned you rather badly." Jacqueline twisted her hands nervously. "Listen, we're not here to start anything or to make you feel uncomfortable. But, as you recall, you made a great point the last time we saw you."

"What's that?"

"You never had family witness the important events in life, Brooke. Your high school and college graduation, your business opening. Honey, we can't get any of these things back, but now, we wanted to change history, if that's okay with you."

Brooke waited before responding. Her heart began to ache. She figured that if all of her friends could change, then maybe not all hope was lost on her. "It is. I won't forget that." Tears started to flood her eyes uncontrollably.

"When Jackson broke my heart, you were there to help sweep up the pieces. You were the closest thing I had to a mother." She had to cover her face, not because she was partially embarrassed by her breakdown, but because she didn't know how long it would take to recover. Jacqueline came in to hug her, but she stepped back. "No, don't touch," Brooke requested with a quivery voice. When she looked up, she saw the face of an aunt staring back who wanted to share the pain. "Oh, hell," Brooke caved. She went in on Jacqueline and allowed herself to cry on her shoulder. Lost in her own world, Brooke embraced Jacqueline, and the idea of a family outside of Jackson, for the first time in her life.

Jackson nibbled Brooke's ear as they slow danced. He stared down at her, holding her hand against his chest. "Are you mad at me?"

"No." Brooke flashed her teeth at him. "I can't be. It feels good to have my family here. I like that you care, and that you're interested. Jackson, you always seem to know what I want before I do." She rested her head against his chest.

"You know, all this dancing is making me hungry."

"Again?" Yanking her head away from him in surprise, Brooke reminded him, "You know we just ate?"

Shooting his eyes around the room first, Jackson leaned down to inform her, "*Not that kind,* Brooke . . . damn." He squeezed her arms. "I'm ready to *eat.*"

Brooke studied him with narrowed eyes. "O-ohhhhh!" Brooke blushed deeply, grateful that her natural complexion hid it perfectly.

"Exactly." Jackson didn't wait for her to resist or express any doubt. He grabbed her by the hand and covertly took her to a corner in the back of the building away from the party room. "Shhh, baby."

Brooke salivated at the idea of having him anytime anyplace. Jackson picked her up from under her arms and positioned her on an empty table. "Jackson," she whispered. "We can rent a room upstairs," she suggested while tapping his shoulders.

"Well, duh," he replied with huge eyes. "But I'm not looking for an obvious way out."

Jackson pushed Brooke's lengthy dress up until it gathered at her upper thighs. Grabbing her by the outer thighs, he yanked her into him without taking his eyes off her. She lifted one butt cheek up at a time to facilitate his effort to remove her underwear. They spoke through their gaze. His told her that if his eyes could devour her, she'd be toast. Hers told him, that she trusted him and could never reject the magnetic pull between them.

Jackson removed her underwear down her legs until he could hold them in his hands. He closed his eyes and smelled the bunched material. "Ummmm. Smells like Brooke." Jackson opened his eyes to a woman biting down on the tip of her index finger wearing a naughty grin. Placing the crotch of the underwear between his teeth, he pushed her legs open and inserted a finger inside of her.

Using his free hand to remove her panties from his mouth, Jackson placed them inside his pants pocket while working her pleasure point with the other hand.

Closing her eyes, Brooke felt her heartbeat pick up, as expressed through her breathing. Without being too loud, she cried, "*Yeah*, daddy. *Yeah*."

"Don't take your eyes off me," he ordered without blinking.

Opening her eyes, his laser stare beamed through her soul, making her feel as bashful as their first kiss. Brooke didn't realize how intoxicating the challenge would be until she was in the thick of it. It stripped her down in a way that going naked couldn't compare. It connected them on a different level now that he was seeing her bare soul for the first time.

"I wanna see what I do to you."

Brooke's mouth twisted as she tried to contain her agony. Caught up in sweet torment, she couldn't express herself as loudly and freely as she normally would behind closed doors. Brooke placed her hands on each shoulder, caressing the sides of his neck, intertwining her hands behind his head, tickling his skin with her red-painted nails.

"You makin' my dick swell, you know that?" Jackson licked his lips, and Brooke wanted to kiss him for that.

When she leaned in, Jackson eased back. "Don't do that. No. I wanna watch you."

Brooke's parted lips and droopy eyelids transmitted a plea to be saved from enforced composure. Why couldn't he just let her do things her way? But when it came to Jackson and his bossy bedside manner, Brooke didn't mind.

Jackson eased two fingers back and forth inside of her. "Yeah, you're so tight, so wet. Mmmmmm, baby. That's it." As Brooke moved her hips to his pace, he said, "Yeah, find my rhythm, baby. Ahhh."

Brooke wanted to bite his juicy, pink, full lips. Restricting her from doing so was like taking all the candy in the world from children. How cruel. She could only continuously caress his neck and shoulders.

Leaning forward toward her lips, Jackson rubbed her clitoris in a circular motion with his thumb. "I wanna bust inside of you. You know that, mamma? I wanna take you over and over until I'm lost inside your pussy."

That! That alone almost made her pussy tingle and pop. This is why she would never want or need another man. Her cheeks tickled with heat, but she had to say something to let him know that he was The Man.

But she could barely speak. His skilled fingers, intense eye contact, and vocalization of desire sent Brooke over the edge. Resting one hand against the table while keeping the other one extended and on his shoulder, Brooke slid her hips rapidly back and forth with pinched eyes and a gaped mouth.

"Look at me."

"I can't. I can't. It feels too good."

"Do you want the dick or the tongue?"

Without breaking stride on both sides, they continued to move in the direction of immediate gratification without showing any signs of slowing down.

"Any of you. Please. I. Want. You."

He grabbed her by the face and demanded, "Look at me. My dick or my tongue. Talk to me."

Barely opening her eyes, she cried, "I . . . can't."

She loved how he was always on top of things when it came to her. He knew that she was on the brink of coming. He knew that she would love to come on his tongue or cock. Without wasting time, he removed his fingers and bent over to throw one leg over his shoulder while hugging her body with his other arm leaving no space between them. Ripping her legs apart like they were on a timed schedule, he dove between her lips, licking up her sweet nectar without missing all the required spots.

Pleasing Brooke with his tongue, her posture snapped loose. Her head rolled back, and her eyes strained to see upward.

"Jackson, Jackson, Jackson," she chanted under her breath. She placed a hand gingerly on his low-cut head and squeezed it with her thighs. "Ohhhhh."

Jackson continued with an, "Mmmmmm," as he worked to please his fiancé.

"Oh! Oh! Oh! Oh! Oh!" She beat the wall behind her head. Reaching her climax, she collapsed and opened her eyes to see a blurry Jackson coming up for air.

Swiping his mouth with the back of his hand, Jackson staggered a little as he drew his body to hers. She felt his budge against her stomach.

Brooke's fine motor skills suffered slightly at the hands of her powerful orgasm. It was too soon to try any movements, but she wanted to please her man.

"Come here, baby."

He grabbed her by the hand to help her off the table. Loosening his Versace belt, Brooke had access to his button and zipper. Getting on her knees, she set his penis free knowing that it was going into her mouth. But then she had a thought. She was submissive to his demands, now it was his turn.

"Look at me."

Grinning, Jackson said, "I got this."

"That's what they all say." Biting her lower lip, Brooke took him into both of her hands and stroked his shaft while playing with his sack. Looking up at him with a loving look, she said, "Mmmm. So long, thick, and hard. This is my Jackson."

He placed a fist into his mouth as he struggled to keep his eyes open. He used his other hand to play with one of her breasts.

"Yeah, baby. This is one of the reasons why you got that ring."

"Yeah?" she teased. "You know I want this long and thick cock." Brooke played with his head using her thumb.

Peering down at her, he nodded with a strained expression.

"You know I want this loooong, thick muscle in my pussy every night, Jackson? Huh? You want it wet? Nice and tight?"

He licked his lips. "Girl you know you gettin' away with murder talking all that trash. Wait till we get home. I'ma really do something about it."

"Don't hold out, Jackson, if you're ready to let go, then let it all out." Brooke ran his tip around her mouth, leaving a trace of glaze wherever it trailed. Then she eased him into her mouth and worked her position with her tongue.

Knowing that she could make him come was a powerful position to own. Brooke Brazile could bring Jackson Sloan to his knees. This man who stood on legs as long as an athlete's, dressed in skin that looked like it was slathered on from a bottle of peanut butter, who peered through eyes that were capable of transmitting sexual vibes even when simply asking what Brooke wanted for breakfast. He was hers, totally and decisively, this handsome beyond belief, suave, confident, and masculine man was all hers. She planned to make this one man happy.

Brooke couldn't carry through with the eye contact game, not when she was enthralled by her mission. She heard his grunts and figured that was enough. Just knowing that she was breaking him down was good enough. Feeling him throb inside of her, Brooke considered backing away, but knew that he'd make a mess out of their fancy clothes, so she let him stay right where he was until he was done. Feeling the salty coating on her tongue, she swallowed, just because it was him. It was her pleasure.

He nodded his head. "Yeah. She's a keeper."

Wiping across her mouth, Brooke grinned. "Damn right I am." Happy to get off her knees, Brooke stood and pulled at the hem to straighten her dress as Jackson fastened up. He reached into his pocket to return her panties back to her. Brooke slid a heel into each opening of her underwear. After they both gave each other the onceover and hand-ironed each other's clothes, Jackson offered Brooke a bent elbow, so she could link up with him.

"Thanks for dessert," he told her with a grin.

"You can tip me later." She linked her arm into his.

He grinned. "I got a tip for you all right."

Summer

Sitting beside Amber, I'd arrived at Brooke's party rather late, and I didn't see Brooke or Jackson around much. But I did manage to spend quality time with Amber. And having the opportunity to wear so many beautiful dresses back to back reminded me why being a woman was fun. I sat in my mermaid chiffon dress, mindful of the material, trying not to let it sweep the floor. Perhaps I should've worn something shorter, but I just couldn't argue with the fact that fuchsia looked so good on me.

"What? No Oliver?" Amber asked.

I giggled at her drunk face. Her eyelids weighed more than her false lashes. "No, hon. No Autumn, no Oliver. Mom went ahead and left, and Oliver wanted to make up for lost time, so he chose to stay behind. Otherwise, he would've been here.

"Aww, Mama Stevenson. Gonna miss her."

"Yeeeeah, she had to cut it short by one day. Hospital needed her."

"Well this is mama's time to go balls out." She jerked her chin at the server. "Have a drink." Amber sipped on her frozen daiquiri.

"And how many of those things do you plan to drink?" I grinned dully.

"You need one." She shoved Emily's untouched margarita my way. "Here. Drink up. This broad don't need no more alcohol."

"And you're a fine one to talk?" I asked playfully.

She nodded with a smile.

"Thanks." I sipped slowly, trying to be mindful of my consumption given the fact that I had to drive and breastfeed.

"Whoooo!" I felt an arm embrace my neck. "My Summertime is here!"

I turned around to see Emily with a hand in the air and a glass in the other. "Hey, you wanna sit here?"

"No." She stumbled as she sipped. "No, no. I came to shake my ass!"

Never before had I been so glad for loud music. I would've been a tad embarrassed by her volume. However, the occasion made it appropriate, and others were having a good time at this very festive dinner party. "You sure?" I offered. She couldn't hear me, so I had to repeat myself even louder.

"Girl, no. No, no, no, no, no, no, no, no, no. I came here to have fun, not to be a sitting duck eating and chatting. Dance tiiiiiiiiime!" Emily moved away from the table and further out onto the dance floor. She grabbed a tall black man and danced with him.

Amber's head snapped back. "Hey . . . hey!" She tapped my knee rapidly.

"What, babe?"

"Look at that." Amber pointed at Emily and then looked back and me through dazed eyes. "I thought she only dated white men. Is she tired of vanilla-ville and curious about choco-city?

I squinted my eyes at her in humor. "It's just dancing, hon. On the other hand, maybe she can't even tell what shade he is with her level of toxicity." I giggled. "But, hey, I'm glad she's having fun and not sitting at home miserable. I want her to seize the night. We'll catch her if she falls—literally."

"Got that right." Amber squeezed a sliced lemon. "I really want some dick tonight. I can't even lie, mama."

"Hey, I am a mama," I teased.

"Horrible joke, Summer. You gonna ride your man's big, juicy sausage? You know you will."

"*Amber*." I didn't know what I was going to do with this woman and her brash ways. "I don't need to know that you know that my man is pleasantly equipped. Okay?"

"Ooops. My bad." Amber said with a careless shrug.

Raising my glass to my lips to take a long swig, the drink covered my taste buds like an oceanic lime with a wave of tequila. Tasty. Setting the glass back down, I saw the server coming my way and flagged her with my hand. "Excuse me!" When she turned her ear to my face, I requested, "A triple-berry sangria, please?"

"You got it!" She nodded and left.

Chalking it up to too much alcohol, at least I knew what Amber knew for sure, and what I'd suspected, but was too afraid to find out: She got an eyeful.

My good friend grinned at me. "We won't discuss how much meat he was given on top of his mashed potatoes."

"Goodness." I rested my forehead against my fingertips. When I looked up at her I said, "Do you happen to know a woman named Boundary? She's good to know."

The server stopped beside me. "Here you go, sweetie."

I thanked the server for my drink.

"Fine, chile, fine. I won't discuss his serving size anymore."

Traumatized, I took a big sip of my drink. Yes! I could start to feel the effects. "Yeah, don't. You're becoming too inappropriate." Remembering that only fools argued with drunks, I changed the subject. "So, how's the apartment thing going?"

"Oh!" She popped my leg with her hand. "I found a place. I'ma-I'ma find out any day now if I got the condo."

Wow! Amber had really bounced back since her days with Daniel. I couldn't be any happier for her. "Really? Where? Tell me about it."

"Well. Can't say where. You gotta wait."

"Okay." She definitely piqued my curiosity.

"But I can tell you about it," she slurred.

"Umm-hmm."

"Okay, well it's a two-bedroom, two full-bath."

"Ooooh. Better than just one, huh?"

She put a hand up to hush me. I knew she was truly twisted. "Summer. Please. Lemme finish."

I placed my palms up. It was difficult to keep a straight face. "All right."

"The landlord is renting it for a great price. He ready to hand over the keys like ASAP. It's like 1200 square feet, wall-to-wall plush carpet, as you, uppity folk say. The appliances ain't top of the line, but they aight. They definitely better than my old junk. My rent is $1500, which is only a $400 jump from my old raggedy-ass apartment."

"Your old apartment wasn't that bad." She eyed me with an expression that warned me not to B.S. her.

"Guess what?" she prompted.

"What?" Listening, I sipped. A heat wave simmered through my body.

"Did you hear that Brooke's peeps are here?"

"No wonder they're missing in action. Then where is she?"

Amber shrugged. "Dunno, boo. But I know I'm lushin' tonight."

Brooke sang, "We're baaaaaaack." She showed up at the table with Jackson by her side. She looked so beautiful in her dress, and Jackson looked like a model, as usual. "Hi, Summer!" She looked out of breath as they took their seats across the table from us.

"Wait." I knew these two, so something had to be up. "What did you guys just do?"

Brooke smiled. "We danced."

"Alone?" Amber asked. "Like, in a corner somewhere or out here with everyone?"

"We were working on our moves," Jackson assured her. "Where's Emily?"

"There." I pointed at the dance floor where she was last spotted. There she was, bending over and jiggling her butt against a man's groin.

"Twerk much?" Amber chuckled. "I ain't mad. Hell. She gettin' that eggplant! I need to go work it. I should be workin' it, too." Amber jumped up abruptly in her mesh-tiered ruffle dress to find a man in the crowd. She was one of the few women wearing a dress that stopped inches above the knees.

Catching a glimpse of Brooke's face, she seemed impressed with Emily's dance moves and free-spirit behavior. "Wow. I've never seen a woman twerk in a Magdalena sleeveless gown before."

I fell over laughing.

"Well, we certainly see what that jerk Eric is missing," Jackson cracked. Brooke flung her hand at his stomach. "What? I'm just stating what I see. She got moves." Brooke gave him the stink eye. "But you can show me yours tonight," he flirted, brushing the back of his hand against her chest.

"Didn't she just do that already?' I joked.

"No comment," Brooke replied with a mock dignified look. Jackson winked at me.

"Brooke, what's this I hear about your family being here?" I probed.

She hesitated with a grin. "Yeah."

"Your thoughts?"

Brooke leaned against Jackson's chest. "I just learned to accept it. You know, one day at a time. We agreed not to press the issue, but to let it happen organically. They'll be at the wedding tomorrow, too."

"That should be nice." Wow. Miracles did happen. This lady was a far cry from the vain woman I met a year ago. I told Jackson, "Be proud of this woman. She is so different than when we first met."

"Isn't she dynamic?" he asked.

"I'm . . . not that different," she replied with a weak grin as she shoved a curl behind her ear.

"Oh?" I sipped on my sangria.

"Well, I get why you may say that, but, honestly, I prefer to think of myself as the same woman."

"No, Brooke." I had to disagree. "You cannot come out of something like this and not be changed. Look at me and what happened to Ruben. My baby's daddy died, and no one saw that coming. I'm not the same after that. In fact, I think that made me a more protective mom. I had to rise to the occasion and quickly, I might add."

Brooke shrugged. Jackson kissed her shoulder. "You are a different woman, Brooke. It's a good thing."

"Well, I liked who I was before, and those guys won't change that."

"No one is arguing that you needed to change, but life events change us, even in the slightest ways." *Does she not get it, or is she reacting to fear that she's lost her old dazzling self?*

"I hear you," she replied. I think she just wanted to retire the topic, and that was fine by me.

Amber came back sweaty and exhausted. "Ohhhhh. Myyyyyy. Gosh! This is how you throw a dinner party." She aimed the "I love you" hand sign at the future bride and groom. "You guys are dope!"

"'Preciate it," Jackson replied.

"We're happy to make your night," Brooke told her.

"I may not get any dick tonight, but, hey—I felt one! Ooooooh weeee! I miss that feeling." We burst into laughter. None of us could help it. "But Amber is a good girl now, and that's what sex toys are for."

"So, are you going for celibacy?" Jackson asked with a raised brow.

Amber flicked a hand at him. "Nah. Just until I find the right man. No more sleeping for cash, favors, or having a one-night stand." She pointed at herself. "This girl rah here, is gonna be a new virgin. Nah, hold up. I hate the 'V' word. Let's just say that the kitty is in the kettle, uhkeh?"

Brooke sipped on her sparkling water, probably inhaling as much as possible to keep from talking. My one look at her challenged her not to laugh.

"I'm on a dick diet," Amber blurted as she sipped on Emily's unfinished margarita. "Or a dick restricted diet? A platter with no bone on the menu."

"Bone?" I echoed in question. "Bone?" I shivered. "Yuck. You have the worst names to reference a penis."

"That's okay, Summer. You will be okay." She patted my shoulder, and I couldn't help but snort with laughter. "Maybe I'm a vegetarian, cuz I won't be able to have no meat."

"Yuck." Brooke pointed at me and fell over laughing. "You snorted."

"Did not!" I lied while giggling.

"No Oliver? Home with my tiny tot?" Brooke asked with a sparkle in her eyes and pouty lips.

"Yeah. She needed a sitter, and he needed that lost time back to be with her."

"I understand," she replied. "It was nice seeing you two at rehearsal as a couple and not as estranged lovers tryna make it work. I thank God you two made up in time."

I smirked. "Who you happy for, us or you?"

Brooke smiled. "Both."

Jackson shook his head. "Ain't she dirty?"

I raised a brow at him in agreement.

"Just the way he likes it," Brooke said.

Then I asked her, "What you gonna do, Brooke, you know, about your name since the public knows it one way?"

Brooke looked at Jackson. I would bet my new Suburban that her hidden hand was rubbing his leg. "They'll continue to know me by my double-B initials for business sakes, but legally, it's gonna be Brooke Sloan. It has a great ring to it. I want to be a full-blooded Sloan." She nodded once, with pride.

"Yeah, baby, I don't want you to be any blood of Sloan. That's incest." He smiled lovingly and kissed her forehead as she giggled. She pressed down on her lower lip with her teeth shyly as she stole a quick look at him.

"You guys are gonna die cute," I told them with an adoring expression.

Amber broke up the mushy moment by sharing her news with Brooke about her move.

"I can't wait to see your new frame. Hopefully it's better than that other box." She smiled devilishly. Yup, the same Brooke still resided somewhere deep in there, I concluded.

"Suck my nuts," Amber said.

Brooke snapped a finger at her. "Still a slut."

Looking away, Jackson shielded himself with a hand. "Whoa, whoa, whoa. Y'all just . . ."

Emily came back with runny mascara and sweat dripping from her forehead. "Whew!" She tried to raise a pathetic fist pump in the air but failed.

"What in the hell happened to you out there?" Brooke asked.

Amber and I studied Emily, who could barely make it to her chair with limbs that moved like Jello and a struggling stare through vacant raccoon eyes. I raced two chairs over to help her land safely. "Thank you, miss. Thank you."

Brooke and I took another suspicious look at one another and burst into laughter. "So, so, sorry," I cried.

"What do you ladies keep laughing at?" Amber asked, looking high as a kite.

Ping ponging a finger between Amber and Emily, Brooke asked, "And, uhhh, how are you guys getting home tonight?"

Amber tilted her head at Brooke and took a break from sipping her drink. "You know I'm a walker."

I raised my hand. "I'll take her home. She lives with me, remember?"

Brooke and I fell into another foolish laughter fit. She held a hand up. "I'm so sorry. I had a bit to drink earlier."

"Maybe you should do that more often," Amber suggested.

"No." Brooke looked at Emily. "Missy, how are you getting home? I can drive your car to your place and drop you off, and then Jackson can take me with him."

"Uhh, ma?" He looked at her. "I don't think we have a choice. Look at her." He started to chuckle.

We all found it comical except for Emily, who was too far out to comprehend much.

"What a stinky bastard!" She started to well up.

"Who? Eric?" Brooke asked.

"Yeah." She threw her hand out like a child and pouted.

I tucked my upper lip inward and poked around on the chicken breast in front of me. A brief glance at Brooke and Jackson showed faces that bore expressions that read, "oh boy." All of our faces were painted with pity. However, it was unspoken that we didn't want her to behave in a way that would leave her feeling embarrassed tomorrow. Earlier, she was having fun, but now things were starting to hit too close to home, and none of that was a laughing matter.

"Let's end this. It's getting late, and we done here anyway," Jackson told Brooke. He walked over to the staff members to relay the message. People were already dropping like flies from the dance floor. The guests were either drunk, tired, or stuffed. All ingredients of a successful dinner party in my book.

"This was like a mini reception," I told Amber. She nodded then bit into her cold steak on a fork. "Get ready, honey." I tapped her on the arm.

Brooke walked to the front of the room to join Jackson once they had everyone's attention. I spotted her family sitting together, happily watching tomorrow's bride and groom. I couldn't find a resemblance to Brooke in her mom or vice versa. Maybe the mom once shared her daughter's beauty, and time had mangled it. I would've actually bet that Jacqueline was her mother, but I dare wouldn't go there with Brooke. The thought that that could be the truth would devastate her all too much. I figured she must've resembled her dad and let it go.

"We want to thank you guys for coming tonight," Jackson said. "I *cannot* wait to marry this woman." He grabbed Brooke so abruptly that she didn't see it coming. He placed a long kiss on her lips. We all clapped. I think he would've eaten her up if he could.

Brooke took the microphone and added, "I hope you guys enjoyed the music, food, and drinks. Come tomorrow, and you can take delight in even more. God bless and drive safely. Thanks!" I watched Brooke march over to her family, and Jackson to his, before spinning around to see Emily. She stood, crying, clapping and nearly falling. I raced to her side.

"Come on, sweetheart. Come on." Grabbing her gingerly but firmly to offer her balance, I eased her across the dance floor and toward Brooke and tapped her shoulder. "Hey. Excuse me, I don't mean to interrupt."

"No, it's okay."

"What do you wanna do with this?" I nodded my head at Emily who was on my side struggling to hang on.

"Wait a moment." Brooke raced to motion to Jackson, and he caught up to us. "Please, help us. I don't know what to do. There's steps, and we have on heels and—"

"Have her sit a moment. Let me send my family off. Hold up."

Brooke's mom nodded at him with a smile. "Brooke, you have such a wonderful man."

"Thanks . . . Lilly. I know."

He returned and asked Emily for her keys. Once she handed them over, he said, "Come here." He picked Emily up in one swooping motion and carried her in his arms. "Brooke, are you ready?"

"Wow. Yes."

Out like a light, Emily's head was cocked back. Her long, brunette hair swung with each step Jackson made. As he approached the stairs, Brooke said, "Baby, be careful."

I eased Amber down with me who, to no surprise, didn't have too much difficulty holding her own.

"Awesome," I told her. "Because my man ain't here to carry you, and I surely can't."

Once we said our goodbyes at the parking garage, Amber and I went home. One thing was certain. I couldn't say that we didn't have the best time together in a long time.

9: together

Summer

I stood in front of Brooke's guest bedroom mirror, admiring myself in my chiffon bridesmaid dress. Brooke wanted us to wear dusty rose-colored dresses to offset her very soft pink wedding gown. Obviously, my friend had an eye for fashion, because I had a hard time stepping away from my reflection. As soon as we'd wrapped up the something old, something new tradition, Brooke had kicked us out her bedroom so that we'd have sufficient time to finish our last-minute touches. Our soon-to-be married friend needed her bedroom to prepare herself with stylists and Haysia.

"I am so glad we get to show some knees." Amber celebrated with multiple quiet claps.

"Hey," I agreed. "Knee-length is the way to go."

Emily frowned. "Did you guys hate the one I picked out?"

I hadn't realized what we must've sounded like to her. "No." I attempted to not sound so dumbfounded. I absolutely loved the dresses she picked for us and didn't want her to think otherwise. I placed a hand on her shoulder. "Do I prefer to show skin? Absolutely. Does it mean we didn't love our dresses? Not at all, so please never doubt it."

Trying to brush away the sadness, Emily nodded and turned away.

"Yeah, we're sorry if it came out like that, Ems," Amber told her. "You know we woulda protested respectfully to your face rather than pretend to love it."

Unsure if we were actually able to assuage her insecurity, Emily nodded and placed a hand in the air. "Don't mind me. I'm just still sensitive. That's all."

My heart ached for my best friend.

Amber placed her hands in Emily's. "Hey, listen up. I don't have a man, nor am I looking, and I hear you're on the market as well." Emily mustered a strained smile. "So, what do you think of us being there for one another? We could go on dates and stuff when others would take their men. But, just please don't try to kiss me." She giggled. "I haven't given up on men yet."

Emily smacked Amber on the butt.

"Careful!" Amber shrieked with a laugh. "I may like it."

"Well, for the record, I'm not writing poems about you at night under the covers either." Emily shook her head at her friend and crossed her arms with a soft look in her eyes. No matter what, we always knew how to be there for one another.

"Amber, what you just proposed to her is what best friends do anyway, you knucklehead," I said, snickering.

"Well, no one told you to get all soccer mom on us all of a sudden." She folded her arms and studied me with mock disapproval. "Man. I just knew you were gonna be my road dog." Throwing her hands up, Amber declared, "Guess not."

"You'll live," I shot back, grinning.

She sighed. "Yeah, I suppose so."

Brooke popped up at the doorway looking like a beautiful bride in a silk chiffon, ballroom-styled wedding dress, with her hair swept away from her face in a low sleek pin-up of curls adorned with a sparkly brooch and tiny flowers. Her immaculate makeup elevated her beauty to a level never thought possible, as pink hues and highlighter made her cheeks pop. I noticed a small envelope in one hand.

In awe, we told her, *"You are so gorgeous."*

"Right?" she agreed. Wearing a proud grin with her hand on her hip, she blinked her eyes at us rapidly, while staring heavenward.

"Oh, Lord," Amber said.

Emily and I shook our heads with a chuckle.

Brooke held out the envelope to Emily. "Emily, here, baby. This is for you."

Emily's eyes widened. "What is it?" She threw her hands up.

Amber turned from admiring her reflection to look. "Open it and see. Good things come in small packages, they say—except penises."

Darting her eyes from Brooke to the envelope with an open mouth, she lowered her arms and slowly removed the envelope from her hand. She stared at Brooke suspiciously as she opened the unsealed flap. Once she pulled out a slip of paper, she exclaimed, "Are you insane? I can't take this!"

Amber shot her bewildered eyes up at Brooke and then at Emily. "Girl, you'll be a damn fool if you don't."

"Wait, what is it?" I asked.

Emily's eyes bounced between me and the piece of paper in her hand. "A check." She turned to Brooke. "But for what?"

"Well," Brooke said, "you didn't get married, so it didn't feel right to take this check."

"But you worked for it, even up until it was cancelled. No, no. This isn't how it works. You did a service, regardless."

Brooke silenced her with a raised hand. "I know, honey, but this is how it works with friendship. I never waste time, and this time, for the first time in my life, I did. Well, Damani was a waste, but at least I got a sensational orgasm out of it and some fun." Brooke placed a finger against her lips. "Shhh, don't tell, Jackson. Even though Jackson blows him out of the water—okay, but this is all beside the point. Emily, it's not right taking money from a dear friend for a second flop of a marriage. I couldn't deposit or spend this. It's fine. Money and I are good."

"No, no. Don't even try this. I'm not pressed for money. Besides, Eric paid for it. That wedding took a lot of time and energy," she told Brooke firmly.

"And I'm just refunding his money back to you. Emily. Please. Just take it," Brooke pleaded.

Amber snatched it from Emily. "Well, somebody better take this damn check, or I will. Black people don't let no unclaimed or *unwanted* money sit around now."

"Amber." Brooke flicked her fingers at her. "Give that thing back to me. Your name ain't even on the check."

Amber froze. "Right." She handed it back. "Ems, you so lucky. Baby, don't be no ding dong. Someone is giving you money. Take it. I hate seeing people reject money. I thought that nonsense only happened on TV. Like giving back an engagement ring. How foolish."

"You know," Brooke said impatiently with a hand on her hip while looking at Amber, "why did I do this with you here? Hush, please."

Amber waved a finger between Brooke and Emily. "Got it. But one of y'all is stupid. If it's Eric's money, somebody betta spend it."

Emily said, "Well, then. Take it as a wedding gift for you and Jackson." Emily took a few steps until she stood in front of Brooke's face. In a soft tone and lowered eyelids, she explained, "I don't need that money. Eric broke me off with some when he left me the first time, remember? When I sold the house, I pocketed a little, too. Brooke, I really won't miss the money. I don't have a family of my own to spend money on, and I don't do a lot of shopping either. I'm a pretty simple girl who doesn't want much. Money has never been the focus of my life. Having a family and teaching are my focus."

"Guys, why does anyone need the money?" I asked. "Why not rip up the check, Emily?"

Emily answered, "Because this check is from Brooke's bank account, so the money would still be sitting in her bank."

Amber pointed a finger at me. "Speak for yourself. You got all your basis covered. Some of us are still single and struggling folk."

I rolled my eyes. "Amber, if you can't make it work after having your debt wiped out by Daniel, a new job, and that birthday gift we gave you, you'll always expect a lifesaver. I think you're gonna be fine now."

Amber placed a hand on her hip. "Rude. Fine." Sighing while crossing her arms over her chest, she jerked her chin at the check. "That amount sure looks pretty though. But you ladies have taught me the value of standing on my own two feet. Done with handouts."

Brooke said, "Summer is right. We're all good now, single or not. Summer and Amber got new jobs, Emily and I are secured with ours. How about a vacation fund?"

I asked, "What do you mean?"

"Look, I don't have much time to discuss this, but, I'll put it in my miscellaneous bank account and every time we do something fun, like travel or take a night out, we swipe from this account. We won't have to pay to hang out with each other for a long time. Thank you, Eric."

Emily's brows rose. "Yessssss. We can take a trip with the four of us one day. We can go to restaurants and stuff." Emily's mood deflated just as soon as it'd spiked. "Wow. Eric paid someone just to break my heart in the end?" Her mouth twisted as she did a slow blink while processing the damage.

Amber touched our friend's shoulder. "Hey. That man comes from a family with tons of stacks. Remember, this was candy money for him. Don't forget that."

"You're right, you are so right, Amber." Emily nodded and plastered on a forced smile. "Moving on. I'm over it."

Amber turned to Brooke. "This is your day, and we're stealing it. Forget the money and all those plans. For now, let's get you married."

Brooke smiled and rolled her eyes. "Hey, Amber."

"Yes."

"You've come a long way since the time I met you. The night we all had dinner, when you wouldn't heed my advice about saving the money you earned from men, I thought you were a lost cause. Glad you proved me wrong."

"Me, too," Amber agreed with a grin. "Never thought I'd see the light either."

In an instant, I hugged Amber tight. "I am so proud of you."

Emily's hands flung at the sides of her face. "Okay, okay, okay, okay people. We gotta mooooove. *Ahora.*"

Tugging once at her sweetheart neckline, Brooke ordered us with eyes of stone, "Get out. Let's move." She spun around hastily with her chapel train choo-ing behind.

We made our way to the Capitol Columns at the National Arboretum in a stretch limo where and Brooke and Jackson would soon tie the knot. We shared a glass of champagne as a pre-celebration to the event. With raised glasses, we toasted to Brooke and Jackson's future.

"To a very cute and happy couple. May they last for a very, very long time," Amber said.

"Here, here to that!" Emily agreed.

"Amen," I added.

Brooke frowned. "A very, very long time? Bitch, I'm aiming at forever. To me and Jackson. The super love of my life." We tapped glasses before we sipped.

"I've never been in a limo before," I admitted.

"Well you have now," Brooke said. "Have Oliver take you in one. Does he even know that you haven't?"

"Uhhhhh, we actually haven't talked about it before. I guess I'll have to talk about it with him."

Brooke tipped her glass in my direction. "Guess you should." She took one last sip and put the rest down on a built-in tray. "That's all for me."

"Maybe more later?" Emily asked.

"With Jackson, definitely." Brooke cleared her throat and leaned forward. "Ladies, listen up, please." We gave her our undivided attention. "I'm not gonna cry, because I can't afford to be ugly before my big moment. But let me just say that I am grateful to have ladies like you in my life. You guys are the best thing that has happened to me—aside from Jackson and my career, that is."

We giggled with her. She stretched out her hand. "Let's get that straight! But no, guys." She simmered down. "I could not have asked for better friends than you guys. I love you ladies, if I never said it before. Thank you for coming and sharing this moment with me. There is no way I would do this without you ladies by my side—literally. No way."

"Awwww," we sang. "We love you, too." Reaching for hugs, I realized that we had arrived when I spied the beautiful scenery outside the limo window. We joined the other limo pulled over on the side of Ellipse Road, which had to have been for Jackson and the groomsmen.

Brooke flattened her hands over her lap. "Well here we are. I *cannot* believe it."

None of us replied. Instead, we waited for her blessing to get going.

I gently shook her knee. "You all right?"

Barely looking up she nodded quickly with a dismissive hand. "Oh, sure, sure. Let's go, guys." Life popped back into her eyes and a smile appeared on her face. "Let's get me married, y'all."

"Thaaaaat's the spirit," Amber said.

Amber hopped out first, and then I followed her, grateful that we avoided a bridal meltdown. Emily came out behind me but took the lead as maid of honor.

"Wow, ladies . . . look what Haysia did." My mouth hit the ground, taking in the visual before me from our limited view.

"You mean look what mother nature did," Amber corrected, in awe as well.

The Capitol Columns at the National Arboretum sat on an elevated span of green grass. Below it was a sidewalk in the shape of an oval that would allow us to join the standing guests on the platform—who waited behind the tall columns—without us walking across the grass. Bushes shaded the space inside the oval. It was a beautiful sight.

On the right side of the bushes, Oliver stood in line with the best man and one other groomsman at the base of the oval. As rehearsed, he stood second in line. Oliver's eyes met mine. They examined me up and down with a look that told me he wanted to do something to me later on. For now, he had to settle for my subtle wave; he winked back.

The girls and I followed the sidewalk on the left side of the oval that would lead us to the ceremony. Wearing a black A-line dress with a fitted bodice, Haysia met us halfway and greeted us with a toothy smile.

"You know what to dooooo," she said. "You ladies are beautiful."

I didn't have to turn around to know that she went to go be with Brooke.

The men began their walk up the sidewalk so that we could meet them and pair off down the aisle one at a time. The bridesmaids stopped at the top of the left side of the oval, and the groomsmen the right. Once Emily made eye contact with Jared, they approached each other until they met in the middle, and proceeded to step between two columns and down the open path split by the division of the bride and groom's family and friends.

Up next, Oliver and I met in the middle, linked arms, and made strides toward the front of the ceremony. The guests watched us inch closer and closer. Jackson's very handsome face came into view. The huge smile across his face had to hurt his jaw. His sister Justice held Autumn, who rested peacefully in her arms. Thank God. Behind him stood the preacher, and to the side of the preacher, stood a college-aged black guy with a microphone. For a moment, I borrowed this moment from Brooke to imagine what it would be like if all these people were actually here for Oliver and me. But, why? What would make me think of such a thing? Puzzled, Oliver and I separated and took our positions accordingly. Admittedly, it wasn't as bad as I'd imagined. It felt . . . right. He felt like a soldier on my arm.

One quick, stolen look at my boyfriend, and my stomach flipped with butterflies. His eyes beamed into mine, as if he were already decoding the thoughts behind my peepers. A shy smirk slowly slid on one side of my mouth. *What is he thinking*? Biting my lower lip, I returned my attention to the wedding. Amber slid her arm into Craig's and marched down the middle to join Emily and me.

Studying the location, with all the twenty-some columns standing on the platform around us, it felt like we were in ancient Rome. Slightly below and behind the preacher rippled a pool about half the size of an Olympic one. The two sets of mini stairs built on the elevation united us to the water. It was quite ironic, the scenery and setup given the bride. Romantic, but ironic. For a high-maintenance woman who made the most prudent decisions, she didn't choose a place of comfort, nor did she choose a place that could shelter us from bad weather. But knowing Brooke, something told me that she and Haysia paid for a back-up plan. There was no way that Brooke would let bad weather take her wedding day down. Having a wedding in a non-traditional, historical location in DC with a pool of water sitting behind the bride and groom seemed to top their list. So here we stood at the end of September under scattered clouds with a sun that played peekaboo. Regardless, Haysia and Brooke made an unexpected move by having a ceremony in the middle of nowhere, and for that, it was lit. The sound of the young man singing into the microphone a cappella snatched me out of my observation and back to my friend.

Brooke

Haysia had stepped up, proving to Brooke what she was made of and that she'd been taking notes along the way when Brooke spearheaded all the other projects. She'd given Haysia the budget and allowed her to choose the location but told her to have at it as long as she kept her in the loop.

Too bad Haysia had to move to a part-time schedule because of college. Brooke hugged her, then proceeded up the sidewalk toward Jackson, with Haysia holding her train along the way. She saw her mom, aunt, cousin, and Jackson's family, too. Brooke and Justice waved at each other.

Jackson whispered, "Hey."

"Hey," she replied.

They gripped hands after Jackson kissed the back of her hand. Her stomach did a backflip. The constant thump in Brooke's chest convinced her that others must've been able to hear it as well. The moment had finally arrived: She was about to become Jackson's wife. After the preacher had his moment, the time came for Jackson to speak.

Turning to face Brooke, Jackson said, "Brooke, before you said 'hello' to me in the coffee shop, I knew you were my queen. One who will never go without. I'm more than just your shoulder to lean and cry on. Baby, I am your armor. I will shield you from any further pain and hurt. I will place you so high the clouds will move under your feet."

Brooke felt the burn in her throat brewing like a witch's stew. No one had ever made her feel protected like this before, not even her own mother. She had her ride or die right here in front of her. This man looked into her eyes from the depth of his heart. He wasn't just spewing words, he was tattooing them into her soul as he spoke. Brooke didn't know how to handle such a remarkable promise. She didn't think her heart could contain all the love that one person had to offer. She bit her bottom lip with tensed brows. Before today, she believed in and knew her worth, but today, validating her choice to never sell herself short below market price, her partner came to take her off the market, ready to pay the full asking price and any additional fees. That was love.

"I cannot wait to make eye contact with you first thing in the morning, every morning. I cannot wait to keep on showing you how a real man treats a real woman. My heart belongs to you, and no one has a chance of making me think otherwise. Brooke . . ." When his eyes faded into hers, he lost himself in her gaze. "Everything that has happened to me has prepared me to be the man for you. This experience is new to both of us, and I promise to love you the way you deserve, until eternity."

Brooke giggled with tears as the preacher called on her to speak. "Jackson, the first time I saw you, I knew I had to have you. I felt a magnetic attraction to you. So, as they say, you had me at 'hello.' No one has ever made me melt at a stare or caused my stomach to flip as it's doing now. When we broke up, I found it hard to breathe, and life just was not the same, and I *never* wanna feel that way again. Before you, I was married to work, and I didn't know my heart was beating out of habit until it learned to beat for you. Waking up every day feels like Christmas, because I know I have you. I will make you happy and take care of you from now until the end of time. I will support you in all of your endeavors. I promise to love my strong, black man like the king he is."

The preacher resumed with the traditional steps. When the time came, Jared passed Jackson the jewelry, so that they could exchange rings and phrases.

"I now pronounce you husband and wife. You may now seal this bliss with a kiss."

Brooke tossed herself into her husband's arms and kissed him passionately.

"I love you, baby," she told him.

"Mrs. Sloan, you ain't seen nothing yet."

Located in DC, not too far from her home, The Hamilton housed Brooke and Jackson's reception in a large dim room with several long tables placed from one side of the room to the other. Repositioned tables presented a large space to be the dance floor for the guests. A stage sat at the front of the room to house a band.

The couple turned down the opportunity to hold the reception at the Herb Garden on the same grounds as their wedding ceremony. They wanted some place where the event felt less restricted and guests would feel unbothered by the outdoor temperature.

"Congratulations, Brooke!" Brooke embraced her Aunt Jacqueline.

"Thank you, Jacqueline."

"Yes, sweetie. Congratulations." Lilly bowed with her head as she clutched her purse. Brooke felt weird not giving her own mother a hug, whereas she easily gave one to Jacqueline. She reasoned that her mother had been respectful of giving her space, and they did pass a milestone in their slow blossoming relationship.

"Thank you . . . Mom." Then, awkwardly, Brooke went in for a hug with Lilly, who hesitated to hug her back. But, as Brooke remained attached to her, she felt Lilly's hand ease to her spine slowly before clutching her tighter, and then with both hands.

"Ohhhhh," her mother cried. "I wanted to do this a long time ago."

"I know," Brooke told her.

The hug. Brooke decided that it wasn't that bad, but it wasn't as easy as sliding on a stiletto either. It was kind of like trying to pull a tight shirt over your head and easing it over ample-sized breasts, but once it straightened out, it didn't feel too bad to the fit. Brooke released her grip from her mother and stepped back to face a glowing Veronique.

"Cousin Brooke, this was an awesome experience."

Brooke waved a playful hand at her cousin. "Ohhh, pshhhhh." She figured that she shouldn't leave her cousin out of the hugging process, so she eased herself into a hug. That hug she enjoyed the most. Veronique was just as much a victim in her mom and aunt's lies, that begrudging her cousin didn't make sense. "Thank you," she told Veronique with sparkling eyes.

Jacqueline smiled. "Brooke? I wanted to give you something."

Surprised, Brooke shifted her attention to her left. "Oh, really?"

"Mm, hmm." Her aunt reached into her purse and pulled out a rectangular sheet of paper. "Here." As it transferred from her hand to Brooke's, she told her, "I want you to have this."

Inexplicably, Brooke felt instantly nervous. Her eyes darted rapidly to all three women as she asked, "What-what is this?"

"Look at it," Jacqueline told her.

Brooke flipped the rectangle over, knowing that she held a check, and gawked at the written amount. Fifteen thousand dollars! "Wait. Why . . ." She placed an astonished hand over her heart. Her eyes shot up at her aunt. "I can't take this." She struggled to breathe. "I didn't work for it."

"Yes, you can. It's our gift to you," Jacqueline stated. "Think of it as your reimbursement for your honeymoon money."

"But-but, why so much? This is too much, and you know I can't accept this." Brooke composed herself to speak firmly.

"Say no again and watch what happens," Jacqueline warned. "I'll increase it by five grand per 'no'."

"Okay, Jacqueline, but you tell me why. Why so much? I'm just getting married. I didn't do a service for you. And the one I did for Veronique, might I remind you that you paid me handsomely for that. So, what's this about?"

"To make up for lost time. What about your graduation and other special moments? We feel honored to be a part of this."

"Jacqueline—"

"By the way, I'm taking your resistance as another rejection, so now we're looking at twenty grand."

"No, no we're not. Gosh, I can't believe I'm turning down money, but you make up for lost time with quality time, not money," Brooke pointed out.

"Brooke," Lilly reluctantly chimed in. "No woman should carry the financial burden of the wedding on her own. Regardless if Jackson paid for something or not, you had to buy your dress and pay your team to do this for you. Use this money toward your business or something."

"Like to hire more team members," Veronique suggested with a hop of the knees and a huge grin.

Brooke stared at the floor. "It just feels . . . wrong."

Jacqueline cupped Brooke's chin and tilted it up. "You've been so independent for so long. I can relate, but there comes a time when a woman needs to enjoy being pampered by others. Aren't you tired of being the one in charge, honey?"

Brooke nodded without saying a word, but she couldn't lie. It was tough being a woman who felt like she couldn't slip up in life. One mistake felt like the end of her career. Being Brooke Brazile never proved to be an easy task. She always had to watch her public behavior, live up to her reputation, and then turn right back around and exceed it. So, she learned to be a taker of free money for the first time in her life. Lifting her arm felt heavy in effort, but she willed herself to stare at the check and say, "Thank you." She beamed at each of her family members and hugged them once more. "Thank you, Aunt Jacqueline."

"Will we have a family day?" Veronique asked.

"Sure, I would love that," she assured in a quiet tone. "You guys being here means more to me than you'll ever know." Veronique smiled and nodded before walking away with Jacqueline.

Lilly stayed behind. "Well, baby." She sniffled. "I can't believe we're here. But we are."

"We are," Brooke repeated with misty eyes. "I have an overnight family." She giggled uncomfortably.

Lilly giggled with her and said, "You are an amazing woman with an amazing man, and I am so glad to call you my daughter. Thank you so much for allowing me to be a part of your life after what I did to you." Choked up, Lilly placed a hand over her mouth to cover her quivering lips.

"No, no." Brooke waved her hands at her. "No more about the past. No more looking back. I'm fine, you're fine, you said you were sorry, and I believe you. Please, let's just move on from here. I'm not that little girl anymore."

"'Kay."

One thing that Brooke couldn't move past was the condition of her childhood home. She and Jackson had a talk regarding options for Lilly. "Listen. Do you need me to rent a new home for you? Jackson and I can buy you something."

Lilly blinked with an averted stare. "You're my child. Parents should not be a burden."

"M-m-mom. If we're gonna make this thing work, we have to start with compassion. We'll talk about it later, but we're getting you out of that home after our honeymoon. Just a heads up."

Lilly looked at Brooke with glassy eyes. "What did I do to deserve your kindness?"

Brooke grimaced. "Deserve can be a false concept."

"Is it too soon to tell you that I love you?"

"No, because I would hope that you do."

"I always did, but . . . I had a rotten heart back then. You saved me by leaving me. Now, I have Jacqueline and she's gonna help me lose weight and refine myself." She chuckled.

Brooke smiled. "That's good, Mom. Improvement is never a bad thing." She pointed a backward finger. "I'm gonna go find Jackson now."

"Oh, yes, I understand. Don't keep that handsome man waiting. Such a good guy."

"He is." Brooke's face couldn't fit her smile. But then it faded when she realized she never told her mom something. "I'm sorry for treating you so badly on my doorstep. I need you to forgive me for that." Brooke felt a weight fall from her chest.

"No, child. Don't you dare feel bad for feeling hurt. I am honored to be in *your* presence."

Just when she saw Lilly turn, she said, "Mom." When Lilly turned to face her, she said, "I love you, too."

Lilly stretched a hand out to rub Brooke's jaw with a pleased expression. Lilly turned. Brooke watched her mom walk away with her slight limp.

"Boo!" A hand touched Brooke's shoulder.

She knew that familiar touch and voice before turning to see him. "Hey, baby."

"Hey, Mrs. Sloan."

She frowned. "No more Brazile?"

"You," he said, pulling her close, "will always be my Brazile." His nose kissed hers before they smooched. His parents and sister came over to welcome her to the family. They were delighted that she could now call herself a Sloan. Brooke couldn't wait to spend more time with them. She couldn't believe that she had a sister-in-law and a father-in-law. It was a challenge to recognize this as her own life, but in a good way.

The DJ picked up the microphone and announced the time for their first dance. Brooke and Jackson led one another to the dance floor to dance to their chosen song, "My First Love," by Avant and Keke Wyatt. She rested her face against his chest. Listening to the words almost sent Brooke into a cardiac arrest. His arms wrapped her tight, his hands careened up and down her back. Chills spiked her skin, hitting her arms and face. This was her husband, Brooke realized. She no longer held a pass in the single life, nor did she want it.

The song lyrics sent tears to her eyes as she reflected on the hurt and pain that she felt when they walked out of each other's life. How disgusting that time in her life felt, she thought. Deciding not to think about it, Brooke reveled in the fact that she and Jackson were each other's true first love, and that made her smile all over again.

Summer

Sipping on wine, I sat with Amber, Emily, Oliver, and Autumn. "This tastes so good." I licked my lips.

"Doesn't it?" Amber agreed.

"And I'm not getting faded like before," Emily claimed with a finger in the air.

"Oh, honey," I replied, "we won't let you." One of Oliver's hand traveled up and down my back while the other held Autumn.

"I got the apartment, y'all," Amber announced.

"What?" I asked with huge eyes.

"I see the delight in your green eyes," Amber said. "Yeah, he left a message on my voicemail."

"You gonna tell us where you moving?" Oliver asked.

"Yes," Amber responded, smacking two flat hands against the table. "Arlington. I'm moving to Arlington on Columbia Pike."

Surprised, I asked, "What? As I recall, you were the one dead set on DC, and northwest, might I add."

"Wow. Then you'll be close enough to babysit," Oliver noted.

Amber placed a hand over her heart with closed eyes. "I know, I know." Looking at us, she said, "Well, I had to realize that it's not about location, but feasibility. Northwest ain't it right now, and I'm gonna live close enough to the 395 exit to get back into DC in a flash."

I leaned forward and warned, "Don't let Brooke hear you say that about her quadrant."

"Well, he said I can move this Wednesday. I'm hiring movers." Amber lifted her nose in the air with mock snobbery.

"Listen, guys," I teased. "Shhhh." They stared at me in confusion. "I think that's the sound of Amber arriving." We fell over laughing.

Brooke came over. "What's up, ladies?" We screamed and stood to hug her. We smashed her with hugs and shot random questions at her after our cheers. She replied with, "This is the best feeling ever! Thank you, guys, for being my bridesmaids."

"There's nothing else we would have rather done for you," Emily stated.

Oliver jumped up with our daughter to congratulate her. "Hey, yo, congratulations."

"Thank you, so much, Oliver." She grabbed Autumn's hand. "Hey, baby. Hey." Autumn smiled at her before turning her head away. I took Autumn to give Oliver a break.

"Thanks, babe," he said.

"No problem. I need to squeeze her." I placed kisses over her face.

Jackson joined us and stood beside his new bride. "What's all this noise about over here?" he joked. We congratulated him as well. He thanked us and passed hugs around to each of us.

"Jackson," Emily called. "I'm so sorry you had to carry me out last night." She giggled. "Thank you for helping a sis out though."

He grinned. "Not even worried about it, but no problem. But soon, I'm gonna have to take this woman away so we can head off to Bora Bora."

"Ooooh," we all sang.

Jackson asked Oliver, "Bruh, what's all this I hear about you guys getting away?"

Oliver answered, "Yeah, we're taking the baby and heading down to Maui. Even though I'm a California boy, we thought it'd be good to go back to my roots."

"You know, since he's half-Hawaiian," I said. "Plus, Autumn will have a story to hear and understand when she's four."

Oliver added, "Summer and I weren't ready to kiss summer goodbye, so we're ready to snag some heat from somewhere."

Jackson stuck out a fist for him to pound. "And Bora Bora will do the same for us." Oliver knocked fists with Jackson.

Pretending to cry, Amber turned to Emily and said, "So I guess we gon' have to marry each other right quick so we can go on a honeymoon."

"I know, *right*?" Emily agreed with her mouth opened in fake horror.

"Maybe y'all should," Jackson agreed. "This time, Amber can have a sugar mamma," he joked.

"*Ouch.*" Amber said. "You told him about my dating disasters?" she asked Brooke, pretending to be embarrassed.

She shrugged. "I guess I did."

"I like living alone, so I'm good," Emily replied.

"Oh, me, too," Amber agreed. "If I really wanted to, I can fart like a man and douche like a lady with no one there to judge me."

"Wow." Oliver placed a hand over his mouth. "Where's the cupcakes?" He walked away.

"What?" Amber asked, looking unashamed and almost surprised by Oliver's reaction. "Men know we do it."

Jackson placed his palms in the air before dragging Brooke off with him. "But we don't like to hear of it."

Standing with just my baby and two friends, I shook my head. "You are *not* supposed to douche."

Amber shrugged unapologetically.

"Should we dance or eat?" Emily asked.

"Eat," we all replied in unison. I took my seat and bounced my baby gingerly on my lap as we ate, danced, laughed, and drank.

Later on, that night, Oliver and I headed home. I changed a sleeping Autumn into a onesie and slid her into her crib. She barely flicked an eyelid. Some nights, I found it hard to walk away after putting her down. She had a face of an angel, who placed a calm inside of me that always seemed out of reach. This would always be the best gift from God.

With both hands gripping the top of the crib, reality slipped away from me with each passing second, just long enough for me to take in the sight of it all. My baby. I'd given birth to Autumn in the summer.

"Hey, you." Two large hands gently slid over my hips. Hands that I'd missed dearly. Hands that had been off this tiny frame for way too long.

My eyes remained on Autumn. "Isn't she precious?"

"Beyond."

I spun around to face Oliver. The need to feel his face transferred to my hands, and so they lifted without command to feel his scruffy jawline. In the dark, the only light that hit his face was from that of our daughter's nightlight.

"Let's get out of here," I whispered.

"Come on," he whispered back.

Like two high school teenagers, we ran to our room and shut the door behind us. Oliver yanked his t-shirt over his head and threw it to the floor. I turned my back to him to remove my shirt, and before I could turn around, Oliver had swung an arm from behind me and crossed it over my chest to grab one of my breasts.

The feel of his lips walked over my neck and shoulder, his fingers imprinted the cushion of my womanhood, covering the circumference with one hand. A pain of thirsty sensation ziplined from my core to my lady canal. It wanted to open up to hold the river that ran deep from Oliver's release of love. The love. The love that I'd chosen to deny, wanted to walk away from, making it more of a headache than the simple token of a genuine space in one's heart.

Resting my head back and seeing nothing but the blackness behind the curtain of my restraint, I chose to focus on his feeling, rather than the seeing. It was that moment that I chose to focus on the way his hands traveled gingerly against my skin, taking care to the task, not wanting to damage his little free bird, yet conquering the assignment of exhilarating my imprisoned senses. Senses that had been dull after delivering life and saying goodbye to another's. Senses that had been dull after being wiped out from all that was familiar and identifying it as a lie. Senses. His touch allowed me to make sense out of my senses.

I sensed this man loved me. It was evident in the way he chose to connect with my being instead of piercing me like a hungry animal. Still, our need was stacked like boxes in a U-Haul truck. Fragile, congested, but nonetheless, handled with care. Because we cared.

And in the blindness of rapture, my mind swam to a sense of belongingness. I belonged somewhere, to someone. I belonged to him. His tender canoodles bent my knees inward, verging on the threat of a collapse. My hand gripped at his nape with the desire to give him a return on his investment, wanting him to feel as electrified as he had me. But, somehow, I think I failed, because as much as I wanted to entrap his senses the way he did mine, the ability seemed robbed as long as he had me first.

What could I do but moan between my lips a song of sensual lyrics? Hitting crescendos, making up my own notes of passion—it was all a symphony of love, all taking direction from Oliver's hand movements.

He spun me around to face him. The anguish in his face hit the lines on either side of his mouth. They formed a narrative, one of pain concocted by lust and long overdue need. The hand he placed on the side of my face whispered to me in its own fashion. It told me that he had my back. That everything was gonna be all right. The look of a torrid examination perforated my existence, cutting right to the chase, and it told me I'd never want to live without all of this again.

Oliver swept me up so quickly, I thought I was going to do a somersault. My hair had grown longer, so its extra abundance swept behind me in motion. We headed for the bed like two topless animals in the wild. This love was about to get chaotic.

The bed waited below me, but I didn't want it. "You. On the bed. Sit."

Taking it like a dare, Oliver smirked at me with a stare of a lion looking at a bird as an easy prey. Capitulating, he nodded, realizing that he didn't always need to take the lead. No immediate plan sat at the forefront of my brain, but something in me was ready to roar. Putting me down, Oliver sat at the foot of the bed with legs wide apart, just like a man who had a lot of wealth in his package. Standing with my stomach almost kissing his nose, he slowly lifted his stare and stopped when it hit mine. My hair waterfalled above him, with the ends resting against a taut midsection which somehow had snapped back into place after giving life. It felt right to straddle him, so my thighs slid like a perfect puzzle piece on either side of his hips.

I gripped his chin with fingers bejeweled by glue-on nails, which, thanks to Brooke, demanded we wear them on her wedding day to look cohesive as possible. They surely beat my normally short and unpolished nails at a time when I felt so much heat. Everything made me feel sexy. This woman had given birth and was now considered a mom. While never considering myself hot, the look in Oliver's eyes told me otherwise, so it felt right to believe it. This woman had her own money, though the means to have it was underhanded, but regardless, this birth-giving bitch had to slide her own pumps on every morning to go make that money using her own brain. This woman was one of the pillars of the all-female monolithic HR tribe who held the responsibility of finding the top talent to bring in the money so that everyone under the pyramid of power could eat. This woman had a sisterhood of women on her side whom she could call at any time of the day when disaster struck, or when a shoulder was needed to cry on. Last but not least, this woman had a man who carried his whole temple on his shoulders. A strong business man with family values who would swing his hammer at any person who threatened to destroy his loved ones. This man, this *father*, who was man enough to take a baby into his arms, even when they didn't have a trace of DNA in common. Was he my king?

Absolutely. Was I his queen? No man would ever have to assign that title to me for me to know it. I was.

Oliver waited for me to say something.

But I couldn't. In a moment like this, no words were necessary. Ramming my mouth into his, my hips grinded into his chest as I stood on my knees, erect, kissing a man with his head cocked back. He placed two possessive hands on my rear, allowing one to roam under my pants and against my bare flesh to explore in between the valley of my two modest humps. I sacrificed his lips to place my bosom in his face. I inhaled between my teeth, causing a hissing sound.

"Mmmmm, Oliver," I cried out in a needful whisper.

"Baby." His fingers slid into my pussy from behind my butt.

"Ah!"

"Yeah, that's it," he said in a raspy whisper. "Let me take care of you."

I lowered myself to come close enough to kiss noses. I rocked against his fingers, against his thumb that hit the sweet spot above it all. My eyes shut down to everything around me. Hiding behind my eyelids, the deep craving prowled inside of me.

"Suck my titties, Oliver."

Of course, he listened. He took one nipple into his mouth and possessively traveled his tongue over the tip. His teeth clenched into my hardened bud, amusing all my nerve endings.

"Don't steal Autumn's food." Rocking backward with my neck cocked back, I cried, "Stoooooop, Oliver. Oh, please, baby." Between his fingers in my world and his mouth manipulating the sensations of my breast, I played with the other one, pinching the nipple to match his play. It must've turned him on, because he rocked us to the side in one motion until I ended up under his body.

He snickered. "I know I tasted some breastmilk."

"You want mama to feed you, too?"

"I want you to do to me whatever it is you wanna do." Oliver's eyes pierced into mine. "Baby, I swear I'll never mess up again."

Instead of moving my lips, kissing him seemed like a palpable choice. We made love with our mouths first, letting our caresses build up the steam once more. Oliver sat up with a heaving chest and stared downward at me. Hopping onto his feet, he jumped out of his pants with lightning speed and jumped back onto the bed. Reaching for my waist, he gripped the waistband of my yoga pants and ripped them down my legs with my assistance. I couldn't kick out of those suckers fast enough. But, when I did, I reached for him with all my might to pull him close and over my body. My thigh rinsed his leg repeatedly, and like a match striking the strip, a fire had started, one that I had no intention of putting out.

With matching breathing patterns, we sounded like two terrified characters hiding from a killer in a horror movie. I couldn't wait for this man to take me. Raising away from me, his hands cocooned each breast with his thumbs scratching over the tip of my nipples. *Sensational.* Oooh, I wanted him so badly. Oliver lined himself up with me, and even from here I could see him dripping for me. He was in as much pain as me. We were like two deprived souls on an island who'd finally made it to a buffet. He was *all* I could eat.

I felt his grip palmed against my hips, and instantly, I missed the cover he provided on top of my breasts. However, he made up for it when he slid effortlessly into my welcoming. What probably should've hurt ten times more, didn't feel as bad, because he was cautious and considerate, despite his torment to have me. He left me with little space to think, because the moment he threw my legs on each shoulder, he said, "Your skin is my home, and there's no other place I'd rather be. But I will make you come so hard, Summer." He pulled his penis from within, dabbed two fingers against his tongue and slid them inside of me. Looking straight into my eyes, he said, "I swear, girl." He winked. "I got you."

Oliver worked his fingers outside of me and rubbed the inside of my lips until he found my clitoris.

My chin flew up, and my eyes squeezed shut. "Ohhhhh." That raw sensation with the one I loved, the one who loved me back, the who had my heart, the one who remained dedicated to me and only me. That drove the sensation to a new height. His skin ribbed against my inner sensitive zone, taking delicious licks with every thrust. And with each move, he could tell that it drove me nuts. He went harder and faster, became more aggressive, and caused the top of my thighs to sit above my stomach as my knees kissed my breasts.

Oliver had me folded up like a suitcase. Something within me snapped, and in a loud voice, I wanted to know, "Am I your filthy whore?"

Oliver had broken into a sweat; he was working overtime. With his chest fitting between the space of my legs, he still couldn't guarantee me perfect eye contact. "Mmph! Yeah. Yeah. Yeah you my dirty whore. Who's your daddy, you whore?"

"You! You my daddy, Oliver. *Yeah*, push, baby." Not afraid to sound like a porn star, I cried, "*Yeah*! Oh, Oliver! Please hurt me, baby!"

"You want me to bang this pussy up, huh?"

That good friction started to build up.

"Control me! Control me! You da boss, baby. You da boss!"

The lid had started to shake, the water was boiling over and puddled onto the stove. The earthquake had threatened the foundation of the house. The lamps started to rattle. The lightbulbs started to pop, one by one. The needle against the balloon barely tapped the latex before it popped into strings of deflated hope. My ship had come in. My ears started to ring, and my body began to float as the numbness rang from my toes first all the way up to my head. I curled my toes so much I thought they'd break. Oliver had permission to peak after he saw me lose control. In my own shielded world, the only action outside of it came as a series of grunts from a man just as starved as me. Tonight didn't need extra positions filled with props and role play. We just needed to unite our cravings for the first time after Autumn's birth. Exceeding my expectations, this man gave me the best orgasm of my life. Not bad for a new mother who was expecting a painful moment since life had given me several doses of that in the past year.

10: sandy times

Amber

Amber placed her hands together in front of her skinny jeans as she surveyed her new home. She walked into her open floor plan, resplendent in her faux-leather motorcycle jacket. "Look at this without the furniture," she told Mr. Wells.

"Here your keys. I just need you to sign a few more papers before I head to London. I'll be back in two months, but I'll email the information regarding where to send the rent money along with my contact information."

"Sounds good," Amber told him. She finally felt like she'd done something right as the fresh smell of paint and new carpet filled her nostrils. She loved her new open and bright apartment.

"Great! Let's get started." They took an additional twenty minutes to review the apartment together during a walk-through and discussed the language of the contract before signing.

"I feel good about this," Amber stated as she looked around with a smile. They stood in her galley kitchen.

"Cool. Okay, just please make the rent on time. If you run into a problem, you need to speak with me with open communication. I'm flexible, because it's paid for, but I do want you to take care of it. Can you do that for me?"

"Oh, I can."

Mr. Wells held out his hand and she shook it. "Take care, Miss Hamilton."

"Safe travels, and thank you, Mr. Wells."

"My pleasure." He eased out of the door.

Amber did another walk-through so she could take in the scenery and space alone. The spacious living room was adjacent to the dining room but was separated by a wall. She finally had two bathrooms: one private, and the other in the hallway. She rejoiced in the fact that Mara could finally sleep in her own room when she came to visit, which meant no more sleeping on the couch to accommodate her sister.

Amber removed her shoes and enjoyed the feeling of her feet sinking into the thick, clean carpet. Yes! she thought with happiness. It was the little things, she reminded herself. A loud knock at the door startled her. She remembered that the movers were right on time. Amber ran to open the door to let in the three muscular men.

"We're here and the truck is outside and ready to unload," one of them told her.

"I'm here. Feel free to go ahead and get started," she told them with a friendly grin. Once they left, she closed the door behind her, but then heard another knock. How could they have forgotten anything? she wondered.

Opening the door, she thought about shutting it again when she saw the person standing in front of her.

Emily

Taking off from work early, Emily charged through her front door, looking flushed as she threw her Tom Ford handbag onto the kitchen counter. The school took her temperature before she fled home, but despite her vomiting, her temperature was normal. Stopping by the drugstore on her way home, she picked up the next best indicator: a pregnancy test.

Emily viciously wiggled out of her purple trench coat and threw it on the sofa. She paced her wooden floors in her purple pumps, debating her next move. Her thick brunette hair would normally be secured in a bun, but, today, it whipped across her face wildly as she bit down on her nails, asking herself: What would motherhood be like?

Emily stopped pacing long enough to study the white plastic bag that held the answer to her future. Holding her head with a sigh, she decided to open it when she felt good and ready. Feeling the tears drive down her face, she wiped them off with the back of her hand. Deciding what to have for dinner, Emily readjusted her pencil skirt at the waistline and headed for the kitchen to possibly feed a party of two.

Amber

Amber gasped when she saw Daniel staring back at her, looking twenty pounds lighter.

"Hi, Amber." He stood there, not blinking with eyes glued on her face.

"Daniel. I thought I told you that I had movers who were going to bring my piano and stuff."

Perplexed, Amber didn't invite him in until he asked. She opened it and he slid through.

"I thought we had an understanding that you wouldn't come to my home. You know, no funny business." She placed her hands on her hips.

"I followed them here once they left my house. I couldn't help it."

"Why'd you do that?"

"I miss you. I've been going to the gym, eating less, saw a holistic doctor about my breath, and you know—I'm trying to do things that would make you see me differently, Amber."

Touched but uninterested, Amber sighed and dropped her arms. She turned her back to him and took a few steps away before spinning to look at him again. "Daniel, that is so sweet. But, really, you shouldn't have come here. Look around." She gestured with her hand. "I told you I would do it on my own, and I have. No help. Sure, my friend let me crash at her place for a few weeks, but I got a new job and regained some of my old clients. My money's coming in. I don't need anyone to rescue me."

Taking a few steps closer, he pleaded, "No, no, this wouldn't be no rescue mission, Amber, just straight up love and respect."

Leaning against the patio window, Amber replied, "Daniel, I just don't love you." She closed her eyes and opened them with crossed arms, placing one ankle over the other. "Or any other man. I don't love anyone romantically on this planet as of now, and I prefer to keep it that way. I'm sorry." She didn't really feel sorry, but she also didn't mean to sound cruel or to hurt him in any kind of way. Daniel did look a thousand times better, but she wanted to remain single.

"Why? Is it because I threw you out of my office that time? How 'bout I take you to my office and show them all what I've got?" he asked with open arms.

"Because when it comes to me, you got nothing."

Her words deflated his posture.

Amber uncrossed her ankles and arms as she straightened from leaning on the glass. "I do like you, but I don't love you."

She had to be honest with herself. She did like Daniel. He may not have been easy on the eyes, but he came equipped with all the right stuff. He loved her, he wanted her, he had financial freedom, and he knew how to treat her, or at least he knew what she wouldn't tolerate. She knew she would have the power in the relationship very easily. All the cards were in Amber's hand, but something inside wouldn't let her play them. She didn't want to play anymore. Winning never felt like a true victory if it meant taking advantage of someone.

"I can wait until you do," he persisted.

"No, Daniel. What you can do is get on with your life, because it's too precious to waste sitting around trying to make someone love you." Amber approached him until she could place her hands on his shoulders. Daniel's face bore a look of despair as he realized that he just might lose the battle. "If I didn't respect you, I would come aboard and take what I could from you."

"Can we be friends then, Amber?"

Amber thought about it. "That may be possible." Her finger pointed at his face. "But don't think that it's an easy pass into Loverville from friend world." She waved a hand at him. "Not gonna happen. I wanna be on my own for a while—just me, my piano, and my sisters."

"Then can I have a kiss goodbye?" he asked with crestfallen blue eyes.

"I guess I don't have anything to lose by doing that." Amber hesitated as her lips aimed to land onto his with the refusal to use her tongue. Daniel took the opportunity to grip her by the arms to keep her close. He covered her mouth with separated lips. She knew he wanted to taste her tongue, and since she didn't smell the bad breath, she decided to let him have fun in her mouth one last time. Their tongues danced as Daniel took advantage of having her close. He moved his hands from her arms and down to her butt. Feeling confused by what was happening, Amber didn't bother to stop him. Her hands moved up and down his back as she found herself allowing the exploratory kiss to keep going.

A knock at the door stopped them. Amber's eyelids felt heavy. She wiped her mouth and stepped back.

"You're right. Your breath is fresh. But I, uhhh, need you to go Daniel, and don't look back. Come in!" she shouted.

Amber saw her baby grand come through the door. She instructed them to place it in the corner of her living room, so she could face the open space of the room when playing or teaching. Daniel nodded and disappeared through her door behind once the movers passed through. Standing in the middle of her living room, Amber touched her lips, reflecting on what just happened. She realized that she had become a woman who had the capability to do the right thing, regardless of what she wanted.

Brooke

Brooke stretched out in the sand of Bora Bora, watching the cloudless, blue sky above as they enjoyed the last day away from home. Jackson joined her with tropical drinks in both hands. Sitting down beside her, he said, "Wake up, sleeping beauty."

Brooke slid her sunglasses on top of her head, enjoying the feel of the gentle breeze blowing her strands. "Thank you so much. I needed this; I'm so thirsty. Are they virgin?" She sat up and crossed her legs.

"Not on our vacation." A mischievous grin covered his face.

"Thatta boy." She winked.

"So Brazile, aren't you gonna ask what's next for us, like a timeline as a married couple?"

"Nope," she replied calmly, placing the straw between her lips.

"No?"

"I learned that total control is a false concept."

Looking impressed, Jackson said, "So I guess our little crazy journey taught us a lot."

Brooke turned to him. "Okay then. Whatcha learn?"

Nonchalantly shrugging, he answered, "I learned that you can face anything with the person you love."

Looking pleased, Brooke said, "Well, that's sweet. But baby, that was my problem, don't you think?"

"Nope. You're wrong already, baby." He leaned forward. "You see, darling, you'll learn that in marriages, one person's problem naturally becomes the other's, but that's only if the other one cares. In this case, I do."

Brooke ran her tongue over her upper lip. "But we weren't married."

"Didn't matter. I was deeply in love with you." Jackson leaned back to continue sipping his drink.

"You know I woulda done the same for you, right?"

"I do, but I wouldn't have married you if I sensed differently."

"I know. And thank you for your encouragement to mend my family. The fact that you kept pushing and never gave up, I appreciate that. Without you, I wouldn't have resolved so quickly."

"It was worth a shot, Brazile. You only get one family." Jackson planted his unfinished drink in the sand and turned on his side to face her. He stroked her tight belly with his hand. "And how many babies are we gonna get out of this stomach of yours?"

Appearing shy, Brooke replied, "I'm glad you asked. One day when I couldn't get to sleep—" She waggled her finger at him, "—by the way, no one knows this."

He smirked. "Okay, what?"

"You and I had a few dates under our belts, and I started thinking of baby names for our children."

Intrigued, Jackson chuckled. "Oh really? Whatcha got?"

"Mmmm, I came up with Br—don't laugh!"

"I won't, I won't." He tried to look serious. "Give it to me."

"I came up with Braxon."

He arched a brow. "Braxon?"

Gesturing with one hand, she asked proudly, "What do you think?"

"But that just rhymes with my name. That's not too special, Brazile."

Brooke's lips pouted. "But I was so proud of myself. It's like mixing Brooke and Jackson."

Humored and trying not to laugh, Jackson shook his head. "Nah, baby. That most definitely will ruin our credibility as a couple and make us seem too awesome to last. Let's do it right and find names with meanings. All right, sweetheart?"

Pouting, she replied, "Okay."

Sipping her drink, Jackson lurched at her to pull her into his arms with one swift move. "Come ride my dick in the sand." Alarmed, she screamed and laughed, trying her best not to spill her drink as her husband took her down into the sand.

Summer

Oliver snapped his suitcase shut on the bed. "I'm done here. Real quick, I'ma put some gas in the truck, since it's empty. Okay, baby? I'll be right back."

"Okay." A sigh from my lips moved a piece of hair from my face as I folded my clothes. Autumns little suitcase had been packed and set to the side on the bed.

"Do you need anything?"

"Umm, sunscreen. Yeah. I can definitely use some of that."

"What number?"

"The higher, the better."

"Cool."

"Hurry back. I still have to meet the ladies tonight."

"All right, baby. Hold it together, sis. Be right back."

I giggled. "Okay. Thank you, sweetie."

"No problem." He disappeared behind the bedroom door.

I scanned the room to see what else needed to be packed. Reviewing my mental checklist, I remembered my bikini. After sifting through my underwear drawer rapidly, I followed the lose strings that led me to my melon-colored bikini top with the bottom underneath.

"Yessss."

The sound of knocking at my door startled me. Throwing the bikini into the suitcase, I headed toward the door, wondering why Oliver didn't just use his key. Did he forget it? Yanking the door open, two unfamiliar faces stared back at me.

"Caaaan I help you?" The older woman with an olive skin tone and petite in height and weight appeared lost or confused. The fairly young lady beside her—perhaps mid to late twenties and a little taller than the older woman but slightly overweight—seemed reluctant to speak. The two dark-haired women stared at me with some type of desperation or need for help. I just couldn't tell.

"Summer Stevenson?" the younger one asked.

Irritated and concerned, I asked, "Well, who wants to know?" I shifted my weight to one side of my body.

"We understand that you knew Ruben."

My heart dropped. *These women wanted trouble!* How could I be so stupid to forget that his family would soon find me? "No, I'm sorry."

The older one spoke with a thick accent. "No, please," she pleaded, placing a hand on my door to block me from shutting it.

"Summer, please, it has to be you. We know you live here."

"Did Fran send you?" Anger scorched through my chest at the mere suspicion that Fran was behind this.

With a mild accent, the younger one asked, "Then you are Summer?" She stared at me, waiting for my confirmation.

I crossed my arms. "And? What do you want?"

"We mean no harm," the younger woman said. "Can we please come in?"

I relented and opened my door to them. My gut didn't flip out on me, so I didn't doubt my decision. "Fine. Something to drink?"

The older woman replied, "Anything you have is fine. Coffee or water would be nice."

"All right. Go on and have a seat." I motioned toward to the sofa. Oliver had already brewed coffee, so I poured two hot cups and placed fixings on a tray and walked it over to the ladies.

"Oh, thank you so much," the youngest one said.

Sliding out of her jacket, the oldest one told me, "We appreciate you opening your home to us."

"Well, I don't even know your names." I stood above them with folded arms.

"I'm so sorry." The oldest one placed a hand on her chest. "My name is Ana."

The younger one spoke up, pointing to the woman next to her. "And I'm her daughter, Ruben's sister, Irene."

My heart dipped. Hearing the confirmation that his family was real and right before my eyes struck a melancholy chord. "What brings you here? What can I do for you two?" I decided to sit on the loveseat to hear out Ruben's family, the Sotolongos.

Ana started. "Well—" She held onto her coffee with both hands wrapped around the ceramic mug, shifting her eye contact as she spoke. "When Ruben died, we didn't know that he had a child. We buried him in Florida, so he could . . ." Her voice began to quiver. ". . . be next to my parents."

"I'm so sorry, Ana," I whispered. Seeing their vulnerability naturally lowered my guard toward them.

She nodded and continued as Irene caressed her mother's back with one hand. "But, uhhh, Fran didn't come to the funeral. She did call us to tell us about you and this lovechild, as she put it. We were so happy to hear this."

Nervous inside and cussing Fran out in my head, I began to panic. What if they demand a lot of time with her? Will they come around frequently? Would my new family need to be uprooted on holidays to accommodate these people? Even though keeping a connection to Ruben was important, with him no longer alive, it felt unnecessary to keep ties to this unfamiliar family. I bit my lips and twisted them underneath my teeth. Oliver was the kid's new family. We didn't need this.

"So, I don't understand. Are you here to impose yourselves on her? She's so young and-and—"

Irene held up her hand. "Please, Summer. This is not why we are here. We are not here to make trouble. We just want to get answers, see her, and think about the future. You know, on *your* calendar, that is."

Perhaps they didn't understand that without Ruben in the picture, I wanted to close the book on my past. I didn't know a thing about his family before, and I surely didn't want to know now. "She's resting, but I suppose maybe I can go get her."

"Wait." Ana placed her mug on a coaster. "Summer, we hated Fran. We don't know what he had in common with her. She used to come around with him during the holidays, but nothing about their relationship felt organic."

"I can imagine that that is true." I had rapid flashbacks of my moments with that woman; it caused me to shudder.

Irene told me, "She was bossy, fake, pushy, and just snobby. She tried to act nice toward our family, but she treated Ruben like crap."

I told them, "It's hard to tell what he saw in her."

"She has money. She knows people. She owns a company." Irene licked her lips. "Ruben wanted us to believe it was love, but no one believed that crap. So, he wasted so much time in his life being in a marriage that he didn't want. No genuine passion. Such a shame."

"*Que lastimar*, indeed." Ana sighed.

I didn't know what Ana said, but I nodded.

Irene sipped her coffee before setting it down on the coffee table. "We know that coming here is not ideal and that you probably don't want to have any connection with us. But it would help us to see what his only child looks like."

Her statement pierced my heart. Before I couldn't empathize with them, but, now, I could see what Autumn meant to a whole lot of people. She touched my life, Oliver's life, and certainly Ruben's family. I released a subtle sigh as I rubbed my legs before standing. "Let me go get her."

One look at Ana and Irene's face told me that I was doing the right thing. Their delightful expressions erased my doubts. Perhaps Autumn could get to know her other family little by little over a long span of time. Besides, too much love never hurt anyone. I certainly wouldn't let her be with anyone else without me anyway.

I eased into her room, careful not to startle her. Peeking into the crib, Autumn's eyes were fixated on her mobile. Good. At least her sleep wouldn't be disturbed. Picking her up and holding her close to my chest, I walked her into the living while placing kisses over her happy face along the way. The two women perked up with awe once they laid eyes on her. Leaning over the sofa, I handed her off to Ana first.

"Ohhhhh. *Mi carita. Mira.*" Ana raised Autumn in the air over her face and then eased her back down with my daughter's tiny feet tapping on Ana's slender legs. My nerves ran thin with worry upon seeing a stranger holding Autumn and not knowing how my daughter would like it.

Resting a hand over her chest, Irene pouted her lips. "She is too beautiful. She has Ruben's eyes. Lookie."

A crooked smile spread across my face.

The elevator opened suddenly. I turned around when I heard the noise. Oliver walked into the apartment with a bag in his hand. He headed toward us with a confused look on his face. He bypassed the kitchen, obviously more concerned about the presence of Ana and Irene.

"Who is this?" he asked with a wrinkled forehead, nodding his head toward them. Stopping beside me, he refused to take his eyes off both ladies as I explained.

"They are Ana and Irene, Ruben's mom and sister."

They each waved and smiled. Ana passed Autumn to Irene then stood to shake Oliver's hand. "Pleased to meet you. We are so happy to meet—"

"—Autumn," I said.

"Yeah, you too." A poker-faced Oliver turned to me. "I got us something to drink, and your sunscreen will be in the room."

I nodded. He headed for the kitchen to put the drink away, then watched us from the kitchen for a few seconds before heading to the bedroom.

Ana tilted her head and smiled. "Summer and Autumn? How cute."

I grinned. "She feels closer to me with a name similar to mine."

"Love it," Irene agreed as she stroked Autumn's chin. Autumn stared back at Irene with a bland expression. Frowning, her eyes met mine, compelling me to take her back. It'd become clear that she no longer enjoyed the spotlight. Before she could tune up, I stepped forward, so Irene could pass her back to me. I squeezed her gently in my arms while lowering myself into the loveseat. We both lowered each other's anxiety.

Oliver returned with folded arms. He sat beside me. "What's going on here?"

I turned to Oliver and answered, "They want to know if they can see Autumn sometime in the future."

With a stern expression, Oliver replied, "Well, Summer and I really didn't have a chance to cover this topic." He placed both palms up. "But I will say this: Our daughter won't be with other people without us present. And these dates have to be arranged."

"We know. We aren't here to cause trouble," Irene assured Oliver.

"Good," he replied sharply.

I rubbed his leg with one free hand. "Honey." He became so intense that I began to feel bad for the Sotolongos.

Ana said, "You know, we just want some time with her even if it's for a few hours every six months or something. We just need to feel like we know Ruben's daughter. We just want to love her, you know, show Autumn her roots. It'd be great for her. Ruben may not be here any longer, but we don't have to be estranged."

"I agree, Oliver."

His face began to soften. "Fine. But unless we happen to be in Florida, it has to be here in Virginia."

"We don't mind at all," Ana said. "I just want her to meet other family members when the time is right, but we don't want to throw her life into a frenzy—or yours."

It made sense, and one day it would to Oliver, too.

"Besides," Irene said, "I know she is new to you guys, too. We feel honored just having this moment. No one in the Sotolongo family wants to harm this family unit at all. Please believe that." Irene appeared extremely sincere and almost concerned that Oliver or I wouldn't believe them.

"Oh, I won't let anything happen to them. Count on that," Oliver vowed.

I passed Autumn to her dad and wrote my name and number on a piece of paper from the coffee table and passed it to Irene. Standing, I told them, "Call me. Over time, we'll work something out. This will be good for her."

Ana and Irene nodded graciously. They stood with tears escaping their eyes. "We appreciate this," Ana stated.

"Yes, you gave our heart something to feel," Irene added. "And, you know, all of this suddenness could have been avoided if Fran told you about the funeral. We didn't know that burying him in Florida and having his service there would take you and this little one out of the loop. We're sorry about that."

A tear fell down my cheek before I could catch it. "No, don't be. Fran did this to be mean. I'm sure she wanted me to get comfortable with Autumn just to say later on, 'Oh, by the way, meet his family.' Fran calculated this mess, hoping to upset me." I grabbed Ana by the shoulders. "But what she doesn't know is that she just opened my baby's world up to more love." Surprising myself, I hugged Ana since I couldn't give my daughter the gift of knowing her natural father. Ana squeezed me back. "So, you're her grandma, huh?"

Ana nodded her head vehemently. "Yes, yes. Call me, *abuelita*." She smiled warmly with tears glistening her cheeks and then made her way to see Oliver. I turned to see her stroke his arm. "Young man, I can tell that these two are your world." Her bony, petite hand brushed Autumn's cheek. "Please, just know we are here on good terms. Nothing else."

When his eyes met mine, I nodded. Oliver grinned slowly and pulled her in for an embrace with one arm. "Then welcome to my world."

Pleased, I let out a breath and turned to a glowing Irene. She hugged me, and we all said our goodbyes.

I told Oliver, "Thank you, baby. Thank you."

"Well, my job is to protect, but who am I to forbid this union?" He shrugged. "Now, Autumn has three grandmothers, and I really can't argue with that."

Exhaling with a smile, I said, "You know, we really can't." But before I could get too happy, an unpleasant idea popped into my head. "I'm gonna call Fran."

Oliver's chin tilted upward at me. "Do it."

Upset by her dirty chess move, I had to let Fran know that she didn't win. Her manipulations had gone on long enough.

"Go put Autumn down," I told him.

Pointing a finger at me from across the room, he ordered. "Wait for me before you make that call, Summer."

"Sure." I plopped on the sofa with folded arms to think things through. Backing down from this fight wasn't an option. I'd taken a lot from this lady, and she needed to know that Oliver didn't need to fight my battles.

When Oliver returned, I spun around at the sound of his footsteps. "Make your call."

I stood and admitted, "I'm ready, but listen. Even though I don't mind the Sotolongos, they could've been bad people on the other side of that door."

"Look, let's do something. I'm going to pay to have the Sotolongos investigated before making good on our word. They're all the way in Florida, and we don't know anything about them. If they are bad people, we won't pursue, but something tells me they're all right. Let's just make sure Fran didn't send us dirty women. Besides, you know I have one of the best home security systems on the market, right?"

I nodded before heading back to our bedroom to grab my cell. Back in the living room with Oliver, he stood waiting with hands behind his head.

I activated Fran's line with one tap on her name. "Hello?"

Recognizing Fran's ugly tone, my stomach churned with disgust. I placed her on speakerphone.

"Fran, this is Summer," I told her with burning hostility. "I met the Sotolongos, so I'm calling you to say thank you. We had a great time together. Autumn took to them very well. Tell me, do you have any other foolish attempts to ruin me up your sleeve? Because if you do, bring it."

"Well, Summer, I'm actually quite pleased that you two had a lovely time." Fran tried her best but failed to mask the irritation in her tone. Inside, I danced delightfully at my successful attempt to piss her off. "Tell me, shall I send over say, uhhh, a pizza the next time you guys meet again?"

I saw Oliver's eyes move abruptly from the cellphone to mine. In a quick move, he stole the phone from me and said through clenched teeth, "Listen here, you raggedy old bitch. I have no problem telling you that if you come into contact with Autumn or Summer, or send anything or anyone to them again, I will plaster those pictures on every pole of Ballston and DC until everyone knows every crease of your cunt. You got me? Try something else. Try it."

I heard her swallow during her long pause. She must've decided to do as advised, because she didn't have anything else to say to Oliver. All we heard in response was a dial tone. Funny. Fran was one of the top recruiters in this area, so it was nice to see that her talent served her well in both directions. While she was good at finding people who could serve her well, she also proved that she was good at recruiting her own worst enemy: Oliver.

"You tellin' me Fran hung up scared?" Amber asked, passing each of us a glass of wine.

We sat on the floor of her second bedroom around a box of New York-style cheese pizza as I caught them up to speed about yesterday. It was the only unfurnished room in the apartment, with only a lonely lamp for decoration. We huddled in the middle, stuffing our faces with pizza and gossip.

I shrugged a shoulder. "I mean, I guess so. Oliver shook me to the core, and the threat wasn't even for me."

"That's my man." Brooke winked with a grin. "Protect and serve."

We fell over laughing.

"Do you think he'd let anyone hurt his two seasons?" Amber joked.

Emily seemed rather quiet and strange all night. When we laughed, she would just crack a dry smile.

"Is something wrong, boo?" I asked her.

Brooke tilted her head. "Yeah. You've been quiet all night. Did my honeymoon pictures upset you? I'm sorry, Emily. That was rude of me to be all—"

"Or did I do or say something wrong?" I asked.

"No, no, y'all. Thanks, but don't be silly." Distracted by private thoughts, she poked her tongue against her cheek.

Concerned, Brooke asked, "Well, can we help?"

"Yeah." Amber lowered herself next to Emily. She rubbed her friend's back. "We all here for you."

"Finish telling us about Daniel," Emily suggested, changing the subject. Deciding not to press any further, Amber nodded with reluctance.

"Well, yeah, days ago, he came over and tried to get me back."

"Ehhhhhh." Brooke pinched her nose at the news as she grabbed another slice of pizza. "Fat with smelly breath. No, thank you."

Holding a hand in the air, Amber replied, "Well that's the thing." She looked stunned. She piqued all of our curiosities. "He was leaner with fresher breath. Daniel told me that he wanted to clean himself up for a sis."

Brooke swallowed. "Stay away. Steer clear from people who buckle down to win you over. It's a trap that they don't even see they set. Once they get you, they're right back to their old habits all in the name of comfort."

My brows crinkled. "Oh, come on, Brooke. Even I can be pessimistic and can say I don't totally agree. For the right person, we want to change."

Brooke shot me a sideways glance. "Honey. It's only been a few months. I got my eyes on you." She winked and smiled.

"Ha!" I said. "Girl, I'm done with the recklessness. Child or no child. Mama had to learn the hard way."

"I agree with Brooke," Emily said. She caught our attention. "Did you not see what Eric did? I fell for his bologna."

"But Eric was a snake in the grass driven by his own agenda," I replied. "Daniel just wants to be with Amber. He misses his slice of chocolate trim."

Amber fell over laughing as she high-fived me. "You know I got the good stuff to keep them coming back."

Emily squinted at Amber and stood to her feet. She marched out of the room and into the bathroom. We all went silent looking like deer in highlights. Brooke dropped her slice of pizza back into the box and sat her glass on top to trail Emily. Amber and I placed our glasses of wine on the pizza box and followed quickly behind.

We all stood at the door in the hallway, watching Brooke knock gently. "Emily, sweetie. Please open up. Talk to us."

"No."

"Why not? What just happened?" Brooke insisted.

"You wouldn't understand."

"Try us," Amber replied.

"You really wouldn't," she answered back.

Brooke said, "Open up, sweetie. We really can't help you if you don't come out. Besides, this is Amber's house, and if you stay . . ."

"You have to go home sometimes," Amber said. "Otherwise, you'll be forced to hear the cries of my orgasms at the hand of my—hand. I mean, eventually, I'ma need that booty bowl to excrete this cheese pizza!"

"*I hate you, Amber*!" Brooke cried holding her midsection with tears. "Get a man, would you?"

"Her only option is a man with booty breath," I wailed in a shaky voice. Succumbing to the humor, we all fell apart on the other side of the door with our backs against the wall and butts on the floor. It had to be the wine.

"Shut up, guys!" Amber cried through her tears. "At least I'm getting some. One way or another, I'm bringing it home, even if it's all by myself."

I fell onto Brooke's shoulders. We coughed and tried to collect ourselves when the bathroom door opened. Emily stood over us with both palms at her sides as she shook her head with a mock look of disapproval spread across her face. "These are the ladies who are here to help me, huh?"

We cried louder with laughter as she stepped over us to head toward the living room. Failing to compose ourselves, we threw out perfunctory apologies. We struggled to stand on our bare feet, but eventually we managed to collect ourselves by the time she marched toward us with her purse in her hand.

With a hand on her hip and hair falling carelessly past her shoulders, Emily stood in the doorway to the bathroom. "Did you guys mean it? You want to help?"

"Yeah, yes," we replied, trying to prove our readiness.

Emily disappeared into the bathroom.

The three of us wiped the tears from our eyes with the sniffles while we gathered in the lengthy bathroom.

Sitting on top of the toilet seat, Emily opened her purse and held it high. "Look inside."

We eyed her cautiously and maybe even suspiciously before following her instructions.

"What do you see?"

Brooke picked up the big box from the almost empty purse. Her eyes widened as she sobered up. "Ems . . . is this what I think it is?"

Amber pointed a thumb at me. "Wow. Summer knows that box all too well."

I eyed the pregnancy box and blinked slowly once. "Yes . . . yes. She may be having a baby." Wanting to correct Amber, I turned to her. "And I did not take one of these. My doctor informed me." My heart pumped its brake for a moment when it occurred to me that the horror in my friend's eyes had to match the same sentiment as mine when Dr. Westin told me the news about my own pregnancy. This was officially, no laughing matter.

"Oh, true." Amber nodded her head thoughtfully.

We eyed each other with expressions that had yet to process the information given while Emily studied us blandly. "Yes, I'm past the shock. Can someone just tell me that it's negative when I do the test?"

"Do you have any symptoms?" I asked. "Or are you late?"

"I am now, and I threw up in class on Monday and every day since. I, of course, have no fever. I've been toting this thing around with no nerves to test myself."

"Then what do we need the stick for?" Amber asked with light humor, but we weren't laughing.

"Give this thing to me," I told Brooke. She passed it to me, and I ripped into it and held the stick out in front of our solemn friend's face. "Pee on it, and Amber will be back to collect the rod."

"Why me?" Amber cried.

"Because it's your home, and that's what good hosts do," I told her.

"You're the one with the baby experience," she told me. "I don't know how to read that."

"Honey." I placed a hand on her shoulder. "Did you take arithmetic? It's a plus and minus. And we all know negative means not happening."

Amber snatched the stick and rolled her eyes. She pointed the stick at Emily and through gritted teeth she told her, "You better be glad I like your butt."

Emily nodded and swallowed. "I need the stick to pee."

Amber paused for a second. "Oh, true." She handed it to Emily before Brooke and I left. I saw Amber turn her back as Emily prepared herself for the big moment. Brooke and I congregated in the spare room with the pizza.

"I think I need more wine," Brooke said as she fanned herself.

"Right?"

Brooke wore a fretful expression. "But which glass is which?"

"I know." I picked up the correct glasses and we sipped.

"Talk about a bad spot." Brooke placed a hand on her hip. "Is it Eric's? Is it Zach's?"

I shook my head. "Zach was a little long ago, so probably Eric's, but you never know. The body is strange. This situation is a nightmare. Let's hope this baby belongs to anyone but Eric. I mean, kids, okay, but to be beholden to dealing with a man for life who left you at the altar?"

"That was just so dirty. So low." Brooke shook her finger. "You know, I knew Eric, too, and I have to say, that was a low move, even for him. Now she has to tell that animal about this baby."

"Maybe she's not pregnant. I mean, bodies are strange, especially for us ladies."

"Right."

Amber joined us with the test on a towel before we could squeeze in another sip.

"Here's the piss rod."

I asked, "What's it say?"

"Too soon," she replied. "We shouldn't be so scared, this isn't our baby."

Brooke wagged a red nail at her. "Nah, sis. We all in this together. Cuz when I get pregnant, you bitches better be there for me." She took a nervous gulp of wine.

I slid a shoulder back as I studied her. "Scared of you."

Amber reflected a dead stare back at Brooke. "Duly noted."

"We should know by now," I told her. "Read it. I'm so scared."

"You? You did the work already," Amber replied.

"That's why I'm scared. I know what lies ahead."

Brooke seemed fidgety. She swirled a nail at me. "Well buck up. I'm sure Oliver's gonna want his own season paddling around the house."

"Umm, could y'all let my vagina snap back into place first before y'all go making plans with it? Sheesh."

"Damn." Amber stared at me with horror in her eyes. "Brooke get so mean when she gets too much wine."

Looking straight and not at Amber or me, Brooke said, "I'm just sayin' y'all. I'm just sayin'."

"A lot," Amber teased. She pointed at me. "And you take it easy, too. You have to drive home."

"You're not that far from me. Six miles to be exact."

"A lot can go on in six miles." Amber peered at her hand holding the towel. "Should we?"

Brooke and I looked at one another before nodding. "Do it," she voted.

Amber bit her lip and opened the towel. Her hand flew to her mouth. The stick stared up at us with an answer. I closed my eyes and swallowed hard.

"No," I whispered.

"Yes," Amber whispered back.

Brooke covered her mouth with her hand. "Shiiiiiit."

"Am I pregnant?" Hugging the edge of the wall and only giving us her face and shoulder, a petrified Emily appeared mysteriously behind Amber.

Amber froze with eyes that darted between mine and Brooke's. She circled her mouth and exhaled very silently before turning around. She answered with a weak, "Yes, Emily. You are pregnant."

"But we will all be there for you," Brooke blurted out.

Emily swung an arm over her midsection as she emerged from around Amber and into full sight. Once she exhaled, she opened her mouth to say, "Okay. I knew it, I knew it, I knew it." While her voice remained low and calm, her eyes told another story. Her complexion had faded, leaving her pale against the canvas of her natural beauty.

I bit my lip but decided to speak up. "Do you know who the father is?" Amber and Brooke couldn't turn their necks fast enough to look at me. When Emily answered, they turned back to her.

"Well, it can't be Zach's, we used protection all the time, and I took birth control. Same goes for my one encounter with umm . . . with umm . . ." she closed her eyes as she struggled to recall his name, "Garrett." Her hazel eyes popped open, but they still looked dull. "It has to be Eric's. I . . . I missed a few pills with him. Okay, I missed a few before he came back. But I would never make Eric use a condom. You know, there's always that one man that you go raw for. And we discussed children for our future. Sperm from the devil himself."

"Don't say that," Amber said. "Please don't put that on a child."

Brooke nodded as she crossed her arms in thought.

Emily looked weak as she threw a quick hand in the air. "Well what do you want me to say?" Subdued more than ever, Emily shook her head. "I am growing life inside of me from a man who ditched me on my wedding day. What a disgrace to label him as a daddy."

"Will you call him to tell him he's the father?" Brooke asked carefully.

Emily didn't hesitate. "I reflected greatly on this. No."

Something deep inside compelled me to speak up. Somewhere from a place of experience. "Emily? This may change him. Don't you at least—?"

"I said 'no,' and I'm not changing my mind," she said quietly, struggling to seem mended as she guarded her stomach with one arm. "A man like that doesn't deserve a child. He will never know."

"And the baby? What will you tell him or her one day?" Brooke asked.

Emily became jittery. "I will tell the kid the truth when he or she is a teenage. I won't lie."

"But what about before that stage in life?" I asked.

"Well obviously there won't be any details but that I'm enough, and that I'm all he or she's got."

Brooke placed a hand on Emily's arm. "Emily, please take some time to think this through. Look what happened to me. Raised around lies. Do you want that for your child? I know the time is not ideal to ask you about this, but it would be remiss of me not to bring it up or not to try to talk some sense into you."

"Stop it, Brooke! Stop it you two!" Hostile, Emily yanked her arm from Brooke's touch.

"I know what it's like to be fatherless!" I blurted with full emotion. "I know what it's like to have the baby's daddy be the last person on your list." I gritted my teeth to fight back the tears. "But, dammit, Emily, you've got to bite that bullet and tell him. *Tell him.* Too many children don't know their fathers. Don't let that—"

"This!" Emily pointed an angry finger at all of us. "This is *not* up for discussion! I never wanna see Eric again. A man who could do what he did is not welcomed in my child's life until my child decides that she is ready to face him. And until one of you gets left at the altar for all to see and sent a recorded message mocking the moment, *you* cannot talk. So let it go!" Emily stormed out of the room; we followed her instantly.

"Emily, please!" Brooke cried.

"Wait up!" Amber called. "Sweetie, don't go!"

Being the last in the line, I saw Emily spin around once she reached the living room. With a finger pointed at her chest and eyes searing with anger, she stated, "*I* will go on to raise this baby alone. I will love, care, and accept this child no matter the daddy, because it is a blessing regardless. I don't need any man's time or help to make this child a dynamic being. If I get a man down the road, then great. If not, I will do it, because I am able, focused, and determined to love this baby like it is the last thing on this earth. *Que sera, que sera.* So *don't.* You hear me? *Don't* bring up the men of my past. I don't need Eric, and I don't want Zach. I want a man who is crazy about me, not just me about him. I want a man who will rub my feet at the end of a long day, after I've come home from teaching children, without me having to say a word to get it. I don't want to force my feelings to have a man, nor do I want to wait for the ball to drop with the other. Okay? My dad will be an incredible grandpa, and that will have to do for now. Understand?"

Standing silently and dumbfounded, we nodded like minions before I charged through the two girls to reach Emily. I gently slammed my body into hers and wrapped my arms around her neck. I kissed her jawbone and held her close to whisper, "I'm sorry," into her ear. She sniffled, and the two other ladies behind me made the same noise.

When I backed up, Emily nodded with a painful grin. She pointed up. "God will see us through," she told me in a trembling voice. She shook her head. "I don't need a man."

I rubbed her shoulder. "You're so right." I stepped to the side.

Not ready to step forward, Brooke rubbed her chest as she silently sobbed. Amber took two steps to meet Emily face to face. She placed a palm on Emily's cheek. "Baby girl? You can do this. Whenever you need that husband in the middle of the night or even in the day, call me and I will help you. Remember around Brooke's wedding?" Emily nodded with a perfunctory smile. "Well I told you we may have to be together." They giggled. "So, as long as you don't catch me when I'm in the middle of my bitness," she pointed to her vagina, "I will come be there for you." Amber gave Emily and me a good chuckle. She hugged Emily, and said, "You know I love you."

"I do. I love you, too, Amber. And thank you for that. I'll call you when I need a *friend*."

Amber let her go and stepped to the side.

Brooke collected herself in time to say, "What are we all getting corny for?" She managed a crooked grin. "No one is dying or leaving, just giving birth. You have my full support, Emily. Time or anything else you need. In fact, I know Jackson's and my kid will be playing in the same sandbox as yours and Summer's." She sighed. "I know I came down on you, but I was concerned, and I did it out of love. But you are the mom, and we have to trust and respect your decision." Brooke embraced Emily.

Emily leaned back. "Thank you, Brooke."

Brooke sighed and wiped her cheek. "I'm not so good with words and affection, but you know how I feel about you, right?"

Emily helped to wipe a tear from Brooke's cheek. "Yes, Brooke Brazile, I know."

Brooke pointed a playful finger. "Hey. Brooke Sloan."

Emily shook her head. "You will always be my Brooke Brazile."

We all snickered.

"True," I agreed.

Somehow, we all knew to grab hands as we stood in a circle in the middle of Amber's living room. We traded glimpses at each other's faces with intricate hands that swung carelessly. Brooke started with, "Summer, I hope you, Oliver, and Autumn have a safe and fun trip. Enjoy your vacation, because once you come back to the States, life and chaos begin again."

I saluted her and mouth a silent, "Thank you."

"I'll miss you, pumpkin head." Amber pouted at me. "But have lots of sex for me. Oh! And do it on the beach. I've never done that before," she mockingly lamented.

"What? You should!" Brooke told Amber.

I giggled and assured Amber, "Oh, I will."

"But I'm not sure how Autumn will like that or CPS." Emily shot me a suspicious side-eye glance with a grin.

I wiggled my neck with a pointed finger. "That's why Oliver is bringing my mom and then his mom. When mine leaves, the other comes. We gonna get that privacy that doesn't come with parenting."

"Whoa, I saw that neckroll, Summer!" Amber hollered. She created a riot of laughter as Emily allowed herself to let her wall of stress down just enough to give into a good time with her friends.

Emily held my hand to her face. "Have fun, sis."

"I will, thank you."

Amber said, "Wait!" She ran from the room and into the kitchen. Confused, we looked at each other and shrugged. She returned with a bottle of wine in one hand. "Hold this." She shoved it into my hands. Leaving again, she returned with four clean glasses and passed them out. After filling Brooke's and my glass with about an inch of wine, she pretended to fill Emily's before her own. With a raised glass, she spoke. "Bitch, you gon have to pretend you got wine with your ole pregnant ass. I ain't that ratchet."

Emily frowned. Brooke and I grimaced then chuckled.

"So, congratulations to Emily on her pregnancy and getting rid of toxic people." Amber looked at me. "You go."

"Congratulations to Amber on her new apartment and leaving her old hole-in-the-wall joint." I winked at her. "Emily?"

"Congratulations to Brooke and her marriage and reconnecting with her family." She gave Brooke's hand a squeeze. "And, Brooke?"

"Congratulations to Summer for locking it down with Oliver, having that precious baby, getting that new job, and to the demise of that bitch Fran." We cheered hard for that. She blew me a kiss. I pretended to catch it.

"Cheers," we all said at once as we watched our glasses click. After taking quick and long sips, we all agreed that it was getting late and time to turn in.

"I know I have to wake up soon," I told the ladies. Can't afford to miss our plane. My mom should be in soon. I should go." I took one last look at their faces to see nods and smiles.

"Me, too. I haven't had proper rest since the return from our honeymoon," Brooke added.

Amber collected our glasses and placed them on the coffee table. "Yeah, I'm acting like I don't have to wake up. Ooh!" Her eyes widened. "Wait, guys." She picked up her purse from the sofa and pulled out a set of keys. When she held up the key ring, we saw an alarm. Our hands flew to our mouths.

"Is that—?" I asked pointing.

She nodded with excitement. "My new car. I picked up my brand new Civic yesterday evening. I'm no longer Metro dependent!" She jumped and clapped like a happy seal.

"I coulda given cheers to *that*," I told her.

Brooke gave her a shake on the shoulder. "Wow. You *are* taking this grown-up thing seriously, huh?"

"It beats living in chaos," Amber replied.

"Yeah, from crazy Columbia Pike to the Pentagon metro stop? It's good to hook right up to 395 with a car, ain't it?" Emily asked.

"Bet. Whew. I cannot believe I got my own set of wheels. My first car! I didn't need one in New York, and I was too broke to buy one once I moved here." She curtsied. "It's my modest start."

Brooke pointed at Amber with a cocked brow. "Just keep your debt low."

"I can say it pays to have good credit." She stuck her tongue out and twerked for a few seconds.

"Here, here," Emily and Brooke said.

"Well, I'm glad for you." I high-fived her.

Emily pointed a finger at Amber. "Hey, well, I may need a ride to church on Sundays. Can you do that sometimes?"

Amber bit her lower lip as she smiled warmly at her friend. "Be happy to. Yeah."

"Awesome." Emily rubbed her stomach. "Well, I'm going to get going. I have a little one to start nurturing."

I placed my hand on her shoulder. "Please, call me if you ever need to talk about the stages, or if you just need to vomit in my toilet." We all chuckled. "Congratulations again."

"Thank you." Emily ran her tongue over her upper lip. "I think your offer sounds good." She plucked some hair back from her face with a hand.

Amber clapped her hands together. "Well, bitches, I guess you can officially get out of my house, so I can get to bed."

We headed for the door with our shoes back on and purses in hand.

I said, "Wait."

They all looked at me when I turned around. "When's our next date? Next weekend?"

"Saturday morning?" Emily suggested. "I'm so in."

"Me, too," Brooke replied. "I don't think Jackson and I will have anything planned. But if he wants me, bae comes first."

A warm smile slid across my face. "Saturday morning, La Madeleine, Old Town Alexandria? I know our old location shut down, but it'd be like celebrating where it kind of all began."

A sentimental look hit everyone's face.

Brooke said, "You know what? I'll make sure that Jackson doesn't plan anything for us during that time. Yeah. That sounds good, Summer."

Amber said, "I'm in. I won't book lessons at that time."

With that, we left knowing that being together next weekend would be a sure thing.

Brooke

Brooke walked through her home to see Jackson wearing boxer briefs while standing in their kitchen with a glass of water at his lips. She headed toward him urgently, causing him to set his glass down immediately as she hugged him with need.

"*Hey*, hey, baby. You okay? What's going on?" He kissed her head and rubbed her back lovingly.

Brooke pulled back to look him in the eyes. "Baby, you won't believe the latest."

"Try me."

"Emily's pregnant."

His eyes got larger. "You kiddin' me."

"Nope. Sis is expecting."

"Okay. What am I missing?"

"Jackson. She's *pregn*ant. Hello?" She studied his face not understanding why he treated the news nonchalantly.

"Emily. Oh." He chuckled. "For some reason I thought about Amber, who I'm sure will be pregnant any given day now. You know how she rolls."

"Hey," she pointed a finger at him, "don't be throwing shade at my girls."

Moving toward the refrigerator, he shrugged with a grin. "Yo, I can't help it if Amber stays open like a twenty-four-hour diner. Just sayin'."

"Please don't drag my friend, especially behind her back. And Emily is pregnant and with Eric's baby."

"Oh." Jackson scratched the back of his head, squinting. "I'm sorry, baby. I didn't mean to minimize the situation."

"You should be, but I know."

He reached into the freezer for the carton of ice cream. "How is she?" Reaching for a bowl, he spooned a few servings of pistachio ice cream and handed it to Brooke.

"Thanks. This is exactly what I need. She's devasted because of the man. But she knows we got her back." Brooke placed it on the counter and stripped off each layer of clothing until she stood in nothing but her lacy red underwear set. She kicked her pool of clothes to the side and leaned against the counter as she began to eat. It'd been a long and stressful day.

Jackson froze as he watched. "Wh-why'd you do that? How can I think?"

Brooke shrugged with a look of satisfaction. "Oh, well." Her tongue toyed with the spoon. She locked eyes with her husband.

Her husband. She liked that. Any physical attention from this man was more than welcomed.

Jackson snatched the bowl from her and before she could protest, he lifted her over his shoulder and carried her to the bedroom. She playfully hit his back repeatedly. "Hey, put me down, man! Gimme back my ice cream."

"You get that ice cream back when you gimme some booty first."

Laughing, her hair swung over her face. She cried out, "No ice cream, no pussy." When they reached their bedroom, he lowered her onto the mattress.

"Mmm." Standing, Jackson towered over her. "Oh, baby, I'm gettin' some pussy." He licked his lower lip. "I've been thinking about you all day. And by the way, I don't wanna hear about other women. Just you. How was *your* day?"

Lying down at the end of the mattress with her bent knees, Brooke's tilted head hinted at her melting from his words. Jackson's hand covered her bare foot, rubbing it, kissing the top of it. She felt extremely touched by his actions.

"It was a good day, baby."

"And, yet, you look worried." He continued to rub. "Why you lookin' at me like that?"

"Because . . . you do put me first, and I didn't even ask about your day first, nor did I say 'hello.' I'm a crappy wife. How was *your* day?"

"It was great. Can't complain." His eyes moved from her feet to her face. "Missed you though. And you're not a crappy wife."

"I love you," Brooke whispered.

"Ditto." Jackson freed his hands from her feet and held them out for her to hold them. Brooke linked her hands into his, and as he pulled her up, he lowered himself and transferred her onto his lap. They stared at each other. "Let's talk about Emily, cuz I can tell it bothered you."

"She doesn't wanna tell Eric after what he did. I feel that she should tell him. Look at my childhood."

"That's her baby, her life, her choice, sweetie."

"I know, I know. She firmly reminded us that that was not our place to call the shots."

"See, there you go." He caressed her thighs.

"But she did say that she wanted a man who would rub her feet without asking after a long day at work." Full of thought, Brooke said, "And you did just that tonight. What woman wouldn't want someone like you, Jackson? I'm extremely fortunate to have a man like you."

Looking pleased, Jackson nodded. "Your love makes me a better man. But if you wanna repay a brotha', gimme some ass."

Humored, Brooke's jaw dropped.

"Then you get that ice cream."

Pretending to be puzzled, Brooke asked, "Ice cream? Ice cream? It's probably melted by now. Your promise is no good now."

"Oh, really?" Jackson tickled her ribs and armpits until she submitted. He moved her to the top half of the bed and placed kisses all over her chest. "You know, Emily's baby gonna need some company."

"Oh, yeah?" she panted.

He paused to say, "Yeah."

"Let's do it, baby. Let's do it."

Brooke enjoyed the feel of his kisses all over her skin. She realized just how rich one woman could be. Quivering under his seduction, Brooke wondered if one could have it all. That question haunted her for the longest time. As a child, she didn't think so. As a single woman, she suspected that it was a possibility.

I love you, Brazile," Jackson whispered as his fingers slid under her bra straps.

"I love you, too, Sloan."

However, now as a happily married woman in love with a booming business, a new connection to her newfound family, and a pack of best friends who felt like sisters, her answer was absolutely, she could have it all! With a grin spreading across her face, she figured out that the trick was learning how to keep it all. Jackson slid into her with one deep thrust, causing Brooke to cry out. She wanted to be like the old Amber since she had the right man by her side. Brooke looked forward to keeping her legs open like a twenty-four-hour diner. Since Jackson made her a priority, she planned to give him all the desires of his heart. With this man by her side, Brooke couldn't wait to see what they could accomplish together.

Emily

Emily sat on her guest bed in an oversized t-shirt as she tipped a big plastic bag from the bottom to watch all the contents fall onto the mattress. Big, blue and pink, wooden letters plopped on her bed to create the two names she had in mind. Getting up to stare at the four walls of the spare bedroom that she now knew would become the nursery, Emily decided to nail the letters on the wall facing the entrance to the room. She wanted the baby's name to be the first thing in sight.

Emily reached for the first blue letter and nailed it to the wall. About ten minutes later, she stood back to admire her work. Then she decided to quickly proceed with the pink letters. Nailing them beside the blue letters, another ten minutes later, she stood back and smiled at her work. Rubbing her belly, it occurred to her that life would be just her and the unborn child, for a while anyway.

The sound of the cellphone ringing in her bedroom broke her thoughts. Locating the phone on her bed, she picked it up. "Hello?"

"Hey, babe."

She smiled. "Let me guess. This must be, umm, Zach!"

She could hear his smile over the phone. "All right. You got me. What are you up to?"

"A lot, actually." Standing with her hand on her hip, she decided to go back to the soon-to-be nursery room with Zach plugged into her ear.

"Oh, yeah? Tell me."

"You wouldn't believe it, but I don't want you to flip out, okay?"

"Talk to me. I'm a good sport."

"Zach, I'm pregnant."

He didn't say anything. "Oh. Is it mine?"

"Do you want it to be?" She wanted to play a little.

He let out a quick, nervous chuckle. "That's cute. But is it?"

"Well, no. But did you want it to be?"

"I would prefer to have you if you were pregnant with my baby. But since you're not, I guess I can quit dreaming."

"But I don't think you would have wanted me and a baby. Just me."

"Nahhh. I was crazy over you. I still am, but you're too foolish to appreciate it."

Taken aback, Emily twisted her mouth in disbelief. "I'm not foolish. But I know what I want, and I—"

"So is it Eric's?"

Emily sighed as she stared at the floor. "The one and only. But I will not be telling him."

"Damn, Emily. I knew it. How does this man get so lucky with you?"

"Well, he won't know he's lucky, because like I said, I ain't telling him nothing."

"Good for you. I don't blame you."

"Glad someone agrees. My friends didn't quite agree at first, but they accept it. They don't have a choice."

"Well, he's not someone I would want around my child. You can do it, Emily. You'll have enough love to make up for his missing half."

Touched and feeling warm inside, Emily said, "Well, thank you, Zach. I do believe that that is the kindest thing you have ever told me."

"I mean it. I just wish it coulda been me. I liked you since the first time I'd seen ya'."

"You and your penis, huh?"

Chuckling, he replied, "Please don't. Remember?"

"I'm sorry. I'm so sorry," she said between giggles. "I'm not going there with you."

"I can't believe it though."

"What?"

"You're gonna have a baby. What a blessing. Congratulations, Emily. Really, I mean it."

"Thanks, Zach. Thank you so much."

"When you need me to do the crib building and stuff, give me a call, okay?"

"I will. And how is everything on your end?" Emily sat back on the bed.

"Ummmmm, Enzo is doing great in school, and he told me that he wanted to buy you a plant or flowers so when you get it, act surprised, okay?"

Emily laughed. "Oh, okay. How sweet. I miss him, too. I'm glad he's doing well. And you?"

"I'm okay, just . . . missing you. That's all. At this point, I'll be happy to be your sex buddy or phone sex partner."

"Maybe you should try dating, Zach. I'm tired, and I'm going to bed."

"You're no fun."

"If I get horny, I think you'll be the first one I call, okay? Sounds good to you?"

"You've made my night."

"Good night. And thanks for calling, Zach."

"My pleasure. Wait."

"Yeah?"

"What will you . . . what do you think you'll name your baby?"

"Funny you should ask." Emily looked up at the wall of both names facing her. "If it's a boy, I'm going to name him Emilio." She traced her finger over the comforter as she spoke. "But if it's a *girl*, then I will name her Amelia."

"Wow. Bears no resemblance to your name, huh?"

Not even pretending to be upset, she replied, "Shut up. No teasing. And I'm hanging up now."

"I do like the names. I do. They're precious. Like you."

"You're too sweet."

"Good night, precious."

"Okay." Emily ended the call and held it to her chest as she stared at the possible names of her child. "You're gonna be all right, girl," she told herself in a low voice. She wore a proud expression as she absently lowered the phone to the bed. Just last year, Emily remembered how frail and unsure of herself she used to be. She remembered how hard it seemed just to wake up. It was inconceivable not to tie her happiness to the possibility of Eric's return.

At the moment, Emily knew that she no longer needed to fit the mode of the woman who needed a big house with a husband and children to feel complete. Rubbing her flat belly with her sight set on the two names hanging on the wall, she realized that despite all the pain, false hope, and humiliation that came along the way, she was exactly where she needed to be. Emily figured out that being alone didn't feel so bad, as long as she took that time to find herself.

Amber

Ready for bed with a scarf around her head, Amber curled up on top of her bed with her keys in her hand as she fingered the ring in disbelief. She set the key down on the nightstand and dialed her sister's phone number while lighting a cigarette. Pinching the cellphone between her shoulder and ear, she waited for her sister to pick up as she took the first puff.

"Hello?"

"What's good, baby?"

"Sis! How-how you been doing? I haven't heard from you in a week! Did you move yet?"

Watching the smoke curl in front of her face, Amber nodded. "I did, I did. And guess what?"

"What?" Mara sounded excited.

"I can come and visit you . . . *in my new car.*"

"What? You got one?"

"Yup."

"Seriously?" she asked in a squeaky voice.

"Not playin'." Amber shared the news about the type of car and the price. "The salesman tried to flirt with me, but I wasn't even tryna have it."

"Oh, no." Mara giggled. "They so fresh and horny, those car salesmen.

"For real. He was cute though. I ain't even gonna front, but nah."

"So, when you gonna pull up?"

"I for real wanna take the girls up there ASAP."

"Oh, that'd be something."

"That'd be lit, wouldn't it?"

"Oh, definitely. How you like your place?"

Amber described her new place. "I feel so lucky to of found my landlord and job at the same time. The good Lord was lookin' out for me, girl. I'm tellin' you now."

"Oh, absolutely. What a blessing. Amber, I'm so glad you're happy and safe. Did you start real estate school?"

Amber squinted. "Soon."

"Oh, okay. And I got some news, too."

Interested, Amber replied, "Yeah?"

"Yes. I'm dating."

"Uh—well, okay, sis, mkay."

"Sis, he's tall, smart, and studying to become an engineer. Bruh not even trying to get into my size fourteen pants."

"Oh! You lost more weight?" Amber put out her cigarette on the tray next to her before sitting up.

"Keeping it moving. And this size is almost too big."

"Honey, that's good, girl. Keep it up."

"I will. I'm loving it. I wanna get fit, you know?"

"You always gon' be my beautiful sister."

"Aww, thanks. And what about you? You dating anyone? Seeing Amit yet?"

Laughing, Amber answered, "Umm, nah. I'm good. I ain't really about that life. I need time alone first. But check this though, Daniel tried to win me back."

"What? No."

"No, listen. His breath was a step up, and he lost some weight, but still I can't. For real, Mara, he really wanted me back. But Daniel did grow to care for me the same time I did for myself. And what I found out was that nothin' really matters anymore except for what I want to do for myself. And besides, Amit was a distraction, not a real possibility."

"Mmm, say less, say less. Well good. You should focus on yourself. I am *really* proud of you. You don't need a man, and you certainly don't need Daniel. I could never forgive him for shaming you at his office anyway."

"Nuff 'bout me though. I'm tryna' hear more about this man of yours."

"Umm, I can give you a few details now and then the rest later, cuz actually, I got a study group in thirty minutes I gotta get to."

"Then how 'bout I get a name?"

"I was about to. Chill. Okay, okay."

Amber could hear her sister's smile on the other end.

"His name is Niram. Niram Jones. He's around your complexion, and he has these deep-set eyes and beautiful brows that I love. Oh! He's slender but got nice arms. He's got a few tattoos on them. It's so hot, he's so hot."

"Sure, sure. It's all fun in the beginnin' though."

"Miss Optimistic, are you happy for me or nah?"

"Yes, yes. Just make sure he stays in college and treats you right."

"Oh, no. The first sign of disrespect, and I'll kick that fool to the curb. Ain't nobody gonna play me. Oh, hell to the super nah."

"Okay. Then it's cool. Stick to that, and you'll be okay. Just put you and those grades first, or you gon' end up like old Amber."

"No, thanks."

"Oh, gee, thanks. She wasn't *that* bad. Was she?" Amber waited with enlarged eyes as she wrestled with whether or not she wanted to know the truth.

"Moving along, I gotta go."

"Me, too. I'm horny, and now a bitch gotta figure out how she gonna handle it."

"Amber. Don't you dare. Stay strong. Gotta go. Love you."

"I love you, too, Mara."

After they hung up, Amber found herself scrolling through her list of contacts. Seeing Crisanto's name, she realized that she either forgot to go back to delete his name or didn't want to admit that she was hoping that one day, maybe they could reconnect and become friends again. Either way, she wasn't too clear on why his name hadn't met the trash can like all the other guys this past year.

Staring at Crisanto's name, she reflected upon the wild sexual encounters that they shared. Then, she quickly remembered just how "busy" he'd become when he started school. She didn't like the idea of begging no one for their time, and he also wanted her just for sex. If she ever wanted to start a family one day, it would be a struggle with law school. Toying with wanting to know how he was doing, Amber thought about calling Cris.

Bored, Amber decided, "What the hell?" Besides, she had something that she kind of wanted to tell him. It rang twice before he picked it up.

"What's up?"

"Cris?"

"Yup."

"How are you?" she asked warmly.

"I'm great. Tired, but great." He grunted and chuckled dryly. "What about you?"

"You ain't gonna ask who this is?" Peeling back the covers with one hand, Amber snaked her body under the sheets.

"I know who this is. I remember your voice, and I still got you programmed."

"Oh." She felt a tad shy. "I'm surprised that you didn't erase me. Were you keepin' your options open or somethin'?"

Amused, he answered, "I'm a man, Amber. I ain't gonna lie."

"Then why haven't you exercised that option yet? Had me thinkin' we blacklisted one another."

"I see you didn't erase me. So, for whatever reason you didn't as well."

"Fair enough. So, how's school?"

"Intense. If it weren't for my passion for the law, I wouldn't do this. I barely have time for much. You tryna come through? But that's right, you have to take the Metro from DC and all."

"Nope. I, too, live in Arlington, and now I got a car."

"You don't say. Well, that's good because you need one. Did you even have a license?"

"Ha, ha. Been had it. Got it years ago."

"I was 'bout to say. So, I'm all tensed up. You wanna come on over? I can play with you on your favorite spot. You know how I used to make you giggle and all."

Feeling her face grow hot, Amber looked heavenward for strength as she raced her bare foot up a leg. "Cris, don't do this to me. I'm tryna be good. Besides, I called to thank you for somethin'."

"And what's that?"

"We had talks about me goin' to school. So, I enrolled at a community college with plans to transfer out in two years. But now I'm gonna do real estate instead. I'm a natural hustler, you know."

"Well. You leave a lady and she grows behind your back. That sucks."

Amber didn't know what to say, so she didn't say anything.

"But that's dope. You're making strides for yourself. *Mujer*, I like that. But I didn't do anything. You did it all, baby."

Touched, she said, "I appreciate that."

"I'm glad that you're doing more for your life. Maybe we can talk here and there, about us, you know."

"Like a relationship?" Amber didn't know how to feel about that, especially since she almost considered herself falsely married to Emily.

"Ehhhhhh. I don't know. I just don't need a woman complicating my life over the next few years."

"Well, you know, I don't either," she joked. "I like the idea of doing me for a while."

"I need a woman like that, a woman to grow with real slowly, but friends first. You know, at least have sex, but give a little more than that, but without all that obligation stuff. For real, I really don't even flirt anymore. What for? What can I do about it? I'm too busy to woo her panties off." Amber giggled. "And I know you. Took your panties off before, too."

His words tickled her vagina. "Not tonight, sir."

"Come on, don't be like that, ma. Don't be no cock teaser, especially when you know how I go down between your legs, though. So, what are we gonna do then? Pretend like we don't want sex? Invite each other over to watch TV? Come on now, don't even try to play me."

"Mmmmmmm, I'm not sure. I really didn't plan on callin' you tonight. Somethin' just came over me, aside from horniness."

"Girl, what's your address? I'm tired of stroking off. Come on. Lemme give you some chimichanga."

Biting her lips, Amber wondered if having a sex buddy would make her weak. She drowned in flashbacks of the way he touched her. Why did she do this to herself in the first place? she wondered. Why did she have to call him? Deciding to find balance while remaining true to herself and not warping into someone she couldn't recognize, she decided to meet him halfway. Besides, this was one part of the relationship that she and Emily agreed upon that they couldn't do for the other.

"Okay, phone sex?"

"Hmmmm? When can we get back into the real thing?"

"Wait here, okay?" Amber dialed Emily without merging the two phone calls.

"Yes, Amber?"

"I'm about to cheat on you. Is that okay?"

"Excuse me?"

"I have Cris on the other line. I'm proposin' phone sex instead of the real deal."

"The Mexican guy?"

"Yeah, him."

"Well why are you asking me?"

"We kind of took a vow to, you know, be uhhh, there for each other. Sex was not on the menu so I'm orderin' out."

Laughing with disbelief, Emily replied, "Amber, if you wanna get laid, just do it. You don't need me to give you permission just because I can't get any. Cuz if I meet a man who can take it to the bridge, oh, honey, I am going all the way, and I ain't gonna call you either."

"Uh-oh." Amber snatched the phone from her ear to give it a quick glance. "Hold on, now. You done broke out the broken English, gettin' all kinds of sassy up in here. You must mean this. Mama has spoken. Thank you and goodbye."

"Yeah, yeah." Emily hung up.

She didn't know what she was going to tell him after she said, "Yeah, Cris?" She didn't hear anything. Maybe he fell asleep on her. She took a peek at her cellphone screen and realized that he'd hung up. Not knowing if she had just made a fool of herself, she decided to call him back to keep from speculating. When the call rolled straight to voicemail, Amber received her answer without it coming from his lips. She didn't want to try to figure out if he thought she was playing games or not when she placed him on hold. What she didn't want was to revisit her past, and this time, the answer was clear.

Holding down his name, Amber chose to erase it when the option popped up. Then she decided to finish cleaning house and deleted Cane's number. When she was faced with Daniel's name, she knew better than to be a fool. One man's number couldn't hurt. He could teach her financial principles down the line or put her in touch with the right people for any professional gain. Amber decided to keep his number.

Amber sent a text to Emily that read: *I didn't do it. Closin' da chapter on him.*

When her phone buzzed, she saw Emily's text: *Good. Good night.*

Amber crawled back under her sheets and placed her phone on the night stand. When it buzzed again, she saw the text from Emily.

By the way, feel free to get your needs outside of this marriage.

Amber grinned and responded with: *Trust me, I will.* She placed a happy face with a wink at the end and sent it off.

Placing her phone back onto the nightstand, Amber cuddled up with the blanket and thought about what reaching out to Cris meant. She knew she had to test herself to see if she could walk the talk. Deciding to give herself a big fat F, she laughed at herself as a scorn for being degraded by Cris' action. She knew better. He'd told her that he was a man. She called when he happened to be horny, and he knew all the right things to say to get her over there.

Deciding that change took more than words, the road ahead appeared tougher than imagined. She had faith that she could stay on course with enough power steering because after all, no matter how, she found a way out of the hood of New York and into her own apartment in Arlington. There was one thing Amber had with her that came from being a resident of the Big Apple, and that was the New York spirit to make it out of any situation better than how she entered. Stretching up to cut off her lamp as she lay in the dark, Amber literally rest assured, knowing that she had her own back—and her front.

Summer

Hawaii was beautiful! Standing in my bikini while taking in the scenery of the stretch of beautiful blue-green water of Makena offered me a sense of peace that I'd been yearning for. I held Autumn at the shoreline as we searched the waters while enjoying the gentle breeze. Pointing outward and into the never-ending water, Autumn tried to follow my finger under the brim of her yellow and black polka dot hat, which matched her sundress. She smiled at me and giggled when I poked her tummy and placed kisses all over her chubby face. This little one made me so happy!

Feeling a large hand rest against my sheer sarong-clad butt, I already knew it belonged to Oliver. I knew his touches so well. The man with half-Hawaiian blood smiled at me with his eyes while flashing me his perfect white teeth. Smiling back, the breeze whipped strands of hair around my face.

Caressing my butt, he gave Autumn a kiss on the forehead. "How do you feel?"

"Hey!" my mom called from close behind. We turned to see her sitting on a towel under an umbrella. "I see that," she joked.

Amused, I replied, "Look away, Mom. I'm grown now."

Oliver chuckled.

"Mmmm, hmmm," she replied as she reclined flat, adjusting her sunglasses.

Pulling out my phone from the tiny purse slung across my body, I reached inside, took out my phone, and held it high. "Selfie—well with you and Autumn, of course." Oliver moved in, and I clicked. I sent it off to my friends and waited for their replies.

"Can I talk to you, sweetie?" Oliver asked solemnly.

The intensity in his face gave me the idea that we should be alone. "Sure. Let me hand Mom the baby." I played with her stomach and watched her giggle as we walked a few feet to my mom. "Can you take her for a moment?"

She lowered her sunglasses long enough to answer, "Do you even have to ask?"

"Great, thanks." I squeezed Autumn one last time before passing her to my mom.

Returning to Oliver who stood watching the waves, I stared at his masculine back. My phone beeped, obviously a response to my shared picture. Oliver turned around to watch me read my screen. "Amber wrote: *Too cute!!! So jealous of the spot.*"

Another beep sounded. Looking at my screen, I saw that it was from Brooke. Before I could read her message out loud, Oliver said, "Can you walk along with me?"

Somewhat nervous by his serious demeanor, I put the phone away and answered, "Sure."

Looking ahead, he said, "Don't worry, we'll bring something very nice but also native to Hawaii for your friends."

"Sounds like a plan. Is everything okay?" The beach wasn't as populated as I'd anticipated, and I couldn't ask for anything more.

"It is, but I just wanted to talk to you." He stopped walking. "Do you have a name picked out yet?"

"Excuse me?" Confused, I bunched all of my hair with one hand and pushed it to one side of my neck.

"Summer, I need to know if you have plans to have a baby with me." He spun to look at me.

Taken aback and almost nervous, I asked, "*Now*?"

"Yeah, but I'm talking later on, in the future."

I exhaled deeply. "Gee, I . . . I . . . I haven't even thought about it." Brooke had just raised this point with me yesterday at Amber's house. Wait till she finds out.

"Well do you plan on having any more children? It feels so right to have a baby with you." He held up a hand. "Now don't get me wrong. I'm in love with Autumn, and I adore her. But . . ." he looked away and then back at me, "Summer, I want our own, too."

Stepping forward to place my hand against his face, I told him, "Baby, I would love that. Of course, *of course.*"

Looking more than pleased, he relaxed and took my hands. "How long do we have to wait?"

I shrugged. "I don't know. What's the timeline supposed to look like?"

"How about a year from now, *after* we're married?"

His timeline didn't sound too bad. In fact, anything sounded better than today. "Sounds lovely. Wouldn't want people to think we felt pressured to get married because I was carrying your child."

"Sounds good to me."

Now that we had some down time, now felt like the best moment to bring up what I'd forgotten to tell him since Autumn's birth. "I have to tell you something."

"What?"

"I had a dream once. Many, many months ago, before Ruben died." Looking concerned but intrigued, he stared at me, ready to hear it all. "I had a dream that I had a daughter in one hand as we visited the graveyard of her father, while I was pregnant with another baby."

"Really?"

I nodded.

"That's crazy."

"Yup. Imagine when how I felt when it played out in real life."

"And you're just now telling me this? Why?"

"It's just that at first, I didn't wanna talk about it. Then I kind of, you know, forgot about it. But you haven't heard it all yet."

"Oh, no. What?"

"The little girl with me…"

"Yeah?"

"I called her Autumn."

"Summer, what the—?" He stared at me like my head was on fire.

"I've always loved that name, so it's no wonder it followed me into my dream. Sh-she was walking and talking, like a three-year-old or something. I had a huge baby bump, and I was touching the headstone of a dead man. It was Autumn's father."

"Okay, wait." Oliver stepped back with both hands in the air waiving like flags. "You're freaking me out."

"Wait." I reached for his wrist. "Her name would be Winter."

"Who?" He looked puzzled.

"The baby girl we would have together. Her name would be Winter."

Oliver's whole demeanor scrambled, going from slightly overwhelmed to delighted. "You sayin' I can live with the three seasons, huh?" He raised an eyebrow. "Do you even like that name? It sounds kind of chaotic."

I poked his chest with my finger. "Hey. We have to be consistent here. The girl would come out and wonder why she didn't get a seasonal name," I teased. I turned my nose upward and folded my arms. "So, Winter it is."

"Fine, fine. And what if it's a boy?"

"Storm."

Cracking up, Oliver held his tight midsection and held up his other hand at me.

Pointing at him, I said, "Hold up, hold up. We can totally Hollywood it and call him Spring. So, we got Spring Hunter or Storm Hunter. Which one?"

"Wow." He pointed a finger at me then pinched my nose. "You a freaking scam artist, Summer."

Genuinely confused, my jaw dropped. "What did I do?"

"Funny how you didn't want a life with children and a man, *especially* children, but you got all these names figured out."

Smirking, I folded my arms over my chest. "Oh, shut up."

"I mean, do I get a vote?"

"I push, I name."

"Now hold on, hold on, now. Y'all all seasoned up, while Daddy gets left out in the cold. How we gonna explain this to the kids?"

I stroked his shoulders. "Now wait a minute. Oliver is . . . kinda natural. Like olive!"

Nodding, he seemed to have been buying my reasoning. He eased toward me with both hands aiming for my hips. Grabbing me, he asked, "So, we're like a natural family, huh?"

"But not too natural, I like a little danger. I mean, I was once a free bird, you know."

He grinned. "I remember that. You were a free bird until you flew into my cage. Never gonna let you out."

"All it took was the piece of bread to lure me in."

"Oh, by bread you mean my money, huh?"

I bit my lower lip. "Well at least it wasn't crumbs."

We eased in closer until we connected at our foreheads.

"You are so lucky your mom is in view, you know that?"

"Mmmm. What would you do to me?"

"Lay you out and pound your ass into this sand. I just don't want Autumn to see her mom getting pounded. Don't want her to think that a man should do that to her before she turns fifty."

A sharp chuckle eased out. "Fifty?"

He grunted. "It used to be sixty. Count your blessings."

Snapping my head back in laughter, I straightened it and said, "Well, if you can control the pressure build-up in your dick until tonight, Summer can bring you a tornado."

"All right. I'll hold you to it."

"Yeah?" I placed a succulent kiss on his lips.

"Yeah." He tasted his bottom lip before easing back.

The love of my life took me by the hand and led us to walk. "How's work?"

"Great, actually. Remember I mentioned Sharon to you? Not evil Sharon—Sharon Quailback—she left. *Thank* God. I'm talking about Sharon Hardway. She's a godsend. She made my transition into the company better. I'm definitely loving my job." That was the truth. My job came with a lot of perks with managers who genuinely wanted their people to succeed. "Turns out, despite everything going down in flames at Dubois Staffing, I learned a lot from Fran's company. Working with Fran did prepare me for this moment. I'm learning so much, but a lot rides on my shoulders. It's good pressure to keep me on my toes, but it's a little intimidating at the same time."

"So the old witch did something right?"

"I loved working for her company, you know, before all that Ruben stuff went down. I was pretty happy there and felt very secure in that job."

"Well, if all fails, you'll always have a job with me at any of my laundromats."

Amused but touched, I asked, "And what would I do?"

"Maintenance would be nice."

I giggled and raised a brow. I watched him talk as we walked aimlessly away from my mom and daughter.

"I mean, I could really use someone who knows how to break apart the machines when they give out."

"Oh, really?"

"Yeah. I have a tool belt that would fit you nicely. I think you could do good at that job." He peeked at me and flashed his teeth. "Interested?"

I patted his defined shoulder. "No thanks, baby. But uhhh, if I ever get laid off . . ."

He patted my butt and grabbed me by the shoulders to turn me to face him. "Just in case you're wondering, I really love being in my homeland with you and our baby. This is the best gift I could've ever asked for in life."

I eyed him suspiciously. "More than your laundromats?"

"Those things only bring me in a ton of money. But you bring me a ton of happiness." Oliver pointed to his right. "You and that baby over there."

"So, I'm doing okay as a girlfriend?" Biting my lower lip, I tilted my head.

When Oliver's chest caved in with his drawn breath, I braced myself for impact. The review was coming. He was about to let me have it but in the kindest way possible. His eyes suddenly reflected a quick glimpse into his heart. Heavy. His heart must've gotten heavy. He didn't want to talk about it. I'd made him miserable before now.

"Summer." Reaching into his swimming trunk's pocket, Oliver shook his head. And then it happened in slow motion.

Oliver dropped to one knee.

He flipped open a black box.

My hands flew to my mouth, muffling my outburst. "Oh, my gosh, Oliver!"

Playing with me, he cupped one hand behind his ear. "What? What?"

"Oh, my Lord!" My mom shouted from the short distance.

"Baby, I know you're not much into stuff like this, and I tried not to go over the top. But when I saw this halo diamond band, it had to go home with me."

My breathing felt compromised under the influence of a drunken heart. The hands against my face shook, matching the vibrating frequency of my knees. If my body gave out on me, the sand would be there to catch me. But somehow, I found strength to stand, by looking into Oliver's eyes.

What had he done? Was he insane? Me. He wanted to marry me. He wanted to marry me? Sure, we'd talked about it, but it always felt like a I-wanna-be-rich-one-day goal. It was something to be desired, but it wasn't something in the forefront of my mind. Not like Brooke. So, what had he done and why?

Pointing to my chest with staggering feet, I asked, "Y-you wanna marry *me*?"

Smiling, he replied, "I don't know what else a bent knee with a ring means."

I placed the space between my index fingers and thumbs against my hairline in place of a headband to pull the hair away from my face.

There Oliver was, anchored into the sand by one knee. His hopeful face waited for an answer. The ring stuck out like a bouquet of flowers given by a man on a first date. But this wasn't a first date. This felt like a make-it-or-break-it situation. Was it a situation? I was sure Oliver wouldn't see it that way. For him, this would be an opportunity.

He said, "This is the best move I've made in my entire life. I hate to say it, but all the bad moments that happened in our lives really led to all the good."

Taking in his words, my eyes fell into a trance, and my mind covered major recent events of the past which included Oliver.

"I'm pregnant! Okay? There, stupid! Ya happy? I'm pregnant!" I jerked from his weakened grip once he heard the truth. "That's why I'm fat, sloppy, tired, emotional, and all that stuff that you hate. Okay? Now what are you gonna do with that?" He tried to process my outburst with a blank stare. My hand flung behind me toward the direction of our bedroom. "Do you wanna go back and look a little harder for those running shoes now?"

"Oh, give me a break, Summer! You haven't grown," he declared with eyes full of disgust. "Are you saying something about this baby not being mine? Do I have to put it bluntly for you?"

"Summer, you haven't put me first the way I do you. You didn't let me help you first when your apartment flooded, you chose Fran. You got pregnant and let me think I was the dad, but your friends knew first. You thought it was more important to share vital information with Brooke

before confessing yours with me, and then you managed to have time to find a man for Amber, when your first order of priority shoulda' been to tell me that I was not the father of your baby." Looking away, he collected his thoughts before continuing. "You didn't even tell me that you slept with that slime ball the same night as me until your back was up against the wall."

"Give me my phone. Let me call him. What kind of game is he playing?"

Oliver said, "You can't, Summer. He rushed to be here and had a car accident."

"What?" we responded in horror. They inhaled sharply while my heart dipped.

"He's dead."

"Put those down," he ordered with a furrowed brow.

Wow. He wasn't panic-stricken at all but rather composed. Had he been wearing jeans, his hands would've slipped right into them, cool as a cucumber. What was I missing here?

"Are you kiddin' me? You jokin' right now? Don't tell me what to do."

"Those aren't for you, and it wasn't any of your business."

My heart dropped like an elevator to my feet. The room started to spin, and I swore that the saying of seeing red was true, because I saw it.

"What the hell, Oliver?"

Oliver knocked me back into the present when he nudged my arm gently with his fingers. "Hey, babe. You good?"

I blinked a few times until my head caught up with the moment. "What?" A sharp breath drew between my lips. "Yeah. I'm sorry, babe. Was reflecting on what you said about the bad times leading to something good. You're so right. We made it."

"Yeah. You weren't sold on a life with me, but I promise to make you happy and to be a great daddy to our girl."

Blinking rapidly, I replied, "Oh, my gosh, I don't know what to say."

Then I heard my mom in the short distance say, "Bitch, you better say 'yes.'"

Immediately giving into laughter with Oliver, my mom snapped me out of my trance-like state of thoughts, concerns, and reasons. Oliver and I looked her way to see her leaning forward in her chair with her sunglasses in one hand and Autumn in the other watching her parents. He and I laughed at her unusual expression of humor. The original free bird arched a brow at me and nodded affirmatively.

Oh my gosh! This was insane. *This was insane.*

"Get up. Get up, get up, get up!" I jumped like my feet were over hot coals.

Oliver struggled to stand on command in the sand, but when he did, I jumped against his torso into a straddled position.

"What does it mean?" he asked.

"I don't know what else it means when a woman jumps on her man with happiness after he proposes."

His jaw dropped. For the first time, his heart beat against my chest. It felt like he was breathing for the both of us.

"Shit, Summer! We gettin' married?"

I nodded so vehemently, it felt like my neck would snap. "Yes! I've been such a fool. I don't wanna do anything alone." I tilted my head and squinted my eyes at him. "Oliver, I am so sorry that it took me so long to come around. I don't wanna do life alone, not when a man like you checks all the boxes. No. I want a real commitment. I can't punish myself based on my childhood. It isn't fair to you, Autumn, or me." Straightening my head, my body jerked. "So, yes. Yes, Oliver! I *will* marry you." I leaned forward to kiss him.

When we pulled back, Oliver said, "Summer, if you thought life was good with a little bit of crazy, just wait. Life will be fantastic with no more unnecessary monkey wrenches. All the secrets are out. We're good. Now, we live, baby. We live."

"We live."

"You're missing something on that finger."

"Oh." Straightening my legs to stand on my own, I said, "That would solidify things, huh?"

Oliver opened the box again to take out the ring. It sparkled on its own with every move he made to bring it to my finger. I held out my hand like an entitled princess. He took it and asked again, "Summer, will you marry me?"

"Yes, Oliver. It would be my pleasure."

Oliver slid the ring to the base of my finger.

"Whooooo eeeee whoo! Congratulations!" my mother yelled.

Smiling, we turned to wave at her and Autumn.

I grabbed him quickly and held him close, gripping him with all my might. "I love you, Oliver. I love you so much, and I'm gonna tell you more often."

"Summer, I love you and that little girl to the moon and back and then some."

"No complaints here on that." During our embrace, his hand ran up and down my back. "I love you, woman. Don't you ever forget that. From now and forever and ever." When his phone rang, he pulled it out of the pocket of his trunks. After glancing at the phone, he complained, "I told these fools not to call me. They should be able to do this job in their sleep. It's a laundromat!" He placed a quick peck on my lips. "I'm so sorry, baby." Holding up a finger he said, "Hang on, okay?"

"Oh, no, fiancé. Take your time. I'm okay. I'll enjoy the view."

"Fiancé." He nodded with a proud grin. "Wait till it's husband and wife." He winked.

Oliver stepped away for a minute to take his phone call, leaving me to reflect on how far I'd come. A warm smile graced my face. Standing at the shoreline with folded arms, my hair blew wildly behind my head as it tickled my back. The faces of my friends flashed in front of me over the ocean with thoughts of how much I would have to tell them about this vacation. Looking around, I couldn't believe that this turned out to be my life!

I remembered to check my phone for Brooke's response. Clicking on her notification, a photo of her and Jackson covered my screen. There the gorgeous couple stood, side by side with his arm over her shoulders. She placed a caption over it that read: *You guys JUST might be cuter than us,* followed by the winking emoji with the tongue sticking out.

I giggled and nodded my head. Yup, that was Brooke. Brazen, not to be outdone, but true to herself. Another chime came in, but it was a second response from Amber. It read: *#relationshipgoals.*

Of course. Always supportive, that was Amber. At least she couldn't see me pout at her message. She and I both realized during the course of our friendship, that being open to love didn't mean that we had to give up ourselves or our independence. It simply meant that someone was going to be waiting for you when you got home after work. Someone would be listening to your problems. Someone would wipe your tears away, take out the trash, cook you dinner. But most of all, it meant armoring up for fights and loving each other through the moments that felt like rock-bottom love.

What I really learned was that this relationship made me a better person with him. For the first time, I wanted to be everything to someone else. I wanted to give him everything that he gave me, wipe his tears away, rub his shoulders, encourage him through his darkest hours. Love was a two-way street. There should never be a sign that said it went one way.

I'd found love, and I'd found true friendship.

I texted all the women a display of my hand wearing my engagement ring. Three women who felt more like my sisters rather than best friends, and I wouldn't have it any other way. They were like my extended family, except we pretty much liked each other and got along—for the most part.

A year ago, I was a woman embarking on life as a single woman learning to live alone after experiencing life as a roommate. Who knew that one breakfast at La Madeline would change my life and lead me into a series of events that would impact me?

I couldn't forget that night I met Oliver at a party, when I felt disgusted at myself for having dirty sex with Ruben against the wall. Thinking of our first date and how we were at ease with one another, as if we'd known each other for months, maybe even years, tickled my heart. It was unfathomable that I had a child—a daughter, no less—who could show me what real love was really all about. Before her, no one could tell me nothing, I had it all planned out. Funny how some of us think careers and achievements will always fulfill us.

The chimes came in almost at once.

Emily: *No waaaaaay! Finally, Summer!!! I knew it! When you get back we need to shop for gowns immediately!*

Amber: *Bitch staaaaahp now this man done bought u a ring that cost mo than my car? Living ur best life 4 real tho sis we gon party when u get back.*

Brooke: *Cha-ching! Umm, I know you gonna hire me as your wp. Right? LOL But really, Jackson & I r stoked. Welcome to my club. Congrats!!!!*

Grinning from ear to ear and chuckling to myself, I turned back to see my mother waving Autumn's hand at me.

"Congratulations, baby!" she called.

With a melted heart, I waved back at them with a tear threatening to boil over. My eyes dropped to my feet. Behind me, Oliver fussed at an employee. Noticing the stick in the sand, something moved me to pick it up to write, 'I WAS HERE' in the sand. The memo was signed with a heart instead of my name. After admiring my work and reflecting on how far I'd come, I threw the stick as far as possible into the ocean.

A sudden touch graced my arm. Turning to meet his gaze, there stood the man who made me believe in love.

"Are you ready to keep walking, babe?"

I nodded with a smile. "As long as you're by my side? Yeah."

A smile stretched slowly across Oliver's face. He wore a stress-free expression that genuinely reflected peace.

Taking one last look at the letters in the sand, I turned around to walk with my fiancé, relishing in the fact that I, finally, was here.

Thank you for finishing the trilogy journey to see how it all ended! Remember to keep a look out for The Capital Trilogy spin-off. You won't believe what happens next when one character gets his or her own trilogy.

Please remember to leave a review on Amazon. I appreciate your feedback!

Follow me @ . . .
Facebook: www.facebook.com/dawn.wright.54738
Instagram: dawnwright_author
Twitter: Dawn Wright@_dawn_wright
Email me at: authordawnwright@gmail.com
Sign up for my newsletters to find out what's new at
www.dawnwrightbooks.com/newsletter/
To learn more about Dawn Wright visit
www.dawnwrightbooks.com

acknowledgements

Proofreader: Dianne McCann
Editor: Richard "Tony" Held
Cover design by Les
Cover Model Photography by Evan
Christopher Photography
Cover Model: Starleigh Caldwell

The Capital Trilogy
Capital Encounters (book one)
Capital Consequences (book two)
Capital Resolutions (book three)

About the Author

Before committing to writing novels, Dawn Wright, spent a decent amount of time teaching and studying business, while having a fascination for the corporate environment.

Determined to someday make the workforce a place where employees would want to work without dread, she made it her mission to obtain her masters in human resource management. However, in her last semester, two classes away from graduation in fact, she pulled out her laptop for other than studying or Internet surfing, and decided to give life to Capital Encounters. Unaware that this book would lead to a trilogy, she set it to the side to keep from compromising her GPA. After years of countless and persistent prayers, she realized that her book didn't have to be second to a traditional career, but that by stepping out on faith, it was just time to say goodbye to what was expected and hello to passion.

Dawn Wright currently lives in Alexandria, VA as a full-time writer. She frequents DC when she and her boyfriend feel like crossing the bridge. Ever since writing her first book, there's never been a time that she doesn't visit DC without feeling like her characters are right down the street.

9 780998 078748